Sheila Fulton was educated at University College of North Wales, Bangor, where she gained a BA Joint Honours degree in English and Drama and was twice awarded the university English prize. She went on to gain an M Litt at Bristol University. After a part-time job at BBC Bristol, she qualified as a teacher and taught for four years at a large comprehensive just outside Bristol. While writing THE HORSE WITCH (her first novel), she was awarded a bursary by Eastern Arts. The judging panel, including Zoe Fairbairns and Leon Garfield, praised her writing as 'unsentimental and powerful, with a strong sense of place and drama'.

She is married to a research scientist, has three children and now lives in Hertfordshire.

The Horse Witch

Sheila Fulton

KNIGHT

First published in 1993
by HEADLINE BOOK PUBLISHING PLC

First published in paperback 1993
by HEADLINE BOOK PUBLISHING PLC

This edition published 2002 by
Knight an imprint of The Caxton Publishing Group

10 9 8 7 6 5 4 3 2 1

ISBN 1 84067 415 6

Typeset by Keyboard Services, Luton

Printed and bound in Great Britain by
Mackays of Chatham plc, Chatham, Kent

Caxton Publishing Group
20 Bloomsbury Street
London WC1B 3JH

To Steve and to Mum and Dad, with love and thanks

Prologue

She killed the owl neatly, so as to please the Lady. Just before she drove the needle in she felt its fear, for all that its eyes had been hooded. There was the brief fluttering struggle, the beak and claws rending air, then the limpness and the warm spatter of blood. Afterwards she laid the body down on the altar stone and murmured the dedication.

Once, in her father's hall, there would have been faces ringing her round and the chant and the thin wail of the bone pipes. Now, in this place far down in the earth, there were only herself and her women, and the child with his nurse.

Yet this was more a shrine, holy, older by far than the other she had known. It was one of the first places and powerful for that. All around, on the walls of rock, the Lady's horses ran, drawn white in curving lines, beaked creatures with blind eyes that stared out in the torchlight. Water trickled in a gully cut in the floor.

Rock and earth and water. The Lady's place, Horse-mistress, Horse-goddess, and Her breathing in the silence.

It was very cold; the torch was set too high for warmth. Already the blood had stiffened on her fingers. She hoped the child would not be frightened. She turned and went to him.

He was very young, not yet in his fourth year, and stared at her solemnly, holding tight his nurse's skirts.

She knelt. 'Hush, lamb.' He must not speak. For all he was a baby, he was male and this was the women's place. Usually the children were older and could understand. She put her finger to her own lips and watched his eyes widen, seeing the blood. They were grey eyes, grey-green but with the black of the irises pooling into them.

'Only a bird, lamb, gone for the Lady. He goes hunting for her now, like Brach the hawk for your father.' He nodded, being brave, then clutched her round the neck, nuzzling at her flesh.

His face felt cold, the skin soft and fresh, smelling of the

1

herb water he had been washed in. His nurse had washed his hair also, so that it shone, silky and heavy, like rough pale gold. His father's hair.

Gently she put him from her. Behind her she could hear the women stir and rustle. There was the clink of bronze bowls and the dribble of thin liquid.

Kneeling on the floor, her hands on the child's shoulders, she was fierce suddenly, looking up at his nurse.

'Does he realize?'

'Yes, lady.'

The women were about her now, silent but with their own excitement. She could feel it, just as she had felt the owl's fear, the knotting of her own stomach, the Lady waiting in the shadows.

They gave her the bowl, with the liquid black in it, and the needle with the owl's blood on it still.

Now the nurse was bending foward, loosening the blanket fastened at the child's neck, gripping his arms tight. For a moment he flinched from them.

Then she began.

Chapter One

Tachga is old and believes herself wise. She says that if you look long enough into water you can see the future there, dimly, like a shadow. She should know. She's squatted often enough, down in the hearth's ashes, to mumble over some crock she's thought full of secrets. But she never told me what she saw, or if she did it was only nonsense to keep me quiet and scare me witless.

The day the messenger came I'd stared at water, black water, the marsh water that goes down deep as seven men or more. Only I'd not looked for the future – though if any water holds it, that does – but for the fish we needed for the winter salting. At dawn I'd gone out to lay fish traps and put down my hooks.

I'd been patient all day, going to the still places out of the reeds that the tench and roach like, but in the end I'd caught nothing. The year's turn was already in the air and a chill in the water. Besides, I had set the traps too high, and the Antlered One, Lord of the Wild Things, wears a dark face in these parts and does not like a fool; the fish stayed put, and would not come from below.

Now it was evening and the mists had begun to rise with the smell of the water in them. I was cold and hungry, with a black mood on me. With no fish my only future was likely the rough edge of my grandfather's tongue or his fist in my ribs when he found me empty-handed. I slung the traps across my shoulder and turned for home.

I hurried. I'd been out too long already. One must take care in the marshes for at night they are no friend to man – nor sometimes by day either. They are one of the First Places where earth and water meet in mud and coarse, long grasses. They keep their own for their own, and the gods here care little for those who walk their causeways. The land is sullen, with the sky hung blind above or held at one's feet in the empty pools. Always there is the lap and suck of water, and

3

when the wind goes through the rushes they sigh together and whisper like sad, thin women. Evening is the loneliest time. You can feel it – at watch for the night to come, a place for birds and frogs and water snakes, making home feel far away.

I was glad to reach the track that led to our farm. I was halfway home when I heard the hooves, a dull thud in the mud behind me. I turned and saw a rider coming up, crouched low over his horse's neck. They galloped towards me, nearer and nearer, while the horse grunted and heaved at every stride. There was foam about its mouth and sweat all down its neck and flanks, but the man drove it on with curses and shouts.

The way was narrow, bordered by bog-grass and water. I stood, waiting for them to slacken pace. Just at the last I stumbled back into the grasses. Metal clinked and a hot horse-stink filled my nostrils. Then I was knocked sideways by the surge of chestnut flesh and a boot near enough in my face. Above the mane that streamed like a pale wave, I glimpsed the rider, mouth thin with laughter, and a flash of blue plaid tunic. His cloak snapped out from his shoulders to flutter and beat like a great leather wing, and they were gone.

I gazed after them into the dusk, shaken and spattered over with the mud of their passing.

A man on a horse, here in the empty lands? The marsh pools could have told me something that day, had they a will to and I had known to look.

Part of me, though, was not quite blind, for as I paused there, my heart a hammer at my ribs and the evening shadows already in my eyes, I remembered the man's face and around me the water went quiet and still as if it drew breath, so that my spine shivered and I was afraid.

The traps weighed heavy on my shoulders, I was aching weary, yet I bounded then like a hare for home.

The track went nowhere, only to our farm, and that was a poor place; nothing more than a cluster of wooden huts, built in the round according to custom but half of them broken down with the thatch off, and a few empty pens. Not many came to us – my grandfather's pride and his temper made sure of that – and those who did were on foot mostly, from over the mountains we could see in the distance, seeking a

4

day's work or two. Once there had been a man with a harp. The salt pedlar alone rode to us, up proud in a cart with a fat, bouncy pony to draw it.

The yard was empty when I reached it. There was no sign of Palug, my grandfather's man, who should have been about, but beneath the doorway of the largest hut which Grandfather called his hall glowed the warm shift of firelight. There were voices too, a steady murmur that rose and fell.

Someone talked softly. I did not know his voice and could not make out the words, only that there was a tone which I recognized. He sounded as the pedlar did when he wanted us to buy more than we could afford – respectful and persuasive together, with a mouth full of oil. My grandfather answered, familiarly gruff. Hearing them I was heedless all at once of caution or even good manners. I opened the door, pulled back the old curtain we hung there for warmth and stepped inside.

My grandfather sat on his bench by the fire, still in his farm clothes, a tunic and leggings, their leather stained with mud and damp; he too must have been surprised. The man who stood before him was workmanlike but much finer. Though his sword was plain and he had only an iron pin to hold his cloak, there was the blue plaid tunic, leather-belted, and his boots were whole and came to his knee. He looked what he was, a client of a rich man, only not rich himself. As the curtain rings jangled he turned to show once more a hard, bony face, scrubbed with beard and narrow about the eyes and jaw. A harsh face, little enough to know him by, but enough to get his measure.

Both of them, he and my grandfather, held themselves upright and watchful, as if disturbed in something. It made me pause – dogs were like it before they fought. I halted and stared back warily.

For a moment no one spoke, then a peat slab shifted on the fire and there was a hiss and a yellow shower of sparks so that the man jumped back. He was quick, as if he had been trained to be so.

As he moved my grandfather's gaze went to my hands and saw them empty. He scowled then, as he usually did at me.

'Well,' he said, 'what do you want? Look at you – all ears and questions in your eyes!'

By the firelight, with the flames leaping, his own face showed red, high on the cheekbones where the small veins

5

spread. A muscle flickered in his neck below his ear. He was excited and irritable as well, through being taken unawares.

Before I could answer him, his frown deepened and he said harshly, 'You're not wanted in here, boy. There's news and it's for my ears, not yours. Go and help Palug with the horse.'

I flushed too as he ordered me about. At his side the man lolled, leaning up against one of the posts that held the roof. He was picking at something in his beard and getting a good look at us. I supposed he thought me some servant; I was young and touchy and it stung my pride.

Then he said, 'The lad should know as well, my lord.'

As he spoke I thought I had been wrong about one thing. He showed no respect at all, not even such as the pedlar gave and that only to ensure his profit. This man's voice stayed soft, making it hard to name what was there, but there was something, as if he swallowed down laughter that would burst from him if he let it. He was sly, calling my grandfather 'my lord', as he liked, but I caught my breath, knowing him insolent, and wondered how he dared.

No one went against my grandfather, not here. He was a big man, heavy about the shoulders and thickly fleshed. He was grizzled now and just beginning to seem old to me, but he had eyes to see straight to the bones of you and it was hard to face him when he'd got his temper up. As a child I'd been taken to see a bull brought down from the mountains and roped for a gift-giving. Two of the local tribes had sealed a pact and their chiefs vied with each other in generosity. It had taken three men to hold the creature while he tossed his head and bucked and bellowed his rage. I'd watched, torn between fear and a queer tight pity, with my ears hurting from the noise. Always, after that, when I thought of the bull I thought of my grandfather too. I expected his anger now, roared out at the man.

He knew what was happening well enough. His eyes changed and darkened and the red deepened in his face. But he didn't shout, only stared and swallowed as if making up his mind what to say. In the end he did no more than snap, 'I told him to tend to your horse. Later we'll see, but in the meantime I'm the one you speak to. Remember that!'

The man was well schooled. He nodded and glanced down at his feet, justly rebuked and with the look of it. Except that the laughter was still there, in his mouth's curve and the twitch of his shoulders.

My grandfather turned back to me, chin jutting fiercely. 'Where's your catch?' he asked, knowing what the answer would be.

I shook my head. It was like him to make a fool of another to save his own face. He growled, making much of his disgust.

'Get out!' he said. 'Do as I've told you or go back to the water till you've something to feed us with. Be out all night if you must – it's nothing to me. Only don't let me catch sight of you till you're sent for and supper's up and dished.'

In the stables, with Palug about his work, I asked, 'Who is he?'

Palug went tight-mouthed. 'You'll learn soon enough.'

I guessed my grandfather had given him his orders already and shrugged to make it seem I did not care. I'd get nothing from him anyway. He grumbled even now, a steady mutter of complaint under his breath as he strapped down the horse.

I went to the animal's head and talked to it. He was a young stallion, perhaps broken that year for riding, and a fine one with a good head and gentle eyes, but his ears kept flickering. Palug made him nervous. He was never one for hard work so he rushed and was rough in everything he did to get it over with. By this time, usually, he would be at his place by the fire in his own mean hut.

For a while I watched him growing hot and sweaty, and the horse fidgeting under his hands. After a bit I could stand it no longer.

'Grandfather told me to do it.'

Palug straightened and gave me a hard look. 'Why didn't you say so before, lazy young. . . .' He added his usual curse and flung over the cloth and a twist of straw. I picked them up and went to the horse, running my hand down his neck. He was hot still and needed a blanket but after a moment he began to settle and nose at my chest. He was used to better treatment wherever he came from.

Palug went and sat in the straw, taking his ease with his legs stretched out in front of him. I felt him watch me, then he said, 'You'll learn nothing here. Horses don't talk and neither will those.' I followed his glance over to the corner of the stall. There were saddlebags, slung down carelessly, belonging to the stranger. If Palug thought I'd meant to open them he was wrong; I'd not even noticed them before.

7

I knew Palug, and his carelessness, and the foxy look he wore. I said, 'What's in them then?'

His eyes widened and he swore again. Then he grinned. 'If you must know, a half-eaten apple and a lump of cheese. Goat's. And not bad either. Nothing else. Nothing to tell about him.' He was lying. It was in his face.

I put down the cloth and took a step forward. The saddlebags lay half buried in the straw, each fastened with a single buckle. It would be the work of a moment to undo them.

Palug said, 'Don't!' and aimed a kick at my ankle. His grin had gone. His eyes had narrowed and his mouth thinned. Where his front teeth should have been was a wide black gap.

'He'll find out.'

He meant my grandfather. He would too. Next time I crossed Palug he'd go running with a fine tale and leave me to face whatever. He had his ways, had Palug. There was no good feeling lost between us.

I worked on, all the time hissing quietly to the stallion. He was a true uplands pony with a good feel to him, hard bone and muscle and shaggy chestnut hair. The stable was warm, like a cave full of shadows. The only light was the lamp set to burn by the door. Beside us my grandfather's own horse, old and sway-backed though good himself once, stirred and nosed for hay. Later, when I'd finished, it would be peaceful here while the animals sighed, steady and dozing, and the polecats slid in to hunt.

But I was restless, hearing all the time the stranger's smooth scorn. When I had fetched a rug and covered the stallion at last, I sat and poked at spiders with a stick and wished that I knew more.

Supper was long in coming. The moon was a sharp sickle, high risen, by the time I went to the hall, but inside the hearth fire burnt and a low table had been put up and scrubbed and my grandfather and the man sat cross-legged on the floor before it.

Grandfather had changed into his best clothes. I had seen him so only once before, when the harpist had come to sing of old times. Now he sat in the breeches and tunic and blue-checked cloak that were kept in the big chest under his bed. They were a lord's clothes. He'd have said his memories were woven into them.

He knew I was all eyes again. This time he ignored me.

He had done more. Always he wore his hair cropped close to his skull as a man who mourns, so there was no need for him to tie it back, only tonight his beard was trimmed and he wore earrings. They were thick ones of twisted gold and to get them in he had re-pierced his ears.

To him it was a small thing. My grandfather had a boar's hide and would have thought it no pain, but blood crusted his lobes beside the bright gold and a thin, dark trickle had hardened on his neck.

I stared and felt, suddenly, my stomach turn and sourness in my mouth. It was the blood, and hunger, and more. I was not so young that much was kept from me, and this at least I'd learnt long ago: that no man will wound himself for the sake of another except in friendship. Or because he has been conquered.

My grandfather nodded at me to sit and almost at once made a great show of the wine. He offered the jug himself to the messenger and poured it. It was pale, thin stuff the salt pedlar got us somewhere. No one knew where it came from; most thought it better not to know, only Grandfather could not have done without it. Tonight it was heated and mixed with honey, which made it better, but still he said, 'Good wine always spoils in the marshes,' and stared at us with a round, fierce eye. The messenger raised his cup and drank as if it had been of the best, but the mockery was there still in the way he smacked his lips and murmured, and when he set the cup down he smiled, slick as butter, to tell us what he thought.

I sat across from him and wished I'd kept my hunger; my appetite was gone, seeing that, and when the food did come there was nothing to bring it back.

Tachga carried it in, swaying fatly, her face all red and shiny with the cook-house heat and stuck across with her hair. She lugged a great, steaming bowl which she set down on the table. I'd never seen it before. It was bronze, green with disuse, a pattern of scrolls round the rim. It must have been a fine thing once.

There were small bowls to match, cold and dusty and sour-smelling. She fumbled them round in front of us. She was clumsy at the best of times but now she sent one spinning off the table. I had to catch it for her and dared not laugh. My grandfather sighed and drew his brows together and in a moment she'd dropped another.

She had done her best, she was too frightened to do otherwise, but she was never a cook. She had made a stew such as we often ate, though I saw it now as the stranger did – a little grey mutton, since we had no fish, barley and beans awash in grease and gravy.

The man took up his spoon and bread and began to eat, very slowly and correctly, mopping his mouth after each spoonful though no doubt he'd been in places where he'd have fallen on such a meal as this and gorged with the best of them.

When he caught me looking he winked and bent over his bowl again, hesitating just longer than was necessary before he glanced again, eyes bright with that crafty laughter and going from one to the other of us.

Worse was my grandfather, frowning and proud and on his dignity, as if we did not really live like this. Once more my stomach tightened.

Slowly I lifted my own spoon to my mouth. Around the bowl was a yellow rim of fat. I swallowed anyway. I could not knock the fellow back into the rushes but I could show him honest manners.

No one spoke. There was only the sound of our eating and the clink of spoons and Nehal the hound yawning by the fire.

Grandfather said, 'Arawn.'

I looked up at him. He had left his bowl though it was still half filled. He gestured to the man to do likewise and swirled his wine round, smiling into it.

He said, light-toned, but with his eyes fastened tight all at once on my face, 'Mhorged has sent for us.'

I remember chewing more and more slowly on a lump of bread while my heart gave great, hard thuds in my chest, and how steady my grandfather's eyes were even though his breathing had quickened and the muscle under his jaw jumped again.

'Eat up, boy,' he said, 'you grumble enough when your belly's empty.'

The bread was hard, yesterday's at least. I dipped it into my wine. It tasted like soggy vinegar.

'Grandfather, why?'

He would not answer me at once. He was busy with the stew-pot, scraping round inside it. Opposite him the messenger smirked, gap-toothed as Palug and knowing as a wolf.

Then he said, 'You think I can see into my son's mind? How do I know? It is enough he wants us.' He put another ladleful of stew into my bowl. A piece of gristle clung to the fat and a long grey hair curled round it.

He waited to see if I would speak then went on, 'Perhaps he wishes to spend some little time with his old father before earth claims these bones of mine. Or perhaps he wishes to hear of these fine lands which will one day be his. I told you to eat, since you're so nice about it.'

At his side the messenger snorted, laughing aloud for the first time. Grandfather's face never changed.

I hated him when he mocked me, more even than when he hit me. I set down my bowl and stood.

'Finish it!'

I glared at him, held out the bread and whistled to Nehal. The dog took it neatly, swallowed and begged with her eyes for the rest. I pushed the bowl along for her and turned for the door.

'Arawn!'

I swore under my breath, just loud enough for him to hear I said something. Behind me I heard him lumber to his feet; I could feel his anger and almost guessed what was coming next. But he didn't hurl the jug or his bowl, nor did he shout. He was simply vicious.

'Be thankful he asks for you as well, you filthy witch's whelp.'

I do not know who first told me my mother was a witch and my father the wanton fool who lost his honour and his clan's and, in the end, his life by marrying her. No doubt it was my grandfather – he'd been knocking the tale of it into me ever since.

That night, lying hidden in the stable straw, I thought of what I knew. My grandfather had good reasons for his anger. His tribe are a mettlesome, wilful lot who take pride in their blood-lines. He could name his own sires back through three times three generations, if he counted on his fingers. So even in the first days he must have nearly died of shame to learn how a son of his had taken to wife the woman who was my mother.

She was called Macha. She was the daughter of some petty

chieftain from across the Wild Sea, and they were Horse-people and she a priestess whom our folk call a witch. My grandfather still spat every time he had to speak her name.

Of her people he would not even talk, except to curse them. They were subtle, shape-shifters, water-snakes, all the bad things a man can name, wailing their prayers at midnight like wolves to the moon; and worse.

But it was she whom he hated, and my father. For between them, by his wedding of her and her sorceress' ways, they roused the fury of the Clan-lord, Cernach, to whom Grandfather owed allegiance, and brought down ruin on them all.

All my life I had heard the stories. Doubly cursed, I was the traitor's son, the witch's spawn. 'Don't get too proud,' my grandfather'd say, 'think what stock you sprang from.'

There were other stories too. The scraps I got from Tachga, and Palug when he was in the mood; they were from these parts, short and dark-haired, with the Old Blood that goes back further than a man can tell somewhere in them still.

Then, one night, the man with the harp came to play for us. He was poor and timid and the harp's strings were thin with fingering but he played, as he was bidden, the laments for the past and played them well, while my grandfather swilled his wine and stared into the fire. Later, greatly daring, I crept over to the cook-house where the man had made his bed. He knew who I was and I suppose it was plain what I'd come for, for it was there, as I crouched by the hearth-stone, he took pity and played me all he knew.

So, from him, in song, I learnt that before my grand-father's people had roused from the Middle-lands, the Horse-folk had ruled even as far as these marshes. They took their name from their worship of the horse, which is an ancient worship of the Great Mother, honouring it for the goddess who rides it to the sun; and their sacred places were by water and stones and caves. Even now, in the marshes, there are quiet parts where Tachga never goes.

My grandfather's people changed that. Land-hungry, in their clans, led by Cernach, they came whooping and roaring with their sharp blades and fierce boasting, their hair twisted into spikes and their war-trumpets – the animal-headed carnyx – blaring. To them horses were for riding and kicking into battle and their prayers were for a good right arm and

12

blooded, smoking iron. Their gods were as powerful, of the fire and sword, the warrior-gods, the Red-faced Ones. To them the Mother showed her dark self, the Raven-hag whose triple name may not be spoken.

The Horse-people were driven back, up into the mountains and beyond to the shores and then to the islands in the Wild Sea. All that remained of them, save from their severed, painted skulls, were memories and talk: of figures glimpsed by moonlight, that flitted by pools still and deep as death; of a white horse which ran in the darkness and screamed a shrill horse scream; of carvings upon stone, figures and lines and circles that twist upon themselves. The peasants know the meanings, though they will never speak them.

The Clan-chiefs, snug in the conquered citadels built on hillsides and mountains, listened to it all and laughed, or else grew thoughtful, for even godless men see shadows lengthen in the night, and these men were not godless.

Later the talk changed. Ships at sea were sighted, sailing back from the islands, little ships filled with huddled people, and the Horse sign reared in the standards and in the mountains the White Horse carnyx blew.

Cernach twitched and snarled. 'A terrible man,' the harpist said, 'whose very breath would put an edge on a sword.' His warriors set to polishing their spears, sang war-songs and got drunk on hopes of fame and better wine than ours. The bard-priests chanted victory and the women danced by moonlight in the sacred maze. At last they gathered at Nam Dubh, the great hill-fortress that guards the Northern pass where my grandfather, Aed, was lord and he greeted them. They rode out in their war-carts, black-browed and battle-hungry the lot of them, and the moon waxed and waned in the time that they were gone.

They were to rout the last tribes, to kill them every one; well, so they did except that Roech, my father, my grandfather's younger, wayward son, fetched him back a wife.

The harpist had a lean face and skilful fingers and his hair straggled on his brow. He had been fed at our table but there was a hunger in him, born of many days, and a weariness also, though I was too much the child then to see it. And he was kind for, in the cook-house, as the ashes shifted and Nehal stretched and snored, he told me what I had not known before. How she was beautiful, my mother, and wild, with her pale hair and eyes that were green as glass and grey as the sea. Witch's eyes. And how, though some said she had bewitched my father – both with women's arts, by dancing and low laughter, and with her magic – others said she fretted for her own kin and longed to be gone. Whatever the truth of it, Roech brought her to Nam Dubh.

If he had stayed away it might have come right but the land was harsh and he was warrior bred with no hearth to own as his. As it was he faced his father's rage, and the Clan-lord's. I used to wonder what it was they feared of her, since her folk were dead and buried. Yet Roech was the lord's son, and young besides; and the marriage pledged according to the custom. Grandfather, in honour, could not turn them out though the Clan-lord sent word he should do so. But my grandfather was not the man to take orders.

She lived there, at Nam Dubh, and in the years that followed she bore me to Roech and outfaced my grandfather and those who stared at her and whispered – until the whisperings grew worse of her strange ways and magic.

The end was swift. Cernach had not forgotten. Once more he sent word, that he would wish to make his peace. With his warriors and his priests he rode to Nam Dubh with gold for her, and cattle for my grandfather, and fine words. He joined in the feasting and drank the wine, and not till the thin dawn light crept under the eaves did he raise up his hand and cry out to his men.

Most he spared, for warriors were precious and to break a man's honour hurts worse than death; that he knew. My grandfather lived, and Mhorged, his elder son, and those who did not lift a finger to help the witch. But by daybreak Nam Dubh was ruined and disgraced, given to the flames as she was, and Roech lay in his own blood, dead where he had tried to go to her. At least, that was how the harpist sang it.

Me too Cernach spared. I was a baby still, or hardly more, and he had naught to fear from me. Already men called me 'bastard', saying marriage to the Horse-witch was no true marriage. In bitter mockery he thrust me yowling at my grandfather to be his burden and his shame. And he, savage as some old bull in truth, took me and left Nam Dubh for good.

So Nam Dubh's pride was broken and if my mother had wished them harm she had done well. They were outcasts – forbidden from the Clan-feasts, the fairs and warfare; even from the gods. Cernach's priest himself spoke the sacred curses. No omens could they seek, no sacrifice make, or even pray. They were the men who walked in shadows. Amid the tumbled walls my uncle Mhorged sat and tried to forget and waited for the time when the Clan-lord might smile again and honour would return. As for my grandfather, I think he took some pleasure from his misery. He drank his wine and swore and sometimes he was gentle but more often cruel, while the years turned and turned again and the marsh grasses grew.

Now Mhorged had bidden us come back, and had sent for me, the witch's son.

In the end she had been clever, had Macha. She had left me something of hers, something to taunt those who had betrayed her and keep me in mind of who I was. She was marked, that Horse-witch, with the mark of her people. It is a circle, perfect, pricked in with blue under the skin, lying just below the crook of the elbow. I know because I too bear it. Such was my mother's gift to me.

Morning came swathed in cold mist. My grandfather and the messenger rose late, both of them white-faced with thick heads. It was not until noon that the man was back on his horse.

I watched him going, standing well back in the gloom of the stable, with the thought that I should not be seen. But at the last instant Palug sidled beside me, to breathe his breakfast of bread and pork fat down my neck. Together we saw my grandfather raise his hand in farewell.

Afterwards he turned. His gaze went straight to us; his eyes were good still. He carried a willow switch. Left to myself I would have run but even as I moved Palug bunched his fist and thrust it into my back.

'Get out with you,' he said, belching. 'Can't you see when you are wanted?'

Chapter Two

If he could my grandfather would have set out at once for Nam Dubh. As it was, there were things to wait on. Palug was sent to the village to see the headman there about the exchange of our few poor cattle. He returned the next day with a sack of barley meal and some blankets and beads my grandfather could use as gifts. Tachga took the meal and settled to baking little flat, hard cakes of bread. Grandfather scanned the skies each morning, muttering, then stalked off to his chamber to sort his things, or else rode out alone from dawn to dusk.

I was glad to see the back of him. Matters were worse than usual between us and if he had much to ponder on, so had I. He'd told me to think myself lucky that Mhorged had sent for me as well but, when I remembered the message, I remembered too the man who'd brought it. With his wolfish, subtle sneering, he lingered like a taste I could not swallow down. If Mhorged sent him, I thought, what kind of man is Mhorged? And Nam Dubh – what welcome shall we have there? By day, going about my tasks, it was easy to believe how anything would be better than the flat, grey marshes but at night I recalled the song-maker's tales of fine, fierce men and my grandfather's of the ruined hall, broken and disgraced; and I bit my lip and could not sleep.

All this I should have taken to my grandfather but would never dare. In these last days he was quiet and brooding, though quicker than ever to anger, shouting out at the least fault, even things we could not help such as when the sow farrowed early and ate her litter or when the goats got free. Besides, after the messenger had left, the beating had been a bad one. He'd thrashed me till his arm gave out, cursing my insolence and blackening my eye afterwards for good measure. I hated him for it and I was frightened too, with a fear I could not put a name to, only knew it sickened me beyond the pain of weals and bruises.

In other ways he made me uneasy. Several times, going about my work, I felt his eye upon me and though I expected him to call me back and find some wrong, always he let me be. Once, at a breakfast we ate in silence, there was a great commotion from the yard outside as Tachga and Palug had a set-to, hissing like owls. He listened a moment then said, grinning, 'Well, lad, would you rather stay here with Palug for your master?'

He'd taken me aback; I could not tell if he meant it. I had not thought to stay, and as for Palug – I would sooner have run away and starved than call him 'Sir'. Bewildered, I would have made an answer, only his grin faded all at once and a light went from his face so that he stared instead, hard and settled under heavy brows. For a long moment he studied me, his eyes on mine as if he sought to read a stranger. Then he gathered his cloak about him and stood and left without a word.

Another time he called me to his chamber where he'd some tasks saved up, stuff to take to the midden heap, some other bits he wanted cleaning. I went, with dragging heels, to find his chest opened once more and him picking through it.

Later, when he'd gone out, I put by what I was doing and went to look. I knew little of what my grandfather held dear. Yet there were only old things in there; an armband and a neck band – a torc – the twisted metal strands dulled and fused together; a couple of daggers still in their leather sheaths, a bronze cup and heaps of cloth that had been garments once. Everything was cold and dirty, smelling of rot, and the clothes had been scorched and stained with water.

I shifted the things about. The torc was heavy. I wondered if it had been his once for only rulers, men and women, and warriors and priests, wear them. Yet though it was rich in gold it was finely wrought and delicate, the terminals worked into small, strange beasts, and more of a woman's thing, a queen's or a priestess's. I put it back and rummaged some more. Towards the bottom I found an effigy, a little carving in stone.

This I had seen before. My grandfather had made sure of that, bringing it to the hall sometimes and sitting it before the fire while he drank his wine. It was small and squat and roughly painted red, though the paint was flaking now. A red woman with a raven's head, the beak turned in profile, the

18

body, heavy-breasted, presented fully. The feet were claws, gripping the dome of a skull.

He'd talked of her too, Battle-hag, the Raven of his tribe, one of the triple Queens who urge men into battle and cry their doom. Her rites are bloody, but they make men powerful and the clans she guards are feared. So once her totem had stood at Nam Dubh.

Some nights still, when the moon was thinnest, my grandfather would leave the farm, taking only his cloak and his knife. Tachga said he went to make his own sacrifice, intoning the sacred words as once he had intoned them for his people. But the gods and goddesses are many, and who knows to whom he spoke?

Now, though, it was an unholy thing to gaze on her too long. I put her back and covered her in the cold rags once more.

Grandfather found me idly turning the cup in my hand – I had not heard his step in the doorway – and, striding past, had tipped up the chest till everything lay spilled and tumbled on the floor. Then he thrust his face at mine and shouted, 'Look there! Dust and ashes! And there'll be more where we are going! Or did you expect different? Too proud, eh, to ask me questions?'

He was beside himself. I shrank from him, dumb, until at last he quietened and drew breath. Even then I did not know what he would do or even what he meant. It was true though. From pride as well as fear I'd asked him nothing. In the end he eyed me narrowly, rubbing at his beard with his palm, and said, 'You have work to do. Take it to the yard. The light is better there.' As I went I heard his wine jar clink.

That was how things stood and then came something more between us, another trouble, though this one I kept close, a secret from him.

That night Tachga came to me. It was very late and I was in the hall, curled asleep by my place by the hearth. I woke to darkness and the slow creak of the door pulled open. A shadow moved and moved again, there was a sense of warmth and familiar flesh and the rustle of her skirts. Her voice told me 'Hush' as she reached out and pushed something down at my chest.

'There,' she said, whispering, 'take it and welcome. It'll be the last time I sew for you.'

The moon was risen and some of its light spilled in at the

door where it stood ajar. I tried to see her face, for her voice was hoarse and I guessed she had been crying. I knew what she brought me: a tunic, an old one of my grandfather's, thrown out some days before. She'd been cutting it to size and patching to make it good. I was touched, by her tears and her trouble, for to sew came as hard to her as cooking.

I reached up and hugged her, feeling her old slack body in my arms and her wet cheek against my neck. 'Tachga,' I asked, 'what will become of you?'

She sniffed and drew away, trying to be brisk. 'Me? Don't fret yourself. I'm off to my sister's folk. They'll have me. I'm not stopping with that oaf!' Beyond, across the courtyard, lay the hut where Palug would be snoring. I was glad for her; it would be better for her than staying. Palug was too lazy to work the farm and fish as he ought, and she too slow and clumsy. They'd have starved come winter.

For a little while we were quiet together. Then she moved in the darkness to wipe her eyes and push back her hair while I thought of things to say I'd meant to keep until we left. I was about to tell her how much I'd miss and think of her, which was true, for she in her way had kept me fed and warmed and hidden me on occasion, when she leant forward again, so close her breath was in my ear, and said, 'Where is he?'

I knew who she meant. 'In his chamber. He went straight after supper. But he'll not be sleeping yet.'

She nodded. The moonlight was full on her. It gleamed in her eyes and frosted a lock of straggled hair. She kept quiet, like a bird that scents a stoat. I said, 'What is it?'

At first she didn't answer; then she reached into the neck of her gown and drew out something on a long cord. She caught at my hand and pressed the thing into my palm. 'There,' she said, 'for you.'

I looked down, wondering. Against my skin it lay, cold and small and heavy. And then, when I lifted it to the light, it took shape and for an instant my heart seemed to fill my body. I saw a creature of lines and curves, not life-like but as a child might work it, a sloping head and back and legs outflung in a gallop. Where its neck met its shoulder was a loop for the cord and it hung and twisted gently, a thing of moon and darkness, shining in the night.

I said, 'Where did you get it?'

'I found it. Long ago. He'd flung it in the marshes but they give back what is not theirs. No one knew.'

'Horse-people's?'

She bridled at that, straightening, and her voice grew arch so I knew she would not tell me, though the truth was plain enough.

'What if it is?' she said. 'It's for luck.'

It seemed then as if I was wise and she the child. I remembered how, some nights, she'd slip away down the tracks into the marshes and how if, turning back, she caught me looking, she'd shake her head and shush. I'd never told; the Old Blood have their own ways and do not like them known.

So I kept quiet, though my mind was full of questions; there were some things best unspoken. I thought of the heap of ragged, spoiled things I'd seen that afternoon with their own mystery, and the beaked red woman clawing at the skull. Then I thought of the marshes where the thing had lain. Afterwards I said only, 'I cannot keep it.'

Her breath hissed between her teeth, her fingers kneaded at my palm. Her eyes were washed stones set in wrinkles. 'You must!' she said. 'It is for you. Who else should have it?'

What she said she meant. She was old and foolish and to her it was what she thought, a luck-spell, as simple as herself. I put out a hand, touching it to make it turn. Once more it caught the light and glimmered silver. The moon-glow ran like water along the pure, cold lines till light and metal seemed to fuse together. I thought, The Lady's horse, whose mark I bear.

All at once a great quietness was in me, and the whole world held still and silent. The horse-charm shone like mist, as if no man's hand had shaped it, only the old tales and whispered shreds of magic. On a breath it moved and trembled and I too trembled, deep within myself, swept with a strange, tight longing for which I had neither name nor knowledge.

But for a moment – no more than that. Tachga sighed, a shuddering sound; across the room the bitch, Nehal, snuffled in her dreams and thumped her tail. I was torn back to myself and angry all at once. It was like being shown what most you want and knowing you cannot have it. All my life I'd heard of charms and magic and what had come of them. The gods were angry and these waters were too deep; I did not dare to try them.

I held out the horse. 'Here,' I said, 'take it! You're mad to

21

have kept it at all. Think what the old man would have done if he found out!'

I spoke roughly, for she should have understood. Besides I was scared already. I'd begun to listen for my grandfather's step in the yard and the room seemed darker now and chilly.

For a moment she did not speak, only peered towards my outstretched hand. Then her voice came to me, sly and artful as any wheedling beggar's.

'Why, boy, if he should find it, what of it? Think of the hurt to him, to know what thing it is.'

I was truly angered then, flaring hot all over. I had to make myself keep quiet. 'If that's your game, you have no sense! You make a mock of me, and this!'

But she couldn't see. For a moment she paused, uncertain, then her own anger took hold.

'Mockery, is it? When he'll take you with him and who's to ask him why? More fool you to go with him with none to speak for you. What'll become of you? Ask yourself that! The witch-woman's brat! They'll make you pay for every prayer she ever uttered. They have their ways even now, with their own gods' faces turned away from them and the Raven-hag croaking high above. You'll be worse off there, you'll see. Ah, trail after him if you must and throw this back at me – but it's a sorry thing you do, to grieve me so!'

She snatched at the charm and backed away, like an old wild cat that spits and shows her claws. I crouched in the rushes of my bed, silent, and frightened though it was not a fear for words. Then she stopped and brought her hand up to her brow. I thought, She means it. She thinks the charm will help. She sets store by such things. And felt ashamed.

I said to her softly, 'Tachga,' and held out my hand. She turned at once, as Nehal would for fondling. 'You know the way he is. You know what he would do.'

She said, 'I'll hide it. I'll stitch it tight – here – in the tunic's seam. No one will know. How could they?'

Still I hesitated. My fear was very real and my back still pained where the willow stick had cut. This thing he'd not forgive. But she came up, rustling in the darkness to take my face between her palms and stroke my hair, and I wondered what she'd mumbled over the charm to make it so important.

'Arawn,' she said, softly as if I were sick, 'what manner of place is it? What does he take you to? In twelve years never a word – and now . . . Have something to call your own at

22

least. Take it home for the Lady. Call on her to hear. It will bring you no harm. I've kept it safe for you all this long while. This pretty thing I could have sold.'

And so she could, for a bracelet or a shawl or some fancy beadwork she could not otherwise hope to own. She was poor and foolish and her face was streaked with tears. It was that which moved me. She held up the charm again and once more I saw the glitter of the silver and the proud sweep of its form. The Lady's horse – to go back to Nam Dubh. I did not want it, but neither did I want her grief to send me on my way. 'All right,' I told her. 'Only hide it well. And don't let Palug see.'

Next morning I stood shivering in the yard. It was early still and across the marshes the mists had not yet lifted, but my grandfather wished to be away. He had been sudden about it, roaring his intentions at first light. He claimed he'd dreamt a dream to bid us on our way but would not tell us what it was. I think, in the end, he wanted only to be gone. Now Palug walked the horse back and forth and Nehal the hound clung to my side. In the cook-house doorway Tachga stood, the tunic in her hand.

I had begun to stamp my feet and pace when my grandfather appeared. He walked swiftly to his horse and mounted. For a moment I thought he would ride straight off but he paused after all and stared around him, unsmiling. The farm looked just the same, mist clinging to the black and rotten thatches, the yard where the pig snuffled and beyond the track and the thick-stemmed bog-grass and the glint of pools. But this place was never home to him.

He gathered up his reins. I drew my breath and glanced at Tachga, shaking my head. Lying awake after she had gone I'd decided I wanted none of it. I had my keepsake, pricked into my arm. The charm could be her own and bring less trouble. I started to walk after my grandfather, whistling up Nehal. Just then he looked back and said, 'No.'

I stopped, not understanding what he meant. He said, 'The bitch stays here.'

I stared up at him, then said, 'She's mine. You gave her to me. You didn't want her.'

'And now she's Palug's. He'll need a dog, even the litter's runt. She can bark, can't she?'

It was useless to protest. Already Palug's hand was on her

collar, pulling her away. She whined and fought till he cuffed her. Afterwards he grinned at me.

In silence I walked forward. Since waking I'd been on edge, hardly knowing what to do. Now, quite suddenly, I was calm. I knelt by the hound and stroked her ears and scratched her throat as she liked. I wouldn't look at Palug. Then I walked to where Tachga stood while my grandfather shouted, 'Arawn!' I took the tunic from her and kissed her. 'Thank you for this,' I said. She winked, coarse and fat as ever, then her lip trembled and she pushed me away. I began to walk after the horse again, out of the yard, with the tunic slung across my shoulder.

The day we came to Nam Dubh it rained.

From daybreak we had walked through forest and since then water had poured from the sky, steadily, grey and icy, streaming down the pathways and dripping from the branches above our heads. The hissing sound of it was everywhere, and the smell – cold and raw and sweetish with leaf mould and rotten bark.

We went in silence, though my belly growled; the last of the bread had gone that morning. In front my grandfather swayed on his horse, hunched and grimly sodden. He'd pulled up his cloak to make a hood and tucked the rest of it round his legs. From time to time he turned and shouted for me to keep up.

Through the mud I did my best. All day he'd been sullen and I knew that mood and what it led to. I wondered if he recognized the silent peaks we glimpsed from time to time through the trees or the river that roared below us and added to the noise of the rain. By now, after nine days on the journey, I hardly cared; the whole world was grey and wet. The way was slippery underfoot and I had water in my eyes and running down inside my shirt. My jerkin was stuck to me and stank of damp fur and sweat. My boots were days since split open and caked with mud; my hands so cold they hurt.

When he shouted again, I fell and swore and stumbled on. I could not hear what he said, nor wanted to, but the trees had thinned and he had drawn rein. I struggled up a mound of soil and roots and then, at the top, the whole mountainside opened before us.

There was a long slope of grass, some rocks, and the wind blew madly. I paused to catch my breath and, as I did,

Grandfather bent and tapped at my shoulder with his whip, saying something. The wind snatched his words and gusted rain full at us. I shook back my hair and rubbed my sleeve across my eyes, half blind with water. Blinking, I tried to follow where he pointed and suddenly, for a heart's beat, the wind changed course, the rain fell away like a torn mantle and I could see.

I'd not expected it; I had not guessed we were so near. Yet some sights stay carved in one as a craftsman carves clean and deep on bone. Nam Dubh was there, distant, outstretched, perched high as an eagle on its eyrie. As the wind gusted the rain I saw the ramparts, the palisade of stone and wooden posts that followed the curve of outcrop on which it stood, all small yet, and if anyone had told me there was more I'd have called him liar.

It stood alone, bare on its long ridge, while to the side the mountain continued its main thrust and the grey clouds massed behind it. Old and gaunt it sprawled, a ring of double walls, clamped to the rocks and dark with water. It looked bred from the land itself, rearing from scrub and heather.

Never had I seen anything so huge. I thought, A giant, surely, set it there – or a hundred hundred men worked the stones and rooted down the posts. It will stand forever.

I began to tremble. I felt empty and sick as I did after a beating, and close to tears. I thought of my imaginings – a head full of great hearths and round halls filled with men. Not this world of rock and cloud and sky. Against my side I felt the horse shiver too. I smoothed my hand down his neck and water oozed between my fingers.

We went on. The horse slipped on wet stone, hooves sliding, while my grandfather cursed. A bird winged up, black against the heavy sky with a long, wailing shriek, and then we had been seen.

High up gates began to swing wide, opening the palisade. My grandfather roused; he coughed and smothered it, and sat straight again, gathering the reins. Then he reached to push back his hood so he was bare-headed. He wore his earrings still, to have a touch of gold about him.

There was one last sharp rise and we were there. The open gateway led into a passageway faced with stone, unroofed and wide enough for three to ride abreast between the walls.

At about forty paces were another set of gates, but while the outer ones were tall and plain, these were broader and decorated. The wooden posts were carved with human heads, staring blindly, while set in each door an eye glared. The blue paint of the irises was flaking and the rim of bronze was tarnished green, like the bowls at home. But old stories tell how a man's soul will stare out of his eyes. These eyes were no man's, and yet they stared.

I must have moved or made a noise. All at once my grandfather leant forward and gripped my arm. He wrenched it upwards, pulling me to face him. Startled, I gasped and met his look and saw something new – a brightness, cold and hard as polished iron – though he was tired and the lines were deep between his brows as if they had been cut there. He could hardly keep himself from smiling, but it was a fierce, thin smile – not for me – the kind a man wears when he is to fight and knows that he will win.

He looked up towards the citadel. 'Nam Dubh,' he said, 'Black Raven; Mountain-hag. I'm back, Dark One, and look what I bring you!'

I was shivering all over and fought to get free. His mouth turned down and he grasped my wrist till I winced.

'What ails you?' he asked.

I muttered, 'Nothing!' and he threw me off, saying, 'I'll get you tamed!' But he watched for a moment longer, glancing sideways beneath his lids.

The great doors moved back on their hinge pins. The bronzework gleamed and was shadowed and gleamed again. Darkness fretted the passage and the rain blew through.

Grandfather laughed. I heard the whistle of his whip as it slashed down. His horse snorted and leapt forward; his cloak billowed out behind him.

I cried out to him, 'Why are we here? Why have we come?' but the wind took my words across the mountain and drove them to the rain.

He entered as he wanted to, the Old Lord coming home.

Nam Dubh. The name means 'The Dark Place', and that is true enough. Once inside the walls could be seen to enclose the whole summit of the outcrop. From rampart to rampart one could have set down our farm and its pastures five times over and still have had land to spare. Yet this was mountainside, not marshland, gusty and wild, with bare rocks that pushed through clumps of gorse and heather and thin, brown-tipped grasses.

There were buildings; Nam Dubh, though cursed, was still a place of men. Nearby, in the shelter of the walls, huddled a cluster of round huts, built as our huts had been of wood and daub only roofed with turfs instead of thatch. Across the way from them were animal pens. A sow and her litter rooted, goats were tethered to graze. Between the huts and the pens the track wound on, down across the stretch of outcrop leading to other huts and was lost behind a rise of land.

It re-emerged to lead to higher ground once more and to the hill-fort itself, distant with the rain and evening's dusk. From where we were there was little to see, save another palisade and a glimpse of a high, turfed roof above it. But further on, raised higher still, where the outcrop lifted once more, was another structure, a vast double wall, built of stone, only ruined and fallen in on itself. Windswept, open to the sky, its toppled walls showed pale against the heather. It circled round and was lost over the breast of the outcrop. I stared up and knew what place it was. And then I looked away.

Men were coming to greet us. They walked slowly through the rain to stand around us, and with them their women. For the most part the men stayed silent, stopping to watch us with steady eyes, but the women whispered and rustled and gathered their children in their dun and muddy skirts.

There were not many of them. They were the farmers from the round huts in the shelter of the first palisade, and they were wary, taking care to keep their distance. But they knew who we were; there was no surprise in the faces surrounding us, only curiosity and a little fear. I saw it when a child struggled free suddenly to point his finger and call out. His mother clouted him and bundled him away, turning back to gaze at us. She had a broad, stupid face but her eyes were wide and pale and scared.

I wanted to move on. I was cold and restless; their looks flicked over us, rough as cats' tongues. They would not talk to us. We could not know what they saw or how they saw us. It would have been better if they had reached out to touch; I could have pushed them away.

Up on his horse Grandfather sat and stared also, but ahead of him, into Nam Dubh which had been his home and his stronghold. His gaze went beyond the wooden wall up to the ruins. There he had raised his sons and marshalled his men,

27

had ridden out to fight and had suffered. Yet none of this was in his face. His jaw was set, the tendons corded below; there was colour high across his cheeks, but it was a mask only, of flesh and blood put on to hide his heart.

The men began to murmur and I saw my grandfather glance down at them, as a big hound notices puppies. Where he glanced they dropped their eyes and lowered their heads.

Still we waited. The track stretched out and grew small before us, with no man walking down. No smoke came from beneath the eaves of the hall behind the wall, and no firelight flickered there. There were only these few people quiet around us, and the rain cold in our faces, and the wind lifting our hair.

Chapter Three

Then we heard a shout. Grandfather shifted in his saddle and people turned their heads. Coming across the outcrop were other riders. There were three of them, two young men, smooth-faced, hardly more than boys, and a third who was much older, a big man with a curled brown beard. They were dressed warmly for the weather, in sheepskins and cloaks, not like the farmers' hotch-potch of rags, and they carried knives, belted snugly at their sides.

Already the older man smiled, urging his horse forward and bringing it round to stand beside my grandfather's.

'Welcome, Lord!'

'Uffa.'

The man had cried out his greeting but my grandfather spoke quietly. The earlier brightness had gone from him. He frowned a little, and now there was a kind of heaviness about him, as if he were ill and drawn inside himself again.

The man called Uffa said, 'Sir, you have been watched for these two days past, but the Lord Mhorged thought you would wish to enter here at your own will, by yourself. Nam Dubh is changed—'

'And he thought I might betray myself. What did he think I'd do, Uffa? Whine and whimper? The old man weep? Perhaps he was right. It is not as I remember.'

He looked up the track, to the wooden wall and the roof beyond and then at Uffa. He shrugged and Uffa looked back at him. Like the farmers, there was curiosity in that look, and wariness, but pity too. He had pursed his mouth before he could help himself.

The young men waited, well trained. They did not speak to one another, or let their eyes wander, and kept their faces stern. Only they sat their horses carelessly, their hands slack and their legs dangling, sure of themselves, and eager for us to see so.

My grandfather gathered his own reins. The four of them

began to move off down the track. As they went I watched the sway of the horses' rumps and the other, easy sway of the riders. It began to rain more heavily, the water blown by the wind like a great, billowing curtain across Nam Dubh; they went on slowly and I followed after.

They brought us through the wooden wall by a small postern gate. In front was the Great Hall whose roof we'd glimpsed, a round, high building, also of wood. There was a paved yard before it and behind more huts, like those of the farmers, larger but with the same turfed roofs. It was to one of these that we were led and there my grandfather dismounted.

He gave his horse to Uffa and for a moment stood before the threshold. Then he reached up and began to fumble with his cloak, trying to drape the drenched cloth gracefully from his shoulders.

'Arawn!'

I stepped forward and tugged till the material went down in folds so heavy they could have been carved. He did not look at me, only set his mouth and stared ahead. At my back one of the boys laughed and murmured something.

Uffa said, 'My lord . . . ?'

My grandfather shook his head. Uffa gestured to the boys and they left us, going back across the yard as before with Uffa in front with my grandfather's horse and the boys following after.

My grandfather did not move. The rain dripped from the eaves. Already the cloak pin had come loose where it gathered the material; I was scared that it would scratch him. I reached up to fasten it and my cold fingers touched his neck. His own skin was wet. For a moment his eyes met mine, bright and hard as polished stone, the lashes stuck with rain. Then he pushed past me and went forward to the hut.

At the entrance a wicker door had already been put aside to show a curtain striped brown and blue. 'Come,' he said, and I lifted it for him and we went in.

Even now, when I think of it, I recall the heat first, and the fire-glow, and the smoke that caught in my lungs and made me gag and cough. As the curtain swung back into place there were, for a moment, only orange flames, licking up from the hearth. Beyond was shadow and all around the close, musty smell of cloth and turf and timber. Then, as I blinked and threw back my head, I saw the man who stood across the chamber from us, waiting in the gloom.

He was big – I could see that much – and fair-haired, though he had combed back his hair and tied it at his nape. Then he stepped towards us and the fire lit his eyes and his cheekbones and the white gleam of his teeth. I thought, This man is my uncle, my father's brother, and felt it like a blow.

He was like my grandfather. They shared their size, tall and broad, and the light hair, and they were similar about the eyes, with a strong jut of bone above and pouched below; even their mouths were the same with a firm, full underlip. My grandfather's face was longer, leaner about the jowls and thinning with age, and their beards grew differently, my uncle's thick and bushy, my grandfather's sparser and straight. But the blood-line ran true.

It was that which shocked me. Till then, all that had gone before, even the journey, could have been a dream to put by from me. What I'd seen today was too vast, those whom I'd met strangers; yet here was something familiar and real in this man's face.

We seemed to stand a long while. The fire crackled and outside the rain hissed down and stirred the curtain. I could hear even the whisper of our breathing before my grandfather sucked in a great lungful of air like a sigh and spoke his son's name.

'Mhorged.'

'Father.'

They didn't embrace. It was twelve years since they had looked on one another yet each of them held back until my uncle stepped forward. Perhaps he meant to open his arms to my grandfather only my grandfather spoke again.

'You should have received me, Mhorged, not sent Uffa with two unlicked cubs. What were you thinking of?'

He sounded as he always did, peevish, querulous and fussing. He spoke to Mhorged as he did to me. I watched, wide-eyed, thinking it his spite; I'd not the wit to know then how grief and gladness take men different ways. But Mhorged's face never changed. There was only the suggestion of a movement halted and begun again. He gestured Grandfather to a rug, one of two unrolled by the fire, and said reasonably, 'Didn't Uffa explain?'

Grandfather glared at him from under his brows. 'Since when have you been so delicate for my feelings?'

31

For a moment Mhorged did not reply. Before him, on a low table, there was a wine skin of cracked, black leather and wooden cups set down by his rug. He filled them, grave and calm, and handed one to my grandfather before he himself sat.

'You've had a long journey. We were not sure when to expect you. We set the boys as look-outs. You could have been another two days yet.'

'We made good going. The ways were better than I recall. Which is more than can be said for this place.'

'You knew it would be different. It changed from the day you left it. You could hardly have believed otherwise.'

My grandfather said, 'I believed nothing! I have not thought of Nam Dubh. One cuts out a sick place, as far as one is able.'

He held out his cup for more wine; he'd downed his at a gulp. I watched it being poured and thought, He is just as he is at home. He'll be swearing next, and saying his drink's overwatered.

But he sat silent, staring at the fire with a scowl on him like black thunder, and I waited with my heart beginning to beat my ribs and the familiar rising fear at what would come. Yet they stayed quiet, drinking their wine, trouble on both their faces. The firelight glimmered on the cups and the leather of Mhorged's jerkin and my grandfather's earrings.

They would have spoken again; the silence was drawn out too tight, like a harp string in the instant it breaks, but before either could open his mouth the curtain was moved. There was a rush of cold air, making the fire curl and smoke, and a flurry of rain. I glimpsed a face, a pale blur in the evening darkness, and a woman stepped into the chamber.

She was not young, perhaps about forty or a little less, and her looks were thin and angular – cheeks hollow, mouth long. Her skin, even in the kind firelight, was yellow as cheese. She was out of breath, as if she'd come in haste. She paused in the doorway, one arm lifted to the frame, but already her eyes were restless. Her gaze searched the room.

In a moment she moved forward and glanced sideways at Mhorged, folding her lips, making them narrow and tight. Tachga would look so at Palug when she was cross or anxious about something but did not like to speak. I guessed this woman was my uncle's wife.

She gathered herself, running her hands down her skirt,

32

and came forward to my grandfather, saying, 'My lord, you are very welcome. Nam Dubh is made great again.'

It was an old greeting, a proper one for a guest, but there are ways of saying it. She spoke it coolly, for show, not for truth. Grandfather knew so. He grinned, fierce as an old hound. 'Gortag. Come to keep me in order. Are you well?'

She bowed her head, unsmiling, and kept her back straight and proud. She wore a long robe of thick wool dyed to a hot, dull red. It was loose upon her, unbelted, going straight down as if she had no breasts, and where her hands and wrists stuck out from the sleeves, they seemed thinner than they were, the bones like knobs and yellow as her face. It was an ugly dress and an ugly colour. I wondered why she wore it.

Then she turned to me and I wondered no longer.

Before, for the fire-shadows, I could not see her eyes, only how her gaze had shifted round the room. Now she stared full at me and my spine prickled.

Men call snakes cold, but that's not true; they'll seek a fire in winter. This woman's eyes were like a snake's, dark and hard and glittering, and the fire was in her. She kept her face still yet her anger burnt at me, from her eyes and her body, wrapped in that blood red dress. She hated me.

She said, 'Is this him?' And my grandfather grunted and twisted round, calling over his shoulder to me as I would call a dog.

'Arawn, here!'

They all had eyes for me then, and I stared back, sullen as I dared, feeling my belly gripe. I didn't move, not so much through defiance, though that was part of it, but because I was caught there, by their looks. I felt naked and raw and sick to my stomach.

Grandfather snorted. 'There you have him, Mhorged. Roech's witch's by-blow, two-thirds grown. They say seed sown carelessly ripens quickest.'

'Save it wasn't a careless sowing. Witch-whore she was, but Roech married her.' The woman spoke again, very harsh and low.

She moved across to Mhorged, going to stand behind him. He had none of her anger, only the kind of cool appraisal one man gives another on the slave block, where you do not see the person but rather how old he is, what strength he might have in his muscles, and how much work you may get from him.

He was easier to face than his wife. I raised my chin, giving him back look for look. He half smiled at that, quirking up an eyebrow, not with humour but as if he recognized the gesture.

The woman too had seen. She reached down to put her hand on his shoulder; her nails whitened in his tunic's cloth.

'Well, my lord?'

She almost hissed the words. I thought Mhorged would have spoken back as sharp to her; instead he shrugged. The easy lift of his shoulders under her fingers made her anger seem a small thing. He said calmly, 'He is like his mother. We might have guessed at that.'

'Like to like! Are we to find that out?' She spoke with her mouth stretched and tight as a cat's.

My grandfather leant forward and spat into the fire, a great gob of phlegm that crackled on the wood. He cocked an eyebrow at me.

'He has her pride, damn him. And he's wilful. As for anything else, don't fret yourself, Gortag. I've skinned his backside for him often enough. He knows better than to give trouble that way.'

She didn't answer, only stared at me as if she'd wielded the rod herself. Then Mhorged gave a quick snort of amusement.

'I'm sure you did. You always thought with your fists!'

Suddenly, for the first time, he and my grandfather were smiling. The smiles became laughter, broadening until they were slapping each other on the back and roaring till the tears came.

Knowledge comes through small things. After the laughter they grew quiet again, and in the hush Mhorged looked full at my grandfather so that their gazes met. In that instant I knew, as clear as if they'd spoken it aloud, that they were father and son, full of understanding, full of remembrance, or love even, for all the long years in between.

The back of my throat thickened. As I watched them I felt a rawness and a tearing hurt as if the inside of me was scoured. I would have run, only there were no wild wetlands to hide in now.

My grandfather glanced across, his gaze narrow. I guessed what he saw; he knew me well enough. Then he reached up once more to loose the pin of his cloak and beckoned me over, clapping my shoulder.

'Come on, you mannerless young cub. Show yourself and

be useful. And there's wine here. What are you about? Pour me some and some for your uncle. He'll want it drunk.'

I did as I was told. Despite his words his tone had softened. The fierceness was gone from his face and he was pleased and fussing. It came to him easy, calling for wine and giving his orders; easier at least for him here, where he'd been lord, than in the bitter marshes. Now he could snap his fingers and there'd be someone at his side. The fire would burn and spears and swords would be set about him, never mind that they were tarnished and their brightness gone. He need no longer fear the gnaw of damp cold at his bones.

I took his cloak, folding it this time and laying it by the hearth to dry. My hand shook as I poured the wine. Some trickled down and made pools at the bases of the cups.

Sitting there they began to talk. They spoke of small, familiar things; people met and remembered for a limp, a way of talking, the handling of a sword. Fights they had shared in – scraps only, hot-blooded feuds over cattle or wives – ended as swift as they'd begun, in the handclasp and oath-swearing. They laughed together at the memory of them; all while their faces were turned to bronze and black in the flames and ragged darkness. I watched and knew them joyful, and all the time the woman watched me with her snake-eyes, thinking to herself of the name that no one spoke.

At last, as the fire burnt down and the flames grew small and deeply red, they turned to me again. Grandfather belched and wiped his beard, and tipped his wine lees into the hearth.

He said, taking care with his words, 'Arawn, here's Nam Dubh for you. What do you think of it, eh? It's a place to be honoured and respected – your uncle'll tell you that. Remember it, or I'll have the hide off you again!'

He laughed at that, glancing across at Mhorged once more to share the joke. This time Mhorged did not smile; quite sober, he looked up at me from beneath his brows.

Grandfather steadied himself and jabbed me with his forefinger. 'Your cursed father failed in his duty. See you don't do likewise.'

What I was feeling must have shown in my face for quite suddenly Mhorged rose. He fitted his palm neatly under my grandfather's elbow.

'Father, it's late. Tomorrow we'll feast you, but for now

35

your clothes are still wet from the journey. I'll have someone show you to your chamber – your old one if you like – and fresh things brought. And some food. A girl too, if you want, to sing for you. Like Eriu, remember?'

My grandfather looked like a child promised blackberries in cream. I felt myself grow hot, though I needn't have been surprised. He was not much above sixty.

They began to move towards the doorway, my grandfather stretching and slapping at his stomach, Gortag with a stiff back and a face as sour as week-old milk. She reached up to pull back the curtain, but Mhorged turned to look at me again. 'Gortag,' he said, 'the lad's wet through. Is there nothing for him?'

There was a pause, just long enough to count two heart-beats in. Then she said, 'What should there be? Can you tell me that?' She swallowed, looking at Mhorged with a smile that stayed at her mouth and went no further. 'He can sleep in here for tonight. There are furs in the chest. He'll be warm enough.'

Their eyes met. Then Grandfather tugged back the curtain. As he stepped out he said carelessly, 'Send him some food as well, woman, if you've a mind to. He's had nothing all day.' And they were gone. I heard their voices caught up by the wind and found myself alone with the dying fire and the empty wine skin.

For a while I sat by the hearth, crouched over the embers. There was some heat left and a little smoke. From outside came the steady beat of the rain, muffled by the turfs on the roof, and there were other voices too drifting in, and laughter and once, far away, a snatch of song.

I was dazed, worn out by hunger and cold and walking, and bewildered also. Still I'd the sense of being in some dream, where things seem distant yet very clear. Yet now, in the shadowy quiet, there were things that were real as well. The weight of Nam Dubh, black with water, hunched its wooden walls around me. The curtain moved as the rainy wind thudded the door behind. On the walls, at each post, were fastened shields made of wood, covered with stained, dark leather. Designs, once bright, now faded, were painted on to them, zig-zags and scrolls. One had a huge eye, like on the Eye Gate, but this one was crimson where those were blue. I gazed at it and thought how other men had looked on it, their hands tight on their swords, and died.

36

And then I thought of what place this was, and of the Dark-mother who had ruled here, the Raven-hag of the battle fields, who perched and hopped about the roof-turfs croaking out her curses. And I thought of my father, if his ghost peered out at me.

For Nam Dubh had ghosts in plenty. In the nights to come I'd hear of hauntings, of the Horse-people who'd set down Nam Dubh's first gate-posts on dead men's bones to please their goddess, and of their warriors given as carrion, crushed and broken by the Clan-lords, rotting on stakes, not sent to their Lady through the earth. The boys who told me spoke as Tachga did, with fear and eagerness in their faces, whispering of shadows and demons tall as rafters.

They were not things my grandfather spoke of, not in the dark or by firelight or to the lapping of the marsh waters. He thought such fears weakness to be driven out.

And who's to say he was not right? For after all, there were no ghosts such as those that night. No slain warriors to walk again. No lords pinned in the earth. Not even my mother, with her long hair streaming.

Yet something crouched with me there. Not of Nam Dubh, no savage residue of battle, no skulls or bones or broken spears. Nothing of what Nam Dubh was built on touched me that night, though the Dark-mother stirred such things like black eels in water. But for then, there was only a knowledge, bitter as gall, that I had not wanted to come, that I was scared tonight in this place, with my uncle whom I did not know and his wife who hated me. I wanted to be home, not here, where Grandfather thought he was a lord again and took a singing girl into his old man's bed. I thought of who I was, and the mark I bore, and what I had stitched fast into my tunic. I thought, Why have we come? and could not tell the answer.

I was very weary; my belly felt shrunk to my spine but there'd be no food and the fire had all but burnt out. I got up and went to the chest my aunt had spoken of. It was made of wood, carved about the sides with hunting scenes. Men like jointed sticks were chasing a bear with dogs through a forest. On the last panel they killed it, and offered it to the god.

There were furs inside, old ones, half-rotten, shedding their hairs and smelling of mould. I stood and held them and thought of my own dog, Nehal, and how she would be crying for me. Presently I stripped and wrapped myself in them and

37

went back to the fire. As I reached it the last embers shifted
and turned to grey.

Chapter Four

I woke early. For a time I stayed hunched on my side and watched where the pale light crept round the edges of the curtain. Already the shadows were receding to the walls and the room seemed larger for it. Between the walls and the bearing posts there was space for a man to stand with his arms outstretched; the darkness had hidden it before.

I was glad of the morning. My hunger was worse and I was stiff all over. The floor I'd lain on was of beaten earth with no rugs to cover it. All night it had had the feel of yesterday's rain in it, but it was an honest cold at least, the sort I was used to, and the place was free of its secrets now, gone like holed-up owls to wait once more for the night. In a bit, as soon as the sleep thickness left me, I roused and stretched and fumbled for my clothes.

I was standing naked when the outer door creaked and the curtain rings moved. A figure stood in the entrance, black against the cool daylight.

For a moment each of us held still, staring at the other. I could make out no features for the light behind but heard the faintest quiver of a breath drawn in too quickly and with it an impression of surprise. Then the curtain was pulled right back and I could see.

He was a boy, rather older than I, tall and lightly built, with a lean, good-looking face, hawk-nosed and dark-browed, with black hair flung back from his forehead. I recognized him from the day before when I'd seen him murmuring on horseback.

Now he looked me over coolly, as my uncle had, missing nothing – I almost expected him to count out loud my ribs and ask to see my teeth. Afterwards he held out something and said, 'Here. Mhorged sent you this.'

It was porridge in a rough, earthenware bowl. I'd smelt it already, the warmth of it curling into the room. I hesitated, for it was not something I'd expected, but the boy said impatiently, 'Take it,' so I did. After that I tried to be mannerly but I ate like a wolf, squatting where I was in the furs. It was good, well salted and savoury; even his looking at me made no difference. I'd have used my fingers if he'd not brought a spoon.

Later, when I'd put down the bowl and wiped my mouth, I looked back at him. He shrugged and said shortly, 'Didn't they feed you in the marshes? Get dressed. There's work to be done.' He sounded sharp and his face was different, no longer cool but sulky.

My clothes were damp and difficult to put on, but I managed at last, even my boots which were broken. He stared again, but there was no help for it. I had nothing else to wear. Then I went out with him into the morning air.

He took me to the training compound which at Nam Dubh is set a little way out from the settlement. There are huts and some large rings, fenced round with wooden walls about the height of a man. Within them the boys are taught to wrestle and handle a spear and the sword and the heavy wooden shields. Half a boy's life is spent there.

That morning all was new to me. The boy opened a gate in one of the wooden walls and beckoned me in. Within were a whole crowd of others, making ready for a morning's training. Some wore thickly padded jackets, others were bare to the waist with rags tied round their heads and wrists to catch the sweat as it ran. They fell quiet as we came in, and stared.

After a moment Uffa walked over and my uncle with him. Uffa gazed me up and down, but by now I was used to this, almost, and muttered a greeting to my uncle.

There followed the worst morning of my life.

Uffa wished to see what I could do – how I could swing a sword and parry, outmanoeuvre and confuse with my shield. Whether I could use sling shot and hurl a spear to a target, and if I could wrestle and pin a man down.

By mid-morning, when the early mists had lifted, he turned to my uncle and said, 'He knows nothing! The boy's untaught! What was the old man thinking of?'

My uncle said, 'Hush,' then, 'what can he do?'

'Oh, he's neat enough, and with a good eye. He moves well and he's steady. With time I'll make something of him. But it's been left late. It'll be the harder for it. A pity.'

Across the practice ring I faced them. My teeth were chattering and my legs felt as though they would hardly bear my weight. At my feet lay a pile of gear: a shield, two wooden swords, several spears and a padded jacket. All were caked, as I was, with drying mud and grime. I was wretched with humiliation and ached all over. Around me the other boys watched, with grins on them like eager hounds.

Uffa clicked his fingers. 'Again! Let's see what you are made of.'

Shakily I turned back to the boy before me. He was thick-set and red-pelted with a white, freckled skin and hot eyes. Earlier, calling him out, Uffa had named him Dearg.

I took a breath and we edged round each other. The mud was slippery and I too tired to be sure-footed but he moved lightly for all his bulk. Suddenly he feinted to his right and as I started, he closed, his arms locking mine behind my back. I was lifted and flung down and held there, face in the mud. 'Whoreson bastard,' he said in my ear.

For a moment he bore down, shifting his weight on to my twisted arms till I had to bite my lip to keep from calling out and then as swiftly released me. Slowly I got to my feet. No one spoke but you could see from their expressions that they knew my history and those amongst them who enjoyed seeing me brought low.

Uffa said, 'Watch Luth with Dearg. You'll see how it should be done.'

Luth was the sullen boy who had come to me in the hut. He threw Dearg neatly, perfectly, twice.

I saw it with the mud stinging my scratches and my throat tight and painful. I had to swallow. Until I had come to Nam Dubh the only fighting I had seen was of fierce things that meant it, the geese hissing in springtime, some dogs snarling over a little vixen they'd cornered and torn apart. Here it was a way of life.

Uffa looked back at my uncle and spread wide his palms. 'What have you done, Mhorged? What have you brought me? A greasy, marsh-land fisher boy?'

Grandfather would have shrugged and laughed. My uncle though was thoughtful.

'You think so? No. A colt, with his ribs staring. Look at him, Uffa. Bridle him, bring him on. Then we'll see what we have got.'

The rest of the day passed in a blur of rain and exhaustion. Everywhere were faces, staring and chattering. I was not used to so many people nor did I know where to go or what was expected of me. In the end I clung like Uffa's shadow while he moved briskly from task to task, ignoring me.

It was he who brought me to the boys' hall that night. Little more than a large hut, this stood apart from the main buildings on a scrubbier part of the slope. No doubt it had been used once for storage. Now the boys had it. There they were a nuisance to no one and could be loud as they liked. Only Uffa oversaw them, and sometimes my uncle.

Uffa fed me first, sparing me the great hall where the others gathered round the cauldrons. He spooned out beans and pork from a pot over his fire and handed me a plateful. Then he too sat and ate, a big man with thick pitted skin on his face and a brown beard and soft curling pelt of hair on his arms.

We made our meal in silence. I thought all the time of the shameful day, and my ignorance with sword and shield and spear made plain before everyone. I could not put it from me and how I'd seemed a fool. But just as Uffa's plate grew empty he said, 'They've been told to lay off. Mhorged ordered it. So don't look for trouble but stick up for yourself. That's the way of things around here.' He sounded gruff and looked straight at me from round blue eyes. Then he ladled out more beans and ate them, staring at the fire.

The boys sat round the hearth, tired from the day's efforts, playing their last games of dice. For a moment I stood on the threshold where Uffa had left me, wondering what to do. They stared back as they had that morning, hounds at a pi-dog. Then someone raised himself up slowly and wandered over. I recognized him. He'd been one of those who'd watched and enjoyed each moment. He was no taller than I, scrawny with hair like greasy tallow, but now he swaggered like a dung-heap cock. 'Well, you marsh-land lout,' he said, winking back over his shoulder, 'what have we here?'

It had begun. I was cold all over, shivering inside and hoping it would not show.

Softly the rest crept forward. Some slid behind me, to push me into the chamber with their fists and fingers. The hut was too gloomy to see them properly. Only a couple stood out –

one at the side of the first boy, also short with a doughy face, a thick-set one with a broad jaw, and Dearg who had fought with me that afternoon.

Tallow-hair walked round me. I felt his eyes probe. He clapped one hand to my shoulder, not gently, and asked, 'Where are your things?'

I kept quiet. A warrior's son should have his dog and his cloak and his dagger. I'd the horse-charm and what I stood up in.

His hand slid down my arm. He flicked his fingers at the stained and ragged tunic. 'Such finery. Luth said as much.' He turned. 'What's this the old man's brought with him? A beggar brat to shame our hall?'

The others murmured, feigning shock, though their eyes gleamed softly. The boy paused behind me and took his hand away. Watching him, the doughy one grinned but I wouldn't turn. Then I got another push that shoved me forward. I whipped round and he cocked his head, smirking. 'Slow.'

For a moment he strutted, a black rook then, pecking worms. He said, 'Perhaps it's worse than beggars.'

Dearg was all eyes. 'Ruarch, be careful. You know who he is.'

'Do I? Who are you, fisher-lout?'

My hands were become fists and my heart pounded though I vowed I would not show my fear. Yet already I knew I was helpless, that they would have ways of hurting just as Palug had, or my grandfather.

They pressed closer. Their arms and shoulders jostled, their tunics brushed my own, their breath was warm on my neck. I smelt the sour taint of strangers.

I said, 'I'm called Arawn.'

Ruarch said sweetly, 'And what did they call your father, Arawn?'

'I think you know his name.'

'We'll hear it from you.'

There was no way out. Some stood before the door. I said, 'Roech,' and met their eyes in turn.

'And your mother?' He asked it like a whisper on the wind and someone sniggered, pressing back laughter with his hand.

'Macha.'

'Say it louder!'

I had to clear my throat. 'Macha.'

Ruarch whistled, long and low. My hands made fists again and the doughy one slithered beside me. He hissed, 'A fisherlout? No, Mhorged called him a colt. We know why. What did your mother mate with, horse-boy, the stallion running in her father's herds?'

For a moment I stared past him, into the shadowy room. Then they shoved me up against one of the bearing posts and held me there. Into my ear the boy's voice rose and fell and all the while the giggling that was like a girl's went on. I was no longer afraid, only filled instead with a great weariness. What I listened to was familiar, lived with from a child. There was nothing in the filth they told me, all through that night, I had not heard before.

In the days after it was the same. I got to know their tricks: the horse-dung pushed into my boots while I was sleeping, the way the bread passed me by at breakfast and how the stew-pot was scraped clean before it got to me. Worse were things that got me into trouble. Objects I had used were found broken; a spear shaft snapped in two, a bowl cracked, my tack repeatedly made filthy and begrimed. Uffa must have guessed but he laid on anyway before them all till I was black and blue. I came to dread his step in the yard and his voice hollering out my name.

There were ten of them, in Uffa's charge. They were the sons of the warrior men who still served my uncle, and we were all of an age. No one was put to Uffa until he was fourteen or thereabouts; until then his father or kinsman could teach him what was needful. Once such boys would have gone to other lords for fostering, to forge links between the tribes and be well away from spoiling. A foster son became as a son, and owed his dues. But since the Clan-lord came that no longer happened. Instead they hardened under Uffa's training.

Of the ten there was Ruarch, of course, who'd made clear he hated me but who'd have hated anyone new, for the sport of it, and his cronies. These were Maelduin, the dough-faced one, and sometimes Dearg whom I'd find watching me, narrow-eyed and sullen. Others like thick-set Benna, with the heavy jaw, and Eraid and Sithlann, ordinary big, hearty lads, would look to see what would happen next, then laugh and turn away. There was Nar also, tall, quiet and lanky, who'd hang about the edges, watching in silence. The last of them was Magh, who was simple and slow in everything but who seemed better hearted than anyone, and the dark-haired boy, Luth. He took no part in baiting but when he looked at me it was with a silent scorn more chilling than mere spite. Yet he was wild and gallant and good at everything in the training rings. Dearg followed him like an eager puppy and they were friends, which I found strange for Dearg I thought was stupid and Luth anything but that. The others looked to him as much as they did to Ruarch; only Ruarch they feared. It was not until later that I found out why.

The days fell into a pattern of work and more work. Those who lived in Nam Dubh were farmers as well as warriors. In the mornings, early, there were the stock pens to be inspected, the sheep and cattle to be looked over or moved to fresh pasture. The smallholders within the outer palisade brought in some goods, chiefly cereal and beans, in exchange for Mhorged's protection, but he had his own flocks and herds. Afterwards, while the women spun or ground corn or tended the geese, we boys waited on the older men, bringing their spears and nets for hunting, or else made fit the hall and swept the stables. After that came fighters' business, wrestling or sword-play or practice with spears or slings.

We had to be fit. For wrestling we stripped to the waist, no matter the cold or the rain which fell too often. Or we ran races up and down the steeper slopes – those who came last served the others at supper and went without themselves. Above all, day in, day out, there was arms training with blunted, notched swords, no good to anyone, or blades of thick wood.

For them it came easy. None had come to Uffa quite unskilled as I was. Pride is a sweet itch in sword-bearing men; the more it's scratched the more it burns, always there beneath the surface. Fathers had carved wooden swords for their sons and shields to go with them, and carried them on their horses' backs even while their mothers still sang them to sleep at night. They'd already had hunting and swordplay and schooling in what was expected. But I had been taught nothing and showed my ignorance.

Those days I floundered on the miry turf, missed my target time after time, was awkward with the sword and round wooden shield. All fingers and thumbs I could do none of it, nor understand any more than I could the noise or the hot, close way we lived together with the squabbling and the laughter. The pain was twofold. I was homesick. I missed the marshes – the emptiness and swaying grasses, the swooping calls of the water birds – and I felt shame keenly, looking up to see the others nudge and wink. When we wrestled I would be down and pinned and desperate, hearing, as always, the hissing words, 'Witch-brat! Witch-spawn! I have you now.' It was then they hurt me, twisting my arms or kicking, and Uffa would look on, unmoved, for such was how I learned.

One morning Uffa called across the yard to me, 'Come. I need to see something. Stir yourself.'

I'd been fetching water to fill one of the troughs. Unwillingly I put down the bucket. I would rather have trudged the long walk down the hill to the stream once more than answer to Uffa. I wondered what fault he'd found out now.

For once, though, we did not go to his hut or the boys' hall. Instead he took me to one of the corrals used for livestock. Within stood a pony, a dun tacked with bridle and saddle-cloth. Uffa glanced sideways. 'Get up, you.'

The pony seemed quiet enough, hanging its head. I approached, watching its ears all the time. They barely twitched when I murmured to it. I ran my hand down its neck and grasped the mane, just above the withers. Then vaulted. The pony stayed put, four hooves rooted. Its looks had not lied. It was quiet.

Suddenly, for the first time since I'd been at Nam Dubh, I wanted, almost, to laugh. I had not yet ridden in front of Uffa, having no mount of my own, though I had watched the others often. Uffa had expected my riding to be as bad as my wrestling. But there had hardly been a time when I had not felt at ease on a horse.

Grandfather had never taught me. Instead I used to take his old stallion secretly when I could, trotting in a pasture of wet grass, or galloping the dryer places in the summer before the day's heat broke. It was dangerous lest he found me out and the horse, when younger, had been mettlesome. But I could not help myself. Riding was something I must do, as a dog must hunt or a bird fly, and I came to no harm. I obeyed what was within me. My mother had served her Horse-queen well.

Now I set my teeth, gathered the reins and pushed on. Unwilling, the pony only grunted so I used my heels, hard.

Soon we were turning circles at a walk, a trot, a canter, while Uffa shouted what to do. After a bit he called, 'Get down now.' I cantered a final circuit and swung off.

He stared across at me, frowning. I joined him and waited. I wanted to ask, 'Was that all right?' but daren't. He was thinking; you could always tell. Not that he was any man's fool, only used rather to action.

Some days later, in a frosty dawn when the sun was barely up, he took me to the horse-field where new colts brought in by horse-dealers were running. Though poor, Nam Dubh still had need of horses, for the chariots and for the warriors to ride. My uncle traded cattle and wool for them. The dealers had hard, shrewd faces and herded the horses from the mountain before barely breaking them. They drove a hard bargain too.

The field was small. The milling horses were restless in the cold morning air, within sight of freedom. Leaning on the fence, watching, were Maelduin and Nar and Luth. I hung back, as I always did, wondering what was to happen.

The horses were beautiful. Bright, early sunlight shone on rough-haired quarters of black and dun and roan. They grazed or else trotted the frosty field, heads up, manes lifted by the breeze, tails carried proud. Neat-hooved, stocky, these were the horses of Nam Dubh, bred on her hillsides. War ponies, chariot ponies, the warriors' pride.

Within me something stirred – not joy as you'd expect at beauty, but a sadness such as I had felt when first I'd seen the horse-charm. It was not a grief that I could put in words, just a feeling that things were made spoilt and wretched. It came urgently – as if my very flesh was tugged at – so strong that if I'd been alone I would have gone away and wept.

Only I was not alone. Nearby Uffa was busy. He handed out head-collars to the other three who had need of new horses, having outgrown their own. They slipped into the field and began to examine the ponies, running practised hands down flanks and necks then standing back to eye them.

Uffa pushed a length of rope at me, his gaze too knowing. 'Don't gawp, you young fool. Get in there.'

I stared at him, and then back at the horses. It was true. I was so surprised my jaw dropped.

At first I was at a loss, bewildered for what I looked for. Then suddenly the horses raced, a headlong gallop that took

47

them up to the far end of the field where they wheeled and turned and halted sharply, squealing and bucking.

I saw him then. Not the showiest but tough and nippy with a fine, tapering head and strong hocks. He'd galloped with his neck outstretched, the movement easy and generous. Now he stood to snuff at the morning air.

The other boys were choosing. Maelduin was up on a bay already while Nar was having a hard time on a thick-set roan. Luth was soothing another bay. The horse I'd seen was grey.

No one else would have him.

A grey horse. I knew what it meant. Grey is the colour of the Otherworld horse, the steed which treads soft-shod between the doors of life and death. I knew it, and Uffa and the boys in the hall and my grandfather and Mhorged would know also. Yet I could not help myself, no more than I could help but wear the charm, and that was grey too, the subtle grey of silver. I wanted the horse, if he would have me.

I climbed the fence. Uffa handed me bread and salt, and a bridle which I held behind my back. More ponies came up and jostled, nudging, impatient for food. There was no time to be cunning. I caught the grey mane and felt him pull away, but I brought my arm up over his neck, reaching for the rope, and swung on to his back.

For a moment I held him, sitting deep, feeling his strength, the quiver of his muscles. He squealed once, laying back his ears, but I made him wait. The boys stood, eyes wide. Then I set my heels into his sides.

He leapt forward like a salmon through rapids. The other ponies scattered or ran with us for a while. There was another grey at our side; his back rose and plunged like a strong tide till we outstripped him. We passed Luth. Over the thud of hooves and the rush of wind he exclaimed and cursed, leaping from our path.

Before us was the fence, and by it Uffa. The day before he'd thrashed me for dirty tack, though earlier he'd seen me clean it. Now he stared, his face upturned, the fleshy planes of cheek and jaw stretched upwards. I saw his arm rise to shield himself and how at the last he cowered away. We lifted and hung a moment above him, and then we turned to the bare mountain.

The pony's hooves thudded; the stride was a steady beat. Beneath my hands the neck arched and stretched as he bore me onwards.

At first I sought only to try him, to judge his pace, his soundness, the softness of his mouth – all the right things one should do. Only it was enough to be on him; soon I had no thought but that.

We galloped towards the sunrise. The air about us shimmered. The sun flamed red as it crested the mountains, while the frost glowed with fire. We rode in gold and silver together, the horse and I, shining while the black palisade of Nam Dubh rotted behind us. He bore me out of myself on that bright hillside, away from all I knew and hated, and all the time the little weight of the horse-charm rode at my side.

We galloped a good way, turning down again towards the lowlands. I had chosen well. He was young and strong and untiring, but at length I stayed him where the trees began at the bottom of the pasture. We waited, warmed from the gallop, under the branches. The pony danced and would not stand. He tried to sit back on his haunches and in his shoulder a muscle jumped and flickered.

The morning light grew. The sky had night in it still, and the moon's high sickle, yet our tracks showed clear on the slope, cut in frost, and the mountains behind were close and black against a blue horizon. Far up on the crag the ruined citadel stood out. The sun's rays caught it. All below was in a slant of shadow, like a long, dark slash scored across the hillside, but broken walls rose from it, purple and brown in the cold dawn.

The horse grew quiet and curbed. I thought, We have ridden in magic – the Horse-queen's magic – I was overwrought and my breath came panting but so it seemed to me, born of the sun and the horse's surging strength. And it seemed too that nothing would be the same again, that the bad things had been charmed away, as if the horse-charm had sprung to life in its own bright glitter, to take shape for shape, scattering the darkness with its hooves as my horse had scattered shards of frost.

I turned the horse for home. We trotted, with him still eager, head up, hooves ringing on the stony ground. But he was obedient, come to hand, though different from the quiet dun as a waterfall from a river pool.

I led him into the horse-field. Once more the ponies surged around. I had more bread, more salt. I had no fear of the swinging quarters, the pushing muzzles. I slapped gently at the hot flanks, scolding them for greed, blew at them, stroked the soft, whiskery noses; and I held him still, the grey, the witch-pony, and he was mine.

I looked across to where Uffa had been. He stood there still and with him Mhorged and my grandfather, hard-faced, without expression.

Happiness slid from me like sunshine into shadow. I slipped off the head-collar and walked across.

Uffa said, 'A grey.' He grunted it out. Then, 'Fair-moving, though. What'll you call him?'

I looked up at them. They would not understand. No one could. I told him, 'Ban.'

My grandfather cracked me hard across the ear.

Even Uffa blinked. Then he scowled, the line made deep between his brows. 'What kind of name is that?'

My grandfather answered for me. 'It means White-face in the Old Tongue. His mother's tongue.'

I met their hot and staring eyes in turn. My own stung, filled with water from the blow. Then Mhorged sighed and touched my shoulder.

'Come with me,' he said.

Chapter Five

He took me through the yard and out on to a track that led up towards the open hillside, going briskly across the rough turf with a steady, easy pace that set his cloak swinging from his shoulders. My grandfather had the same walk, though lately he'd caught his breath sometimes as if it stuck like flesh to his ribs and pained him. But you could tell again they were kin.

He paused once, and told me to look back. We were on a rise of ground and I could see into Nam Dubh. It was very quiet. Within the palisade only the geese flocked and some pigs rooted in the midden heap. Smoke curled from huts where breakfast cooked but no one was about. There was nothing grand, nothing of gold or heroes. The muddy yard and rotting, dripping huts, the wretched bothies and the sties, were all familiar. I saw what I knew best – a farm, poor as ours had been.

My uncle said, 'What is it you see?'

'A yard. Huts.'

'No more?'

I shook my head. I was at a loss for what he meant.

He raised his bent head. The corner of his mouth tightened and looked ugly. He said, 'There is something I would show you.'

We walked on, going high until the land began to even out once more and a light wind blew. He halted. Before us ran the remains of a deep, curving ditch and beyond that lay an enclosure.

At first there was only a wall, a grey mass built of stones and rising up twice the height of a man.

The track ran to it and followed it round. In places the wall was breached, the outer part cast down. It had been built as a double skin, two walls held together with timber lacings and rubble between.

It curved on steadily, girding an outcrop, until there was a

51

break and the remains of two great wooden watch-towers, their gates gone. Some time past they had been fired and the timbers were cracked and blackened, rotting now. Some had crashed down, lying split and overgrown, just where they had fallen.

Days past, on the journey here, gazing from the forest track, I'd known what place this was. This morning, waiting on horseback under the trees, I'd seen it also. Now the joy of that ride was gone. Sick at heart, I stared back at my uncle where he stood motionless a little way behind me, with the wind stirring his hair and the sunlight all about him. He said, 'Go on.'

I walked forward, crossing the turf, stepping over broken slabs and boulders until I came to the walls. They reared above me, though the stones had shifted and lay aslant or jutted like teeth knocked out. The place was very old and the fire had spread into the walls themselves. Where the flames had been, some parts were reddish and shiny, the stones melted together. Others were only scorched so that the charring had flaked off to show a crumbled yellow surface beneath.

I stepped between the broken watch-towers. Within the walls were galleries and passageways for men, defenders, to scramble through. They hung ruined. Supported still, by heavy lacings of black wood, they sagged above, open to the sky, and in them sparrows squeaked and fluttered. Most of the stonework had fallen so that the space between the walls was littered with rubble, and the flagstones beneath had fissured. Between them tall weeds grew, swaying heads of pink frosted flowers. Once more I looked back at my uncle. This time he said nothing, only raised his hand as if to drive me on. I pulled myself on to a pile of broken slabs and clambered over.

Before me lay the place of heroes, of fine warriors and women bright with gold. I saw the painted halls, once hung about with severed heads and chariot wheels and pony masks; and it was worse, much worse, than what lay quiet below.

In front of me, within the circle of the walls, was a settlement indeed, but twelve years deserted; another cluster of round huts, some small to act as pens, some larger for habitation; one, largest of all, larger than Mhorged's in the citadel, would have been the hall. All were built in the old manner, of stones, and their wooden doors and turf roofs were long gone, rotted with the seasons. Their walls too bore the marks of burning.

I thought, It was here. It happened here. The Clan-lord raised his hand, and my father died and my mother. And I was a child and knew this place when it was whole.

I stood there, gazing out at that wrecked and ruined settlement. The only sounds were the sheep that grazed nearby on the open hillside and the wind sighing in the stone circle of the walls. And Mhorged had brought me here today, having seen me ride and be happy, and heard me name my horse Ban in my mother's tongue.

This was my punishment. To see what she had brought them. Yet I felt nothing. Not as I had felt fretful, uneasy things that first night. It was too open, too deserted for that. What tales it had to tell were spoken to the earth and the grass and the sky, not to me. There was only its loneliness, and a wonder that something so vast should be so empty. It had gone from men who had raised it, back to the wild hillside. It was itself, as an eagle is, or a tree, or cold, hard rock.

I began to walk between the huts. Beyond, where the wall continued, a stairway ran up its side. Once it had led to view points at the top. Now it led to empty air.

I climbed the steps warily; I had to test each one before I put my weight on it and then, where the outer wall fell away and reached only to my waist, I halted.

Under my hands the stones were pitted and cold, lodged tight. Kneeling on the broad wall was like being on a cliff top, high and exposed.

There was movement on the rocks below. My uncle stood there.

'Once,' he shouted, and the wind caught his words and brought them to me, 'there were men here who talked and laughed and spoke their thoughts aloud. How many men live now, do you suppose, down in the citadel?'

I cried to him, 'I do not know.'

'Twelve. Twelve men to serve me, with their families. The proud men, the fighting men of Nam Dubh. My father had three times that number and more.'

The sunlight shimmered. The frosts were melting. At times, in the marshes, you'd have thought the silence was a living thing, pausing at rest. Almost it was like that now as his words died away, but not quite. The marshes take you to themselves. You can crouch in the reeds that are as tall as men and watch how the same sky stretches over grass and water and the thorn trees that twist back upon themselves and claw like beggars. Here I was pinned on the hill's bare back, lonely as the hawk's prey, with the cold bright slopes around and the grasses blown like water. Only these great walls rose up, scaly with lichen and the marks of their burning.

He called again, 'Our gods are gone from us. No lord will foster our sons and teach them what is right.'

I looked at him. He said, 'Come down,' and turned his back and began to walk round once more towards the track. I waited a moment, with the sun on my shoulders and old grief in my heart, and then, slowly and with care, I made my way back through the gaping ruins to join him.

When we were on the track we faced each other. He said, 'There were our past times, the fire and sword and gold, our glories. Know it well since you're to live with it.'

I said, 'There was no need. Don't you think he didn't tell me all of it, often enough?'

'Yes, but now you've seen. You've seen the manner of our own gods' cursing. This place, with the living flesh torn from it – so much carrion for the War-hags' birds. And below – cold as corpse-rot.'

He paused and met my eyes again. 'The Dark-mother of our people no longer speaks to us – but she watches, even now. Look there.'

There were ravens, perched croaking on the battered watch-towers.

I looked back at him, into his face. There was no anger, only heavy thought. He said, 'What else did he tell you? Did he tell you why you are here?'

'No.'

'He told you nothing? No mention of reasons, or what would happen to you?'

'No.'

'You were nine days on that journey and he said nothing? Did you travel in silence?'

It was near enough the truth, yet still I held my tongue. Whatever answers he wanted I did not know them, but his eyes had widened to show their blue.

He said sharply all at once, 'Come now. Surely you were

curious as to why you've been brought all this way? You know who you are. Did you expect such a welcome from us then, or are you so stupid you do not care?'

'I care,' I said. 'Grandfather had no mind to tell.'

'And you would not go against him, or ask him again?'

He tried to make me out a liar. He stood here on this wild outcrop and I remembered how my grandfather had sat in his little, rotting chamber, making his ears good and bloody for some man we'd never seen before and sitting after, with his wine, grinning across at me, smug with his secrets. My uncle should have seen him then.

My anger flared until even my ribs felt hot and tight. 'Would you?' I said. 'He told you how he schooled me and you know what he is like – close as a bird's backside and twice as ugly! Anyway, as I heard tell, you were the dutiful one. When did you last try him?'

He stared at me. I looked for rage to brighten in his eyes but he only waited, long enough to show me insolent. Then he said, 'Your grandfather is old. He plays sour wits and slack muscles against a beardless face. He was not always so. But I can see why he does it. You're touchy as a girl when her wedding fires are lit.'

I flinched. He had meant, carefully, to hurt. Grandfather had struck me already; this in its way was as bad.

I turned away, back towards the ruins. I heard his step tread quietly on the grass and swung round. In the same instant he caught my chin in his palm, tilting my face to his, murmuring, 'Macha's boy.' For an instant I met his gaze, considered under folded lids. Then I jerked back my head like a startled pony and wrenched myself away. I could not help it; he handled me as if he owned me and I remembered how he'd looked at me the first time. I found myself paces off, breathing hard. He stared and said, 'I will not harm you. What are you afraid of?' And if he'd put half a mind to it he could have guessed.

He paused but I would not speak to him. He said, gentle all at once, 'You have to know the way of things, how people feel. It is hard for you here.'

I said, 'I know!' Suddenly I wanted only to be away from this place. A distance off, bodiless in sunshine, came the thin wail of a child, mewing on and on. Caught on the wind, it rose and fell through the gaunt walls that surrounded us, and flicked me on the raw.

He took another step towards me and I cried out to him then, after all, because I had to, 'Why did you send for me? There is no welcome. Your wife hates me!'

Startled, his face changed and frowned and cleared. 'Gortag? She remembers your mother. There was ill feeling between them over small things as there can be with women. And you bit her once, on the thumb, through to the bone. It went bad and festered till she had it lanced. She bears the scar still.'

The blood rushed to my face; he'd shown me a self I did not know and made of me a child. I could not match him, and he knew it.

He said, 'Do you dream these nights? What dark things do you imagine? No, don't look like that. I can guess. But hear this, the simple truth. Your grandfather rotted too long in that place. He's old and aching, and when's pride a match for that? Do you blame him for seeking comforts before the Death-hag comes and wraps her skinny arms around him?'

'He vowed never to return.'

'Only words. Noises made to the empty air. Little nephew, you'll learn. A man keeps faith with what he needs to. No more than that. Remember it when you have to.'

He looked away down into the citadel. The wind, blowing about us, still brought the child's cry and lifted the loose strands of his hair and tugged at his cloak.

Perhaps he was right. Whatever my grandfather's reasons, they were unimportant set against the fact of our arrival, like yesterday's hunger when one's bowl is full, or a hurt scabbed over. Perhaps my grandfather was no more than an old man lonely for home.

Some part of me was eased, as after a fever when the body grows cool and can sink into sleep. For the rest I was in a mist, stretching my hand to meet a familiar wall and finding empty air. I reached and reached but could not make my way.

I felt worn out. But there was one more thing that I should know. My uncle had been eager for the rest, only not for this.

I said, 'What was he like, Cernach? How could he do it?'

My uncle stayed still. His hair hid his face. Then he said, 'He is the Clan-lord. He does the goddess' bidding in battle or the land's own laws. He is what you might think him.'

He looked back. He met my eyes and said, 'Does any of this scare you? Try not to be afraid. You are my brother's son. There's that much owing to you. You'll live as a warrior's son should, with honour. You have my pledge on that.'

Together we walked down the hill. We went in silence. My uncle had spoken what he needed to and there was little I could say.

Just before we entered the settlement he stopped. He said quietly, 'You are not to go there again. It is forbidden. You can understand why.'

I could. I had sense for some things. He went on, 'I mean it. You must not go there again. Dark things happened and they are remembered – not only by men. The Raven is jealous. She knows who you are.' I nodded. He looked a moment longer shrewdly and afterwards said, 'Well then. Understand how you should name your pony wisely.'

Later that morning, about some chore with several of the boys, I crossed the courtyard. Two old women were there, cutting away turfs to reveal a cooking pit going down the height of a man, with lumps of smooth charcoal at the bottom.

Benna called out to them, 'What's this for?'

'Hakos's back,' answered one, 'and his fair bride with him. Mhorged had word last night. How'll you like that?'

The boys exchanged looks. Ruarch smirked. The other woman said, 'His lot will keep you in check. It'll be quiet ways from you, and skulking and manners now, and that's something we'll like to see!' She dug her neighbour in the ribs and they both fell to cackling like hags round a bonfire.

We walked on. Then Sithlann said, 'Well, it's about time he showed himself. Just how long does it take to be married?'

'Long enough,' said Luth, 'if you've a bride such as he has. My father says she'll bring gold and a strong alliance and it's the best anyone could have hoped for. It'll save us yet, he says.'

Dearg spat. 'Save us! What, a few more head of cattle? Some bits of gold for the women to wear?' He minced a step or two, swinging his hips. Then he turned.

'What do you think, marsh-land lout? What'll he bring you? Your cousin has a score to settle, you know.'

I said, 'Cousin!'

They stopped, staring. My voice had told them. Luth said, 'Yes. Mhorged's son and Gortag's. Didn't you know?'

57

I shook my head, and shrugged. They all looked at each other.

For a moment I thought Luth would speak. Then Ruarch said, 'Hakos is well bred at least, so keep your marsh-land manners to yourself when you meet him, won't you, lout?'

Chapter Six

A day after the cooking pit was opened the men went hunting in the forests. Next morning they dragged back a great boar strung up on a pole and carried between the horses. After that two fat sheep were killed. The women brought out hangings from one of the huts and laboured from dawn to dusk with ashes and hot water to get them clean. In the evenings they talked quietly together of gentler things, sitting on the rugs and heather in the hall and telling of the bride, Nemair, whose home was in the softer, eastern lands. The boys talked also, their voices low and troubled. I could not hear their words, though Ruarch laughed loud as ever and swaggered, his arm round Maelduin's shoulder. For the rest, a shadow lay on them.

Nights went by while the dead boar, gutted and held by the heels, hung in the game hut for its cold flesh to darken. The days themselves were bright and golden, strange to me after the marshes where winter wears an honest face. There the land dies as the year does, the reeds bleached and wet and broken, and the water rimmed with ice. In this place the woods were all fox reds and browns. Each leaf and branch stood out clear in the sunlight as if the women had woven them in place with rich wools, one colour laid carefully upon another. Yet it was the trees' own death they flamed with, like a fever. The marshes were sad enough in winter; here was a different grief.

On a day such as this my cousin returned. We boys had gone to throw blunted spears at wooden posts set up in the lower pastures. The air was hazy and we'd started the long climb back to the citadel, making heavy going of it for we were tired, when Eraid shouted out and pointed. Coming out of the trees beneath us, taking the main track at a canter, were a number of figures mounted on war-carts and horses.

We stared, watching them come on. I'd seen nothing like it in my life before.

Up the slope they galloped. The ponies sweated and pulled, yoked in pairs to the light little wickerwork chariots. The ground was rough and stony – the wheels bounced and lifted and scattered clods of earth – yet they came flying on. Within each cart rode two men, one who leant forward to urge on the sweating ponies, the other standing upright, brandishing his weapons – the long sword and the spear.

They were a fearsome sight: bare-chested, their hair swept up in spikes or else streaming behind them. They had painted their faces to seem like masks, rimming their eyes and cheeks with whorls of blue and scarlet. The dying sun glinted on the iron work of their weapons, on the gold about their necks and arms, and on the bay and dun and black of the straining ponies.

They were all colour and noise. Above the hiss of the wheels and the clatter of the hooves, the men whooped and roared. Behind them galloped others, their cloaks of green and red and blue fluttering. Someone sounded the carnyx; it blared, hollow-toned and hideous, a war-cry across the valley.

For a moment we stood, poised to flee. Then the boys too were crying out and running up the slopes, cheering the warriors into Nam Dubh.

As we reached the postern gate I fell back. Till then I had been caught up with the rest; now I faltered, wondering what was to come. I stayed in the shadow of the gate and peered within.

Everywhere was bustle. The men were opening the main gates, swinging them back on ropes; the women shooed the geese clear of the yard, clutching each other and laughing. I saw my grandfather stand in his doorway and then go in again to make himself ready. Only in the moments before my cousin entered did the whole place fall still and hushed and it was then that Mhorged walked out before the hall, and Gortag with him.

We heard the hooves and the spinning of wheels; at first a steady drumming and after a clatter as the track became paved before the gates. Then they were inside the palisade, with flashes of rough flanks and ironbound wheels and the swirl of their cloaks and painted flesh. Everywhere was movement and noise. The horses turned and shifted – the yard was full of them. Once more the evening sun caught their harness. I drew back further and looked on.

The first confusion cleared. Someone was shouting for the horses to be led away and the riders were springing down. I saw the men were young, new-made warriors, striding gladly to their families to be hugged by mothers and clapped on the back by fathers. I watched the boys I worked with run to greet them also.

My cousin had come in first, on the best horse, but I could not see him clearly. When he dismounted others were in the way and afterwards he'd gone with Mhorged and Gortag into the hall. His bride was only a dark shape, muffled up in mantles, stepping from a cart surrounded by his men.

Soon after the yard was clear, save of the baggage waggons that had trundled in and servants unpacking them. Families had gone to their own huts or to the hall to talk and drink with others. Of Hakos and his bride there was still no sign. Some of the young men stayed about, bellowing orders. I slipped behind the hall to one of the work huts which would be empty. There I crouched by a bench, a lamp by my side, mending a strap on Ban's harness. As I stitched through the leather the yard quietened and at last grew silent.

That evening we feasted. The boar was skewered through on an iron spit and set to roast across the cooking pit. From the hut I watched the other lads gather round while the huge bulk jerked and turned, glossy with juices and fragrant with the warm, bloody taste of the meat. Some girls from the farms tended it, hoping for leftovers. In the darkness their faces and bare arms were shiny and shadowy and touched with gold and their hair stuck to their cheeks and necks. The boys drank cold ale and gave them some, laughing every time the fire spat sparks to the stars, and the girls squealed and clung to them.

Later, when the boar was taken in to be divided, before the bride-showing, I slipped into the hall.

Inside it was yellow with the flaring pine root torches and hazy with smoke. Fresh heather had been put down and rugs laid over. People sat around in circles and ate already from pots of mutton and barley. Everyone was fine; the women wore their dresses of softest wool and the men had combed their beards free of knots and put on neck rings and arm bracelets. Even the children had been caught and scrubbed.

I moved quietly to where the boys had gathered round one of the bearing posts. Now they were subdued, the elation gone, huddled and anxious like birds on a winter branch. I shrugged down the feeling of being shut out and set apart – their troubles were their own – and went to a space beside Dearg who scowled and drew away. I ignored him and looked about once more. Some evenings, when the men had been hunting and were not yet back, we boys had the place to ourselves. The hall was large then, and dark and empty, and kept us quiet as if old warriors sat there, breathing coldly at our necks.

Now the place was full and my grandfather and Mhorged were together by the hearth, with Gortag in her usual place. I gazed at her a moment. I could not be used to her though I saw her often, crossing the yard to the women's quarters or busy about her work. Most nights she would sit after supper with a lap of combed wool and spin with her women. Yet she never worked for long. For a little time the bobbin would twirl, then her hands would drop to her lap and her fingers begin to pinch and pleat the wool still there, and her robes. She'd twist her yellow face about, this way or that, and peer with her dead, dark eyes as if she saw things in corners. If by chance she felt me watching, she would turn slowly till her look would rest upon me, cold as river clay. Afterwards she'd work again, speaking sharply to her women above the hiss of the twining wool.

Tonight she did not spin but was herself drawn tight. While her women chattered and gazed around the hall, she was still for once, and taut as cat-gut though now her eyes were bright.

The noise rose. Wooden platters clattered on the low tables, a woman screeched as a dish overturned in her lap. The men drank ale, strong stuff mashed from wheat or barley; our own was the second brewing, the thin, bitter drink of children.

I took a round of bread and dipped it into the nearest pot, scooping bits of meat. The boys murmured together, their voices low. I glanced at them, and noted that for once Ruarch was not holding forth among them. Then Benna said, 'What are you staring for, witch-brat?' and the rest looked up, hard-faced and scowling. I'd gone back to the bread and meat when there was a flurry of movement at the double doors which still stood open. Voices died away and suddenly rose up again in a great cheer. Golden and lit by flame, my cousin Hakos entered.

Barely glimpsed in the yard, now he was on show. He drove a two-wheeled war-cart right into the hall. His horses were matched roans, curbed and fighting for their heads. Their pony harnesses were hung with tokens that glittered and flashed and the war-cart was painted red. Beside him swaggered his warriors, holding high their torches. Clad still in their battle-garb they were bold. Their cheeks were painted, their eyes gleamed, their chins jutted fiercely. But it was my cousin who drew the eye.

Some of what I saw I'd half expected. There was much of my uncle in him. He had a dark gold beard, neatly trimmed, and lighter hair curling to his shoulders. His nose was Gortag's, strong and hooked. But, unlike my uncle, he also was painted with whorls and swirls of woad and ochre on his cheeks and brow and hands; and was richly dressed, with a plaid cloak woven in russets and moss-greens and foxglove purples, fastened at his shoulder with great, worked gold pins. For the moment he stood in his cart, upright and laughing, and in that moment I glanced across to my grandfather, who was his as well, squatting in the heather. He watched him as a starved man watches the stew-pot, empty heart and belly in his eyes.

Dearg said nastily, 'What do you think of him, toad-spawn? He's fine, isn't he? Good stock runs true they say.' I swung round and there must have been some look in my face for his eyes widened. Then he flushed, the red blood flooding upwards from his neck, and reached over for his cup.

Slowly Hakos drove the war-cart round the hall, his hands hard on the reins while the horses stepped high and fidgeted their bits. He halted before Mhorged and my grandfather who stood for him. The warriors slipped away to find their places.

The hall hushed again. Everyone was happy and expectant. Hakos's was a fine homecoming. Now the bride was looked for.

There was silence. Then from outside came the dull beat of a drum, slow and hollow-sounding.

People fell quiet, the silence growing tight and strange as if they listened in the dark. No one laughed or ate or tilted back their beer-cups. Even the dogs stopped scuffling in the heather and pricked their ears.

The drum thudded. Steady and slow it beat, a foot-fall, a

sea-sound. It drew close, with something relentless in it. The rhythm never changed, only loudened as if it kept pace with what came near. My own spine crawled.

Like a ghost a dim shape moved in the doorway. The darkness took it back and afterwards it was there again. A woman.

A dark woman come from darkness. She stood there, Hakos's wife, framed in the doorway, her back to the night sky and the stars, but still in darkness with the night coiled like smoke around her.

All around the people murmured and now there was fear in their voices, rising as a wind will rise across open water, ruffling all before. She paused, white face, pits for eyes, and then stepped into the light.

Hakos had been fine but she was finer. She shimmered with gold, from threads in her red-brown hair to the border woven at the hem of her gown. She wore her diadem and torc, her bracelets and belt, even anklets that chinked as she walked. But the gold was set against black – the true black, the sacred black, of these people. For she wore too a cloak of feathers, raven and crow, shot through with green and purple and blue, a dark rainbow in that hall of yellow, smoky flame.

Slowly she walked, the feathers stirring and lifting at every pace. Behind, to attend her, walked a child and an old, shuffling woman. They passed by us, she small and slight with thin bones, the heavy gold circling her wrists and neck like chains to weigh her down.

Like Hakos she came round the hall before the tables. Her face in profile was calm, the nose straight, her brow arched, her chin soft and a little heavy. Moisture clung in tiny beads above her lip. No one spoke. She moved with grace and pride. A good match, Luth had said. She was a princess, and let us see it with every step she took.

Hakos had left his war-cart. The drum-beat ceased and they stood together before us all.

The silence was deep as darkness and they were there, in its heart, with the people looking on; Hakos with his spear and chariot, his bride with her cloak of black feathers, the child and the old woman. And in the silence it seemed as if something should be spoken, something solemn and ritualistic, for it was an ancient thing we witnessed – the warrior and the raven; maid and wife and crone. A mystery come back to

Nam Dubh, that had been stripped of its mysteries long years since.

My hands were damp. Cold sweat trickled between my shoulder blades. I was confused and afraid, but without understanding my fear, like an animal sensing a change in the wind or the sky or the shadows on the grass. I thought only, She serves the Raven-goddess – whom the Clan-lord forbade to them. How is she here? The gold and black burnt at my eyes, my blood felt thick and cold. I put my hand to my brow and when I looked up I saw Gortag with her eyes on mine and my grandfather staring on the girl, and his own eyes were empty and filled with the night.

Still there was the silence. Others were afraid. One could smell it, sharp as fox stink, and feel it and hear it in the cold and the shudder of long-held breath; and with fear came anger. Softly, like a growl, the men muttered in their throats.

Gortag moved. Swift as a snake she slipped from Mhorged's side and stepped up before the war-cart. She put her hands to her neck and drew out a token. Something shone, not gold but with the blighted gleam of yellow bone. She held it out, dangling from her straightened arms.

Beneath her gown her breathing was quick. Her ribs sucked in and out. But her face was bright in the torchlight.

'See,' she cried, 'look on it! Fit for the Lady who comes back to us. All will be well.'

We saw what she held, a raven skull on a leather string, dry and fragile as thin, peeled birch bark. She turned, bending a little to Hakos's wife, then stepped back and the thing hung between the girl's breasts.

'Welcome her!' she cried.

Still there was silence. The tribe were uncertain, swayed and driven like cattle before the winter slaughter. Then Mhorged stepped forward and clasped her in his arms and Gortag touched her lips to her brow, for custom's sake.

Suddenly there was laughter, the women crying out upon her dress, her looks, her youth, the men calling for more drink. Yet even in the noise people caught each other's eyes and frowned, and some of the older men drew close together.

Shaking, I drank down a cup of ale – good ale now. The boys celebrated with the rest.

The feast went on. The great boar was dragged on a hurdle into the hall and the women set about it with knives, apportioning the joints. The drum-beats sounded again, harsh and quick. Once more the ale came round and the hall grew hot and stuffy with the torch-smoke thick about us and the smell of men and meat. I glimpsed the girl in her black cloak seated in the heather, served by her women, and Hakos, watchful as a fox.

The boys had become noisy, flushed with drink and excitement. They talked eagerly of what they'd seen, listing the gold and Hakos's weapons. Then Sithlann looked up and nudged at Benna, the laughter dying from his face. I followed their gaze.

The young warriors had begun to swagger, and people drew back from them. They had brought daggers into the hall – narrow-bladed ones with enamelled handles, sheathed in coloured leather, like the one I'd seen in my grandfather's chest; bride-gifts from the lady's father. They took them out to display, twisting the blades to catch the light, and afterwards started a contest, throwing them into the nearest post and whooping loudly. Then, as the meat went round, they raised their voices and gestured to one another, claiming one another's share. There was one, thick-necked, splendid as a stag, with blond hair lying on his shoulders, who was the loudest.

Time after time he'd spring from his place, and laugh and shout, going the rounds, challenging each of his companions in turn. He wrestled with them all, and sprawled and grappled on the rugs and heather. After a while the older men urged them on. They made a circle and cheered him, yelling his name: 'Arax! Arax!' It was the first time I'd heard it. My grandfather stood in his place, bellowing with pleasure. But the boys watched in silence.

At last Mhorged put down his cup and nodded across the hall. Someone scuttled forward with a haunch of pork and gave it to Arax who cracked it open between his fingers. He began to eat, the juices running down his chin. Around him people laughed and slapped his back and sat down to their own platters again. I looked and started. I said, before I could help it, 'Ruarch's with him!' and Dearg said, his mouth twisting, 'He's his brother.' Then Mhorged clapped his hands.

It was time for music. From our midst Luth stood up, a wooden harp in his hand.

The boys drummed with their fists upon the table. They

were proud of him and he had a clear, true voice. He sang sometimes in our hall at night, with the others joining in or else inventing new words for old tunes. Now he was nervous, taut and quivering slightly, but he waited till we wcre quiet and then, in a moment, struck up a ballad with a strong beat. We listened between mouthfuls of roast pork, savoury with gravy, and ale. He sang others like it, with people calling for favourites, and then he slowed the pace and sang of love and sad things.

Dearg said, to anyone who'd listen, 'I tell you – his heart's in this more than throwing spears or working in that stinking ring. And he's good.' I wondered at that, though Dearg would know. Then I looked at Luth and understood. He sat by the hearth where a great log burned, looking grave and proud, with a frown just creasing his brow. His clever fingers plucked the strings and the sweet notes soared.

The torches burnt low, dripping resin. The young warriors' gold glinted. The air was heavy and hot. Hakos, who had been talking across the earlier songs, stretched out his legs and leant back on his rug and listened.

Only once was there a disturbance. My grandfather threw down a bone to a favourite hound and another, lying beside the bride, growled and went for it. The girl shushed it and it came back to her straight off. I saw her face full on then. Her lips were firm, her gaze straight.

Luth never checked. The music went on until he drew the last, sad note out and then, before people could applaud or call for more, he pulled his fingers harshly across thc strings and went straight into a song fit for a wedding feast. There was a great roar from the men, and laughter, and Mhorged gestured for him to go on.

They were shouting the chorus when someone tugged my sleeve. I jumped, staring up to find that a man my grandfather had as servant stood there with something in his hand. He said, 'The old lord sends you this. He said to tell you that since you're seeing fine sights tonight you'd best be decent, like the rest. Here.'

He held out his hand. I caught sight of a soft, shadowed gleam and took what was offered. It was an armband of beaten bronze, worn thin and very old and not very wide.

I stared at it and felt the smooth metal resting on my palm. It was quite plain. I pushed it on to my arm, over my elbow where it fitted, and heard Benna say, 'So you're a favourite for once.' I paid him no heed but looked up the hall to speak my thanks. But the servant was gone and when I searched for my grandfather's place, that too was empty.

Much later, in our own hall, we had more music. Luth played, his face dreamy, another old haunting tune, half-familiar. The notes floated true as birdsong and his voice murmured on.

Most of the others were asleep, curled in their blankets on the floor or sprawled together on the wide beds set against the wall. Those who were awake had settled by the fire watching the flames in silence. I sat in my place by a wickerwork screen, hugging a goatskin round me, not yet ready for sleep.

I thought of the solemn, bright-haired girl – Hakos's bride, with her cloak of ravens' wings. I wondered how she saw us and if she was afraid. I remembered her stern young face, and the bright gold about her neck and forehead and arms, and how she'd snapped her fingers at the hound.

I thought too of my cousin, bold and bright as the heroes in Luth's songs. Like a hero he had eaten and drunk his fill, and held it well as was expected; and when he'd laughed his friends had laughed, and when he'd smiled they'd watched and smiled also. Yet it had not been he who had fought.

I had no gold, but I had my armband and that other gift, more beautiful yet but shameful, glimpsed by moonlight and hidden ever after in close, thick darkness. I could reach and feel it there, pressed into my flesh. The one I could wear; the other never. But which of the two was my talisman then I could not tell.

I should have learnt Uffa's lessons better. The blade, he told us, bites no gentler for the jewels on its hilt; even foxes grin and wag their tails. So it was with Nam Dubh. That night it had worn the sheen of gold, but when I woke it was to its darkness, and a pain and bitterness that touched me to my soul.

I had no warning of its coming. There was only the crash of the door, flung back upon its hinges, a cold rush of air and bright flames dazzling in my eyes. I reared up from my blanket and glimpsed faces and heavy leather shirts. A hand pushed me back and I was kicked, hard, in the ribs. I rolled and twisted and began to fight, tangled in the blanket. Someone yelled out, 'Get him!'

There were more flames, thrust down towards my face. They stank of pitch and smoked so that I could no longer see. Someone kicked again and I cried out then, because I'd not expected it. The swing of a cloak, heavy with mud, caught me full across the mouth.

They were all around me. Half-blind I crouched against the wall and shivered with cold and shock. My blanket slipped from me and my skin was prickling; I heard my own breath sob in my throat. And now it had gone quiet.

I gazed around, blinking because my eyes stung. The boys stared too, Luth, Dearg and the rest, eyes wide, mouths agape, broken from their sleep and drawing back to one another. I understood then – too well. The silence became a hush, racked out between us all; except I heard the blood-beat, thick and fearful, like a deep echo in my ear.

It was the young warriors who had come – seven of them – and they watched us as we watched them, but with the swagger of those already men, hands on hips, flicking glances at each other. One of them was Ruarch's brother, Arax.

They didn't move. One stood apart, holding up a great torch. He held it before him so I couldn't tell who he might be, but the torch fluttered like a scarlet rag in the night wind. Two others had torches also. They stood with the rest in a semicircle, clad still in their finery. At their sides the bride-gift daggers winked. Cloaks hung heavy from their shoulders. They wore their gold about their throats and wrists and their shadows were flung huge on the floor and walls behind them.

Still they waited. No one moved or spoke. Even to swallow sounded loud. I looked across to where the others were. Fear lay like a cold sweat upon my limbs and they were huddled, their own faces, even Ruarch's, scared and gleaming, and their fear made mine worse. They watched as horses do when wolves pad by at midnight to run the weakling out.

In the yard the dogs began to bark. Someone called sharply and the man at the doorway turned and called back. His torch flared, cutting a high arc and flames streaked the chamber like water. I heard the door pulled to and tied.

Arax stepped forward. He pushed between the others who gave way for him and stood before me, gazing down. I thought of how I'd seen him at the feast, as he'd called across to others and cracked his jokes, and of his boasting and his fighting. There, at a distance, his looks had been full and bold. Close to he was thick-necked, with a high colour, and his eyes were set close like a fox's. He said, smiling, 'Easy, little colt, little cub. We only want some fun.' And reached for me.

Till then, dazed, blurred still with sleep and shock, I think I had not understood why they were here. Now, at his touch, I was terrified. From being blind I saw too clearly. I flinched away, trying to ward him off. He was neat, though, as a cat, despite his size, and we'd had the same teacher. Briefly we struggled but the wall was at my back and the others came to help him. I could not get free or beat him away. At last he held my wrists in his big hands, panting and laughing. Then he hauled me on my knees towards the hearth.

He stopped just before we reached it. The others gathered round; even the boys stirred from their blankets. He glanced towards the embers, still burning in their ring of stones and for a moment I thought he meant to drag me through them. But he'd only looked to see that the others watched. He'd something else to do to me.

He no longer smiled. His mouth had tightened. Nor did he look any longer in my face and I knew then what he wanted. Slowly he began to harden his grip on my wrist but I was ready for him and tightened back. He kept on though, with a careful flexing of his sinews as if he pulled upon rope. My arm began to ache and the muscles quivered – I was no match for him but I found some strength from somewhere. Then he gave a grunt and twisted his hand. A pain shot through to my shoulder. He held my naked arm outstretched before them all.

He'd known what would be there. It was no secret, nor had I ever tried to keep it hidden. At least that way no one could call me ashamed or coward. Yet you'd have thought he'd laid bare some horror. He stared around with a dropped jaw and bright eyes, like a woman come upon mischief, and beckoned to the others. Already they were laughing and pretending to be shocked. They jostled round me and one pinched the mark and after shook his hand and sucked his fingers to make believe that it had burnt him.

At last Arax waved them back. 'Well,' he said, speaking so everyone could hear, 'you were right, little brother, we've rotten stock among us!'

He flung me off, as hard as he could, on purpose to hurt

me more. Then he wiped his hand upon his cloak. I'd landed at the others' feet, across the hearthstones. One kicked me and said, 'Crawl away, marsh-frog. Find a hole and hide there.'

I would have if it had done some good, only they'd have had no mercy. Instead I got to my feet, seizing what pride I had left as another might seize a sword. It seemed that all along I'd known this would come; if it was here the least I'd do was face it and make it their shame, not mine.

Arax came up again. This time he did not look at the mark but to see if I wept or not. I didn't, though it would have pleased him better if I had. I stared back and saw something that was cruel and ugly peer forth from his eyes.

He said, 'Why have you come back, you hell-hag's puppy?'

I had to pause to make sure my voice was steady. 'Mhorged sent for us. He wished to see his father and care for him. And me.'

He grinned once more at that, looking to the others. He said lightly, 'Is that what he told you?' And they laughed.

Afterwards it was quiet again. Across the chamber the boys kept tight and huddled by the wall. Only Ruarch stood apart, watching his brother. The rest were afraid.

Arax had not yet done. He watched me narrowly all this time and suddenly took hold of me, pushing me backwards till I fell against one of his cronies who seized my arms and held me fast. When he saw I could not get away, he cried out, 'A charm, a charm, witch's boy!' He made his voice high-pitched and nasal, like a peasant whining to the village wise one.

The rest began to snigger, muffling their laughter behind their fists, eager for more. The boys stirred again uneasily though Ruarch had crept nearer. Arax knelt in front of me, making play his knees ached. He had the part off well, twisting his fingers together and ducking his head. Somewhere he'd seen it done.

He spoke again, still with his whine. 'There's a girl I want, sweet as honey, ripe as an apple . . .' He added some more, all of it filthy, while his friends roared louder. 'She'll have none of me, witch's boy, so work me a spell. Ask something of that *cailleach* of yours!'

That's how they name the Mistress, the Horse-Queen, my grandfather's people. They will not use her proper title, only

71

sneer, though *cailleach* is Old Tongue, true enough. But it means 'the hag'. It's what they always call her.

He was smiling as he spoke, with white teeth and narrowed eyes. He was older than I by years. I stared over the top of his head to the door beyond where someone else still stood unseen behind his smoking torch. I thought of the 'honour' Uffa urged on us and wondered what honour there was in this. Then he got to his feet, and the thick bulk of him blocked out the torch and he leant over me. His underlip pushed out, like a man's squaring to fight, and his voice became his own again.

'What do you need, witch-brat? Spittle? Clay? Wax? What binds a spell and keeps it fast? We've heard. Look, I've brought you some pretty hair. Isn't that what your mother used?'

He flapped something down in front of me. It took the torchlight down its length and shone, wiry and rough and grey. Horse-hair. A whole hank of it, tied to a switch. They'd have pulled it from poor Ban. Arax threw it into the ashes and it moved, sluggish in the heat, to curl and settle there.

Whoever had hold of my arms tightened his grip and shook me. He said, 'Arax, he's very quiet. Won't he do your bidding?'

I stared again into the hot, blue eyes and saw what a taste he had for this. My mouth was dry and bitter; I could barely swallow down my fear and all the time I thought, What will he do to me?

He must have seen me flinch. He peered into my face and said, 'Won't you?' He'd dropped his voice so the others craned to hear. 'Won't you make a charm for me? I want that girl.'

As he wanted me, skinned and salted with shame, crying at his feet for him to stop or muttering nonsense for them to jeer at. I could feel blood drying on my face from where the cloak had cut me and the pain in my arms where I was held and knew that in a moment it would be worse. Almost I struggled to break free but there was no one who would help me. I was alone with only my own self to answer to.

I flung up my head. My voice trembled but it rang clear. I said, 'Can't you do your own wooing, Arax? It's a brave man who admits he cannot please the girls. Doesn't she like your kisses on her? Your mouth is big enough!'

From around came a kind of gasp and a sound, not quite of

72

laughter, but as if some smiled or raised their brows at each other. From the corner of my eye I saw the boys crane on tip-toe to see.

Arax too made a noise, deep in his throat. I had thought he would hit me straight off, but he'd caught himself back in time. Now he stared with the blood high in his face and his thick neck corded. When the storm broke it would come howling. He leashed it in for it to madden further.

He stared round for quiet. The others murmured and took a while to settle and someone said, 'Truth there, Arax!' But afterwards they hushed to see what else would happen.

Arax turned back to me. His narrow eyes were hot and hard, like a boar's before it charges. He said, 'No magic, witch's boy? See here. Perhaps you will like mine!'

He spat then, right into the hearth. There was no hiss or bubble, only a little pool of froth sliming the ashes. He took up the hank of horse-hair and dabbled it there.

'Ha!' he said, and pointed to the wet, grey circle. 'Here's magic for you!' And flicked the hair straight at me.

I stood there, with his spit and the ashes dribbled on my face, and his laughter and his friends' laughter in my ears, and in that moment I was taken out of my fear.

A great anger welled up in me – not wild and burning like the torches, but cold and clear as spring water. I saw myself as he did, held tight and helpless, and him with his sneering mouth and swelling throat and the others pointing at me. I saw too the chamber, streaked with flame, and the huddled, frightened boys and the old rafters up above where the shadows moved.

Within me something stirred and gathered, like great wings beating in my brain. It was beyond myself and what it was looked at him and thought, You are an oaf and a brute, through and through. There's no more to you than that. And you know yourself. You hate what you cannot break and what you can you hate as much. What hope is there in that?

I thought of what he'd done, and his ugliness and cruelty in this place, and there was in me the knowledge of how this place had been, lived in and sacred time out of mind, longer by far than my grandfather's hall or his father's father's before him. Then the grey stones had risen, high and proud, and my anger was not just for myself.

Still he laughed. What was part of me, and yet was not, saw through my eyes the ashes all befouled, and around us the

73

darkness and the flames, and in my head the wings went on beating. I found myself standing free – how I got loose I do not know – and facing him and crying out with all my strength, 'Fool, to look in dead things! What can such as you see there?'

He quietened, the laughter choked off, and stared. Around him the rest fell back. I saw their eyes widen like scared children's and I felt their fear. My own anger died, and all at once I was lost and afraid. I felt that I had played at ghosts and stopped to find the shadows thick about us. I had spoken out of myself and did not understand what I had meant – only that what I said was true. He was an oaf and a fool and what he'd done was wrong.

The silence should have lasted. If it had taken root he and the rest would have shrugged and turned to one another and in the end have gone. By morning they would have told themselves they'd had their fun and believed it.

But just at the last Arax snarled like the animal he was. To him I was the stranger, the witch's boy, cornered tight, half-naked. Like any brute he could not help himself.

He sprang for me. In his outstretched hands was all his anger, and his fear. Someone – Luth – called out, 'Oh, don't!' with horror in his voice. But the big fists swung.

The fire was here again, swooping down, a wild bird's flutter, yellow and bloody red between us. A cool voice said, 'Arax! Remember yourself. He is the lord's nephew. And the old man is back.'

He almost did not stop. He could have broken anyone, snapped them like dead wood. But the speaker stepped forward from his place by the door. He was quite calm, carved slender and spare in the darting torch-light. My cousin Hakos.

He said, 'Touch him again and you'll answer for it. You've had what you wanted and more besides. People expect horse-play on a night like this but no one will be pleased if they find you here and the boy beaten senseless at your feet.'

He spoke pleasantly. His face with its hooked nose and golden beard was guileless until the light caught the gently lifted brows and long lids. He played Arax like a fish.

There was a pause. On Arax' face was drawn his thinking; you could see how his thick rage cooled and clotted.

Hakos turned. He did not look at me, only flung down the torch into the hearth where it flared and died. As he left I saw

74

the tattered clouds driven before the moon and the dark bulk of the citadel under them. Then my cousin passed into the yard and for the first time I saw that he limped, his foot turned inwards so that he lurched with every step he took.

At my side Arax gripped my shoulder. He said, breathing in my ear, 'Don't sleep too quiet, witch-spawn. You're back but they've brought the Raven also. Ask yourself why. And listen. Have you ever seen a battle field when the killing's done? The ravens hop about the dying ponies, pecking out their eyes.' His fingers tightened, to bruise; then he too was gone, and the others after him.

Chapter Seven

Sometimes at home in the marshes the river tide runs high and floods the fields and hovels. Then the women weep and howl for it is a dreadful thing, and whisper again the old prayers such as Tachga knows. Once, I'd stayed awake and listened to the river lap the reeds. Yet in the end, for all my watching, it had come in silence, and lain its fingers and broad pools across the floor as if to say, 'Look. This is what I choose to do. Did you think that you could stop me?'

So it was with the dawn that crept as dangerously at the edges of the doors while I lay sleepless on my pallet. Yet in the end I did sleep, for I was woken after day-break by a hand on my shoulder. Luth bent over me, dressed for the hillsides. He said, 'I've been outside. Your grandfather saw me and asked for you. When you're ready you should go to him.'

I roused straight off and sat bolt upright, though he'd spoken hardly above a whisper. He stepped back a pace, startled. No one else stirred. The hall was half in darkness. The doors were pulled to, even the side one we mostly used, and the only other openings were the little smoke holes set just beneath the eaves. The morning was grey. It was a mean, thin light that showed in them.

I drew a long breath to clear my head and nodded at Luth. I remembered everything; even in sleep I had not been free of it, and the blanket was hot and damp against my skin where I'd sweated in some black dream or other. Now, awake, there was no blurring, only the emptiness that comes after rage, and no comfort. I was sapped and beaten. The morning found me on my knees.

It was very cold in the hall. I dressed quickly, pulling my clothes on anyhow. When I'd finished Luth had hardly moved. He stood there as if he had to, from duty. He said, 'Arawn, you'd better wash your face. There are marks on it.'

He sounded awkward, not mocking, and tried not to stare.

It had been him who'd called to Arax when he'd gone to strike me down. I remembered the way his voice had sounded. I said, 'I thought I'd rubbed them off.'

'You have, but there are some smears left, there – along your cheekbone. Without a mirror you couldn't have known.'

I had to draw water from the courtyard well; the pails were empty and kicked about in the fun last night. I brought up a big bucketful and needed most of it. Alone in the yard I scrubbed my face. Nam Dubh was hushed. Behind the rough walls people hugged their blankets, or sighed and stretched.

The worst they had were sore heads to plague them. For myself, I paused and stared at my reflection in the water, at the dark rise of head and shoulders with the sky behind. I was afraid – afraid of Arax and his cruelty and afraid of the girl in her raven-wing mantle and afraid too of what had come to me in the hall. The fear and the anger and shame had bitten deep until I could swear even my looks were changed, as if they bore upon them everything I felt, in stiff, cold scars. The water – less cold – helped a little.

My grandfather's chamber lay on the western slopes, about three hundred paces from the main hall. In the old days, before he'd left Nam Dubh, it had been his, built upon one of the high places in the citadel. Though it took no shelter from the walls, and was open to the winds, it had the best views and he'd been pleased to have it back. From the doorway one could see the yard and across into the wooded ravine where eagles sometimes flew and beyond to the ring of mountains. He had another reason for liking it as well. He could see far below on to the track that led to the Eye Gate out of the woods and notice everyone who journeyed there, even before Mhorged. For him, the Old Lord, that was fitting. More than anyone he knew what was his due.

He was sat by the fire snug enough, though he grumbled over his shoulder at me to close the door as I came in. That, at least, was familiar. These days I was not often near him, but even at a distance he was changed. He had his pride back and an air about him, glimpsed the night we'd arrived in the warmth of the hut when the wine was served and he was easy and sure of himself. Now he was neat and clean with a taste for finery. Today he was dressed in clothes of new wool, a tunic and breeches dyed the colour of birch buds. He wore them well; in the marshes he'd been less careful of himself. Yet the change was not all good. His face looked gaunt and his cheeks more veined and purple and some things about him were the same: the ale pot at his side and the narrow glance he ran over me. I noted it wearily, with a sinking heart, and thought, His temper is no sweeter. He'd heard something, I could tell, and meant to have it out.

He did not speak at first. I waited by the door and watched him busy with his drink. The chamber had been made comfortable with a rug woven in reds and blues and a bed to sleep on, piled with skins. There were hangings on the wall, though they were faded. I looked at them and at his hands as he heated his ale and stirred it. From time to time he glanced across, eyeing me. I could not meet his gaze, though he tried to make me. Usually, from pride, I stood up to him, then took what came. Today I did not know how I should bear it. I'd no strength left to fight him.

He lifted his mug and drank great mouthfuls to get the taste of ale. The hut smelt of the spices he'd crushed into it and woodsmoke from the fire. Afterwards he threw me another glance from under his brows.

'There's a face on you.'

He spoke sourly. I stood like an idiot, wondering what he knew and biting my sore lip. He waited just long enough, then said more sharply, 'What's got your tongue?'

I mumbled at him, 'Nothing, sir,' and heard his bark of laughter.

'No? Then you're sickening for a fever.'

After that he was silent, watching me with bright, curious eyes. I braced myself and felt the well-water cold in my hair and a trickle of it down my cheek.

He was not, though, a man who liked to seem too eager. He settled back, resting his shoulders against a bearing post, drank a little more and waved his hand at me.

'I see you wear it. That was more than I hoped. I suppose Uffa's thrashed manners into you at last. Were you pleased with it?'

I could not think what he meant until I realized he spoke of the arm-band. I reached up, hesitating, and touched it where I'd pushed it over my sleeve. Before I'd come to him I'd glimpsed it where it lay almost buried under my blanket. Last night, angry with everything, I'd vowed I'd never wear it but this morning I'd slipped it on despite myself. For all its age, it had been a good gift, shining and burnished and precious, the first I'd had from him.

I was glad now that I had worn it. I said, 'I meant to thank you, sir, after we had eaten and when the songs were finished. I looked for you but you had gone.'

He snorted. 'I've no time for verses such as those. Some perhaps, but they went on too long. There's only so much a man can take of love-songs and maidens pining. Still, the boy had a good voice, that's something.'

He paused again and stroked his beard. The fire crackled and outside birds cheeped in the yard.

His eyes had never left me and I was scared. What had happened in the boys' hall was something strange, like a dream of warning, barely sensed, waiting like a shadow upon a shadow, an echo sounding in my ear. I could not put what I had felt into words even for myself. But I knew what my grandfather would make of it.

'Well now,' he said.

I stirred, thin-skinned and restless, the door at my back.

'Last night, it was good to see Nam Dubh restored to the old ways. You saw?'

'Yes.'

'It took me back, with the cauldrons full and the young men gathered round. They've done well. I had their fathers serving under me. A good lot mostly, and their sons the same.'

I could not even nod to that though his pale eyes narrowed. 'Come here.'

Slowly I walked across the chamber and stood two paces from him.

'If you wear bronze,' he said, 'as I have given you, let's see what you are made of. Show me your hands. We talk of warriors and a warrior must have good hands, and strength, there, in the line of arm.'

I held out mine, awkward with fear, and he took them by the wrists. His own were strong, big and square like the rest of him, with thick, blunt joints and hair curling on their backs. He wore rings on his fingers now, heavy and carved as my uncle's had been.

He turned mine about, looking where the palms were roughened from the work with staves and felt the pads at the base of each finger. My wrists were bruised right round where Arax had dragged me and he stopped when he noticed and rubbed at the marks with his thumb. His touch was cold despite the fire and ale.

'There's no spare flesh on you. Skin and bone. You're growing up too fast. Uffa works you?'

'Yes.'

'And this. Did he do this to you?' He meant the cut in my lip. I shook my head.

His eyes, blue and shrewd, looked into mine. Quite suddenly I felt the prick of tears and, shamefully, my mouth quivered. I stared down at his hands and then up again into his face.

There was a pause. He said deliberately, 'Your cousin – what did you make of him?'

'He was very fine.'

'Is that all?'

He had hold of my wrists still. I told him, 'Yes.'

'You should be full of it! What else have you seen in your life? Mud and waterfowl – fish when you're lucky!'

That was too much. Helplessly I rose as so often before. I said, 'And to see him was a favour? Well, how should I know more? He wore his gold and he limps. What more is there than that? Nothing you saw fit to tell me! But tell me of the bride. What of her?'

I broke off, seeing his mouth. I'd spoken very loud.

He grunted and let go of my wrists. His face was grave and thoughtful, frowning a little and guarded. He pointed to a rug rolled by his bed. 'Bring it and sit down.'

I did as I was bid, pulling it out and coming to sit at the hearth. I was clumsy and trembling and could not hide it. He ladled more hot ale into another mug and I recognized the spoon he used, a big one carved from dark, translucent horn, with flat-footed birds strutting down its length. Palug had fashioned it long ago.

My grandfather said, 'Take it. You're nervy as a colt. I suppose I know where you get that from. And you lads have no stomach. Up puking in the night as well, no doubt.'

I shook my head. I could not talk of it with him. I crouched above the fire and held my mug in both my hands for warmth. Often as a child I'd sat so, though then alone. Now, through my thoughts, I heard him take a deep draught of ale and swallow and brush his hand across his mouth.

'Arawn – no good in silence, boy. You won't keep it from

81

me. I'll have it out of you one way or another. Besides, I heard them in the yard. Which one of them was it?'

I shifted from him, shoulders hunched. If I spoke I did not know how my voice would sound.

'Not Hakos?'

The fire was hot in my face, as the torches had been last night. I lifted my chin. He could see only the back of my head but I would not have him think I wept. I said, 'No. He stopped them.'

He said, 'That's something,' and cleared his throat. He did not press me further. We sat while the steam from the ale curled up from the mugs. We'd hardly ever been like this together, sitting in a way to make old women smile; only a few times when both of us were weary to the bone and the long, marsh evening stretched ahead and the world was no more than a small peat fire flickering in the shadows.

But here it was morning with a whole day ahead.

I rested my head on my arms. I no longer cared what he saw.

My mouth was sour with last night's ale; I was sick and wrung out. I thought, Useless to tell you, Grandfather, how your feast is far from me as moonshine. Except it was, fragile and golden and distant, masked by cruelty and the strange, dark knowledge that had come, the other sight that was still my own, peering from my eyes, my skull, the sockets rimmed in bone.

I was far gone, wandering in my thoughts, when his great burst of coughing shook me. It came upon him suddenly so that it seemed at first he choked. There was a dreadful gasp as if he was being pulled apart and the breath tore from his body in deep, anguished spasms. For a moment the sight held me. I could not move, gripped stupid while his mouth yawned and gaped and the awful purple colour mounted in his face. Then I was on my feet, moving swift as I've ever done, to take his cup and help him. I held him and felt his ribs wrench against mine as he fought to breathe.

Almost at once it was finished. The air sucked back into his body; under my arm his spine shuddered and jerked and strained.

When he could talk he said, 'It was the drink. It's bitter. It catches in the throat.'

He lied. From his eyes I would have known it. Besides, his

82

coughing had come from deep in his lungs, as if he'd spew them up. There was blood too on his tunic, and flecks of yellow bile and froth.

I said, 'I'll get one of the women—'

'No!' The coughing had forced water from his eyes. He began to wipe away the wetness from his cheeks and beard and scowled up at me. 'I need no one's dosing. Do you hear?'

He shivered, rubbing his arms to warm them though he was right by the fire. I said, 'You're not well, sir. You need someone.'

He swore, bent over to ease his breathing. He looked like a hunched owl, glaring on its branch. 'Stop your fuss,' he said but coughed again and tried to choke it down. His eyes filled once more, so that tears squeezed beneath the lids and ran down his face.

I made for the door, telling him, 'You must have someone. I'll fetch Gortag.'

His voice, sharp with spite, halted me. 'Arawn! Why must you always go against me? I told you no! And least of all her!'

The latch was under my fingers. Another moment and I'd have pulled it up. Instead I turned back. Unspoken, our thoughts hung between us.

I'd known before that he disliked her. Now, when he was weak and shattered, there were some things he could not hide. He hated her as I did.

I caught my own breath. In the silence something stirred in me and was gone, like a snake slipping through grass. I thought, What does he know of her? and opened my mouth to speak.

His wits had not left him though. Already he was putting his clothes in order where the ale had slopped and stained the green. The moment had passed.

I came away from the door and stood and watched him, as so short a time ago he had watched me. He was brisk, smoothing his beard and pulling at the front of his tunic. You'd have thought nothing had happened, save that his hands shook.

His eyes met mine and slid away. The wrinkled lids creased. He knew what I had seen. I said, stubbornly, since I guessed he would be angry, 'It must hurt, to cough like that. It wasn't the drink at all.'

'You call me a liar now? I'm surprised you care so much. Have you some feeling then, for your old grandfather?'

I stared at him and he scowled back but afterwards stretched and breathed deeply through his nose. The blood rose in my face. I did not know what to say.

His breathing grew quiet. I thought at least I should ask how long he had been like this and if anyone else knew of it. For a time he sat at rest, half lying on his rug. The purple colour had gone, except on his cheek bones where the skin was thinnest. There it remained in small stains.

The fire burnt down. I put a log on to keep the room warm. Outside the birds still twittered and someone shouted from the hall.

I wondered if I should cover him or help him to his bed but he seemed quiet and easy and to put blankets on might fret him. I sat on my rug and listened to the breath whisper in his nostrils. He might sleep all morning but I did not like to leave him. Yet it felt strange too, to see him so, as if I'd stumbled upon something shameful – a grown man weeping or the like.

Some time later I pulled the armband from my sleeve. Over cloth it was too tight for comfort. I turned it in my fingers, seeing the light catch on the smooth bronze and little pits and scratches. I wondered about it, whose it had been and why he had given it to me. I thought up some fine stories, till a prince at least had worn it. In a bit I felt my grandfather watching me. He had not slept after all. Now, quietly, he had moved until his back was once more against the post.

He said, 'It came from the chest at the farm. I kept it with me when I left Nam Dubh. I don't know whose it was. It lay where it had fallen, in the rubble.'

In my heart I'd guessed at that, though it might have been his own. He met my eyes steadily as if he had naught to answer for and briefly his memories and the old tales stretched out before us. Nothing had changed. I said, 'If it wasn't yours, why did you take it?'

'Who lets good things rot? If I had need, I could have sold it. They were dark times, Arawn.'

So I knew, as all my life he had made sure I would. Only I thought of what I had seen in the chest the day before we left. Things had rotted there. I held my tongue and asked instead, 'Why did you give it me?'

'It was fitting. Last night you looked a beggar or a slave, and this is your home despite what you may think. You should remember it.'

He spoke carelessly, as if it was no great matter. My face

84

grew hot once more and I turned away. My clothes were not my fault and this was not much home to me – still less so since last night.

I said, 'If you are better, Grandfather, I should go back. Uffa does not like us to be late and there's clearing up to do. We boys must help with it.'

He almost let me go. I put away the mug I'd used and rolled aside the rug. But when I reached the door once more he said, 'Wait.'

I did as I was told. I could do nothing else. He kept his gaze on me, pursing up his lips. Yet he did not seem angry; more like a man dragged unwilling to some task he must do. Then he said, growling, 'How is it here for you? Are the others very hard on you?'

I hardly believed I'd heard him right. It was like when he'd asked me if I had some feeling for him. I was so shocked I almost laughed aloud. Without considering I said straight at him, 'What do you think, Grandfather? A clap on the back for the witch's son?'

He said, scowling and gruffer still, 'You're treated well enough, aren't you? Uffa is a good man; he always was before.'

I could only nod, grown wary all at once and confused as if someone crept behind me. Yet he was not a man to hold back thoughts or anger; always what he said he meant. He paused and swallowed, shifting on the rug to ease his buttocks.

'Arawn,' he said at last, then stopped while he searched for words. He went on, 'Fight if you must. It's expected of a lad your age. But otherwise behave, no matter what. Leave well alone. You'll have me to speak to, or Mhorged else. Do you understand?'

Slowly I asked, 'Has Uffa complained? I ride and wrestle and do what he tells me. What else should there be?'

'Nothing. Only there are things we all must do and make the best of.' He turned his face away to show the long hollow of his cheek and the slant of his brow and his hair.

I went cold all over. Suddenly, in all of this he was a stranger. His hesitancy, his touch of pity, I could not recognize. The echoes of the night sounded still, no longer clear, a thing that slipped away from us, almost touched, almost glimpsed, but clouded in thick mist. It passed, as last night had passed and he sat cross-legged in his bright new clothes, reaching again for his cup. Yet it had been enough.

I said, 'Grandfather, what do you mean?'

'What I said. Behave yourself!'

His harshness was back. Another moment and he'd be calling for his stick, but I was raw already; not just from the night. I remembered his anger snarled out for no good reason before we left the marshes, and before the messenger smirking at our table; and Arax, in the torchlit, smoky darkness, hissing cold with spite of the raven and the pony. None of it I understood but Grandfather did, who'd brought me here. I'd feared his anger for what had been last night but now I was webbed and hung in ignorance, and harried on all sides. The hurt went home like a blade snapped fast into its sheath.

I went and stood over him and swallowed down my fear. He gazed into the yellow flames.

'Grandfather.'

'What is it you want? Go away now!' He whined like an old man while his fingers plucked the tunic laces at his throat. But his hands were steady and his mouth set grim; besides, he'd have shown me no mercy and what I'd learnt I'd learnt from him.

I said, 'Tell me.'

'Tell you what?'

'What is it you keep from me?'

'You're a fool. I keep nothing from you. What secrets could I have?'

Not an hour ago I'd seen him ill. When I'd held him he had clung to me. I'd seen his face and what was in it. Because of that, he could have told me any story and I would have believed him; yet in that answer I knew he lied.

My throat went closed and dry. I felt, despite myself, a sudden pity, the kind that youth must feel for age when it is stripped of wisdom and dignity and all it holds too dear. I thought, He is unwell. I've watched him frightened and it's that he hates.

I knelt by him, hardly knowing what I did. I should have cleaved fast to my anger but I think instead I meant to beg him for whatever thing it was he held from me. He looked at me then, like an animal that is big and hurt and cunning looks to see which way the little hunter dodges. He said, 'What difference would it make?'

And I, with my flesh still cold and the memory of the ashes bitter upon it, and in my ignorance and folly and close,

86

nameless fear, gave to him the very thing that would anger him the most. I said, 'I do not know, Grandfather. But last night, in the hall, there was something – a feeling of what was not right. It was here, in my heart and my bones and my blood. I feel it still. I cannot tell you more than that.' I faltered it like a scolded child, knowing as I spoke what I had done.

The sick old man was gone. He was himself again. Cold scorn lit his eyes, his head thrust forward. He said, 'You talk to me of feelings. What right have you to that?'

He paused and his face settled, sneering. 'What went on in there last night? Do you think I didn't see them afterwards, down in the yard, coming out with their tails between their legs and heads together, muttering? There are things I could ask you – think on that before you bother me with feelings!'

I said, 'They held me down! The big one – Arax – mixed ash and his own spittle and flung it in my face!'

'What did you say to that?'

I shrank from him then. I felt only fear and horror and did not dare to speak. He saw and grinned again, his lip pulled back like a great, fierce dog's. He said, 'What do you expect? Remember who you are and bear it as you should! Don't crawl to me to help you!'

I cried out, 'I never did!' and heard my own voice break.

For a moment more he waited. I watched the cruel grin die before he spoke and the dark thought born slowly in his face. He said, 'No? Yet you take what I will give you. You're bought, lad, and there on your arm's your price. Did you think to sell yourself so cheaply?'

I hardly knew how I left his room. I think he called after me but it might have been the wind off the mountain or a shepherd in the vale below crying for his flocks.

Chapter Eight

Those days were my bad time. The year turned. We were worked hard enough. By day there was little time for brooding as we helped dig out the grain pits or cut and stacked wood. Yet I'd grown wild. I was no longer quite the green boy who'd been brought here. Some fighting skills I'd learnt by now for I was naturally neat and quick, with a good eye; before it was only ignorance that had held me back. I had not yet the polish but I had the will. Where I was hurt I hit back – the others were less ready to be set against me in the ring and less free to mutter of the witch's boy. Besides, they remembered what had happened with Arax.

As I did. I remembered it all. 'The ravens peck out the ponies' eyes,' he'd said. At night, while the little watch-lamp burned and the boys breathed and snored, there was in me a darkness and a fretting that was like a great, starved emptiness; only it fed from me too, like a worm snug in the entrails. That one can cure, however deep, with drinks of herbs and birch-bark, but I had no cure for this though if I could I would have taken a knife and cut it from me.

Arax I was powerless against; my grandfather I could defy, and did. He had been keeping to his chamber with a woman brought up from the farms to tend him, and had been ill for some days. On the evening he came back to the hall for supper he ordered a great pot of wine steeped for everyone to share for his honour's sake. When the jug reached me I emptied my cup on the straw where the dogs got it. So much for his honour, I thought, let him see how I hold that.

There were other times. Once, in the courtyard as I sharpened blades on the whetstone, he beckoned me. I would not go but instead gathered my things and walked away. At home he would have called after me or come over; here he had his dignity and would not make a show. Yet it did not go all my way. Going past the women's quarters I met Gortag at her doorway. She paused a moment, standing there with her heavy skirts held close to her body as if she'd twitched them from the mud. To me she said nothing, but from the way her mouth moved she was pleased to have a tale to tell. Sure enough, in a while Uffa came to find me and, when he got me alone, cuffed me and meant it. Even then, with both ears ringing, I'd had no sense but raised my chin to him. He hit me again and said he'd met such games before. I'd called it courage; so puppies yap till they're kicked.

In such ways it went on. I felt as if everyone's hand was against me, though I did my best to prove it so.

Some mornings, while the rest ate breakfast, if I made do with a fistful of bread I could leave our hut by the side door and be my own man till I saw the rest walk down to the training compounds.

Those times – and they grew more often – I had begun to ride to the ruins of old Nam Dubh. Though it was forbidden to us, they were close enough for me to see them each day and, when we rode over the crest of the hill, the walls would be below us, desolate and hard and grey, with a great space of sky behind.

If I'd been found out by Uffa or Mhorged or my grandfather, I'd have been the first to say, bold-faced, that I went there from defiance. In part that was true, though I never quite dared to cross the ditch and enter between the ruined watch-towers.

Instead I would take Ban on higher to a rocky plateau above the ruins where I could sit and gaze down into them while Ban cropped the grasses. Then I would play a game – I, who was far too old for games.

I would say to myself, There was a hearthstone, and there a place for the loom. On that side the passage ran, and there the women's chambers. From the edges of the walls and the blackened struts, I could count the huts and guess their shapes. Then, in my mind's eye, I would try to see them whole again and think, They feasted here, blazing and proud with their gold and their laughter, and the stern warriors drinking from the cups. Or, How was it, the night it burnt? Did they know how it would come to them?

Sometimes, when I was sad and quiet, I'd think I almost saw, as if a curtain was drawn across a doorway and lamplight shining through while I stood outside before it. Yet I understood how, if I tried to lift the curtain, it would slip from me, like clutching water. Afterwards I'd feel empty and a fool, as a jewelsmith who finds his silver a pale shadow of what's in his heart, or a poet whose words make his fine visions only small, and the Nam Dubh below more a place of rot than ever.

In the end, of course, I overstepped myself.

Since their return the young warriors had been our bane. The boys were frightened of them. Most days they hunted or had their own work to do, but when they were around they delighted in baiting us. Not far from their own time of training, they gave out orders, shouting and claiming they did not like to see us idle. They were cruel too, devising punishments for those who disobeyed or who were clumsy or slack.

One day their butt was Magh, the simpleton in our hall. To look at he was a great, shambling fellow, with a gentle, empty face, grown so ahead of his wits he could not tell his left hand from his right. He was conscious of it, and blushed if the older boys or men spoke to him though he was a head taller than most. He liked best to be with animals. At night, in the great hall, it was to him the dogs came. He'd feed them all with choice bits from his own bowl and rub their ears and under their chins while they squirmed and loved him.

We had been put to chop wood together, a long business, dragging out boughs from a pile while one of us steadied the log and the other cut it. The afternoon was cold and wet but soon we had to stop to wipe our faces and catch our breath. I had been cutting and went to draw us a drink.

I was gone a while. When I returned with Magh's cup he had taken the axe, and in the meantime some of the young men back from riding had gathered round.

The axe was an old one, and faulty. The head was fixed with a piece of wood rammed between it and the haft. I had checked it several times and it had stayed fast through all my efforts. But Magh would not remember to look again. As I called a warning he bent and straightened and struck out with it.

He was much stronger than I – his shoulders wide as Uffa's already. The axe head bit deep into the wood and needed all his strength to haul it out. As he did so and it came free, the head went flying.

The heavy metal blade turned in the wet air and landed

ringing on the courtyard stones. No one was hurt. But children were about, playing in the mud, and some men over by the byre. For a moment the axe blade, spinning to rest, held their eyes; then a little girl, scared senseless, bawled out and her noise brought people at a run.

They gathered round since the child pointed at us. What with her noise and the muttering and hard looks from the women, everyone grew angry.

Arax and his lot took charge. They strode up, seizing Magh and questioning him. Then they crowded closer, pushing him, which he hated and shrank from. They spoke at once, shouting, though they could see it was not the way with him; they knew how he was. He stared back at them, bewildered. I don't think he realized what he'd done. Someone picked up the axe haft and waved it at him and he reached out to try and take it.

Frightened, he began to lumber round the yard like a half-grown, frightened bear while the young men chased after him, whooping and roaring. Then he fell against a doorway and a wicker screen came down.

There was quiet. It was Gortag's chamber. Slowly she came across the threshold into the yard. She looked thin, brittle as dead wood, and watchful. 'What is this?' she said.

No one spoke. Even the young men were quiet. Gortag was feared. Then the child's mother pushed forward and screamed how Magh was like to kill someone with his booby ways, and struck at him with small, hard fists.

If one has been in grief, it takes little to remind one. I watched with the old, tight feeling gathered in my chest.

My aunt looked down at Magh where he lay, sprawled against the screen. There was a look on her face, with her mouth drawn down and her chin poking, which I knew well from Grandfather. It said, 'I have you now.'

She drew breath and paused. Then, while the young men laughed again, she raised her hand for quiet. 'The lackwit,' she said. Her voice was cold as winter raindrops. She stepped up close to him, staring into his face. 'Your father should have strangled you at birth.'

Magh gasped and flinched. His mouth trembled like a child's; then he covered his face with hands that were like big paws and wept.

The gorge rose in my throat. He wept as though he was in truth a child, with huge, noisy sobs. He had no shame in it.

His shoulders shook and he heaved his anguish up from deep inside him and laid it bare before us. I could not have wept so, not while they looked on, yet beside it all that I had felt seemed a small thing only. For a moment I was still; just the blood-beat, hot with anger, thudded in my chest and ears. Then I cried out, 'Don't! He cannot help his wits – nor Hakos can his leg!'

I saw their astonishment, and Gortag's. Her head jerked back, her eyes black as pebbles and wide, her mouth fallen open.

There had been times since the night in our hall when, halfway through some task or other, I'd stopped without my realizing it. Instead of a horse to tack or leather to clean there was Arax, striding from the darkness, swinging down the yellow flames to touch my flesh, and the others with their boots and cloaks and wide-jawed grins. Once again I was in a ring of those same faces who wished to see. My fear came back a hundred times worse. I shrank from them, a whole pace back; I could not help it, flinching like Magh though no one had laid a hand on me. I moved on instinct, not understanding, until I saw how Gortag's face had set. She looked straight at me and the sharp, reddened face was like those of the dolls the young girls play with, pinched crooked out of clay. Only her tongue peeped out to moisten her lips with its tip and her eyes gleamed hatred. It was then that, clear in my mind, I heard my own voice whisper: 'She will scream at you as she has at Magh.'

For Magh, poor, frightened Magh, I should have stayed. Instead I broke from them and ran. I could not bear the words that she would say.

I halted only once, when the ruins were in sight. I had a pain in my side from the running; we were taught how to go steadily, especially over scrub, but I had no care for that. In the end I had to bend and clutch my ribs. As soon as it passed I went on.

The track I followed became lost in dock and thistle and the way was steep and rough. Sheep, bunched in the wide ditch, cropping the short grasses, cantered away from me, sometimes when I was almost upon them. The pain returned, so bad and sudden that I stumbled.

I landed on my knees and stayed there, gulping air as if I too sobbed, and staring round; and then I bent, crouched over, and rested my head on the ground, and all the time I saw the way that Magh had looked.

I do not know how long I lay there. In the end the very quietness roused me.

I was there in the ruins. All around were the long, silent walls. The empty gateways and fallen stones gave them such a blank-eyed look they seemed to stare. In front the shattered walls rose up and up and at their foot the lumps of smashed, burnt stone lay anyhow, as if some huge hand had seized and hurled them down.

My legs were heavy and trembled but I stood and made myself go on though now I walked slowly. At last, when I was in the midst of the ruined settlement, I sat to rest on one of the fallen boulders. The flowers that had grown there before were all dead. Only a few broken heads hung on their stems and the thin, straggled grasses stirred in the cracks in the flagstones. Before me was the long wall. Against the sky it showed ragged, licked with the long, black scorch marks and all sloped and tumbled in a fall of stones where the fire had been hottest.

Rain began to patter; there was no shelter and a light wind blew in across the turf. I huddled in my clothes. From being hot a shiver ran in my flesh; my throat was raw with anger and my side was sore. Through doorways the broken structures reared up from the empty hillside. Archways gaped to cloud and grass. Above me stonework hung and glistened in the dull, wet air.

And then I looked. I looked for the shadows, for the ghosts, for the bright firelight and the feast, for my grandfather laughing in his place, and my father and my mother. I looked for their youth and the gold about their necks and I listened for the music and the voices of long dead men. I looked beyond, for the Horse-people themselves and their high walls and painted stonework, the horse-crested helmets and the spears.

But there was only the rain and the grey stones and the sheep. What the Clan-lord had done.

I grew calmer, spent and weakened.

The shock began to go, like the tide on the turn. I felt as if I should see clearly now, as in a mirror when you rub the breath mist from the bronze. I understood how in the past days I had flayed myself with my own nerves, that I had neither eaten properly nor slept a full night through since

Hakos's return and that, though I had run from hearing words, it was words that came back and back to me.

My grandfather had said, 'You talk to me of feelings. What right have you to that?' He'd meant, There is nothing here. Nothing to know or understand or long for. Believe that. Nothing left. All the old ways are dust and ashes. The sky will spin from dusk to dawn and there is nothing here for you, the witch's boy.

And so it was.

I picked at the grass heads, waving at my knee. The sheep had returned with fine rain glistening in their wool. Somewhere a thrush sang. I raised my head and saw the citadel below. Smoke drifted in small curls from the cooking fires. The women would have finished setting supper on to boil and there'd be bread to eat, still warm, with cheese. Soon Uffa would bring the other boys back in. I thought of them, laughing and grumbling and hanging their cloaks on pegs to dry. I found out then my anger was for myself.

I thought, He is right. There is nothing, not even here. I cannot see it as it once was. One cannot give back flesh, or see men walk again, or make walls whole.

The game I'd played was like the shadow game that children play upon the walls; they use their hands to conjure birds and beasts from firelight and people smile to see them and show them more.

I looked around. Nam Dubh was no more to me than it was to any man. The stones and toppled walls were as much part of the hills as the grass and rocks and the wind. They were only themselves, gone back to the earth that had borne them. I could not look for what they had been, or anything that was graceful or fierce that they had known or carried within them. It was not to be found.

I could not even say, This was the Horse-people's place, and yet they will not answer me.

I stood alone in that great, quiet place that other men swore was haunted. The wind brushed the grasses at my feet, the clouds that filled the sky were a mass of grey, the cold walls stayed still and broken. Within me the child I had been wailed and was silent.

Much later I climbed the long wall slowly and carefully and sat once more. I reached for the horse-charm hidden in my tunic and held it tight through the thin, worn cloth. Then I pulled at the hem until it tore. I felt the touch of silver, smooth and warm from my holding, and lifted my arm and flung. The charm spun upwards in an arc. For a moment it was there, a dull gleam, and then it was gone, lost among the grasses.

I shook the wet hair from my eyes and wiped the rain from my cheeks with the heel of my hand. I was very calm and lonely and filled with a sorrow for past, unhappy things. I thought of Magh, a little; and how when I came to the ruins again it would be different, in duty as was their right. It would be as one visits long dead ancestors, with hands full of flowers or gold to place on their graves, but empty-hearted so that it seems no more than a chore.

A bird screamed, a black, ugly bird with ragged feathers, flying past. I seized a stone and threw. My aim was good. The bird wheeled once and toppled from the sky.

There was a noise below and I turned and looked. It was the time of lamp-lighting, when everything that is pale shines out for a last, brief span. In the dusk I saw their hands and faces as they climbed, white and hard as bone.

There were only the two of them, Luth and Dearg. They waited on the path till I was down. Dearg said, without ceremony, 'Are you mad? To go there! You know it is forbidden.'

I made no answer. I pushed past them and if they'd touched me I would have struck them to their knees.

They did not call me back or run after me as I'd expected. I went down the track alone. Soon I saw the others gathered about Uffa, trudging to the hall. I paused, watching while the darkness thickened and they were black on the curve of the hill. Then I shrugged and spat and went to join them.

Chapter Nine

The year turned and it was Samhuin.

Samhuin – the dark time which opens the gates of winter. The time of beast-slaying and the Otherworld and of the dead when spirits are called back to the halls of men and speak what is to come.

In the marshes the peasants had their rites. With the early darkness Tachga would slip away, paddling her coracle into the waterways, between dying brown reeds. By daybreak she'd be back, limp and heavy-seeming, and sometimes with the smell of blood upon her. The water gods give much, but so too do they take.

At Nam Dubh there was no propitiation, no appeasement, no prayers or sacrifice. While the Raven-tribes gathered with their priests according to the custom, in forest groves long days' ride away, Nam Dubh stood and faced what came alone.

That year the day was foggy. Cold mist clung about the yard. When there was light enough the women left their hall. Gortag led them. In her hand she had a knife and a bag of salt. We watched in silence as they walked from the yard, going to the stock pens out on the hillside to choose which animals would over-winter and which would be led down for slaughter. As they left the menfolk turned and went indoors. It was women's business and no good thing to watch.

The afternoon was damp and dim, the air full of the cries and lowing of animals. The fog crept in to our clothes and touched our bones. Then came the night.

As darkness fell people sought the hall, slipping quietly to their places, sitting huddled for no fires were lit. Once the heads of enemies would be gathered together and tapers burnt before them to light them on their way. Now no skulls grinned from the rafters or gazed before the hearth. Nam Dubh was still a place dishonoured.

Men and women sat apart. Women are more powerful at Samhuin, for birth and death are but two faces of the whole.

They wore black and had stained their hands and faces with yellow, the colour of the Otherworld. The doors to the hall stood wide for entrance must be denied to none, fleshly or fleshless.

The warriors crouched, their weapons idle at their feet. The women keened, wailing and moaning. Nemair, Hakos's wife, the Raven-priestess, rose up among them – she who of us all was not accursed. She stood, lifting her face and arms, bared where the raven cloak fell from them. In her right hand she carried a pair of shears. Down the hall Mhorged walked, slow and burdened. He knelt before her and she cut his hair while we watched and saw the whiteness of his naked neck and the dry, grey-blond locks as they fell to the floor. The shears hissed and clicked as he made the penance.

Across the room Gortag made a sign. Uffa gripped the cloth of my shirt and hauled me to my feet. She pointed and he dragged me forward. Nemair looked towards me. Uffa pulled me to her and I smelt the strange smell of her: a cold fragrance of earth and rooted, growing things. Briefly she hesitated. I guessed this was unlooked for, a working of my aunt. Then the feather cloak stirred and whispered as her arm came up before me. Uffa bent my head and the shears clipped at the back of my neck, a touch of iron. At the last moment I looked up and saw her eyes. I looked for the ecstasy that comes to the wise when they do the gods' bidding, but hers were filled with a lost, dark look. And I remembered the nature of the Raven-hag. It was as if Nemair gazed on battlefields and the slaughtered lying in their bloody wounds.

Again the shears snipped. I shuddered. Their feel was like the cold peck of the raven's beak. Another penance.

The night drew on. The women mourned. They mourned the dead and the deaths that were to come. The keening was dreary, lower in pitch. Nemair sat folded in her cloak. Gortag rocked on her heels, her eyes closed. The yellow on her face was painted in lines, like scratches.

Fog drifted in at the open doors. The little tapers sputtered. They lit our faces and made ghosts of us all before, one by one, they died.

In the cold dark we waited. The ancient fear clutched us, closed round our hearts; the fear all men know, of the nameless things that cluster at the door. I rested my head upon my knees, my eyes fast shut. By my side Sithlann shook with dry, tight sobbing.

So the long night passed. At some point the young warriors slipped from the hall. We heard them shuffle by.

Then in the dawn, out in the yard, a light showed and another and another. There came the noise of stamping feet. Out of the darkness they leapt, over the threshold into the hall, the young men wearing masks and bearing lighted torches.

They danced the Fire-dance to drive off bad things and light the way for good. Naked they danced, but for their neck-rings and amulets, in a swirl of yellow flames and hot smoke, blue and stinking in the cold air. From the dark they leapt, lithe and sure, their flesh gleaming with sweat and gold. Their eyes and mouths were black holes cut in leather; antlers tossed upon their heads. They screamed and whirled their brands, dancing face to face while the wooden sticks struck together and sent up showers of sparks. They danced as if in a maze, pacing out the steps, quicker and quicker, while drums throbbed in the yard and all around people laughed and clapped their hands.

So passed Samhuin. As the day broke, people staggered off to sleep and by evening there would be pork to eat and ale to drink, and in the days and nights to follow the dark, fallow time of year would come when the earth would rest.

Afterwards, in the nights that followed, in our hut after supper, the others would snatch brands from the fire to try it out for real. They'd clear a space to make a circle and laugh and clap each other to it, but always it came to nothing. The sticks were too short and broke in a shower of sparks when they hit together. They thought themselves daring though and made little of any burns or scratches. Magh had his hair singed but that was the worst of it.

When it was over they would flop down, panting, and gulp ale from the jug smuggled in from supper, and catch their breath from laughing.

Nights like these I watched from my place by the wall where I had my goatskin. It was a hard winter; the days brief and icy, the nights blackly frozen, and we shivered in our hut. The tasks of the citadel did not stop; the food stocks needed watching, the women wove on with stiff, cold fingers, the men went out with the dogs and their spears. We boys had the animals to tend, our endless sword-play and wrestling, wood to gather. Uffa drove us and we stumbled through our tasks, clumsy and miserable, with itching sores on our hands and feet. We longed for the end of each day, for the hearth fires and for hot broth and meat. Yet now, seeing the others close and happy, I understood why we were kept together, and how the work we shared so hardily and custom would bind one man to another.

There were other times also. After supper in the great hall grown men would talk. When the pots were empty, we young ones would sit and listen as we were supposed to, but with half an ear while watching the girls go out. I'd hear the others talk sometimes of those they fancied and how it was for them. Mostly the young men went down the hill to the farm girls, who were willing enough. It was the custom and the babes they bore strong and healthy. Our own girls were kept close. I'd seen the women's chamber only once when I'd twisted my ankle. It was too bad for Uffa to tend and there was a woman like Tachga who made poultices of herbs and earth that always worked. When I got there I was kept outside till she would see me but there was a gap in the side of the curtain. Behind was a big room with skins on the floor and rugs, and plants hung upside down from the rafters to dry. There was a clay oven in the middle and by it my aunt had her rug. The others sat round her on the floor. They'd been busy, stitching cloth, and everywhere was neat. I thought my aunt must rule them hard to have them all so silent.

That was for the day. The girls of an age to marry had their own chamber to sleep in but with older women to watch over them. Shut up in our hall, we had no one. Yet winter had cooled even our blood. Some evenings the boys would play dice awhile or Luth would sing again. They would gather round him, wrapped in their blankets, watching and listening, or join in till the torches guttered out and only the watch-lamp was left. With full bellies, dog-tired and sleepy, there was contentment too in that. Nam Dubh had weathered winters time out of mind; she held each one of us close to her even yet.

As I looked round at my companions I saw in the way someone threw back his head or laughed or told a joke that, after a fashion, I knew them and they me. For in fighting you learn the feel of a man; by his laughter what is in him.

Usually after dark we were left alone. It was rare for anyone to come while the doors were still unbarred and sit with us but one night, not long after, we had a visitor.

That evening the boys worked once more at the Fire-dance, pacing out the steps. It was rough, hot work, and the burning sticks from the hearth kept splintering in a shower of sparks. Tempers were up when we heard a cough from the shadows behind. A man stood there; he must have used the postern door, we had not heard him enter.

Some days before he had arrived, driving a horse and a traveller's cart with a hood of skins to cover it. My uncle had greeted him courteously, as if he knew him.

He was short, only as tall as Maelduin who was smaller than any of us, but fat and bald with a line of black hair over his ears and the back of his neck, and a beard. He'd coughed, not from necessity but to let us know his presence; there was no telling how long he'd waited.

We stared up at him, open-mouthed. Eventually Luth at least recalled his manners. He got up and offered the man his own place by the fire. The man stepped forward, all smiles. He had a big pot-belly which he thrust before him as if, for all the world, he was with child, and though he was smooth in his manner there was something that was coarse as well. He looked the type to scratch his backside and bow together. When he reached us, he paused and seemed to hesitate, and if he had been a woman, I swear he'd have hitched his skirts.

He glanced at the floor where we sat and then around – the meaning was unmistakable. Luth, his colour high, fetched a rug.

When he was settled there we waited for him to speak. He was a guest, though uninvited; it was not for us to question him. But he said, 'Go on. To disturb you was the least of my desires.'

From the way he spoke we could have been an audience. His courtesy was elaborate and his voice was deep with a richness to it as if he'd had to work to make it so.

We paused, tongue-tied and shy. Then Benna, whose arm was blistered, cast one look sideways at the man and burst out to Sithlann who'd burnt him, 'You fool, you're like to kill me!'

Sithlann played the fool and thrust the branch back at him, nearly in his face. The rest howled with laughter and urged Sithlann on.

They had almost laughed themselves out when the man shifted his great belly and leaned forward, as far as he was able. 'Don't be too quick,' he said to Sithlann. 'I've seen such a dance as yours, and a man die in it.'

He chose his moment well. He'd held up a finger to shush us but had no need. He could watch our faces as the laughter went from them. After a moment Benna said, 'How?' He scowled and his tone was the one he used with us; from anyone else he'd have got a clout for either.

The man's gaze slid to the fire. He pursed his mouth, making it small, and shook his head – as if all the sorrows sat at once on his shoulders. His beard was only a thin fringe along his jaw bone but it glistened where he'd combed it; above, his cheeks were full from good feeding and pitted all over with pock-marks.

'The time it was danced, when I was there, the warriors were fine – young men, each one of them. They wore their jewels, their torcs and belts, their amulets for luck. They wore their paint too and had oiled their bodies to glow in the firelight. It wins applause; the women like it, and the gods.'

He paused, taking his time. 'What happened was this: the man who died oiled himself too well. And he was slow. The flames touched him and he roasted.'

No one spoke. We all believed him. In a while he shrugged to break the mood. He looked at the fire again. There was a quirk to his mouth as if he found some humour in the tale, then he turned his head away.

Luth said, 'When was this?'

The man looked back, out of blue, smiling eyes. 'A long time ago. The last time it was danced. Here. For the Clan-lord himself.'

All around I heard an intake of breath. Someone said, 'Here? That night? What did the Clan-lord do?'

The man shrugged. 'What could he do? He knew it was a sign. Usually it is lucky, the Fire-dance. But not at that feast. There were flames in plenty to follow, and Cernach roaring them on.'

I recognized the silence that came then, just as I recognized the sidelong glances cast across at me, and how the man noticed them, his own blue gaze darting.

Ruarch said, 'We have no Clan-lord now.' He spoke coyly, stirring as a beetle stirs up dung.

'No,' said the man. Then again, 'No.'

For an instant the memory of the old flames hung on a breath, the ghost flicker, dim as the wraith-lights of the marshes. The boys watched him, crouched and eager, the flames of our own hearth bright in their faces, waiting for the dark things to rise and him to give them form.

He smiled round again; he had a grin like a dog's. I stayed

102

where I was. I would hear it out. I thought, He will tell us of him. And what it was like. And then, quite suddenly, Magh, who understood nothing, said to him, plain as a child, 'Why have you come back?' And the moment went.

The man barely faltered; he was good at what he did. He answered, 'For food. You have your grain pits and your meat stores salted down. Even game in the forest. What are my poor skills beside that?'

His spell binding was broken and he spoke truly. The meat was tough and stringy, even when boiled for half the day – we boys called it jaw-ache – but everyone valued it. Already the hill farmers had begun to trudge up from the slopes below to barter with ewes' milk and cheese and turnips and wool for the women to clean and spin. They were rough and hard and scabby, like the hillside itself, but when they came to my uncle I never saw him treat them with anything less than courtesy. Their people were of the mountains and his had come to it; he held them in trust, and their dignity, as a thing unbroken. And he was generous. Plainly other eyes had noted it.

I stood up. The ale jug had gone round twice at supper and I felt I could go out now. Besides, by the fire it was hot and stuffy and the man had scented his clothes. Perhaps in better places it was expected, but he'd used cheap stuff. He stank of something sweet with his own smell underneath.

As I passed him he caught my wrist. His hand was hot and greasy and his grip firm. I shied away and stared at him. His mouth was pursed up, very red and moist in his black beard.

He smiled. Then said quietly, 'You were there. Do you remember?'

His touch sickened me and so did he, with his sly eyes and heavy, bloated looks. I tried to pull away and he dropped his look deliberately to the mark on my arm.

Someone coughed. Uffa was there, waiting by the door.

The man said, 'A good-looking boy – fine-boned but hag-marked. I watched him this morning. He moves well. Who is he?'

'You know. What do you want with him, Cumair?'

'Mhorged, perhaps, would be well rid of such a one? And I could use him.'

Uffa's beard jutted. There was colour high in his face but he said only, 'No doubt you could. Anyone could guess how. It's as well that you are who you are, Cumair. We do not put our youngsters up for sale.'

The stranger's smile widened. The red lips parted and showed his teeth. He said, 'Forgive me. I had heard otherwise.'

Afterwards I did not go straight back. I leant against the wooden wall and thought. All around the night hung quiet. A great spill of moonlight lay in the valley like an upturned bowl of thin, blue milk. I could see the dark mass of trees and the mountains beyond. Against their black the sky looked deepest blue and full of stars. Nothing stirred; the citadel buildings threw down long streaks of shadow, the whole world was sunk in slumber. Only the frost and the stars glittered and the shining moon was high and cold and white as mist.

I let the cold run through me. It felt good after what had been in the hall, and my flesh was hot and prickly. Yet such things were not new to me, and my skin was thicker now. I was no longer the shy, bewildered boy who'd come to Nam Dubh.

And something had happened that day. Mhorged had watched us at practice again; nowadays he made a habit of it. Uffa had worked us as usual, and all had gone well. There were times now when I found my blood was up and to fight became a joy. I'd been put with Luth with whom I worked best. We had fought and the steps had been intricate and right, and the swords had gone swinging through the air so that we were strong and sure with a wildness that coursed like wine through us. It was like being hawks in the moment when they stoop or hounds leaping for the stag.

Afterwards Uffa called us to him and clapped us on our shoulders as a father might. It was the first time for me. His glance flickered up and met my uncle's. A long look passed between them till my uncle lidded his eyes. I understood then. This, a hand laid on my shoulder for all to see, was a reward.

Mhorged had smiled. His gaze shifted and looked me up and down. He blew through his nose a small snort of amusement. Then his face went still again.

I'd known what they thought. The look said, Well done, you've got him tamed. And so I was. These days I took whatever was on offer and no longer stirred the shadows. Something had died in me, that time in the ruins, quenched in the quiet, indifferent rain and by the flood of grief that was my own. Yet afterwards, in the driven days that followed, as I'd slashed and hacked and stumbled through my training, I'd taken to myself a new knowledge, a comfort even, buried deep and always there – that when a man is skilled in arms there are places where he can name his price and have it counted out to him in gold.

So now, when I dreamed, it was not of the great, burnt walls of old Nam Dubh and the flames and what had happened there. But I dreamt still – of wild places blown by the wind and other halls, gilded and painted, or long shores with the grey tides running. In my mind I would walk among them and have my sword safe at my hip, its weight in its scabbard or clasped two-handed in the death-blow. That was my reward, bought with my blood and tears and, seeing Mhorged's smile, I could have yelled it at him.

The side-door jerked and stuck. Someone cursed and got it open, then stepped out. It was Luth.

He stood there, his tunic laced for warmth and head uncovered. His hair fell in black strands across his forehead. His face was intent and troubled, honestly so. I saw his eyes when he flicked back his hair. They were wary and widened, the way they were when we fought and he guessed I'd win.

It was like the other time, in the ruins; he'd come on purpose to find me. He said, 'Uffa wants us in.'

I moved away from the wall. Although we fought, we never talked. I could have said something to make it easier for him; I stayed silent.

He didn't press me. He turned to step inside once more. Before he went he looked back and said, 'The man's gone now, if that's what you wanted. He's a bard, a song-maker. No one likes him, though he's good. He comes every year to nose around. Some say the Clan-lord sends him to spy out what we do. Perhaps he came to scare you. He always says how terrible Cernach is.'

He paused then added in a rush, 'Tomorrow Dearg and I are hunting. Join us if you wish. We're leaving early.'

Yet we did not hunt the next day, nor for some time after, for by the morning I was sick. I had taken a fever, with sore joints and an aching head. All day the fever grew and by evening I was raving.

I remember little of the illness and what I do seems only as scenes carved on a sword blade, each separate from the other. I know I was carried, burning hot, and laid somewhere soft and cool: and then came a blurring of days and nights so that they ran all together. At some time I was lifted up in bed and my head bent over a bowl of herb-scented steam. Another time there were women chanting and the scarlet flicker of burning pine roots. Yet another I was bathed with water so cold against my scalding flesh that I screamed and begged for them to stop.

One thing I do remember clearly: a girl's face looking down into mine and her braids brushing my cheek. Their ends were bound with small gold beads. She said over and over to me as if I could not understand, 'Drink. You must drink,' while behind her another woman stood, all in black, with a painted face like the women at Samhuin, only this face was daubed with red all over, like a bloody mask, and her hands were reddened too, up past the wrists. The woman laughed while the girl spoke, a laugh so full of mockery and hatred that I knew she wished me dead, and afterwards she seemed always with me, half glimpsed like a shadow looking on from the corners of the room.

The sickness passed. One day I opened my eyes to find the world once more familiar about me.

I was lying in a small chamber. Above I could make out the painted beams and the turf roof. The door curtain was pulled back a little way and through it wintry sunlight streamed. I lay on skins on a wickerwork bed with a linen sheet draped over me. I felt weak but quite comfortable. Close by someone pounded at a mortar and sang.

I turned my head to see. A woman sat with her back to me, working at the hearth where the fire was lit for warmth. Her hair, neatly braided in four long plaits, was glossy red-brown, with gold beads glinting at the ends. Her gown was bright green, checked with blue. I watched her a moment and glimpsed the stone bowl and the pestle she used. There was a scent of willow bark in the room.

She heard me move. She turned, and it was Nemair.

We looked at each other long enough. I saw her clear grey eyes, and the silky brows above, and her firm mouth. A calm face. Yet I remembered too the touch of the cold shears at my neck, the brush of raven feathers; Nemair as I'd first seen her, far off in her mind, serving her goddess. What she saw of me I do not know.

She did not smile but gathered her skirts about her and rose smoothly, coming up to my bed. Then she laid her hand on my brow, feeling for the fever. Afterwards she held a bowl to my lips. The liquid it held was bitter. 'Drink,' she said.

'What is it?' My voice was a croaking whisper.

'Willow and sage and borage, steeped in wine. And a little wild garlic. Not pleasant, but it cures.'

I drank and almost straight after fell into sleep, so perhaps there was poppy in it also.

When I woke again it was nightfall. The curtain was drawn across and the smoke holes darkened. The fire glimmered in the hearth and threw warm shadows. This time she sat spinning, her white hound snoring at her feet.

I watched her a good while, and then I slept again.

So it went on. The next day was the same. She tended me while I was too weak still to do more than sip at what she brought and lie beneath the coverlet upon the skins.

By daybreak I was stronger, strong enough to make some order of my thoughts. She saw so at once. This time we faced each other, wary as cats, mindful of who we were.

I asked, 'Did you nurse me?'

She nodded.

'And another woman? Where is she?'

'There was no one else. Mhorged came sometimes, and Uffa, and your grandfather once.'

I knew what I had seen. I shivered a little and pressed back against the skins.

Her gaze was cool and thoughtful, with little liking in it. She knew who I was, well enough. Abruptly I turned my face from hers, looking towards the fire. It came to me that I'd been healed by my enemy – a bitter healing with no good to come of it, like a sore with the skin grown over but festering beneath.

After that the memory of the dark woman hung about me. I could not be rid of her. I thought, the *badbh* was here, the ill-wisher, the Raven-hag, and Nemair summoned her to haunt me. When I slept I was restless and murmuring, waking with a start. At the last time Nemair stood over me.

'What is it?' she said.

I said, 'A dream.' She shrugged and made to straighten the coverlet upon the bed. I was naked under it and at her touch my flesh shrank.

She mistook me. Her fine brows lifted in mockery. 'Do you think,' she said, 'I've never seen a well-made boy before? I am a married woman, and have healed many.'

With the mockery there was pride. She was young and conscious of her dignity.

I was too weak and witless to keep my counsel. I said, 'It was not that! She was here, whom you serve, to suck my soul and wish me ill. If that's your work you may be proud of it!'

'My work?'

I stared back at her, confused. Still I saw her as she had been, at first in her gold and black and later with the snipping shears and the dark, lost knowledge in her eyes.

I said, 'The Raven-queen drinks the blood of men. I've seen her reddened face and the darkness of her standing by the bed. You serve a cruel Lady.'

She made to speak again, her mouth opening. Then she paused. Afterwards she said quietly: 'Do you think I am the same? In my tribe I was priestess and healer both. There can be no death without the life before. Who should understand that better than the Mother who watches the beginning and the end?'

Fresh sweat had broken on my brow; I was very weak still. I said, 'The Mother! That's not as I know her!'

'Know!' she said. 'What can such as you know? The Old Lord's disgraced grandson! They tell you came with bruises black as dirt upon your skin and rags upon your back! You have naught but ignorance to guide you on your way. Beware of that!'

Her scorn was bitter. I stared at her, not knowing what to think. She said only, 'You have been sick. Perhaps you saw what was never there. I have not ill wished you.'

'For all I am the witch's son?' I too had bitterness in me.

She turned from me, so her braids swung across her cheek. 'I only serve what I must, as did your mother. Her I cannot judge.'

She went back to the fire and then out to fetch some wood. Later it was not she who returned but the old woman who was good with herbs. In a day or two I was on my feet again, and soon I had gone back to Uffa.

Chapter Ten

In the dead of winter we hunted together, Luth and I, but when we did it was for bigger game than we'd yet dared to try. One morning something shocking happened. At day break a swine-herd, driving his pigs into the forest, found a woman there, dead of wolf bites and frozen on a fall of leaves.

In the days that followed the talk was all of hunting wolves.

Dearg said, 'Mhorged will have to kill it. Suppose it got into the cattle pens?'

Benna said, 'Of course he'll kill it. But will we be allowed to go?'

That was what all the boys were hot for since a wolf hunt is a test of wits and craft and cunning. Hunt a wolf and you're somebody. I watched and listened and learnt that there'd been no hunts for many winters past; not since the forest pack had been driven by hunger this side of the mountain after weeks of snow. That time the boys could recall their fathers setting off with the wolf hounds and their spears and nets, and some tales of the chase – how one man, Sithlann's uncle, had fallen when his horse stumbled, hit his head on a root and could remember nothing for a month.

Afterwards Dearg said, 'But even if we go, can we hunt? It's snowed most days. On foot's no good with wolf.'

Luth had been stringing his harp. He looked up and said, 'It'll be clearer on the upper slopes, if it gets up there. The wind's taken most of it away though the ground's like iron. Only Mhorged won't let us anyway. He didn't before.'

Someone else said, 'Oh, we were too young,' and Ruarch said, 'Ask him, Luth. You're the one everyone listens to.' His eyes went to Luth's hands. 'Take your harp,' he went on, 'and strum to him. Sing as well, if you're in voice.' He said it smoothly, straight at him, but with him everything was an insult.

Luth barely raised his brows. 'Ask your brother. Arax howls like a wolf, and slobbers like one too when he's angry.

Kith to kin. We've seen him. Mhorged could use him to sniff the other out and we could go and follow.'

The rest laughed and Ruarch scowled. I sat at my place by the wall and heard them bicker. It went on harmlessly for a while and then they turned to other things, to dice or to polishing up the spear-heads. I pulled my blanket round my shoulders and thought of the young woman on the frosty leaves and the wolf, sloping along, full-bellied, licking its reddened jaws.

The next day Mhorged sent out two scouts to track it to its lair and Uffa, who knew us through and through, found fault with everything we did. When we'd been cuffed and shouted at, he took us out and made us wrestle. By nightfall we thought no more of wolves but only of our aching limbs, the supper pot and bed.

Yet it was Uffa who spoke up for us some days later when one of the scouts returned. He'd news of the wolf which he brought to my uncle and then repeated to the men. They'd found the lair and the other scout, Tuan, had stayed to keep watch. We were kept ignorant of it until at supper Dearg, who had ears for everything, overheard Uffa say to Mhorged, 'The boys are wild to go as well, sir. They've been cooped up as it is, doing what they hate, and besides it's time they earnt their keep.'

My uncle replied, 'Yes then, if you think so. But a couple, not all of them. Two who can sit a horse half-decently and won't fall off. Pick them yourself, but leave it till daybreak or there'll be nothing but squabbling and ill will.'

There was squabbling anyway, when Dearg repeated what he'd heard, and a fight between himself and Maelduin, which he won. Afterwards the others talked again, for it was plain the hunt would start tomorrow. I wondered who would go, though I was not much interested. Whoever was chosen would preen himself and get black looks from the others. Dearg fancied his chances. He sat by the hearth, oiled the shaft of his spear and smirked at Maelduin.

So I slept and knew no more till I woke into the soft spill of lamplight and found Uffa stood nudging at me with his foot. 'Up with you, lad,' he said. 'There's a wolf to find and that savage little horse of yours to catch. Stir yourself.'

For a moment I blinked up at him, hardly believing what I heard. Then I raised myself on one elbow, dazed with sleep and staring round. The light was steady and yellow and by it I saw Luth over by his bed pulling on his tunic and around him, rolled in their blankets, the others stretched sleeping. Only Dearg was awake, watching. He looked like a beaten hound. Uffa nudged me again. 'There's plenty who'll come if you won't.' That roused me. I reached for my breeches and began to dress.

A little later I went out into the yard. From the high wooden walls pine root cressets flared for it was very early with no dawn as yet to lighten the eastern sky. People were about, talking quietly; men led horses from the stables; women fetched cloaks and spears and little packs of food. The cook-house door was open and inside I could see the oven fires, red and flickering within the clay. I went over and noticed that Luth was already there. More women were inside, putting the day's bread in to bake and stirring great pots of porridge that had been left to soak all night.

I helped myself and went to stand in the doorway, spooning in the salty, hot stuff and shivering.

More men came out. I recognized a group of older men, friends of my uncle, who stamped and laughed together as they waited for their mounts. From his hut Mhorged emerged and greeted them. His hounds were with him, one couple only, a wily old bitch called Flidais and her brindled son, Dua. They stood up to my uncle's waist, shaggy and lithe with rough, clever heads and lean-boned limbs. The young one, over-eager, flattened its ears and whined with pleasure.

There was movement behind me. Uffa came up, a bowl of porridge in his hand, and with him Luth, silent and serious.

Uffa said, 'Both of you, listen. It'll be a cold, bloody business this. It's not like hunting for sport, or even for meat. This is what'll happen. We've to surround the lair and Mhorged will send the dogs in. They'll do what they can to keep it at bay and then we'll come down and finish it. We're not here to chase him or be first in at the kill. Leave that to those who know what they're about. All you've to do is stand where you're told and keep your mouths shut. If you can manage that I'll be well pleased.'

He broke off. There was a roar of laughter in the yard. Turning, I saw my cousin Hakos limp from the stables, a white hound, Nemair's, at his side. With him were his young warriors who hailed the waiting men. They were got up as they had been the night of the wedding feast, their hair

111

spiked with limewash and in their brightest clothes. They looked bold and brave. Foremost among them was Arax, casting his gaze around with a grin to split his face apart.

Uffa clipped my ear. 'Pay attention. Now go and catch your ponies. The rest of us'll move off. Wait for us on the track.'

He strode off to join the others. Always brisk, there'd been excitement in him though he'd tried to hide it. The rest were the same. It was in their laughter, the eager clasp of the spear, the way they handled the horses as they were brought out to them. It was dark still, though the darkness had begun to pale and the cressets flared less bright; yet here, within the black, decaying walls, the men were truly awake. More, I thought, than I had ever seen them.

At my side Luth said, 'You heard him.' He sounded sulky. I came to myself and we went first to fetch the bridles and the saddle cloths that we used. As we came out again the yard was even fuller. I think I realized then that it was real danger that we faced. My grandfather was in the doorway of his hut; it was too far to see his face but I guessed he must make me out. I turned away hastily, lest he be the one to turn first. I don't know if he stayed looking after me.

We rode all day, moving mainly at a walk or trot to save the horses. First we had to traverse the valley, going down nearly as far as the forest margins, passing the place where the woman had lain. From there we could skirt the foot of the mountain and begin the long climb into the next range. The way was hard. The wind, soughing from the north, had swept clean away the snow, save in the gullies, but the soil was frozen and unyielding. For all the day was fine, with a high, white sun, the wind blew still and by noon we were chilled through. My own cloak was old and threadbare, brought with me from the marshes, and I'd remembered to snatch a blanket and some cord to put in my pack, only when I came to tie it round the cord was too short, so I shivered and felt a fool instead.

At last we halted to eat in a sheltered place behind a ledge of rock. I saw Luth steal a glance sideways then step a little nearer. His father hunted also, a tall man, handsome as Luth was, with a hawk's beak nose and the same black hair. But beyond a nod of recognition he'd not acknowledged his son, nor would Luth have expected it; a man must make his own way and no father would have his son seem weak or begging on favours. It could not be so in battle.

Presently Uffa beckoned us to him. He had some bread and cheese and a flask of milk, heated on a fire they'd got going from twigs piled up on a stone. When we'd drunk and both pulled a face, he grinned and said, 'Anything stronger heats at first but the warmth soon goes. You know that. You'd feel colder after.' He paused and looked me up and down, staring at my cloak and trailing blanket. I flushed scarlet, knowing he did so on purpose and expecting him to say something. Instead he handed me a pin from his tunic and helped me. Afterwards he tutted through his teeth and said, quite gently, 'What good'll you be, eh? Dead with cold. Why didn't you ask?' Just then someone called to him, which was as well for I could not have answered.

Nor had Luth and I spoken. Yet now we sat and munched our bread together. Without words we each of us knew we were boys in a man's world and not to draw attention to ourselves. We listened to the joking and the laughter, rough and eager, and the sort of talk the women never heard. At night it was the same in our hut; but now, wide-eyed, shy as young mountain cats, we listened and watched and held our tongues.

After we had rested Mhorged set a faster pace. The land had opened out on to the high moors and the way was easier than before. There was a change too among the men. They were quieter and their faces had hardened, knowing what they were about. The horses sensed it, pulling and plunging. Luth and I kept to the back and my arms began to ache. Then, as the day's light faded, Mhorged drew rein.

We looked across the land. Before us stretched scrub and heather, dark under a darkening sky, and outcrops of rock and heavy, rounded boulders. The place had a grey and brooding feel, a kind of empty wildness. Save us, no living thing stirred but nearby, just off the track on a patch of bare earth, lay a jumble of little bones, thin and fragile, a bird's or a hare's.

Everyone was quiet. In a little while Mhorged moved on, with Hakos riding at his side. We followed, turning downwind into a gully, and waited once more until we saw a movement amongst the rocks and Mhorged raised his hand. Presently a man appeared, climbing carefully, picking his way over the boulders. It was Tuan, the scout who'd stayed as watchman, well wrapped against the cold. He went to my uncle and they spoke together and then to some of the men. Soon after Uffa came up to us.

'It's like this,' he said. 'The lair's nearby, under that overhang there, and the brute's been gone all day. According to Tuan, it'll be back soon if it runs to habit. Till then we stay put.'

We tethered the horses and watched as Tuan went back up the gully, keeping low. Mhorged handed round a flask. This time it was not milk, but Uffa was right; soon after we were cold again.

We waited a long time. The dogs lay down and dozed but the men stayed silent or talked in whispers. I leaned against Ban, feeling his warmth, and watched the young warriors.

Now, for all their fine clothes and upswept hair, they were sober, gathered round Hakos, checking their nets and weapons. I was so intent on them I did not hear Luth till he was close behind me, and then, turning, saw he too had come to watch. After a moment, without taking his eyes off them, he said, 'They're like iron, aren't they? Glittering at first and then hardening off, like a sword. They're more deadly then. Wait till you see them go.'

I did not know what to say to that and we stared on, having nothing else to do. Then Arax turned suddenly and caught us looking. Both of us drew back against Ban but he made a gesture anyway, with his fingers, obscene and threatening. Afterwards Luth sighed and shrugged. 'Even iron,' he said, 'will rust.' Suddenly his mouth twitched, and for the first time we met each other's eyes and grinned together.

Not long after came the signal, clear and sweet, a wild bird's whistle. For a moment we held still with only the wolf-hounds' whimpering in the hush. Mhorged beckoned and the men began to creep together up the slopes. Luth slipped in beside me and we followed after. At the top we saw it.

It was a huge beast, trotting unconcernedly to its lair. From its jaws hung a piglet, slack-limbed and bloody. As it reached the rocks it stopped and began to eat, head down, worrying at the meat. Its tail hung low; its forepaws splayed across the carcase. It was an old wolf, gaunt and stringy, the rough fur grizzled. From time to time it raised its head. We could see the fresh blood on its jaws and how it scented the air.

Mhorged said quietly, 'Uffa, stay with me and Tuan. In a

moment I'll let loose the dogs. The rest of you mount up but stay down there. If it breaks free we'll need to chase it after all but I doubt it will come to that. Hakos, keep the white bitch with you – she won't know how to work with the others. And see our horses are brought up if we have to ride. Come to the ridge once the dogs go.'

Carefully we moved down again. No one even whispered. The cold dusk was thick about us now and the stars were in the sky, glittering like ice. In the thorn trees the birds cheeped and puffed their feathers; our breath smoked in the purple air.

We reached the horses and soothed them and swung on to their backs. Under me Ban was warm and comfortable. He turned his head and tried to nip my ankle through my boot. It was a gesture only; if he'd meant to he would have.

Hakos said to Luth, 'Sit easy, damn you!' and I saw Luth flush. He was tense and his horse sensed this and finicked. It was hard enough anyway. Mhorged was on the ridge still, with his dogs beside him, and Uffa and Tuan with the nets and spears. I clutched my own; it seemed a paltry thing with which to face a wolf.

All at once, the dogs' heads reared up. Mhorged sprang to his feet in one smooth movement, outlined against the sky, and Tuan with him. There was silence measured in a heart's beat and then he cried out loud, 'Go hunt, Flidais! Go hunt, Dua!' and unleashed the two great wolf-hounds.

We set heels to the horses. I felt again Ban's lovely, sure, leaping bound and the scouring rush of wind. Then we were at the top of the ridge and reining in to see what lay before.

The dogs rushed down the slope in long, smooth strides. For a moment the wolf stood still, its sharp head lifted, ruff of fur raised on its neck and the length of its spine. Then it too was loping down the mountainside towards the safety of the forest.

At my side I heard Hakos shout and urge on his horse. We began to run again, galloping down the valley which shone with frost. Ban stretched and I gave him his head, lying along his neck. In my ears was the thud of hooves and in my face the dusk and the icy air. Suddenly it was glorious. Close by, Luth laughed aloud.

Below us the lean forms stretched and reached. The wolf ran steadily while behind the dogs bounded, ruthless and smoothly questing. Through the shadowed air the rough flanks and lean, strung bodies worked and we too were borne onwards, hurtled down the slope in a hot, coarse surge of mane and tail and horse flesh.

The noise of our coming reached the wolf. Its steadiness faltered, the practised muscles slowed, and it veered, running briefly back at an angle to the dogs to make them check. There was a flurry of fur, grey and brown, they parted and the chase renewed as the wolf made again for the forest.

But the gap had narrowed and Flidais, the old hound, the good bitch, knew it. She ran on instinct, the hunter's line bred true within her. The whole of her seemed to draw out and lengthen so that she flew over the frozen ground, dark and lithe, a shape that lolloped and sprang in her own sure rhythm of bone and sinew. The wolf sensed it. It twisted again in front of her, up towards the lair. My uncle shouted and the wolf-hound sprang.

She missed the first time, and rolled to the stony ground, but in an instant she was up with the same, stretched staunchness. She was blind now to all but the wolf-form of her quarry, deaf except to the beating pad of paws. And now, once more, she gathered herself and this time they closed, wolf and dog, and snarled and yammered and twisted together. The hound straddled the wolf's back with her teeth in its scruff; their paws scrabbled each other's flanks and the wolf strained round its head to bite. Dua, the young hound, bounded round them, wild with excitement, eager and ignorant.

Mhorged cried, 'Circle them!' He sent his horse forward, spear up, balanced to throw. At his order I set my heels in Ban's ribs, turning him. Around us the others did likewise until we formed a circle of men on horses, surrounding the struggling beasts.

We waited, reining in the shuddering, plunging horses, our spears held high. I smelt again the hot musk of animal fear and watched in the moonlight the supple twisting bodies, coiling like otters at play, save these bodies grew bloody. For a moment Flidais' head came up, her grip broken. Her jaws opened, glistening and strong, to seize again, but the wolf broke free, rearing, and turned on her with a snarl. She crouched, teeth bared, ribs heaving, her flanks compressed to spring, but the young dog, Dua, leapt instead. He fell shrieking, caught by the throat and worried. Then the wolf stood and the hound lay still.

For a long moment the wolf waited. In the moonlight its eyes were pale as flames and its pelt like silver wire. Its sides sucked the night air, blowing out hot gulps of steam. Still crouched, Flidais was at bay; a thin trickle of dark blood stained her coat. She too was hurt.

No one moved. No one spoke. Above us the sky was black and the stars glittered. The moon was a nail's paring of silver.

The wolf's head cast about. The jaws opened, the pale eyes gleamed. Nearby a horse whickered and under me Ban shifted, starting back. His quiver drew the creature's eye. The muzzle wrinkled and the black lips lifted, laying bare strong, curved teeth. In its throat was a muttering snarl. As Flidais had done, it hunched to spring, a slow, careful gathering of itself; and as if through water, clear and magnified, I saw what was to come.

Ban shuddered and jerked in terror. In my mind, cold as beating drops of rain, a small voice said, 'Hold him. Don't break the circle. Or else the wolf will run you.' For in an instant Ban, whom I had brought to this, would gallop in an agony of fear with myself on his back, and the wolf leaping after to tear us apart.

Ban fought, sitting down on his quarters. With every morsel of strength I possessed I set my knee and calf against him and forced myself deep into his back, for his sake and mine, for if he went we were finished. Both of us, horse and rider, faced the wolf. Its jaws were open, filled with bloody spume and the scarlet, lolling tongue. The hackles rose like a great cuff of iron fur and I closed my eyes.

A voice spoke as once before, light and hard and quick. So I'd heard it then and knew it now. It said, 'Be easy, little cousin.'

I opened my eyes and looked. This time he was more than a voice and a presence, barely glimpsed in flaring torchlight. He sat his black mare, a man no longer golden but silver, his hair and beard bleached by darkness, the jewels about his throat and ears and fingers catching sparks of moonshine. His little mare snorted and plunged. About her bridle he'd hung his amulets and tokens, to ward off evil and bring him courage. They jingled, bell-like, in the hush and the wolf crouched down and panted.

Across the circle my cousin smiled, the self-same lift of mouth and chin and brows. I saw but could not tell what

117

thoughts showed in his eyes. And then, with care, he closed his legs about his horse's sides.

He drove her on. In the boys' hall he'd played with Arax, to bend him to his will; now it was the same. The pony skittered, dancing in her fear on thin, delicate legs. I remembered his own, the halting limp and dragging foot that would not bear his weight. Yet here he was strong. Before us all, deliberately, step by step, he forced the black mare forward.

Briefly, the wolf cringed. From its throat came another noise, not quite a growl; but it too had courage. It drew back, and leapt.

The great, hard body rose high into the air. Just at the last it twisted, held between the earth and sky, bathed in moonlight. So too did the white bitch – Nemair's hound – who knew wolves as she knew her own, and tasted of their hunger .

The breath died in me. Released at last Ban squealed and jumped and now, when I could have sat him, I tumbled sideways, scrabbling on the ground with barely wits enough to clutch the reins. Someone – Uffa – leant down and steadied me and pressed me up against his horse's shoulder. Held in his steady grip I gasped and stared and saw what was before us.

The wolf was dying. The white hound's jaws had bitten deeply. Yet now she stood apart, obedient to her master. The wolf lay on its side, its hindquarters made useless by the bite. Hakos raised his spear.

The mountainside was very quiet – a place of frozen rock and grass and stars. For the last time the wolf lifted its head. The pale eyes blazed, the long throat lifted, bare and vulnerable, and it howled. The ululation was not of pain or despair nor even of defiance, only the voicing of itself, unchanged, eternal, the wolf-cry that bound it to its gods as words bound us to ours.

Hakos flung his spear. It flew singing in the air, and the wolf yelped and whimpered and died.

Afterwards, as the body settled, the young warriors shouted, taking Hakos's honour as their own. The older men were practical – already talking of the skinning and the fineness of the pelt. But some were quiet and thoughtful, gathered round the body. I slipped away from Uffa, who held me still, and joined them. Mhorged was there, staring down.

Close to the wolf was bigger, still terrible, not really pitiful. It stank, hot and musty, and the fur was coarse over strong, raw bones. Yet the Antlered One who is lord of the wild things had heard; death had come cleanly. I thought of the dead girl, of Dua, even the little piglet lying in its blood.

Mhorged stirred. I looked up at him and he caught my movement and met my eyes. Almost he spoke, but he turned his gaze instead to Hakos, who wheeled his mare about and about and waved his bloody spear while all his warriors cheered him.

It was too far to ride back to Nam Dubh that night. We camped in a shepherd's bothy over the ridge and got a fire going and some broth warmed up and the drink went round. Much later, before we slept, Luth stirred beside me. 'Arawn?' he said. I turned to look at him. He was flushed and heavy-eyed with beer. He said, 'Have you spoken to your cousin?'

I shook my head. Hakos was very drunk, surrounded by his men who were making a poem to him, and laughing himself sick.

Luth paused, trying to think. Then he said, 'Did you enjoy it today?'

My own speech was slurred, but I saw everything very clearly. I said, 'No. Not really. Not at the end. Did you?'

He shook his head. 'But it had to be done. It killed the girl. And it might have got to the stock-pens.'

'Besides,' I said, 'it was an outcast.'

His eyes met mine, dark and considering, more sober than I'd guessed.

He said, 'It's not that simple.'

'Perhaps it is.'

He shook his head. 'No.'

The jug came round again. Afterwards he said, wiping his mouth, 'Flidais would have gone in anyway. She was not that much hurt. Your uncle was all set to send her. And you did well to hold Ban like that. Better than I could have done. Uffa will tell your grandfather.'

I laughed. 'Who cares?' I said, and soon after slept.

Chapter Eleven

At sometime between midnight and dawn I awoke, roused by a noise. I sat up and looked around. The bothy was not too dark for there was no door to close and outside the night sky was cloudless and lit by stars, with a bright frost besides. I could make out the sleeping forms close by me and hear their snores and mutters. It was very cold and I wrapped my blanket tighter and meant to settle down again. Then, from the corner of my eye, I glimpsed a movement outside. I stared, wondering, for the hounds had not given tongue, and saw it was a man who limped on the hillside among the rocks.

I guessed of course who it might be, though not what he was doing. It seemed strange for him to be picking his way about, alone, in the bitter night. I was curious and half-fuddled with sleep and ale and it came to me that I had a duty to him, for what he'd done that day. I thought at least I should be able to speak with him, face to face, with no one else to hear us. I did not stop to think he might not wish to talk nor that what he did no one should see. Cautiously I stood and stepped my way over the sleepers.

Outside the cold caught my breath and cleared my head and made me shiver. I scanned around and saw how my cousin had crossed down, past the outcrop where the wolf's lair had been, out on to open ground. Beyond, the moorland lay dark under a crust of frost and the rocks cast long, black shadows. It was deepest night yet the air had a pure, cold, brilliance, and he was touched with silver. He moved quickly, for all his limp, and I lost him where the ground dipped away. Then I crested a ridge and found him again.

I think, by then, some part of me knew where he was going. He walked on purposefully, keeping straight across the hill, and then he halted, right where the wolf had fallen. After it had died there'd been no time to skin it before darkness came, so they'd built a cairn of stones over it, to keep it safe until the morrow, for the pelt was too fine a thing to waste. My cousin paused beside it, then knelt, stretched out his hands and began to pull the stones away.

I wondered what he meant to do. A man may return to a fallen enemy to gloat, or rejoice, or even to mourn. He worked steadily, crouching over the mound, wrapped in himself and busy.

Seeing him so, the hair on my neck lifted. Strange things are told of wolves – how some men run with them, clad in their fur, serving the Stag-god who outruns them and leads them to his shrine – and stranger of the dead. Besides, I knew not what manner of a man my cousin was. I had seen him perform only, in his glitter and his jewels and his posturing, as the song-maker did in his. The substance of the man had stayed hidden as paint on a statue hides the clay beneath. Here, suddenly, was something shocking – born of night and solitude, and the wild, frosted mountain. My heart felt like water within my ribs and I wished I had not come.

He worked on. The stones grew to a pile behind him and the body of the wolf lay exposed, a black hump of fur and stiff, dead flesh. Now it seemed a lonely thing he did, touched with sadness and aching with the cold; he who had ever had his men around him and the wolf that had snarled out his hatred and fought outnumbered and had died.

My cousin stood. From his belt he drew something. The light from the stars and the thin little moon glimmered on it and picked out the shape; an axe, a small one to use one-handed.

I looked and the breath died in my body. He raised it up and the blade shone aloft under the winter stars. Then he brought it down in one sure swoop, cleaving the wolf's head from its corpse. Briefly they were locked together, the one to the other, by iron and wood. Then the head leapt and rolled and at last lay free.

I let out my breath, trembling. Far off, in the valley, a vixen screamed. My cousin stood a moment, his shoulders slumped. Then he knelt again and began to pile the stones back into the heap.

Some of my fear had left me. I thought I understood a little. In battle one takes the head of an enemy if he has been worthy, to display and boast of and to set his soul free so he cannot haunt you. They'd told me the Clan-lord had taken my father's head that way from fear of what might be. Also you take your enemy's strength for yours. But this had been a private thing, not for witnesses, nor in the heat of battle. It seemed a darker ritual and I wondered where he'd learnt of it, and who had taught him to have such secrets in his heart.

He finished with the stones and the wolf lay once more hidden. He stood, then stooped again and took up the head. He carried it by the loose fur behind the ears and began to walk back the way he had come, going past its lair.

I did not know what to do. In my belly was a twice-tied knot. I almost crouched down and hid but at the last thought, No. That is the coward's way. I've seen him and nothing can change that. I owe him honesty at least. So, when he was near, I stepped out in front of him.

He started, I had not stopped to think how I might appear to him, and then he frowned. I half expected anger, an outburst familiar from my grandfather, who was his also, but none came. He only eyed me thoughtfully.

Now my moment had come I could not begin. I was shy and awkward and dazed with the night's mystery. He had the axe still in his other hand and, after the first moment, bent and wiped the blood from it on the grass. When he had finished he straightened and looked into my face.

Never before had I been close enough to him to speak. He was taller than I by several handspans. In the starlight I saw his eyes, long-lidded and dark, and the strong planes of his cheeks and forehead, like his father's, with the lines running from his nose to the corners of his mouth. He was perhaps seventeen or eighteen. His beard made him seem older than he was.

About us there was no drift of night wind; only the still, cold air. Into the silence he said, 'Well, then?'

I paused, trying to gauge him, to search for mockery and find if it was there; yet there was no lift of brow or chin, and as I stared at him so he did at me.

I swallowed and caught at words and said, 'I did not mean to see tonight. I only wished to thank you, for what you did. I could not have held on much longer.'

His face hardly changed. He said, 'You think you owe me that?'

'And for the other time before.'

'With Arax?'

'Yes.'

He stepped forward; I had to tilt my head to meet his eyes and my heart jumped in sudden fear.

Earlier he had been very drunk. Even now there was a slackness about his mouth and eyes. I watched him smile and slowly, wantonly, with all the familiar mockery, he let me see him as he was, his guard all gone. He stood revealed, as Arax had been, but plainly, as if in crystal, with no sense of gathered, dark things as had been then. For a moment he was like winter itself, cold as bone and hard as the ground we trod on. Nothing could make him yield. He gave me the knowing of it and sickeningly I understood why he had taken for himself the wolf's head.

I must have flinched; I had to stop myself from running and suddenly he laughed. It was true laughter – a yelping gulp that shook and bent him double. Shocked, I stood fixed before him and through it he began to speak.

'You owe me nothing, cousin! Do you think that because I didn't let Arax strike you to the ground, or that brute leap to kill you, that I am any less your enemy? The wolf could have had you for all I care, and Arax smashed every bone in your body.'

He spoke in gasps, wiping water from his eyes and bending over me while his long mouth curved. But I heard every word he said.

'No,' he went on, 'it was not for yourself I saved you, little cousin. Not for your bright hair and eyes and courage, nor for your strong, straight limbs. My dear, I saved you because of what you are, the mark on your arm, your mother's son. You are very like her, did you know? For that I would save you from worse and more! Remember that next time you strip and see yourself!'

He caught his breath, swaying. And then, soft all at once, he said, 'What did you think when you saw me tonight? That we were bound by other things than blood? What nightmares run in our veins, cousin? What dark things do we share?'

He paused and looked at me as if he searched for wounds. All at once he raised his arm and I thought he meant to strike me but he pushed me from him instead. Then he turned. In his right hand he held the wolf's head still. He flung it at me, savage and bitter all at once, and the thing caught me in the chest and bounced away.

'There,' he said. 'Perhaps you were right. Perhaps we both have knowledge of a kind. We are each our mothers' son. Take it. It is as much yours as mine. A filthy trophy to hang above your bed!'

He went off, laughing, and I was left. For all that bright, starlit night my eyes stung and, as I stumbled to my bed, it was as if the marsh mists lapped once more about me to make me blind and falter.

The next day we returned to Nam Dubh. The men were cheerful and full of the victory. From the young warriors' talk the wolf had grown into a monster. Hakos had its pelt rolled up behind him on his horse; he must have gone out at dawn to skin it. My uncle carried Flidais before him. She'd been bitten deep on one shoulder but with nursing she would mend. The white hound trotted and coursed among us.

Early on Luth rode beside me. He asked some questions. I found it hard to answer. My mind was all with my cousin. Today he was himself again, as he rode among his men, jewels glinting, elegant and fine. But I saw him as he'd been last night – a shadow slipped behind a mask, the dark ghost peering from his brightness. I shivered and felt as if I should be ill and presently, when Luth had gone from me to ride with his father, Uffa came up and asked if I was well. He thought, perhaps, that I was shocked from yesterday. I was, but not from what he believed.

We made good speed, not having to save the horses, and by afternoon we were in the foothills before Nam Dubh. It was here that Luth rode back again. Still we rode in silence until, looking down the track, he cried, 'There's Dearg!'

It was he indeed, waiting just off the main path to the citadel, and I saw he had dogs with him also, and a net and boar spears so it was plain at once what he wanted. Sure enough, as we came up, he pushed his pony on to meet us and said, 'Long days past, Luth. Had you forgotten?'

He sounded sulky, like a child forbidden from its toys, and his face was red under his freckles. He sat, stocky and stubborn, astride his horse; he too had wished to hunt the wolf.

Luth said, 'I hadn't forgotten. But now? Have some sense. The horses are tired out. Can't it wait until tomorrow?'

Dearg shrugged. He fixed his eyes on Luth's as if he tried to speak through them. He said, 'We need the meat.'

Luth sighed and I knew, for their friendship's sake, he would go though he would rather have shared in the hot wine and cheering of our homecoming. He reined in his horse. 'Tell Uffa,' he said to me.

125

Dearg spoke again. 'And him.' He pointed at me. 'He comes as well.'

For a time we rode, keeping the horses to a walk. In front the dogs searched with their noses and wove back and forth across the track. As we entered the wood the way grew narrow, plunging down a gully and doubling back. Great trunks rose up from the earth banks on either side, wound round with thick ropes of ivy. Overhead the branches tangled and hemmed us in. I thought of the day before and the windy mountains. Here nothing stirred, only the dogs and us. We snapped dead twigs as we passed and with our spears held back the undergrowth that reached across the path. Everywhere was rimed with frost and the cold vapours hung. It was the waiting time of winter, when no birds sing.

We went in silence, as we'd been taught. We hunted the small, wild pigs whose flesh makes the sweetest eating. Twice we found spoor and a place by a hazel thicket where the earth had been rooted yet never a sign of the living creatures.

The sun was pale and cold, glimpsed through the branches and the wood was full of small noises and silvery light and shreds of mist. Somewhere a stream trickled, a secret hidden sound. We rode now above a slope and all below was thick with shadow.

Later we came to a clearing in a part of the wood that was young still. The trees had smooth, narrow trunks and there was a stretch of grass and frozen mud. It was here that Luth drew rein and sucked at a scratch on his wrist. Presently he glanced about him for the dogs, then at us.

He said, 'We're out of luck.'

That was true; we'd known it from the start. It was too cold to hunt. It was not like yesterday, tracking a beast that must be killed. Anything with sense laid low in holts and burrows and waited for some warmth to touch the ground. But we had not, in truth, come here to hunt.

Dearg said, 'Do you want to go back? Perhaps we should. It's time.' He'd an edge to his voice which made me look up.

Luth said lightly, 'What do you think, Arawn? Shall we go on?'

'Why not?' I answered. 'We need the meat.'

The track wound upwards and grew more difficult, trailed across with strands of bramble that caught on the horses' tails. Once more the wood was ancient, the trees grown close together, their branches broad and heavy. Underfoot the leaf-mould crackled and I felt the cold within me, like sleep or a sickness.

We rode on again in silence. Dearg and Luth had gone ahead but Luth went first and they did not speak together. When the dogs gave tongue the noise shocked, as if someone lay close by who mustn't waken.

We took up the chase. It was fast-paced and brief. Clods of mud flew up about us and thin, whippy twigs brushed our backs, but in the end it came to nothing; a large bird struggling in a bush. As we saw it, it got free, squawking, and flapped away.

Dearg dismounted and went to look. His pony, a mare with a good head, stood waiting for him. The dogs sank on their haunches.

Some feathers lay on the ground, long brown ones and lighter fluffy down. I thought again of yesterday – the men intent and fierce, the savage courage of the wolf – it seemed a world away. Dearg crouched a moment and took one up, smoothing it with his fingers before he straightened. He said, 'It wasn't worth the taking.' He spoke to Luth.

'No.'

We waited for him. The place was narrow and awkward. On one side the earth had fallen away and formed a slope. The frost had not reached it and the soil was black and rich, pushed through with strong roots. On the other, the ground rose steeply to a rocky overhang. Trees arched across the path and through their branches the pale sunlight fell in slants.

Dearg said, still to Luth, 'I remember that song you sang, at the marriage feast. That was about a bird.'

'Yes, but not this kind. A raven. And a girl.'

They looked across at each other. Dearg stared up. The winter light was full on their white, cold faces and their hair, red and black.

Then Luth smiled. 'There was a girl afterwards too. She slipped out to be with me. Did I tell you? Except her mother saw.' He was a good mimic. He made a tale of it, glancing between us. It was very rude. Almost it had me laughing.

Afterwards he was quiet. Dearg stayed where he was and turned the feather in his hands.

The pause stretched and took hold. I watched Luth

smooth his pony's mane. The dogs whined and wriggled their rumps and bellies.

There are ways of speech. One can say things without words. Friends do, and enemies. I heard more in that silence than in all Luth's clever stories.

I said, 'What is it?'

The silence deepened. All about me I knew small things: the sound of water again, the mists that stirred and shifted in the trees, the cold, wet smell of black wood and moss and rotted leaves; yet it was apart from me, held back by the waiting.

Dearg said to Luth, 'Ask him!' He swallowed and the red blood washed in his face.

Luth said, 'Arawn, it's nothing.'

He began to turn his pony, a slow, careful guiding of wrist and knee, to go back down the track.

He would have to pass me. He hesitated, working his lip with his teeth.

Dearg stood behind. He watched Luth as a big, uncertain hound will watch his master. Then he cried out, 'Ask him! You wanted him here! You want to know! Ask him! Ask him why he went there!'

He jerked his thumb. There was a gap where the trees thinned. Beyond, through the cold haze, were the mountains and Nam Dubh, the southern side, with the spread of the citadel and the ruins broken on its back.

He cried out again, more sharply.

'He went to the ruins. No one else does. And we heard him that night with Arax. Everyone knows what people call him.'

His colour had deepened. Now it was me he looked at, not in honesty, or even in anger – but in defiance. He had no right to ask.

'We know whose son he is!'

My own blood ebbed like a tide within me. All my life I'd heard those words, and all the scorn and hatred that went with them. They sounded like an echo, dim from childhood. As Dearg had spoken them, so too had Arax, and my grandfather; the boys had whispered them, and Tachga, and everyone I'd ever known or loved or loathed. They were bound to me as flesh is bound to bone or the witch-mark deep into my skin. There was no freedom from them, ever, and in death those words would sound the man of me as the waves will sound the sea.

I threw back my head. He but spoke his fear. For all his boldness he was like a babe scared of night-time shadows. But we were taught to give no quarter, ever.

I pushed Ban forward. Dearg held his ground then shifted back, still staring. His eyes were blue and there was sweat on his upper lip, caught in the new down there. I waited till he blinked, then said, 'Is it that much bother to you? What do you think I did? Conjured ghosts and demons? Muttered curses on you all? Do you think she had time to teach me anything, or does she speak now from the dead?'

He swallowed. His mouth worked as if he tasted bile. I pulled Ban's head round. I was afraid I should weep. A toad will spit poison but this was worse. Dearg, for all his arrogance, I'd thought had sense.

Luth called, 'Arawn!'

I turned and faced him square so he could not think I ran away. Ban fought and threw up his head. For the second time I held him hard against his will.

Luth frowned, a quick tug of his brows; his hands were white on the reins.

'Arawn.'

He was older than I by a year or more, but this time he sounded a boy. It shocked, and brought me to my senses.

He said, 'I'm sorry, but listen.' He gave me no time to answer. 'I fight you every day in the ring. I know the feel of you, how you fall, how you feint to the right twice as often as to the left, the way you reach to throw. You carry a shield too low and you're much better with a sword than a spear. I saw you yesterday. But I know nothing of what's in here.' He tapped his brow. 'We live and work together. How can that be right?'

His words were tumbled and eager. He was a story-teller and knew his happy endings. He hoped, I suppose, for me to go to him, hold out my hand and tell him everything.

Only I'd learnt different lessons, from different sorts. And at Nam Dubh life is simple; they have it no other way. What they do not understand they hurt until it breaks.

Dearg had spoken first, but it was Luth I answered. My words served them both. I said, 'I do not know.' Deliberately I raised my brows and smiled. 'But that was well rehearsed. Set it to music and make a song. You'll have all men lay bare their souls.'

He winced. I thought, He'd rather I'd struck him. No one's spoken to him like that before.

For a moment he stayed quite still. The wood was quiet so that when his pony moved its head we heard the bridle clink. In the end he flicked his eyes away. He shivered a little and glanced around and up at the sky. He said, 'So be it,' and touched his heels to the pony's flanks. He did it well, like wiping dirt from his hands.

My throat thickened. I felt young and reproved, as shocked as if I'd drawn blood from Uffa. In my mind's eye I saw Luth at the wedding feast, with his sudden pride, his head raised to us while his voice caught our heart-strings and plucked them like his harp.

Then it seemed worse. Once I'd broken a glass drinking cup. The grief had flooded me – not for the trouble, I hid the pieces well – but for the beauty, all smashed and useless in little, jagged shards, good for nothing. I had buried them, smoothing over earth. And soon, like the earth then, Nam Dubh's gates would close behind us and nothing would be changed.

I called out – I could not help myself – 'Luth! I thought it would make it better, going there.'

Behind me Dearg said harshly, 'Did it?'

He had mounted and ridden up. Now we were so close the mare stretched her neck to nibble at Ban's neck.

Through the tightness in my throat I answered, 'No.'

He laughed. 'How could it? What did you think to find there?'

I lied and said again, 'I do not know.' Then, seeing his eyes, 'Something. To show me they had life, once.'

His breath hissed softly between his teeth. The wood had winter sunlight in it, the gold of dead men's masks. His hair glinted. He said, 'They had life enough. But, Arawn, the old ways are past. We do not want them back. Remember that before you seek them out.'

'My grandfather told me that.'

'He's right. There's nothing left. Even if there was, what good would come of searching for it?'

His eyes were still on my face, contemptuous. He'd put his fear from him, hearing me cry out, yet he knew nothing. And we were taught another thing – to go down fighting.

I said, 'Perhaps I looked for ghosts. But a place itself will have a soul. Don't you understand? When I was a child there was a place I used to go to fish. There were no trees, only mud and reeds and water, a great waste, shining to the sky. One time I stayed out too late and I was scared of going home, so I sat there and baited the hooks and looked at the water. And when I looked up again the sky was dark – not with night but clouds. There were no birds and no one anywhere, just the reeds, whispering and swaying, and the water. I was frightened then, of that place – more than of going home. I ran, and when I was home I wept myself blind and said that I'd been to an angry place. The old woman who nursed me understood.'

The wood was filled with cold shadow and cold sunlight. A little chill ran down my spine. I felt dull and tired with my strength all gone. Dearg sat his horse and watched me, his face narrow and suspicious. He'd made nothing of what I'd told him.

'Dearg,' I said, 'the ruins are not like that. They are empty now. You were right. There is nothing left, and nothing to be frightened of. The Clan-lord saw to that. But I had to know.'

I moved Ban off. Presently I heard hoof-falls and Luth came to ride beside me. He said, 'When I had my first harp Arax laughed at me. He laughed at everyone, even Hakos.'

'Hakos!'

'Yes. For his limp. But Hakos is good with words and Arax is frightened of him now. I had a place to go to, to practise. Dearg will not come but I'll show you, if you want.'

It was a pool, fed by one of the forest streams. We had to tether the ponies and reach it wading on foot, following the stream bed with branches and brambles twined above our heads. We halted where it opened out.

Even now I remember the feel of the water, flowing cold and slow as grease against my legs, and the way it lapped before me. It was black and open to the sky, rippled with silver where the breeze stirred it and with ice at its margins. All around grew trees, not close together but standing apart, thin and twisted like the beggars you see, who wander the marsh-tracks with their cruel faces and hungry, clutching hands.

Afterwards we clambered on the bank. A little way along there was a great, toppled boulder, half buried, roughly hewn into an oblong. There was a carving on the side, poorly done and ancient – long, stretched lines that made the outline of a horse.

I said then to Luth, 'You knew.'

'There's more.'

We wandered on. Further along we found a stake driven deep into the ground, the wood of it carved with a head, worn and cracked and bleached; but the eyes still stared and the mouth was a straight and ugly gash. Luth said, 'The Clanlord put it there. To keep the Horse-queen in the earth.'

I looked away from it, across the broad stretch of water. I thought, It will be deep. A little shiver of wind fell away and left it flat and still. I thought how at Nam Dubh a man would take a staff, wrap it round with rags soaked in pitch or tallow and hold it in the hearth for the flames to take. Then he'd use it not for torchlight, set high on the wall, but, dancing, as a sword thrust full in another man's face. And I thought of my cousin, striking a wolf's head from its body to have its strength for his.

But beside this place Nam Dubh, and all that was in her and of her, was no more than a passing fancy, a whim of men, brief moonshine on a hill.

In a little while Luth said quietly, 'Arawn, what do you see?'

But I shook my head and would not answer him.

Chapter Twelve

Spring came and the days took on a new pattern. We were kept to our training, but afterwards there'd be games that the men would come and watch. The favourite was played in teams, with a pig's bladder blown up for a ball and hit with sticks across scrub ground into a hole. It was rough, hot and often bloody. The men would bet on us or the young warriors would swagger up and have their own game while we stood by.

Those times Arax would play, red and sweating, bellowing in rage or triumph, and I would think again how much I hated him. My cousin never played; he'd stand at ease and smile his hard, carved smile and comment cruelly on his men. Yet he always wagered on them and always won.

For me it was a strange time. I never went to the pool. I'd put it from me and did not even think of it. Yet the knowledge of that quiet water was always with me as once the horse-charm had been. Perhaps I had an instinct as birds do, or animals, for what was right or wrong and where to venture. When Luth tried to talk to me about it, as he did in the first days after, I was short with him. I shied like a colt from a heavy burden and then, wilfully, I forgot.

Sometime over the winter I had turned fifteen and though I was two years still from manhood, I had filled out a little and the fighting skills which I'd found so difficult came easier now. Uffa spoke well of me and my uncle was kind. He stopped to talk to me occasionally and once, after a horse race I'd won, said I rode just like my father.

Still there were some who looked askance. My grandfather ignored me, except to curse into his beard. He'd coughed and hacked his way through winter, keeping to his chamber and possets. I only saw him when I must, for duty's sake. As the weather warmed he brightened and grew stronger. He came into the hall to eat, taking his place with a body servant close behind him, and he'd go sometimes to check the horses in the stables or watch the men put through their paces. Afterward he'd make a point of giving orders over small things, a piece of tack uncleaned, a man's demeanour he found wanting, to make himself seem lord still. Mhorged saw he was obeyed.

My grandfather I knew through and through. My aunt I had no understanding of. From her hard looks my presence rankled still. Most days, being always outside, I could keep out of her way. She never spoke to me but I had some sense she meant to do me harm and would not chance her malice. I crossed the courtyard when I heard her voice scolding the girls or maids and thought, boy-like, I had grown wise.

But my nature was my own, hot and rash. If indeed she meant me harm she had only to watch and wait, biding as a spider on the edge of her web; and so it came about.

One night Cumair came to play for us, entering the hall quietly and settling in a corner. He stayed there till my uncle signed for silence and waited for the hush. Even where he was, in the shadows, we could see he'd got himself tricked out. He'd put on a long tunic, fringed with some gold stuff that glimmered when he breathed or moved, and over it a mantle of fine, purple cloth, worn loose to hide his belly. There was bronze at his wrist and throat though he kept his fingers bare, the better to pluck the harp he carried with him.

After we had settled and taken up our cups he stepped forward and stood a little way from us, between a pillar and the hearth. He was a man who understood his craft. Half of him was lit by fire and half stayed in the shadow. On purpose he'd made himself seem strange and rare, not one of us at all. The sweat shone on his forehead and lip and his skin looked bluish, with a bloom like a plum; black hairs curled on his bare arms; he'd dressed his beard with oil.

He waited until we'd quietened, then made a gesture, opening wide his hands. He said, 'My friends, tonight I bring you songs.'

Luth was good, but this man was better. His voice was strong and true and filled the hall. When he sang of a maiden gone to her grave for love he made you believe he felt in his own heart all that he sang, and that you felt it too. At the end no one moved or spoke, as if the girl had really died. Afterwards he played brief familiar tunes and airs we'd heard before. None were of his making, nor did he sing for long. He knew better than to make a feast of it. Who values the windfall in the summer glut? The nights stayed long, he'd hope to sing again and keep the best till last.

At the end he would have left us straight away, though from the applause they loved him like a kinsman, singing of their deeds. My uncle stayed him and gave him a present before us all, and my grandfather, not to be outdone. At first Cumair made a pretence of the gift being too great – whatever passed between them had the flash of gold – but he took it anyway. Later, when he thought no one looked, he weighed it in his fist.

After that most evenings he sang for us; we grew used to having him around. I wondered sometimes why he stayed since he could have had a welcome in any hall he chose.

Each night, when he had sung, the gaming boards were brought out and the dice. While the women sat with their spindles by the hearth we would play and the song-maker and my uncle talk, for Mhorged was interested in most things and he too could sing. Sometimes he would murmur some lay or other or try a tune over. Luth, though, never played. Since Cumair had sung some light had gone from him and his harp was no longer in its usual place in our hall.

One night the dice were turning well. Gortag was pouring ale for the men; my grandfather had left. Since winter he expected Mhorged's arm to the door; from pride he would not use a stick. We had stood for him till the doors were closed, then settled to the boards once more.

I was busy and forgot the man. When I looked up next it was to call for our ale jug. The fires were dying and most of the older folk had followed my grandfather out. Mhorged had not returned and soon Uffa would call us to our beds.

The big room grew quiet and cold. The dogs lay down together and watched with sleepy eyes. In the corner Hakos and his men polished tack and talked softly of the next day's hunt. The women put aside their spinning and gossiped. The song-maker had lingered; no doubt his hut was bare and empty, bleaker still after the riches of his music. He had no servant of his own though always my uncle ordered a fire lit for him. Now he had drawn up a rug near Mhorged's place.

Luth threw the dice. A little group were playing 'black raven', which is a game both of chance and skill. It was not clear yet who would win. He threw badly, cursed and pushed the board away. Then I saw him look up and frown and look back at me.

I asked, 'What is it?' and followed his glance. The song-maker was in his place still but now a group of young women stood about him. Some of the other boys and warriors were there as well, hanging on the edge and peering over. There was something on the floor that they were looking at. Then Ruarch, who'd pushed to the front, said, 'Arawn, come here.'

He sounded too eager but those days I was not one to ignore a challenge. I got up and went across, with no idea what I should find.

They had drawn into a circle round the song-maker. No one spoke. He sat in the centre, leaning over to gaze at the floor. Beside him, on the stool, was a pouch of soft, worked leather. In front, on the rushes, were pebbles, polished till they shone. Some I could put a name to; blood-stone, black onyx, even a little pitted lump of amber such as kings wear.

From the hush it was a new thing for the others, but not for me. I knew what he was about. I'd seen it done before. At home, in the marshes, when the water-sight failed her, Tachga would cast the stones and read what lay in them. She'd go where none could find her, lest my grandfather or Palug should chance by, though when I was small and in her charge she'd take me with her. I used to peep from the dark corner where she'd put me, with my belly cold and crawling and a chill brushing my neck. Afterwards she would gather up the stones and rattle them and give them to me to hold and play with. Yet she preferred the water-sight and never used the stones but when she had to. I think they scared her; perhaps she saw too much. Nor would she talk of them after.

Seeing him, my fear came back to me – as a child I'd been half-sick with it though I'd never taken my eyes away. I wondered how he dared, in this godless place; besides, of itself it seemed too deep and heavy a thing to show in front of others. I stole a glance across the room to where Hakos and Arax sat. They'd noticed nothing but my aunt stood rigid with her dark eyes turned towards us.

Cumair beckoned to one of the girls. She came up, a soft, silly thing, giggling and looking behind to the others. He held out the stones and she took them and he clasped her hands in his awhile. Then quickly he pulled her hands apart and stones tumbled down before them, anyhow, glinting and flashing in the heather .

Cumair held up his hand for silence. Everyone craned

forward to stare where the pebbles lay. In the hot, close hush Cumair closed his eyes. From deep in his chest he sounded a long note, letting it grow then fade away. Afterwards he opened his eyes and peered down.

The stones lay, a jumble of black and amber and red and blue, fallen anyhow. He put out a fleshy finger and prodded them, stirring them about. Then he plucked one up, holding it before the girl's round eyes.

'A fine husband, my dear.'

She gasped and giggled again.

'And here – look.' He pointed at a group of yellow stones. 'Sons. Good sons, healthy and strong.'

All around the girls gave little shrieks and coos, and so it went on, with him casting the stones over and over and telling them what they most wished to hear. No doubt he'd seen it on his travels, performed by a pedlar or tumbler for a slice of mutton or a bed for the night. He did it well. Almost he made of it a harmless thing, but his fingers, fat and greasy, picked up the stones and turned them, and the sweat broke afresh on his brow and there was something greedy there, as if he sat gorging at a feast that was not his to eat. And I remembered the chill little hut where Tachga used to throw her stones and the way they had fallen, not bright and haphazard but gleaming dully, lain in threes or sixes or nines, and her gaze, eager and frightened together, as she bent over them.

My spine shivered. I backed away and looked round to see if the door was open and as I did so someone moved behind me and stared into my face.

Nemair.

She stood on the outskirts of the group with her women about her. She must have stepped up quietly to see with none of the jostling of the other girls nor the giggling.

Since she had healed me of my fever we had not spoken. Now I saw the same mouth and her eyes of clear, cool grey. But her face looked tired. We looked long at each other until she said quietly, 'Are you better, Arawn?'

I nodded. 'I no longer see the *badbh*.'

'I told you it was not I who raised her.'

'Who then?'

She shrugged, as she had once before. 'Perhaps there is another with older powers than I.'

I was uncertain of her still, of what she thought. I said, 'Do you not go to him, to have your fortune told?'

'Do you?'

I shook my head. 'No,' I said, 'this is not for me.'

Just then Gortag called, 'Daughter!' She spoke pleasantly but Nemair frowned and the firm mouth tightened. She looked a moment longer at me, her brows drawn down as if she was puzzled or anxious, then she swung round and went back to her place. She bent and took up her spinning and suddenly looked up again, straight at me, and smiled. The smile was the sort one gives a servant to say, 'All is well. You are dismissed.'

I turned back to the song-maker. She had put me out of countenance and I did not want to leave the hall directly in case she guessed and made more of it than there was.

Cumair had kept at his trade. By now people were tossing him beads or rings to make him cast for them and someone was at his shoulder to fill his cup every time he drained it. I was closer now and could smell his smell again. There were damp patches under his arms where he was hot in his robes and his face was red and glistening. All the time he smiled while his eyes followed where the gifts fell. Some of the boys were coming forward now, wanting to hear how they'd be brave and famous. I heard him promise Dearg a sword that would never need sharpening and some girl a prince to marry. Dearg was drunk enough to believe him and the girl, from her shining eyes and cheeks, wanted to. He did it well, with his wild talk, for his business was words and, sung or spoken, he was at ease with them and understood their power. I drank more ale and tried to put aside my doubts.

It grew late. The women yawned and rose to leave the hall. My aunt clapped her hands to summon the girls. Of the boys Nar had left already and Sithlann dozed over his mug. Luth, quiet and gloomy, finished his drink and stood. He was slipping off when Dearg caught his sleeve. Flushed and grinning from what he'd been promised, he said, 'Wait, look at that.'

The song-maker was gathering his things. His had been a good evening. Just at the last a girl, one eye on my aunt, pushed through and asked for a fortune.

I knew her a little. Her name was Brua and she served Nemair. She was a big, dark-haired girl, bossy and loud and not much liked. Now she stepped up boldly and held out a string of glass beads.

The other girls went quiet, not giggling like before. She looked at them and us with her fierce dark eyes and put up her chin. Then she threw back her hair.

Dearg gulped more ale. 'We can go now,' he said but this time Luth shook his head, watching the girls. I wondered which one he fancied. The song-maker leaned forward. Under his sweat and bluster his eyes were sharp as ever. He took the girl's hand between his thick fingers and kneaded the palm. He said, 'Here's one who knows what she wants,' and the girls laughed nervously.

He shook the pebbles out. They looked pretty in the firelight – glistening as if they were wet from the stream. The girl licked her lips and stared round. Nemair had gone. My aunt stood near and watched since the girls could not be left alone. He began his nonsense. The girl said nothing, not like the others who had exclaimed or sighed and thought it wonderful.

The song-maker looked up at her. Perhaps in that moment he took against her. His gaze went round us and I saw him think, considering how we felt. Suddenly he pulled her close and whispered in her ear. I saw her pull back, her eyes wide open, trying to snatch her hand away. Until he'd touched me I'd thought him womanish and fussy but he held her wrist in a tight grip while her fingers picked at his hand.

She did not speak but the colour came high in her cheeks and neck. He said loudly, 'There you are, my darling. Such as you are always the slyest,' and slapped her rump.

Beside me Luth began to laugh and Dearg belched into his mug. The girls around did not laugh but a kind of rustle went among them to show that they were pleased. She had enemies there. We got up to go. I had a last mouthful of ale and I paused to drink it, a bitter, young brew but wet enough. As I set the cup down the girl went past, pushing in front of the others. She would look at no one but there were tears in her eyes and she'd caught at her lip with her teeth.

I did not like her. She had brought her trouble on herself and she cried because it came hard for one such as her to be humbled. Perhaps, though, I remembered too well the feel of the man's fingers on my flesh and his words about me. Something in me stirred. Without thinking I lifted my cup as if in salute to her and said, 'Never mind. His mouth's as fat as his belly!'

She heard – I'd spoken clearly – and the muscles in her

139

neck jumped but she would not look at me. The girls went past with my aunt scolding them for lateness and they'd heard too for I saw their sidelong glances. The song-maker smiled still and gathered up his things. If my words had reached him he did not show it.

I walked back with Luth and Dearg a little way behind. Both were quiet until Luth said, 'Why did you say it?'

'You know why.'

'You had a grudge to settle!'

Dearg said, 'Challenge the man, Arawn. It would be like wrestling a greased pig, but he'd enjoy it!'

I stalked off rigid. Then Luth called wearily, 'I'm sorry, Arawn. Don't be so touchy. You should not offend someone like him. He has influence. I would give anything to sing like that.'

All along I'd guessed the reason for his silence. I came back and said, 'One day you will.'

He shook his head. 'Do you think so?' There was little light to see by, for the night was cloudy, but I saw how he looked and said no more.

We neared the hall, stumbling as the way grew rocky. Ahead, through the darkness, we could hear laughter and see lamplight round the door. Luth had his hand on the latch when a voice called, 'You, boy! The witch's son!'

It was a woman's voice, shrill with age. Luth pushed open the door and at the same time she stepped forward from her place in the shadows. We saw her clearly in the lamp's glow – an old woman clad in a rough cloak. She was my aunt's woman. All evening she had served her.

She scuttled up. Her hand when she reached for me was like a claw, bones and skin and nails shrivelled and bent. She took me by the sleeve and peered up. She came as high as my shoulder; age had shrunk her. She said, 'My lady's after you.'

Dearg whooped behind me. 'What's she got warm for you then, Arawn? She heard, you know, and she'll sting you for it.' He was glad. He hated me still.

Luth said, 'You'll have to go,' and indeed there was no help for it. My aunt was Lady here.

The old woman said nothing. I followed her as she hunched and stooped her way back to the hall, dragging along like a creeping bat. Then she slipped off and left me in the yard. No one was about. Even the hall seemed dark. I paused a moment to gather my courage. Above the moon gleamed. It rimmed the clouds with silver and then was gone again. I pushed open the door and went in.

Chapter Thirteen

She sat at the hearth. Someone had put a fresh log on the fire and the bark had caught. From the bed of ash the small flames lapped and hissed and made the only light, like a little golden pool. The torches were out and the walls and high rafters lay in darkness.

The old woman had followed after all. I heard her pull the door to and fasten it. Her skirts rustled as she went past, scurrying like a beetle to its hole.

I stood and waited. My aunt kept her face turned from me, cowled by some shawl she wore. It was a sign of her displeasure to hide her features so; there was only the curve of her head and the long fall of cloth to her feet. If she had heard what I had said then she would mean to punish me. All the way down the track I'd wondered how it would be – a hard task to bring me to heel or some petty, paltry thing for the others to jeer at – and how best to answer her. I'd words to say and ways to speak them. Now, across the wide room, she looked small, squatting by the hearth, half in shadow, but she'd put herself in Mhorged's place. From there he gave judgement, which men must respect. I did and held my tongue.

She had heard me enter; some stiffness in her told me that. In a little while, when she thought fitting, she shifted and leaned out across the fire's brightness. The flames touched her brow and chin and cheeks with light, but her eyes were two black pits. She was like a water-bird, craning her neck to hunt.

After she'd searched me out she sat back once more and rested her hands on the rug beneath her. Tonight they were still, turned palm downwards on to a pattern of reds and blues. She kept her silence and I did not move.

Presently she said, 'Had you no offering, Arawn, to have your fortune told?' Her voice was harsh and flat. She spoke just as she did to her servants, as if I was no one and worse than useless.

My colour rose and the fine words died before I'd uttered them. Then I said, 'I had an offering,' and raised my chin.

'But not for him?' She was too far from me to see if her face had changed, only how she stared.

'No.'

'He is your uncle's guest.'

I said, 'Is he so?'

She was quiet then as if she considered the matter. I had clenched my fists in case her anger flared and I drew a breath to steady myself. I would not have spoken to my uncle like that and she scared me worse. It was not courage though that made me goad her, only a kind of nerviness. Once I had been riding in the hills, far from Nam Dubh, with a black storm about to break. We had outrun it, Ban and I, galloping under clouds with the wind and rain at our backs, reaching the gates as the first lightning split the sky. It was like that now, as if the storm-light still crackled on my skin.

Gortag moved. She beckoned the old woman who shuffled from her watching place and bent her ear. When they had murmured together my aunt put back her shawl and the old woman took it, folding it in her arms where she stood. The fire was young yet, and dim; the shadows flickered and were close about them. They were careful in everything, and deliberate, so that my nervousness increased. It was as if they made ready for some ritual, some dark and hidden deed.

My aunt said, 'Come here.'

Halfway over she showed clearly. The fire took hold; flames, amber and gold, spurted up and lit her where she sat.

Truly she was ready. Earlier she had dressed in a gown lined with fur up to her neck and embroidered. Now, despite the night's cold, she wore the blood red dress once more, fastened low at the breast with a long pin. Round her neck she had a circlet made of little, beaked raven skulls and her hair was unbound. It tumbled down her back like a wild girl's, coarse and brown, streaked through with strands of silver.

And like a girl, another girl, she wore the cloak of feathers, the raven cloak with the night shimmer and the darkness coiled like smoke within.

I halted, staring as if I'd taken root.

Her face was the same as ever, sharp and yellow, so thin you could see the bones stretch the skin but I had seen her, day after day, cold and formal, instructing others in their duties; or by night, spinning with her restless fingers. Though I feared her, in those guises she was familiar. Now another woman peered from her eyes, a woman of the night and of dark, secret things. But I knew her, the *badbh*, the ill-wisher, laughing by my bed.

There was more. Before the fire she'd drawn a circle, chalked in white, such as Cumair had used to cast the pebbles in.

She had seen me looking, raw and ignorant as I was, though I tried to master myself. Softly she said, 'Once a cloak such as this was mine to wear, till the Clan-lord's priest forbade it. Yet even now the Dark-mother comes to those who call, for she is in all men and women and she roosts in the hearts of those who summon her.' Her words fell on me as stones fall into bright, cold water. Still I paused, for my pride's sake, and when I walked to her it was slowly, on purpose.

She held me with her eyes until there was only the fire between us. I stood there, out of her reach and glad of it; facing warriors you get the other's measure – here it was the same.

So she too watched, with her mouth thin and tight and curving. Afterwards she said, 'A fine, upright lad with the world before him. Yet he does not wish to see his future and insults the man who would do so. Brave words, Arawn!'

She was spiteful as ever. I said, 'He was cruel. And it was nonsense.'

'You think so?'

I stared beyond her into the darkness. At my back came a breath of cold air, a rustle and the soft hiss of breath. I whipped round to look and saw Nemair there. She stepped quietly and no longer smiled. She was clad for the bedchamber, her hair unbound, lying disordered about her shoulders. Yet for the first time I saw her as she was, young and confused. Her eyes looked bewildered.

My aunt fell silent, thinking. Once her eyes lifted quickly to mine with a black look before she lidded them. She spread her fingers to the fire, in the gesture that says, 'Ah, well . . .'

For a while she watched the flames. I waited. Outside an

owl hooted once, then again from the woods; the fire shifted. The old woman, standing apart, swayed slightly with the cold and hugged the shawl about her.

Gortag did not move. The fire-glow lit her where she sat. Her head downturned, she stared into the flames.

Smoke curled between us. I shifted to ease my shoulders which were stiff. We'd been all day in the saddle and Ban still pulled.

Gortag moved, a slight shifting in her place, coming back to us. Her eyes gleamed.

'Arawn,' she said, 'Mhorged speaks well of you, of your riding and sword-play. He tells me you work hard. Uffa is pleased too, and your grandfather.'

'My grandfather?'

'So he says, when you cannot hear him.'

Some change had come upon her. Before she had curbed herself as a man curbs a horse. Now her mouth curved as if she told a secret to bind us close. She'd moved forward a little, in her place, and showed her arms, thin and naked, under her sleeves and the hollows beneath her collar bones where the pin pulled at her dress. A shudder, cold like water, ran through me and I made myself be still.

She asked, 'Do you like it here?'

'It is better than the marshes.'

'Why?'

There were a hundred reasons but I was too proud to tell her so. I set my mouth and made no answer.

She did not press me. In a bit she asked, as if the idea was new to her, 'What will you do, nephew, when you are grown? Will you be here with us?'

I guessed what she would wish to hear. Neither would I give her that. 'My uncle sent for me, Aunt. Why should he bid me gone?'

She laughed. The sound broke from her, shrill as a girl's, and she rocked with it, back and forth, on the rug. Still from the shadows Nemair looked on. My aunt calmed herself, pushing away her hair and staring up. A chill hand seemed to clutch my heart. Her eyes were black as marsh pools and when I looked into them I thought I saw some dark and ugly thing that moved like a fish's flicker, waiting to break the surface.

'Do you know,' she said, 'what your uncle tells me? He says, "Listen, Gortag, Arawn is a good boy. Only look at him and you will see. Forget your fears.""

Outside the owl hooted, flying in the night. Fire glimmered on my aunt's face. Her breathing had quickened; at her breast the gold pin flashed and moved, the bleached skulls tapped together with a little, hollow, knocking sound.

'He says that to me. And I look but what do I see? Only wilfulness and disobedience. And the past come back to us.'

She spoke slowly and kept her voice low though so harsh that I stared, pricking as an animal does at danger. She was hunched over, bent to the fire as if she were sick, craving warmth to nurse what lay within her. Then she turned up her face to mine, pinched and narrow-eyed, the jaws tight as a cat's. For the first time high colour stood in her cheeks.

It was a look I knew. I'd lived with it from three years old though a man had worn it then. In bitterness I thought, We've come to it. It is the same as always. A scolding and a curse for what has been, and blows, like as not, to follow.

It seemed hard then – for all her mystery and robes and magic things – she'd done no more than watch her chance to blame me; to thrust back my faults with the weight of things long past.

Hot anger washed me. Flaring, I turned on her. I cannot tell what I would have done; more, I think, than speak my anger – I was out of myself. But she was no green girl. Her eyes widened and she poised on a sudden, rearing like an adder before it strikes. My words stuck in my throat. I flinched, stepping back from her as if from a blow indeed. Silence hung on an instant between us until, all at once, she gathered herself and cried aloud, 'You tell me, Arawn. Who sees true? What will you be to us?'

Our eyes met. I saw the hot, hard hatred and the way her lips drew back. The wild hair fell half across her face and the stretched skin gleamed gold.

Afterwards she kept her eyes on my face. When she'd cried out I'd felt it through me as a hammer rings upon metal and then is still; now the quiet seemed heavier and the shadows deeper. This was no show. Dark things breathed beside us here this night. From the corner of my eye I saw how once more the *badbh* waited. Presently the old woman shuffled forward, saying, 'Lady . . .' But my aunt waved her aside and put her hand to her brow. Behind her Nemair had come to stand. Clear in the firelight her face showed, remote no

147

longer but wondering and her hands were clasped about her belly as if she were in fear. For myself I had no words to speak. I was as a child hearing others quarrel, crying in the dark because he does not understand.

In a while she raised her head and said, 'Look.' She had something in her lap, hidden among the loose folds of her robe. She took up whatever was there and threw. There was a scattering on the floor around and I saw pebbles, not bright and pretty like the song-maker's but rough stones such as Tachga used to gather. In the firelight they had a dull gleam, like ancient gold or bronze.

She bent over them. In some anger burns and then is quenched, cleansing the soul as hot salt does a wound. With her it was not so. Whatever was in her she had grown old on it. Her nose was a white ridge of bone and deep lines ran to her mouth. Where her robe gaped was full of shadow and her thin breasts hung. I thought, She is like a stone, carved upon as the stone cutter pleases, to make her what she is. Then I remembered what the cutters say, how their hands are guided by what is in the stone already. The one will shape the other.

She sensed my gaze. She lifted her face and read what was in mine. Her eyes were cold and she did not trouble to cover herself. She said, 'It is fear, Arawn, makes women ugly. Your mother was beautiful, but that night, when the Clanlord came and they caged her in her wicker shrine and put their torches to it, she was beautiful no more. You understand?'

If a man had said that to me I would have struck him down, though they had killed me for it after; she cleaved the tongue in my mouth. I could not speak, but in the end nodded.

She poked at the stones, turning them with her finger. 'Yours,' she said, 'I cast for you. Once I could see, till the Dark-mother turned her face away. Now the sight is gone but some things I know. It'll be a hard road for you, and tears and an uneasy bed, I tell you that.'

She sat up. Tonight with her hair about her shoulders she was strange, a wise woman or priestess; I did not doubt that what she said was true.

'Ah,' she said, 'you're all eyes and ears for me now, but you do not look at what's before you. Come.'

She waited. At her feet the stones glinted, laid in their patterns, telling of life and death, of fortune and misfortune,

148

of the fallow times and the reaping, the future and the past; and all was interwoven and interlaid like the threads on a loom or the swirl of coloured glass on gold.

The old woman stepped forward, wrapping my aunt in her cloak and fussing her quietly. Through their murmuring the darkness beyond seemed full of muffled ghosts, waiting for what would be. I thought of Arax in the boys' hall and Luth at the pool saying, 'What do you see?'

I began to tremble and could not quite be steady. My hands were damp and cold. At Gortag's side the old woman had fallen silent and watched, blinking eyes red and wet with rheum.

My aunt said, so smooth you'd think her kind, 'Why are you afraid? If you see anything it is foretold and will befall you, come what may. If nothing, how can that harm you?'

Again she waited. It was very late. I felt as if I'd stood there all night before her, with the firestains on me and this sickness in my heart, yet still I would not look.

Then she said, 'You – with the horse-mark on you!'

She spat it out. All her hatred was in those words, flung at me like black rags at a beggar. I knew, as I had always known, what she saw; the mother's sins reborn in the son, the line of blood flowing from the parent to the child, tainted and accursed; and all around the soft clasp of old sorceries, binding as a lover, floating on moonshine and darkness as once the horse-charm had floated before my eyes.

The flames crackled. At my back the hall was icy.

'Lady,' I said, 'I want none of this.'

Her voice came soft and clear, low with spite.

'Do you know the way of it, Horse-boy, the mating of a Horse-witch? When they coupled what was he to her, do you think? Her stallion, her wild one? What did she feel – hoof and hide and bone and hot, hard sinew? And he – riding his mare, his witch, his whore. From that you are sprung! Look and you will see.'

Their three faces stared at me, pallid as hags'. I heard once more the sneerings of my childhood, hissed out in spite or shouted in blind rage; the hints of guilt and wickedness that I had borne in ignorance and fear. They had no form or substance, nothing that I could picture or understand; only the mark pricked into my skin, the goddess mark that made me what I was.

Horse and Raven – two faces of the one. The mother of the

tribes, life-giver, life-taker, sower of the corn, shedder of blood, and sorceress.

I cried out, 'This is witchcraft!'

'Ah!' she cried. 'And so it was for her! For Macha. And so it is for you! Now look, and you will see what is your burden and your shame!'

I bent my gaze. My head seemed filled with the beat of plushy wings, the owl's drift, the night-bird, corpse-bird, that casts men's dreams and gives them flesh. I saw the feathers, the beak and claws, and from long ago the orange eyes looked into mine before the lids of skin came down and hooded them.

The heat of the fire stung. I blinked at dazzle. The patterns of the stones were like ripples in mere water. They drew my sight as the moon will draw the waves. I was cast out, lost in the calling of my blood, treading the maze of what was in me.

So the dog-fox answers the vixen's shriek and the act of night is done.

The firelight glittered on the stones. They crawled before my eyes and now I looked for what was there, to teach me who I was.

Yet there was nothing. Nothing to see, only pebbles fallen all about the hearth. There were ten altogether, two under the burning log, smothered in the ashes.

Later, when I had raised my head, she drew in a long breath and straightened a little, tightening her lips. She said, 'Pick them up.'

I did as I was bid, though all my limbs felt heavy as if I had a sickness. It took a long time. I could not get at the two under the log.

When I had done she put out her hand for them. Nemair said softly, 'She no longer has the way of it. No one should set god against god, goddess against goddess.'

I looked straight at her and said, 'She threw them wrong. She cast an even number. Tachga always threw an odd.' And ran them into Gortag's palm. She closed her fingers over and did not look at them again.

She said, 'Your mother had her secret places. She thought on her sight and spells. But the stones she cast she hid from us.'

Her hands had begun to move in the old familiar way, pinching and pleating at the red cloth. She took no notice. Her eyes dwelt all the time on me.

'You are straight,' she said, 'and will be strong. She suckled you on mare's milk, though the old man forbade her. That is why you ride so well. As well as my son.' She paused and said again, 'My crooked son.'

A great weariness was upon me, as after a day's toil or a long bout in the arms' ring. The fire burnt low and the wood shifted into ash. I thought, She wanted to know. She believed I could see as my mother could. Her present words came as in a dream while I listened, dumb as a dog who knows only that he is at fault. Yet I had a little understanding that whispered in me as the night breeze whispers in the reeds.

My aunt stood and wrapped her shawl close. She was shorter than I by a handspan. Her face was her own again, a shrew's, hard and sharp.

As she went out she stopped by me. Her mouth twisted as if she had the taste of gall and her voice dripped poison. 'Arawn,' she said, 'the song-maker made complaint of you. You were insolent. I shall tell Mhorged. He will have you whipped.'

Then she was gone, with the old woman at her side and Nemair following after.

Mhorged came for me himself next day, waiting till the morning was well through – on purpose I supposed. We had fed the stock and swept the yard and were sat round, to grease the leather shields, when he walked in.

He strode up, lithe and easy, familiar in his cloak and boots. As he passed Uffa he paused to speak a word with him, then gestured with his thumb to where I sat. Slowly, before he could order me, I got to my feet while the boys pricked like puppies and asked me what was up. Luth stood as well and caught my sleeve, saying quietly in my ear, 'Think of the wolf – you've weathered worse.' He'd kept awake until I'd returned from the hall and I'd told him a little of what had happened. But not much. Only my aunt's last promise for me, and he hadn't asked me more.

My uncle looked across and beckoned. Luth tapped my arm, smiled with his mouth and looked pity with his eyes. My legs had gone to water but I went over. Behind me the boys fell silent and Uffa glared. I could feel their eyes at my back.

I wondered if my uncle meant to beat me there and then

before them all. When I got to him, though, his hands were empty and he said, 'Come with me.'

I followed him across the yard. People were about, working or chatting or glancing across; some tale had got about already. Then the smith came out with work to show my uncle. I had to wait while they finished turning it together and the man had been well praised. Mhorged watched him go back to the bellows and only after turned to me.

I faced him. I wanted it only to be over. I felt very sick, but without much to throw up – I'd had no taste for breakfast – and cold with a chill that ran right through me. Yet my words to the song-maker seemed a small thing to what had been. A simple beating for insolence I could bear and some part of me it would hardly touch. That part stood in the hall still, clad in the night's thick horror. Compared to that a whipping would be nothing.

He stood, legs apart, big hands resting lightly on his hips. He did not tease, cat-like, before the kill. He said directly, 'What is this with Gortag?'

I drew a breath and tasted the heat and tang of metal from the forge. He was very like my grandfather.

I set my teeth. 'I was rude to the song-maker who is your guest. She chided me for it.'

'That is all?'

'Yes.'

'Liar!'

He said it quietly but he meant it. I stared up at him, to meet his gaze. Then my heart gave such a thump it shook my body. I had not thought that he might know the rest of it; it had been too much a thing between my aunt and me. Still clear before me lay the tumble of the stones and the way I'd looked at them. Some sense I'd had all morning of being dazed and numb and weary to the bone dropped away. I felt as a thief must with everyone's finger pointing 'Guilt', and that even the shadows had had eyes and ears and mouths to whisper of what they'd seen. My aunt must have made a fine tale of it, or else the servant gabbled.

It was too much to bear. I could remember too well how it had been with Grandfather – no pity given or excuses heard. I turned my face and hunched from him, as if he struck the blows already.

152

Chapter Fourteen

None came. There was only his silence and his hillsman's eyes, searching me over. Then he said quietly, 'It's not the first time you've flinched from me. What did she tell you I'd do?'

My face flooded scarlet. I opened my mouth to speak and then could not. I was hot all over and sick with shame. I tried to turn away but he caught me by the arm and hauled me back. His dogs, which were always with him, sat up and pricked their ears.

Then I was angry, with myself more than him. From his words he knew nothing after all; had meant only that Gortag would not be content with scolding. I'd been a fool through fear, and my fear had set him now to wonder. I thought, in bitterness, He can do as he likes, and spat up at him, 'Can't you guess?'

'Perhaps. A chiding, eh? She's scared you witless!'

He let me go. He had made a sore place on my arm where he had dug his fingers in. I did not rub the hurt away. I had betrayed myself and could have wept with rage but whatever he would do to me I'd take in silence.

I scowled at him as if I'd had the thrashing. I was too overwrought for sense. His cool blue gaze held mine until, carelessly, he reached up and brushed back a lock of hair fallen across his brow. He looked irritated and at a loss, as if he'd hunted one thing and caught another.

He said, 'Half a year here and you're just the same – a polecat, all teeth and snarls. Well, you have no need to fear me, Arawn. I told you that before. I haven't sent for you to give you the hiding it seems you deserve, or to starve you, or string you up by the thumbs, or whatever else she threatened. Gortag's tongue is sharp and Cumair is an oaf. Besides I do not like scoldings in the dark, nor threats. It is not my way, nor should it be hers. She should have sent for me straight off. You'd have got what she ordered then and known about it! It might have done you good.'

He watched to see how I would take this and afterwards went on, 'Yet she is Lady here and needs be respected. You will say sorry to her and the singer in the hall tonight. And, understand, she will need to have it seen.'

I would have preferred the whipping. I gazed across the yard, at the turfed roofs of the huts, and thought of her gloating and the fat smirk of the song-maker. I felt sick again and worn out. Mhorged thought only that I was scared of his belt and his fists and his whip. So I was, but it was not the worst fear and a whole skin did not make it better.

The smith began to hammer, loud blows that rang through the yard. Ruarch and Benna, on an errand for Uffa, hung about a doorway close by, straining their eyes and ears. I made a gesture, so explicit no one could mistake it. Ruarch made it back, but they went.

My uncle said, 'Arawn.' My heart sank. I'd thought we'd reached the end of it.

'There is another reason why I wished to see you. I have something for you.'

I followed him wearily back through the yard which was empty now save for the smith and an old man clearing horse-droppings. The scent of barley stew hung on the air and in their hut the boys would be eating. We left the yard and went out to join one of the tracks that wound upwards from the citadel.

This time I studied him as he walked. His head was bare, hair rough and lit with sunlight and today he wore it loose upon his shoulders. He walked swiftly, with no hint of breathlessness despite his middle years. I thought again of my grandfather. His strength was back. Several times he had been out riding the hills. Yet still he coughed from time to time and his colour was often feverish and high.

We went on climbing the hillside. The only sounds were the sheep as they cropped the new grass and the thin, high lark-song.

My heart began to quicken. We made for the ruins, though by a different route from the one we'd used before. Already the great stones were before us, hurled down, lying like blackened hulks within the grasses, forsaken and alone. I thought, despairingly, What now? and wondered why he'd brought me here, who'd forbidden them to me or any man.

154

The noon-day air was sweet and the sunlight warm but I felt all at once quite desperate, as if he took me into darkness.

Mhorged cut across the outcrop, going past the walls and on to one of the huts. This one was more whole than most of the other buildings, though very small, with the door remaining and bolted through with a long pin of iron.

He went to it and stood before the door. Slowly I came after him and waited at his side. He worked at the bolt which was rusted to the keep. He had his knife out, scraping at it.

Specks of rust fell into the grass; the metal was black beneath. Finally he freed it and pushed with his shoulder at the door. It gave reluctantly, catching on the hinges.

I peered over his shoulder. A lozenge of light brightened on a clay floor. The door opened wider. There were shapes, indistinct and grey, standing among shadows, and the scurrying of small creatures making for cover.

The hut was circular, the walls curved over in the most ancient manner. All around were wooden shelves pinned up with rivets, and on each shelf lay piles of debris; old leather and wood and metal, and bits of broken armour.

A storeroom, full of the waste and rot of fighting men's lives.

I stepped inside. Heaped on the floor before me lay rusted helmets, with great gaping eye holes on each side of a straight nose piece. Above were swords, stacked lengthwise on the shelves.

Mhorged murmured something. I turned and gazed wide-eyed. He stood with his back to me, in front of a post which stood behind the door. The wood was painted red and fixed on the top was a skull, the jaw dislocated and hung awry and with locks of red hair still clinging to the scalp. My uncle had placed something small and bloody before it.

I looked away but not before he'd seen. 'The Red-lord,' he said. 'He no longer hears, but one day he will and ride with us again.'

I should have known. The Red-lord was the war-god, and the bleached, fleshless head a battle trophy. Some man had died well to serve him and now watched in this place.

For something to do I walked forward and began to pick up a piece or two. There was a sword, good once but notched and pitted all down the blade's length, with a little, roughened pit in the handle where a jewel had been prised out.

Moving round I saw spears and a battle horn, a carnyx, with a silver mouthpiece and a rearing head shaped like a dog. Everything was thick with dust and sour with age and the smell of cold metal.

My uncle said, 'Try this.' He held out a shield of wood with a leather overlay, split and faded. It had straps to slip over one's arm but I could not undo them and did not want to fumble them before him. I put it down and began to prowl again, curious and uneasy. Some of the spoil was very old, old perhaps when the ruins were whole. The lines of shaft and blade were warped and spoilt, the sheen of metal dulled. No trace remained of the warriors who'd borne them and hurled them into battle. Like the ruins those men were cast down, left to the earth and the long barrows of their graves. Again I shivered, recalling the past night and an ancient magic that should also be long gone. Speaking soft behind me my uncle said, 'Are you cold?'

In the end I asked straight out why he had brought me here. He answered as if it was the simplest thing. 'It is time, Arawn, you had some arms to call your own. The others have. It is not fitting that you should lag behind.'

I considered this. It was true. Gradually the other lads were acquiring their arms, from fathers, brothers, uncles, according to the custom. Old bits and pieces, most of it no better than what lay here, were handed on, to learn with and teach the weight and feel of ironwork and how it handled in a fight. Such weapons taught caution too; a blow from one of those hurt more than wood.

I leant across and lifted up a helmet. It was different from the others, an upturned bowl with a short peak, beautifully cast in bronze, the metal raised in scrollwork and crested by a boar with tiny red stones for eyes.

My uncle said, 'Choose what you like. If it's broken or doesn't fit the smith can rework it.'

It was too much then, after what I'd expected. I sat down on one of the benches, pushing aside the clutter. I stared at the floor. I could not look at Mhorged.

'What's the matter?'

'Nothing.'

'Make a start at least.'

I picked up the helmet I had cast aside. 'This will do.' I looked round and reached for a short spear, the handle mostly rotted away. 'And this.'

156

He laughed; true, honest laughter. 'Most boys would have been through this like dogs after a weasel, making sure what they had was best. Now, listen.' He stepped forward and stood over me. 'About everything else do as you like, but there's no need to bother with a sword, and don't be indifferent. You might like this.'

He turned away and reached up unerringly to a high shelf. From it he drew a long package, wrapped in skins which had been soaked in oil. He laid it on the floor and began to unwrap it. Beneath the skins were more wrappings of woven cloth, the colours, dun and green, darkened with age but preserved and tied round with thongs. He cut them, rolling back the cloths, and from them drew out a sword. It was quite plain, but whole and polished – the only thing in this place that was.

He held it out. Wondering, I stood and took it. It was quite light, a young man's weapon, only a little heavy for me. Its lines were clean and whole, the blade flowing unbroken from the hilt.

'Arawn.'

He was standing, watching me with the light behind him, the way he had watched the first day, months ago.

There was a little silence, hardly more than a breath. He said, 'It was your father's – Roech's – as a boy.' His voice was quiet and easy, as if he remarked on the weather.

The world stood still; and then it went on again and nothing was changed, from my uncle standing there to the sparrows cheeping on the roof. Only myself, standing with the point of the sword resting on the ground and my hands clasped on the pommel. Something in me stopped and waited there, crouched and at bay, for what would come.

Mhorged said, 'Roech's. It was his.'

And I said, 'You kept it?' The blood began to move in me again, throbbing slow and steady in my brain and heart and belly, only sluggish, like a weed-choked river.

'He was my brother.'

He paused, the pale eyes holding mine, and went on gently as if he searched a new-made wound.

'I could tell you of him.'

So this was planned, with intent and care. I wondered how long he'd meant to bring me here; if he had thought of it before last night or if Gortag had urged him to it.

I spoke before I could help myself. 'You tell me!'

157

He could have been angered then but no more than a flicker passed over his face. I knew how I had sounded – incredulous as if I'd heard the stag praise the hunter as it died. My uncle bent and took back the sword. I did not try to stop him.

'Last night,' he said, 'what really happened? Something brought that white face and shadows beneath your eyes. And you were very frightened.'

That was true enough. He turned the blade as I had turned the helmet and I looked down at the floor, at the cracks and the sunlight and the scattering of pale dust that lay everywhere.

My throat felt thick and clotted. I wondered what I could say to him; how all night I'd lain awake and thought of my aunt and what she'd wanted from me. How, in the darkness, I'd been touched by what was cold and cruel and taken into it. I had not understood all her words; part of me had and part had drawn back and whispered, 'No.' But she had made me step into the reek of magic, seeking to condemn me, and I had done as I was bid, without fight or protest. Here, with the sunlight streaming in, it was no better. Something in me was lost and bewildered, caught on the edge of a wasteland, and I could not speak of it to him. I could look for no pity, for it seemed to me I'd get none.

I stayed quite still. I no longer saw the floor, only my uncle's knees and boots and the point of the sword, turned and turned about, as he sat and waited. I could not raise my face to his.

He said gently, 'Was it so bad then?'

I nodded.

'She threatened you?'

I said, 'It wasn't that. She spoke of her – my mother.'

Once more there was silence between us until a bee droned by, going from flower to flower outside. At last he said, 'It might help you to know her if I tell you of him.'

I had been right. He was wise and understood men indeed. He went on, needing no leave.

'He was as tall as I am and you will be, broad but not quite filled out. His hair was darker than mine. You have his nose and chin. His eyes were blue, set like your grandfather's. He was very like him. Did you know his looks before?'

I could say nothing, having no words to speak. I knew my father in my own way – a boy's safe dreams and fancies. I'd imagined him a little as my uncle had said. I don't know what I would have done if he'd been fat or swarthy or his teeth were bad.

My uncle's voice was quiet. Yet I had no power to stop him, no more than the rocks have power to turn the tide though it wears them into nothing.

'He was my younger brother. You have none so you cannot know what that means. I taught him what I knew and mopped his knees when they were bloody and his nose when it ran. I hid him when he was in trouble, which was often; he was too wild. He rode out on Father's horse once, it bolted – he was barely turned eleven, and another time let loose a hawk because he did not like to see it caged. It was my best. We fell out over that.'

I asked, sullen because I could not help myself, 'Did he ride well?'

'He did. Better than I.'

I reached forward then and took the sword from him. The wrappings had protected it. It shone like new – the handle was barely worn, only a little smoothed in places and the blade still honed. I liked its plainness, more honest than the broken, fancy ones.

I looked again at my uncle. I saw him clearly as he sat there with the doorway's light on him. His eyes were pouched and he'd stubble on his jaw. There was sorrow and weariness there as well. He too had gazed on shadows.

He smiled. The moment felt fragile, like holding a cup or bowl from the potter's oven before the glaze goes on. I thought, no one has spoken of my father to me before, except to curse him. I was scared too much would show in my face. Perhaps it did, for he considered me and went on, 'Roech was brave and skilful. It will not shame you to wear his sword, no matter what the others say. Later he had another, up to his weight. That went with him. But he did what he thought was best, always. No one can say otherwise.'

I found my tongue. 'Grandfather told me he was obstinate and a fool. He said he was cross-grained from birth and that I took after him in all those things.' My bitterness was spoken freely for once, without fear. It startled me.

I remembered the first night here at Nam Dubh and what had been said then. 'I have his nose and chin, but not his eyes.'

'No. You see with hers.'

I said, 'Others think so. Gortag . . .' But the horror of the night was close now, laid between us as a knife between enemies, thin and glinting with the blade up. My throat closed tight and I choked.

He paused, feeling his way. 'Your father was a boy in love, only a few years older than you. He thought he could right old wrongs when he brought Macha here. He was not to know.'

'He knew what she was?'

'He knew she was a priestess of her people.'

I said at last what I must. 'No more than that? Why then does Gortag blame my mother for Hakos being as he is?'

He stared. 'Did she say so?'

'Not in words. But last night I understood.'

'So there was more?'

'She believed I could read the stones, as the song-maker does; only truly.'

'Could you?'

'I thought I could, but she threw them wrong. I do not know.' Then, 'Is it true about my mother?'

The room was quiet. About us stood the cluttered spears and swords and empty helmets. Strange that all here had once turned blood to water and dealt out bloody death. Now they lay quiet with nothing to tell of pain and fear; it is only in men's mouths that things may find their voices.

Mhorged said, 'Arawn, the old ways are gone. Remember that. Come home to us and do not seek to tread those paths or look for what's no longer there.'

He cleared his throat; the dust was thick in the air.

'As for your mother, she came here as a bride and Gortag was in her seventh month and frightened, hearing the tales. Some weeks before she had fallen.

'And I will tell you this. Had I been your father I would have done no different. She was very lovely and with him she was full of laughter. What man would have seen wickedness in that?'

He said no more and in a bit he left, telling me again to take what I had a use for. But I did not forage. As before I took up this piece and that, hardly noting what I handled. When I was ready I went back to the sword. I raised it up and felt the pommel fit close as friendship into my palm. I thought, This was my father's. He stood as I stand now, holding it. Then: It is as much his still as it can ever be mine.

I went outside, past the grim and bloody stake, and swung the sword, to test its weight and action. It went sweetly as a bird. So he had used it, and clasped a shield close to his body. I felt nothing of him, just as I had felt nothing of those others at the ruins or today, handling the weapons. Neither did I seek for him. It was enough to swing the sword and cut lightly at the air and watch the sunlight sparkle down the blade. I looked for no more and for once something in me was stilled and at peace.

Chapter Fifteen

That summer the days were long and hot and bright with colour. On the hillside the grasses grew green and sweet. White flowers shone on the nettles in the margins of the forest; the heather was purple on the high moors.

It was a better time. By day we grew brown and loose-limbed from being always out of doors. At night a great fire would be lit outside in the yard under the stars and through the gate one could see right down the valley to the dark forest below. Then boiled pork would be lifted from the cauldron and jointed and the ale would go round and, after we had eaten, the men would talk and sing, old tales that I had never heard before, of battles and single combat and heroes and gods. Their eyes would shine in the firelight and the women would speak softly together and watch the children or rock the little ones to sleep in their arms.

We boys were wild and headstrong then with youth and the sweet mountain air. Our only woes came from Uffa who drove us hard, with an edge to him as if he sickened for a fever, and from the young warriors who were ever our bane. Of late there'd been more trouble. They found fault with everything and cursed us with it. We were 'Curs, whelps, good-for-nothings!' and all accompanied by blows. Sometimes Hakos would order them off and sometimes he'd stand by and laugh. Yet me, who had more cause than most to fear them, they never touched. Only Arax said once, 'Your turn will come!' before he strolled away.

Most days I rode, slipping out early of a morning to gallop along the high moorland tracks with the wind tugging and the steady beat of the hooves sounding in my ears. Afterwards I used to think that I understood why my mother's people had worshipped the horse; not for magic but for joy in its swiftness and beauty.

Several times Luth came with me. We two had never

spoken of friendship, but it was there, grown from bare beginnings in the yard when he'd called me to my grandfather and from the wolf-hunt, and from the other hunt in the forest. At first he had begun from pity, no more than that, but of late he had changed, and now I thought I understood. For Luth fighting and arms-play and the wrestling in the ring were never enough, for all his skill and grace. Always he fretted after something to which I do not think he could even put a name, only it had grown worse since the song-maker played. That unnamed sense, of something searched and longed for we shared; the only time I was free of it was as I galloped on the moors, and in each other we caught an echo of ourselves. From that came our friendship.

Other things were hard. Though I outfaced my aunt I could not forget her. She had gloated when I had appeared, contrite by my uncle's orders, before her in the hall. She tugged my hair, suddenly familiar, as if I was a chastised child and her people smiled at each other behind their hands. To me she said nothing but her fingers in my hair pulled sharply so that I had stiffened and drawn away and her face was narrow and spiteful as she looked. She thought herself hard done by; she knew my uncle had not taken a whip to me.

So for all the bright days there were dark things even now that squatted on my shoulders. Then I remembered the little silver horse, my talisman I'd cast away, and wished I had it still for comfort.

One morning four of us rode out together, Luth, Magh and I, and for once Dearg, who was scowling and sullen but who wished to be with Luth and would not keep away. We went to the woods where the air was fresh and cool and the world about us green and new made. We did not hunt, merely rode for the sake of it, galloping where we could down the pastures and once in the wood slackening pace and going wide-eyed for what we could see. Once I'd come on badger cubs tumbling and growling in the sunshine – a gift, for badgers are as shy as deer though they can break your arm with a bite.

We had ridden for some time, quiet at first, then with laughter for Magh had a puppy with him, a gift from Nemair whose hound had whelped, a white, soft thing he loved. He brought her with him everywhere though she fell over her paws and mostly had to be carried. After a bit I recognized certain trees and a huge, hollowed trunk where wood ants swarmed. I thought, Beyond there lies the pool.

Around me the others talked; the ponies went soft shod on the leaf mould, Magh's puppy panted. I heard Luth ask Dearg what he thought Uffa would have us do today, and Dearg grunt that it would be the same as always.

I held Ban back a little. The others went on, thinking I rode behind. In a moment the wood had taken them; the branches swung back over the path, the sound of their talk was muffled with leaves and overlaid with birdsong.

I waited while my heart beat faster. I could not make up my mind. My aunt had talked of my mother's secret places where she'd worked her witchcraft. I knew where she meant right enough. I had seen it in the frost and under the grey skies, cold and silent with the stake and the crude-carved horse-stone.

Today, in the cool, green brightness, I hoped I would make a lie of her words. But I was not so sure that I did not hesitate.

A bit clinked, there were hoof-falls on the path. I looked up, serious. I did not need to smile. He knew me well enough.

I said, 'I go this way.'

Luth grinned. 'Dearg's for breakfast and Magh's gone with him.'

'You'll come though?'

'Why not? It was my place before I showed it to you.'

We took the downward path. All the time Luth talked, joking, of girls he liked, of our horses, what the high summer would bring. 'Gnats,' he said, 'midges worse than fleas, that drive you mad with itching.' I laughed and said it had been the same in the marshes, only there we had leeches that were worst of all. After that he rambled on. We followed the path until we reached the stream bed. The water ran full still; summer's heat had yet to parch it.

I halted again, and tried to see the way ahead. Luth came beside me. He too stared before him. He'd fallen silent. His hand smoothed his pony's mane and he scowled a little and shook back his hair.

'Luth,' I said, 'what will become of us?'

He turned, searching my face. 'Why? What brings this on?'

165

'Nothing. Hearing you talk, I suppose. What do you want for yourself?'

I watched him thinking and hesitating, all his lightness gone. Then he said, 'If I could have my way I would live as the song-maker does.' He caught sight of how I looked. 'Not like him, but singing for men.'

'It's hard, trailing from hall to hall and living by men's whims.'

'Not for those that are good at it.'

That was true and Luth would be good; better than anyone, with practice.

I asked, 'Have you spoken to your father?'

He stared, genuinely shocked. 'Are you mad? He would never hear of such a thing. We are warriors at Nam Dubh. Nothing else will do. Don't you understand that yet?'

That stung. For a moment we both were quiet then he sighed and said, 'It's what I wish for more than anything. I've not even told Dearg. Don't speak of it, Arawn.'

I thought of him singing in our hall at Hakos's wedding, and how he chose his songs with care, first to wring our hearts then make us cry with laughter, and then of him fighting in the ring, good at everything. I understood then, a little, his restlessness, the sense of yearning.

He smiled at me suddenly. 'What of you? What will you do?'

I shrugged. I knew that the skills I had learnt were more than ever I could have hoped for if we'd stayed in the marshlands and that my grandfather no longer hounded and tormented me, though I'd spoken of that to no one. I said, 'I suppose what befalls Nam Dubh befalls me. Isn't that so with all of us, even you, if you will not pick up your harp and leave?'

'Yes.' He quirked his mouth as if he'd a sour taste in it. 'And what is Nam Dubh? A place for warriors? For farmers rather! Oh, I did not mean that as it sounded.'

Dapples round as deer spots lay on the twisted path where the sun shone through. The stream flowed steady and deep beneath us and the weeds moved in the current like green hair. Fish flickered, brown and quick; the water was clear enough to see the freckles on their backs. I said, 'I think I am cleansed of their guilt.'

We moved on, picking our way slowly to where we had dismounted the time before. I thought as we went. What I

166

said to Luth I did believe, though it had taken words spoken aloud to teach me. I wanted no part of my mother's magic, if magic there had been and not the gossip mongering of stupid old women and my aunt, pregnant and fearful. If I bore her mark, why, she had given it me, inflicting it unasked. Blue dye pricked into the skin could not make a man what he was not. As for my father – 'a boy in love' was what my uncle called him. For that he'd suffered enough.

For the rest, what was there? A charm, which no one saw, cast back into the ruins from which it had come; ashes thrown in a frightened boy's face; stones cast by firelight. Things that had hurt. What longings I had were not for those.

The day stretched before us, golden and bright with promise. I thought of breakfast and hot oatcakes with cheese and the gallop across the meadows to Nam Dubh.

I pulled Ban up. 'We have no business here,' I said. 'Let be.'

Later, as we ate in the boys' hall, Luth said in his straight, serious way, 'You were right, Arawn.'

'Oh,' I said, 'what do you think we would have seen?'

He grinned. 'Nothing but wild duck paddling at the reeds. But it is forbidden. There are things that should not be disturbed.' He became serious again, touching my shoulder as he got to his feet. 'Remember.'

I wondered afterwards if he, with his song-maker's soul, had sensed what was to come or if his words were only lightly spoken. I never asked him. In the end the day was not glorious. Treachery came, hidden in the sunlight and green leaves and the sparkling water, and turned them all to bitterness.

It began with what was cruel and ugly and grew worse.

Much later several of us stowed arms in the main store whose entrance faced on to the yard. We took our time, for there was cleaning with oil and rags to be done, but we had almost finished when a commotion at the far end of the yard, near the horse troughs, made us stop and wander out.

We looked over. There were a couple of our lads clustered and shouting and some jeering. We thought it was a simple fight. By now it was dusk and growing difficult to see.

To keep boys from a fight is like keeping dogs from a hare.

We glanced at one another and then ran, heedless, across the yard; one or two of us still clutched the stuff we were meant to put away.

We pulled up before we got too close. We could make out all at once who was there and from that and the sounds we heard it was no clean fight. Already Sithlann and Nar drew back and beside me Dearg edged away. He growled in my ear, 'Come back, you fool!'

He was right. It was no place for us. We could see some of our lot, Ruarch and Maelduin – who found trouble as flies find dung – but the rest were Hakos's men and their fun was none of ours. We guessed what we risked by staying.

Almost I turned with the others and followed them; just as I did there came a great shout of laughter. I swung round and, in the same instant, a swathe of bats streamed from the eaves of the empty storerooms. Black as ashes they flitted up before us into a sky blue and dimmed with evening. The moon had risen, thin and bright as if carved from new gold, and a star rode the horizon.

For a moment everyone was hushed and staring. Then, in the silence, someone moaned aloud as if he were sick or in a fever. His keening struck cold and urgent, running as the hubbub started up again like an undercurrent in a stream.

Dearg pulled once more at my sleeve, saying something. Before us the young men surged and parted as a wave upon the shore. There were not so many of them as I'd supposed; the dusk had made them seem more, but they were the rough ones who liked to hurt. They hung about our hall and taunted us. Now, as they jostled, a figure huddled on the ground before them. He hid his face and wept. Yet they did not strike or kick him. They'd better sport to see.

Arax stood at one of the troughs. In the half-light he looked bigger than ever, broad as a tree. He was hunched over with his arms plunged into the water up to his elbow and his shoulders tensed. He was drowning something.

He was quite cool about it. He hardly moved. He stood there with his big feet splayed wide by the trough, solid and rooted, while what was under his hands struggled and splashed and writhed, with its death throes on it. I was too far to see properly, only how it tried over and over to heave itself up and sometimes something broke the surface or Arax let it go, showing in a glimmer of white. When he did he paused a moment before he thrust it back, scrabbling and desperate, and the others cheered. It was taking a long time. He saw to that. Even now the memory turns my stomach.

There was more. All at once the figure who had lain so pitiably in the yard sprang up, rushing forward and clutching at Arax' arms before he was seized and dragged back again. He cried out as they took him.

At my side Dearg moved; already the others had shown a clean pair of heels. He drew in his breath sharply and when I looked he'd flung back his head, wide-eyed. I cried out at him, 'What? What is it?'

He made to run forward but looked back as if he did not see me and said, 'It's Magh!'

Now I too knew him, though nightfall made it difficult and the press of young men round. And we too were noticed. Across the courtyard they gazed in our direction, broken from their sport and watchful. Fear, like sickness, stirred in me. Arax gazed too, smiling. The feel of danger was like a knife scraped across skin. I wanted none of it.

It was too late. Magh had turned at our call. Now he stared at us as I'd never seen him stare before, like a blind man with a face twisted to the light.

They flung him down. He stumbled to the ground and crouched there on his hands and knees. The heart was knocked out of him for fighting; he was spent and gasping and what wits he'd had were gone. Only he cried out to us, 'Dearg! Arawn!' begging us to help.

We could not let him down. There is honour in one's name and a man of your hall is a comrade-in-arms. Yet there should be wisdom too. Always we'd been told, 'Keep a cool head and be steady. What's courage when it's lying low and bloody? Weigh your chances.' We stood shoulder to shoulder Dearg and I, and faced a pack, careless as wolves. We had no chance and we would not run.

Then Arax lifted what he had held in the water to drown.

Chapter Sixteen

At the end he had been grim, the laughter gone from him, a common murderer intent on what struggled in his hands. Now he raised up the body by the scruff and held her there, hung like a trophy between the earth and the glimmering sky. The paws dangled and the rough white coat was smoothed and sodden. Water ran from it in streams to the ground. She had fought bravely for her life; there was blood on her jaws and muzzle.

There fell a hush, and straight after more talk and laughter. Arax dropped the body and did not even glance at it though in life she'd been worth more than he, a hundred times, and in death also. He strolled off, shrugging his shoulders to seem clever and winking at his friends who clustered round. Almost he got away.

Only Magh lay on the ground where they had thrown him, and wept. Now he raised his head to peer through his hair. Poor Magh who had needed to do no more than be himself, humble and bewildered, to bring Arax' viciousness upon him. His face was swollen with crying, blotched and pitiful. While those about him bayed his eyes searched the courtyard, believing it over and no harm done. He saw what lay before him, limp and draggled on the ground, and crawled towards it. When he reached it he put out his hand to touch the white, wet flank and began to stroke the water from it, murmuring the while for the body still settled into death, the flesh not yet stiff and cold. I gazed at the stones then but I could not shut my ears. All at once he cried out, a great wail that reached up and up to the stars. I said to Dearg, 'He cannot understand,' and when I looked again he had his dog in his arms and rocked and cradled it as simply as a child.

I could not bear it. His sorrow touched my soul as a flame is touched to pitch. As once before I burnt with anger for him, till I was white hot and my heart swelled fit to burst.

I ran across the yard. There was a wide swathe of light that streamed over the stones from where the hall doors stood open and when I passed through this the darkness seemed blacker after. Then I was face to face with Arax and shouting at him and he broke off his laughter and narrowed his eyes at me.

We fought. It wasn't clean. We rolled and kicked and scuffled in the dust with no care for holds and falls and what was proper. Once he got me down and held me, his arm about my neck, his knee deep in my stomach. We were as close as lovers and I saw his lips pull back and the flecks of spittle on his chin. Then I set my teeth in his arm and bit into the flesh and filled my mouth with blood. As he cursed I twisted free.

We struggled a good while. I do not know how it would have ended. Arax was heavier than I and stronger and had played this game before; I felt it after and my ribs and all my side were black for days. I didn't mark him so badly but had my rage in me like a living thing and who can tell what, in the end, that might have done?

All the time we fought the others clamoured, to drive us as they drive on boar hounds when they battle. It sounded as a tide sounds, a constant ebb and flow of noise. Then, after a time, a quietness crept over, stealthy at first, growing then so we began to hear our blows striking on flesh and the harsh suck of our breathing. I was barely aware of it till Arax faltered.

Some men command even when they are stooped and lean on sticks. My grandfather stood unaided today, unbowed, and he was such a man. He must have stepped from his chamber, hearing the uproar. By the time he reached us his presence was known, the others had fallen back from him and were silent at once. No one stood in his way so he watched us unhindered, gazing where we wrestled and seeing all.

Arax pulled away first, sensing some change. As for me, I was raging mad and cared for nothing but the circle of the yard and the hot, fierce tangle of the fight. Even when he stood I'd have gone after him, except someone grabbed me and pushed me back.

My sight cleared. I found myself sitting on the stones, blinking up. Before me were my grandfather and Arax, covered with dust and dishevelled, all the fastenings of his

172

tunic pulled undone and his face mottled. I stared at him as in a dream and then I considered myself. I was in a worse pass even than that, my shirt and tunic half ripped from my back and bruised all over. But nothing hurt yet, and my grandfather waited for me to rise.

He regarded us both, his look measured under level brows. He had dressed for supper. His robe was dark blue and heavy, with paler thread worked in at the hem and sleeves; his hair combed back and neatly clipped. He looked his age and sick, for where the gown opened about his neck deep hollows showed beneath the collar bones and there was no flesh on his face, only loose skin at his eyes and cheeks and chin. Yet every bit of him was lord and his eyes were shrewd.

He'd come to judge. Here, with others to see, it would please him, as in past times when he was lord in truth. All about the watching boys gaped, hang-jawed, and at that I tried to steady myself a little, for he hated such shows and would be sterner for it. The knowledge cooled my blood, but I panted still and was almost choked with dust.

He spoke to Arax first, low-voiced and brisk. The rest craned their necks and tried to hear.

'What are you about?' he asked. 'Is this the way for one of your standing to behave? Explain yourself.'

Straight away Arax shifted his gaze to me. I'd always supposed him stupid. Now, seeing what was in his eyes, my heart sank. He had cunning, as a weasel has, or a big hunting spider that squats in the top of its web.

He spoke, though, as if he was honest. 'Sir, it was only sport. These young lads need lessons sometimes, hard enough not to forget.'

My grandfather said, 'Lessons! What has he done then, to deserve what you were giving him?' He looked across to where I stood and I thought, He is better in work clothes. Not so old. The thought came from nowhere and I had other things to think of only I had not seen him close to for days and now saw him afresh. But I kept my mouth shut. His own was a thin line turned down to his beard. He would think what he chose. No words of mine would sway him.

Despite his smooth tongue Arax was nervous. He rubbed with his arm his forehead where the sweat ran down and fidgeted like a horse. The body of the dog lay for everyone to see and Magh sobbed from time to time and watched us, too overawed to speak.

My grandfather shook back his hair and pushed his thumbs in his belt. He had settled to wait. He'd have waited all night for his answer. I knew that from past times.

I was shaking slightly now and had begun to ache and could not be rid of the salt taste of blood. Above, the moon was risen and torches flared on the walls. I began to take notice of those around us; Ruarch and Nar had slunk back and brought others of our hall. Big-eyed and whispering they watched.

In the end there was no wait. Arax stepped up. He flicked a look at me again. Then he laughed and held open his hands to my grandfather, man to man.

'My lord, surely you would not take his part against mine? You have another grandson whom I serve. For his sake, trust me to have some honour.'

My grandfather said, 'Indeed. And what has Arawn?'

He too had begun to smile. His teeth gleamed in his beard, close-jawed and hungry, an old dog fox grinning at a goose.

'Him?' Arax also had seen the smile. It made him easy as if they shared a joke. 'He fought like an animal. Here, sir.' He thrust out his arm, torn and bloody where I had bitten him.

The wound was deep and oozing. Around us his friends sighed and made wide eyes as if shocked, playing mealy-mouthed girls at each other.

My grandfather said, 'Move closer,' and beckoned tetchily. When he was near he bent to examine the injury and clucked and shook his head, muttering of herbs and bandages. I thought, The old man stoops. How Arax loves it.

So he did. He waited till my grandfather had straightened, then put up his hand to quieten the rest. 'An animal,' he repeated, 'as befits him.' He lifted his voice so that it carried; other folk stood round now. His eyes went to them as if it was to them he spoke. He cried out, 'Do you forget, sir, the mark he bears?'

Into the quiet stole a deeper silence. Hunters wait and watch so, holding their breath, while the prey steps down to drink. A stillness was upon me, and a shiver at the nape of my neck as though someone whispered there. My grandfather turned his head to look at me. Above us a taper flared and hissed and sent up sparks. The flames' light played upon his face and made of it a mask of gold and shadow, old and young by turns, such as dead kings wear on to the pyre. We'd trodden this path before; the knowledge of it peered from my eyes, unsurprised, bleak as winter. His own as he watched me stayed hidden, untouched by the light. What lay in them he would not let me see.

He turned back and said to Arax, 'You say that to me?' His voice had no more chill in it than when he asked if his midday meal was cooked.

Still Arax smiled and shrugged and raised his brows. He said to my grandfather, 'Only for that you are old, sir, and might be deceived. He interfered in what did not concern him.' Then at last he showed the spite, grown in him like a canker. He spat out, 'Horse-boy!' to my face.

My grandfather moved, swift as a striking snake. He seized Arax' injured wrist and clamped his fingers round it.

For a moment they were quite still. As figures in a dream they stood, ringed by the watching boys, with the little moon above. Their flesh was pale as lamplight, their garments dark. They could have been old carvings made of wood and paint, set in a sacred grove. Then Arax made a noise in his throat and his breath shuddered.

My grandfather held him in a grip of iron. He'd strength left; no one could doubt it. It ran in him as slow sap runs in a weathered tree. Fresh sweat beaded Arax' forehead, a pulse throbbed in his neck. All the time my grandfather tightened his grasp. Together they were of a height. My grandfather was tall today, not stooping to cough.

He bent his head until his mouth was by Arax' ear. Even then Arax could not draw away though he flinched as they touched, cheek to cheek, the grey hair spilt on to the gold.

Very quietly my grandfather spoke. They were so close his breath stirred the mingled strands. He barely moved his lips but I heard his words as I was meant to; over the slope of Arax' shoulder Grandfather's eyes met mine.

He said, 'You forget, he is of my kin. Remember that and do not raise your hand again to one who is your better.' For an instant his fingers squeezed till the sluggish blood oozed between them. Then he opened his grasp and set him free.

For a heart's beat Arax never stirred. He was caught, surely as a bird is trapped in lime. Then he snatched back his hand and pressed it to his chest. His mouth opened, seeking words, but he had none. He had not looked for this, nor could he match it with his savage ways, only struggle with himself before us all.

My grandfather stepped back. I looked across to him and tried to seem grave though my heart leapt in my breast. I thought, He has spoken for me before them all, and put it from me that no one else had heard. His words shone in me even while the body of the dog lay where it had fallen and Magh wept still. I grieved for them, but joy and grief ran together as wine is mixed with water.

My grandfather said to Arax, 'Go.' He went, turning back when he was past to give me one last look; it had daggers in it – he'd have stabbed me dead there if he could. His friends moved aside as he went, and some hid smiles behind their hands, glad, like curs, to see him bested.

I waited for my grandfather. He had begun to walk towards me, straight and splendid with his dark robes swishing and a bold, fierce grin. I swear he meant to praise me, to chafe me and clap me about the shoulders perhaps. I had never seen him so pleased, though a fight of any kind, even of cunning, was meat and drink to him, and this he had won. I raised my face to his and paused, listening for his words, only in doing so I forgot others. Uffa had warned us, 'Watch behind you on the field; the coward's spear is longest.'

Safe on the margins of the yard, among his own again, Arax found his sort of courage, worthless as the rest of him. Now, where we could not get to him, he stabbed us in the back.

'Aed!' he called. Everyone looked, pricking through the twilight. He hung on the outskirts, caught like a shadow, pulled two ways by his hatred and his fear.

For a moment he stayed. He stared through the gloom and the flickering torch-light. Almost he did not speak – only caught at his lip with his teeth. But my grandfather moved back, raising his hand in mockery to dismiss him, and Arax snarled his venom out.

'Aed!' he cried again. 'What have you to be proud of? You are old – there's grey in your beard and your breath is stinking! Why did you come back, and that witch-spawn with you? Remember what you know and tell us before you cough your wits up along with your rotten lungs!'

The torches flared and turned him all to gold. Then the darkness swept back and he was gone, running through the yard; we could hear his footsteps fading.

Everyone had heard. Shocked they waited, but they were

eager too. Ill fortune savours in another's bowl. I thought again of the wolf-pack, who bring their own king down when he is old and spent.

My grandfather was close by. I put out my hand and caught at his sleeve, saying, 'Sir—'

He stood with his back to me and out-faced them all. At my touch he turned and gazed as if dazed or deep in thought.

I said again, 'Sir' and, 'Grandfather'.

He came to himself. He swung round. I glimpsed what darkened in his eyes and cried out. He summoned his black mood as the old gods summoned cloud and storm to hurl their rage from heaven. Before, with Arax, his anger had been quiet and still. Now all of him was fury. I had no time to draw back or shield myself. He raised his arm and struck me, back-handed, across the face, so hard I could not stand against him.

I tumbled on to the stones. In my mouth I tasted blood and tears of pain. I thought, I must not let him see, and tried to turn my head, but already he'd seized me and wrenched me up towards him. His robes swirled like a bird's heavy wing; they beat about me and I could not get away. With one hand he fumbled at his waist, drawing out his belt, and I buried my face in my arms and crouched before him while he hit again and again and flogged the senses from my body.

He hit me for a long time. The buckle cut with every lash. At last, when he was spent, he stood off as a wrestler does who's felled his man. All about was silence as if everyone had taken breath at once. A wave of sickness rose from my belly. I lay on the ground, cold and retching, and heard him shout. His voice was cracked and seemed to come from far away; he panted as he roared but his words were clear enough, for everyone to hear.

'He was right! An animal! You young brute – will you always bring me to shame?'

My face and back were numbed and bleeding, but the wrong hurt more. It was not for shame that he was angry. I had brought him none, not then, with Arax. I raised my head and met his gaze full on.

He'd known I would. He thrust forward his face, to dare me to defiance. His lip pushed through his beard, his hands were knotted still and clenched, his hair lay loose on his shoulders so he seemed wild or mad. But there was something in his eyes. At first I did not understand, and then

177

I did. He raged as a warrior before the battle; behind the mask the man is thinking.

His glance went round the boys. Their noise had died and they were hushed and frightened; when their gaze dropped he had them in his palm. Then he took a step towards me and hauled me to my feet. He kept me there, thrust before his body, in front of everyone, and I saw them staring and the thin, bright moon above and a sprinkling of stars.

Against my back his chest moved. He shouted aloud like a king proclaiming. 'Have I forgotten why I came back? That one – Arax – never knew the years when Nam Dubh was my own. He should have asked me rather why I stayed away so long, and here he'd have found the answer!' He shook me as a dog shakes a hare, not finished even yet.

He gave me a push and said, loud in my ear, 'Tell them, boy. Tell them what you are sprung from. Speak up to them or you'll have worse to weep for!'

I could not answer; there was nothing I could say that was not known and my throat was thick with swallowed tears. I wept indeed from pain and shock and older hurts I thought were healed, but I could not bear for him to see.

Behind me his hand moved and swung the belt. Sickness once more clutched my belly. I tried to get away. I fought him off and stumbled on the stones, but he fell on me again and dragged me back. Then, in terror, frantic as a cat, I twisted in his grip and cried out the first thing in my mind. 'No, sir!' I cried. 'No excuses! Surely they are for you to make?'

He let me go. I fell back to the ground. His hands were stilled, the belt dangled. It was his good one, the leather dyed a dull red and oiled to keep it supple, the buckle of heavy wrought bronze.

I waited and tried to be still though I trembled all over and my breath came in short, ragged sobs that hurt my ribs. He did not move, only jutted his head and asked, 'How's that?' And, 'What do you mean?'

I hardly knew. Sick and dazed I'd only wanted him to stop and meant no more than that. Yet part of me stood back in the old, familiar way and watched as all around the others did, sober and unspeaking. That part remembered the time in his chamber, and the other time with Arax. I thought, I have said more than I knew.

My grandfather took a pace forward. I flinched but kept

his eye and said, 'Think what you will.' I struggled to my feet and faced him.

He stared, a hard, shrewd look, then settled his robes. He was angry still, and dangerous, but wary too like a mountain lynx with prickles in its paw. I thought, quite clear through all my turmoil, It's some great wrong he's done, or knows of one and even now he hides it.

Too well we knew each other. He must have seen some understanding in my face for all at once he caught me back to him. He pulled me close and for a moment held me as he'd held Arax. His breath was hot and rasping, his narrow eyes searched. I could see how the grizzled hairs of his beard grew and the web of fine lines about his cheeks and the pit marks in his skin. Then his lip curled. Between his teeth he hissed, 'You hold your tongue!' and after gave me a great shove backwards.

There was no help for it. I stumbled away, heedless of the grey and quiet dusk and those who watched. I barely felt Dearg's hand reach out to touch my shoulder.

Chapter Seventeen

I went to the stables. I could not face the boys' hall and the mockery and the glances.

I went by the rough way to the rear entrance where no one would see. Once I fell in a clatter of stones yet nobody called out or followed after so I was safe. When I got there I pulled back the bolt and dragged myself in and searched out an empty stall. Then I stretched out and rested my head on my arms.

For a time I knew no more than that I was hurt and beaten. The pain was a darkness that I could put my hand to and touch. I felt very ill.

Suddenly from the courtyard below came a drift of noise, like people muttering, and my grandfather's voice bellowed out. Straight off all was quiet again but it had roused me. Trembling, I lifted my head to listen.

It stayed quiet. I stared down through swollen eyes at my forearm. Through dust bruises showed, red and angry, not yet darkened.

I could not be warm. The cold clutched my flesh and ran like water in my marrow while I stung and ached as if I had once more the fever. My back felt flayed; there was a mist of red in one eye and a bloody swelling below where my grandfather's ring had scored my cheek across.

I was sick then, twice in a bucket, and afterwards the tears came. I cried not because of the pain but because of how my grandfather had turned to me and then, the instant after, struck me for Arax' words. They were tears of anger – and I tried to hold them back, but they came anyway, sliding hot and salty between my fingers.

Later I lay on my belly, against the stable wall. There was no sound now from the yard and in the stables just the little, patient horses stirred in the stalls beyond mine. No one was about. The night was young and the groom had yet to begin his rounds. In the dusty passageway, the night-lamp gleamed, set high and dim in its niche for safety, the beams falling on the rough walls and rafters. I shivered, pressing my hand to my injured cheek, and watched till the flame was like a small, clouded moon burning through the shadows.

I could not sleep for pain. I dozed, then roused myself at once when the groom came round, but he was old and only checked the horses and never thought to look beyond their stalls.

Sometime later the door-latch clicked and a step sounded on the flagstone. In a moment the passageway was filled with a bright, clear light, the colour of amber. I made a guess at who it was and braced myself and drew back against the wall, thinking that I should die sooner than beg his mercy.

Only it was not my grandfather. The figure who stood in the doorway with a lamp in his hand and a blanket slung over his arm was Dearg. In the glimmering light he hesitated, watchful but holding back, so that we stared at each other till I knew what he was seeing and turned away.

At first he too was silent. I dropped my head back to my arms. He waited a moment then said, 'I've brought you this,' and threw the blanket down. It landed in the straw by my feet. I recognized it. It was his own, a good one of heavy wool, woven by his mother in thick stripes of red and blue. One day in spring, when the doors to the women's hall were open, she'd been at work on it. I remembered, and how she'd sat close by my aunt.

I looked up. Above Dearg's outstretched arm his face was pale and grim with marks like dark thumb prints under his eyes. After a moment he said, 'Are you all right?' I nodded.

He walked over to the empty manger to set the lamp where it couldn't be knocked. It was so quiet we could hear something run across an old black beam above our heads. Briefly he bent over the flame, checking the oil's level, before he looked again and said harshly, 'How can you be? You look dreadful and there's blood all over your face. He cut you.'

He spoke as if he were a grown man with a right to chide me and I would not take that from him. I put up my chin and said, 'Are you surprised?'

His glance slid away. He turned, saying, 'I've brought some other things,' and went to the bucket in the corner. He peered in, then took it away and rinsed it. When he came back it was full of fresh water and he drew a piece of cloth from his belt and dropped it in, swishing until it was soaked.

Afterwards he wrung it out and came back over. I said, 'Dearg,' but he took no notice.

I knew what he meant to do. He knelt close enough for me to feel his warmth and his breath on my shoulder. His face was hard and drawn and the lamplight sparkled on his red hair and freckled skin and eyes that were blue and guarded.

He reached out and lifted away the rags of my shirt and tunic, torn from my back. They stuck to my ribs and down my spine where blood had dried. He paused and scowled and wiped with the cloth. He was gentle, which I'd not expected, yet it made no odds. I loathed him still, fiercely, and the feel of the cloth, his hands, the way he was with me, wary and stubborn and angry, as if I was some kind, hurt beast he was half scared of. If he had said, 'Come be a man,' or sworn or laughed I could have borne it; as it was it shamed me. I struck off his hand and cried out, 'Don't!'

He started as if he had been touched with flame, and stared, the bright red mounting in his face. His hand tightened on the cloth – to fling it at me – then he put it down, too carefully, and his throat moved as he swallowed. He said, 'You don't change, do you? Only you needn't be so proud. I was there too. I saw what happened.'

I said, 'And now you come by so faithfully?'

His mouth turned ugly, sneering. 'Yes,' he answered, 'like a dog, you mean?'

He knew what he was saying, right enough. All my anger came back and I cried out at him, 'Tell that to Magh, you bastard!'

We faced each other, with only the straw and the cloth and the blanket between us. Yet we were both still and gradually the hot, angry colour ebbed from his face and his fists began to slacken.

He looked down at his empty hands. He said, 'It was horrible. All of it. Arax and the old man. You'd done no wrong. Why did he do it?'

I could not speak. Beyond him, unseen, the horses moved and whickered at their feed. The place smelt of them, their warmth and dung, and of hay and the sweet, brittle deadness of last year's flowers. There were other scents also, a salt-tang and musk, blood and sweat and the stink of vomit. After a moment he bent and picked up the rag and went over to rinse it. When he came back he handed it to me and I held it to my face where the cut had opened, running freely.

183

He asked, 'Do you know how it began? It was so stupid. Benna told me when I got back to the hall. Magh was on his way to supper with the dog. The poor brute got under Arax' feet. Benna said the worst bit was when the dog wriggled round and licked Arax' face and Magh was in tears and pleading with him. No one thought Arax would go so far, except his friends goaded him to it.'

'Why doesn't Mhorged stop them?'

'They're Hakos's men. You know that. It's for him to do it.'

'Could he have done?'

'If he'd a mind to.'

I paused. From nowhere I saw a figure step limping from the shadows and heard a voice say, 'Leave him, Arax.'

After that we were silent, each of us with our thoughts. Then Dearg gave a great sigh and came and sat down beside me. He picked up a length of straw and twirled it back and forth. The lamp was burning still and hissing in the manger.

Under the cloth my cheek stung and throbbed and made me restless. I moved to ease myself and had to catch my lip between my teeth. There was a deeper pain in my back, low down, where Arax had kicked me. Dearg looked then said, 'There's talk. Ruarch's stirring.'

'About what Arax said?'

He got to his feet. In his fingers he still had the length of straw. He went to the manger and held it in the flame and watched it burn.

I said, 'Tell me.'

'There's more than that. Nemair spoke for you. She saw it all. She told the old man he'd done a cruel thing for no good reason and he was wrong. He was very angry.'

'The pup was hers. She'd given it to Magh.'

'He told her that Hakos knew how to offer up his dues, but you would come to do so. And then he laughed.'

The straw powdered to a fine ash and fell. He saw it out before he turned. I said, 'What do the others say?'

'Can't you guess?'

It was cold. I touched the edge of the blanket and slowly drew it round me. I tried to think. I could not be rid of what had happened. I saw the dog as it struggled and drowned, Arax shouting in the torchlight and my grandfather with his heavy fists that clenched and hammered and the red-bronze belt he'd used on me. The pain was very bad still. Yet it seemed also that there were worse things and that behind my grief lay an old fear, familiar and stale as a cloak worn through winter. Arax had spoken plainly, asking, 'Have you forgotten why you are here?' And I knew nothing, save that look on my grandfather's face, sharp and cunning and guilty, telling me more clear than anything, of a mischief he had done.

I thought, He said Mhorged had sent for us, as a dutiful son should his father and kinsman. And Mhorged has been good to us. He gave me back my father's sword. Yet all this time some mist lay thick upon my eyes and through it the sly, white face of fear was peeping. I was lost and afraid and did not know which way to turn.

I said, 'We should go back. It'd be better over.'

He'd not expected that. His head lifted, too quickly. 'No. Not tonight. Don't go.'

I guessed what they were saying, and he was right. Under his cap of springing hair, his face was taut with misery and I was tired and sick and sore and could have slept for days. But his own questions stood unasked in his eyes. He had not the guile to hide them.

I winced and turned away. He waited and then stirred and walked to the stall's entrance. His back was to me. The light from the lamp which had been hidden by his shoulder streamed out in a long beam across the floor. He said, very quietly, 'You never told us. That wasn't the first time, was it? Nor with the belt. Why didn't you run away? Anyone else would have done, if they were treated so.'

The trembling had begun again, deep in the pit of my stomach. I said, 'You do not know the marshes.'

'Were they any worse?'

I thought of the reed beds and the grey pools lapping for ever. I told him, 'They're flat and boggy. There was nowhere to run to and in the villages about they knew my grandfather. They called him the Old Lord and would have sold me back to him if I had asked for food. He would have paid to get me.'

'And beaten you again?'

I had some pride left. I said, 'What do you think? Only his duty was to raise me. It was not all bad. He'd not have seen me go begging, or a slave to some peasant, grubbing in the fields.'

Far away an owl screeched. Dearg turned another piece of straw between his fingers. Around us the night stretched like water. He said, so softly I barely caught it, 'Out there he threw you to the wolves and never cared.'

I turned then and looked full at him and he held my gaze. I remembered him shouting at me in the wood and this morning, laughing at Magh's puppy. And I thought of him and Luth and the way he'd looked when we'd gone off to hunt the wolf.

I said, 'That time in the hall with Arax, I saw nothing, only knew him, what he was, quite suddenly. Now it's the same with my grandfather. He's scared of something he has done. He believed Arax would speak of it, and it's bad.'

'Yes,' he said. 'Don't you think I know that?'

He stared at me and his eyes were brilliant and haunted as mine were. All his thoughts were there, in his plain, anxious face; in the set of his jaw and the line between his brow and his eyes. It was like having a mirror of polished bronze held to my fear, for his gave shape to mine, and it peered back at me.

I was the witch's son, come to honest men unasked and unlooked for. I was hung with her darkness and the quiet shreds of her magic, but I had no secrets and no answers and those who had both kept their counsel and would not tell.

All this I realized then, and Dearg who had hated me did too and pitied me, and that was worst of all.

In the night I woke to the sound of a cry and found my face buried in my arms, hot and soaked once more with tears. I had dreamt and the fringes of the dream were with me still. In sleep I had seen the old ruins on the hillside, clear and ghostly under a bright moon, and thought I myself sat in them. Then presently a figure, very tall and dark, walked towards me across the sheep pastures. His face was hidden for his hood was up though he passed by so close I could have put out my hand to touch him. He went on in silence and I knew suddenly that I must speak with him. I began to run after him but, even as I did so, he drew off further, slipping between the empty walls. I glimpsed his cloaked and hooded form again and again, always going from me as I scrambled on the rocks. At last I saw him, far off, upon the moors, still walking soundlessly. I called out 'Father!' and it was that cry which wakened me.

I lay for a while, shaken as if it were real and listening in the dark to hear if Dearg had woken. I thought perhaps he had for his breathing was quiet and light as if he too lay with his ears pricked, but he said nothing and later I slept again for when I opened my eyes it was to full morning and an empty space in the stall where Dearg had been.

The morning passed slowly. I was sick and feverish and haunted by the dream. Bad things seemed gathered round me, fretting in the shadows. I was like an animal in truth, in pain and sensing storms to come.

My body felt weighted, as if in chains, but my head was light and empty. I could not be still. The feeling of oppression grew. Presently I eased myself up from the straw and limped outside. The air was cool and helped to clear my head. I began to walk – not very steadily – through the pastures, towards the ruins. If anyone saw me I had no care for it. I was the witch's son again, going to his place.

Today the old stones shone in sunlight and once more the sheep cropped the short, sweet grasses. The air smelt fresh, of thyme and heather and the mountains. High above a hawk hovered.

I sat and watched the bird hunt awhile and then looked round. I thought of how I'd come here before when I'd been in trouble. Then I'd found no anger to answer my own, only the quiet peace of rock raised from rock, grown long apart from the dead hands that shaped it.

Today there was no peace, only a sense of danger, of things unseen and waiting. Ravens hopped about the walls and cocked their heads, watching me with bright, black eyes. My own head ached; I felt hot and cold by turns; my flesh was dry and sore and burning. I remembered how the stones had looked by moonlight with the hooded figure walking by.

I stood and wandered through the ruined walls. As in the dream I began to search clambering about the rocks, scrabbling and seeking. But it was no man for whom I sought. I was goaded, driven by the hopping birds. I sought for what would help me: my talisman, my silver horse.

I searched a good while. All the time the cold sickness grew and the pain of my riven cheek and back grew worse. The air was full of the ravens' cawing. The feel of their eyes was upon me.

I was weak and clumsy and at last slipped, sprawling across an upturned block of stone. The ravens screeched. I reached out to save myself and saw on my outstretched arm the mark, my mother's mark she'd made on me.

I lay where I was and stared. A small circle, no more than that, pricked in blue. When she had made it, how had she hoped to shape men's hearts? What power did she work as if I was her magic? If she had left me clear of it, would my grandfather have loved me better or hated me worse?

Blue as midnight, night circle, witch-mark. Dirt under the skin – what had it done to me?

I was finished. The ravens circled above my head. I stood, swaying and trembling and could not go on. The ruins had the horse, taken to themselves. There was no help. I had given it freely and could not claim it back.

Chapter Eighteen

Later I stumbled down the hillside. I looked back once. Something stirred there, half seen among the stones. It might have been a sheep or one of the half-wild dogs that hung about the compound. I went to the boys' hall. I thought it would be empty and a refuge, but when I stepped inside Uffa was there, resting his shoulders against a post.

I tried to stand and face him. Outside the boys were chattering like starlings, fetching wooden shields and spears. Uffa said, 'How are you?' He seemed far off and I had to hold on to the wall. Then he was beside me, his hand on my forehead, an arm round my waist.

Later, when I lay face down on a pile of skins, my back and cheek salved and cool, a cup of some herbal drink beside me, he said gruffly, 'It will be all right.'

Muffled into the skins I said, 'Will it?'

He paused then said, 'I saw you just now. Up there. And what I see others can too. Take care, Arawn. Let well alone.'

I made no answer. He waited a moment, then sat by me on the skins.

'Arawn, Arax is a fool. He stirred up something from nothing, from malice only. As for your grandfather – put it from you. You're not the first to have rough treatment. You'll live.' He sounded gruff and awkward. I'd never known him so before.

He got up as if it was over. The others laughed in the yard at some horse-play. Still he waited, standing by me. I looked up suddenly, seeing his eyes widen. 'Uffa?'

For a long moment we met each other's gaze. Then he turned, swift on his heel, and when he was outside I saw through the doorway how he went off alone and the others fell silent as he walked by himself down the hill.

After that I slept, and woke in the evening better but with a raging thirst. It was supper time and the cooking fires were

189

lit. I wondered what to do; the doors of the great hall stood open and people were going in. It was simple cowardice not to join them.

I got up and crossed the yard and went in quietly. Everything was as usual. People had helped themselves and sat in small groups, cross-legged in the heather. I looked for Luth and Dearg and found them set apart. I fetched a bowl of stew and joined them.

For a while we ate in silence. I kept my head down and picked at some meat, trying to feel hungry. Across the hall the other boys were together – they never looked our way but sometimes their laughter, very loud, reached us. Gradually the evening drew on. The doors had been opened so we could see across the mountains. The day's light was dying. In the west the horizon was bright gold with the evening sun and the sky softly barred with rose and grey but over in the east clouds were gathering, heavy and black. The air was close. I thought, There'll be a storm.

By now I felt a little easier; no one had come up to me and any whisperings were out of my hearing. All seemed just as usual. Near the hearth Cumair cleared his throat and tended to his harp. My uncle was laughing with Dunadd, one of his best men, and my aunt was with her women and my cousin at her side, talking softly. Nemair had her own people round her and her hound lay stretched out with its nose on her feet.

Luth stared at my face. He said, 'The old –' and called my grandfather a name not even I would say of him in public. Afterwards he asked, 'Are you better?' And I nodded. The fever had passed.

I looked at them. Both were quiet and Dearg was as pale as before with his freckles standing out and the same dark marks under his eyes. I wondered if he'd been in trouble for staying out all night.

I asked, 'Where's Magh?'

'In Uffa's hut. He's still upset. Your face looks terrible. How can you see with that eye?'

We talked on. I had more ale and more meat from the stewpot, and the serving women joked about my looks, and my favourite hound, which reminded me of Nehal, came to beg for scraps. Gradually the day-long tightness that had gripped my belly loosened until I could even look about for my grandfather and saw him hunched like an owl on his rug, clutching his cup of wine. Of Arax and most of the young warriors there was no sign. I thought nothing of it. Often they ate in their own chamber, rowdy as they liked.

Sometime afterwards I stood to go. Now I had drunk and eaten I could sleep. I was still very sore but the edginess had slipped from me. I wanted my bed with my old blanket and goatskin and a dark, heavy dreamlessness to take me. The worries could wait till morning.

I went out into the yard. All was quiet and peaceful. The geese had been shut in for the night; from the coops came a sleepy honking. I began to walk towards our hall.

I was halfway across the yard when I saw what had been done. Before the threshold of the boys' hall lay the smashed wreckage of something that glinted and shone in the red sunset. I went up slowly and bent and took up the ruined pieces. My father's sword had been hammered into bits.

There was more. Before the threshold stone others had been laid in an intricate pattern, set in lines that twisted back and round on themselves, a pattern difficult as a maze – a witch-maze that stops a witch from entering in.

Stealthy footsteps trod behind me. I whipped round before I was touched. Ruarch stood there and with him Benna and Sithlann. They paused a moment, then came up until they were so close I could smell the day's sweat on them.

They were nervous. Benna fidgeted, shifting from foot to foot and Ruarch licked his top lip with his tongue. He looked as dirty-haired and narrow-eyed as ever. Though it was a long time since he had held me down at wrestling, I was wary of him. He was cleverer than Arax and more sly.

He looked me over, sullen and scowling, his gaze dwelling on my hurt cheek. Then he snarled, 'You're a hero, Arawn. It's a shame not everyone thinks so.'

I didn't answer. I was watching Benna and Sithlann and they looked towards the hall. I followed their gaze and saw the other boys sidle out, in ones or twos, just as usual, only I knew from their quietness, as one knows anything bad, that this was something thought on.

They crept up. Rays from the dying sun shone through the clouds and touched them with red-gold. Their eyes gleamed as they moved their heads and whispered softly. Nar and Sithlann slipped beside me, one on either side.

They had given Ruarch courage. He said, more loudly, 'What angered the old man so, Arawn? Was it something my brother said?'

I shook off Sithlann's hand which was laid on my shoulder. 'Couldn't you hear, skulking in your corner? Ask your brother!'

Benna said, 'He's gone. Hakos sent him off because of you, like a thief in the night, on some errand to Nemair's people.'

I shrugged. 'I pity them. What will he find to murder there?'

Someone laughed and said to Ruarch, 'He still bites!'

They were all around me, scenting like dogs uncertain of their master. Ruarch licked at his lip again, a lizard flicker of his tongue. He wanted to hit me but was not yet sure of the others. They might go either way. Arax had been hated. But I wondered what Ruarch had said last night to bring them this far with him.

There was the sound of people running in the yard. Luth and Dearg came up breathless. Luth said, 'What's going on?'

Ruarch was frightened of Luth. When he spoke the whine was back in his voice, sulky and defiant. 'Can't you guess? Or do you know anyway – you're so thick with him! Why's he here? The old man had plenty to hush up last night – everyone could see it! But Arawn had better tell us.'

I looked him straight in his ugly, weasel face and said, 'Had I?'

'You had!'

Dearg said, 'Stop it, Ruarch,' and Sithlann gave a great bray of laughter.

Ruarch snapped his head round. 'You say that! You've changed your tune. Dance with him then, and Luth with his fancy ways and graces. But we never wanted him. At least Arax is one of us!'

Some of the others called out at that but Ruarch was ready and shouted above them, 'It's true! And Arawn knew something – he told me so – and what he knew Arawn surely must and he should tell us! Why has he come back?'

He paused and drew breath. The others watched, on edge and anxious. They had the look of those who wait to be led, not sure of what is best or what will harm them. I thought, If I were them I'd heed Ruarch. I'd think, what brought the witch's son to Nam Dubh? What secrets does he hide?

But I could not tell them. I had no words to say – could only plead my ignorance and I was too proud for that. I thought of the early days and their savage, secret cruelty: the horse-dung in my bed and boots, the hurts inflicted blatant in the training ring, under Uffa's nose, and I wondered suddenly, would I tell them even if I could?

Yesterday I had stood before them, brought low and stricken, and felt their pity. I could remember too well what I had felt for Magh, how he was maimed and set apart because of it. So they had felt for me, seeing my grandfather beat me. But I was not like Magh, and the words would not come to tell them how I'd been dragged here, unknowing as any brute beast is brought to market.

They waited in the hot, thick dusk while in the east the storm clouds rolled and churned and cast a darker shadow on the hills. Not one of them would meet my eye.

Dearg said sullenly, 'Ruarch, you have no right. He knows nothing. And it's true – you took to your heels fast enough when it suited you!'

Ruarch grinned, then he sniggered. 'At least my skin is whole!'

He stumbled backwards as Dearg hit him. From the ground he glared up, his mouth thinned and vicious, his narrow face sharp. 'Touch me again,' he cried, 'and I'll go to old Aed and tell him why – and we've seen how dear he holds his grandson and what he'll do to him if he finds him the cause of trouble!'

There was silence. Dearg swore and dropped his hands to his sides. Someone said, 'That isn't fair,' but with little heart to it. I stood there with a great emptiness in me and a sorrow I could not put a name to, as wide and grey as the sky.

Ruarch got to his feet. His eyes darted from one face to another. Some nodded back. It had gone beyond mischief; several of the men had come out from the hall and were watching. I had to speak.

I stepped forward and from my heart I caught at what I knew. I said, 'We came because my grandfather made his peace with Mhorged. Everyone was told that.'

It was a hollow truth; they knew it, as did I. The light showed from the hall, a clear, steady brightness, nothing like the flickering of the courtyard tapers. Above us the storm clouds were like curds and a wind had began to blow. Then Ruarch laughed. 'Witches,' he said, 'are known for lies.'

No one moved. Watchful as cats they waited, just as they had watched last night when they would have torn my grandfather down.

Slowly I reached out. I did not need to look. My fingers felt the cloth of my sleeve and pulled at it. I said to Ruarch, 'I know what you are about. I owe you nothing.' I held out my arm.

Free and naked the flesh gleamed pallid in the storm-dark, as it had gleamed in sunlight before. The horse-mark was there, blue on the outstretched crook of my arm. Beneath ran the quick pulse of my blood.

'For this,' I said, 'I know only that my mother gave it me. I don't know what it means or why she did it. And of her I know no more than you.' Almost I added, 'And that is too much for me', but in the end I didn't. Last night I had been denied. Even now I would not do to her, who had no one to speak for her, what had been done to me.

They stayed silent. I pulled down my sleeve and faced them all. The trembling was back, deep in my stomach.

I looked straight at Ruarch. 'I'll tell you something else. My grandfather was right to strike me – it was a shame to fight Arax, to me and to him who raised me, and dishonourable, and to raise a hand to you would be the same!'

He glared, but played his games as his brother did. Slowly he slipped his hand into his tunic and took from there a pouch of leather. Something in me shrank away; my soul understood before my mind. I could only watch as he shook it upside down till on to his open palm tumbled what was bright and glinting and silver: Tachga's charm, the running horse.

He held my eyes. The smile was back, open and triumphant. Once more the lizard tongue touched his lip. Then he took the charm up by the leather thong and dangled it before the others while it turned for him as once it had turned for me.

They knew what it was. They gasped at first and hung back but in a moment crowded round. I said, 'Where did you get it?'

'I found it. In the ruins. Where you were seeking for it.'

I said, 'It is not what you think.'

They stared, hard-faced. I saw Dearg, bewildered, looking at the ground, and Luth frowning and trying to understand. But the charm was Horse-people's, Horse-mistress, the Queen-mare, mother and sorceress and soul-taker, and her powers were very great.

I said, 'I've told you all I know. What do you want from me?'

There was real fear in their eyes, and hatred. I was a fool not to have better understood. All the stories they'd been told returned to them. Then Ruarch flung the charm down in the dust of the yard.

He said, 'Ask him. Ask the old man why he brought you here. Ask him why we have witch's blood in our hall again and witch-charms when our own goddess once more flies among us. Ask him now. And if you will not, I'll throw this in his face!'

I bent to the ground. Though it had been hidden for so long the charm was bright and polished and smooth to the touch. I picked it up and looked at it. I'd seen it by moonshine. Now the green storm light played about it so that it glowed like rotten wood. Yet its beauty caught my heart. I thought how it had been with me, hidden fast in my tunic, a symbol of something I did not understand but yearned and hoped and looked for. And I had cast it out.

Ruarch snatched it. No one tried to stop him. He sneered now, openly. I watched his fingers close tight and the thong of leather dangle from them. It was as if once more I watched a living creature die within another's grasp.

'Go on,' he said.

The walk back to the hall took forever. When I was there I went in and began to make my way between the groups of those who sat and talked. Behind me the boys slipped in and waited by the door. They had an air about them which signalled trouble. As I passed him Cumair struck a chord and glanced up. After I felt him follow me with his eyes.

The talk died away. My aunt saw me first and sat back, raising her hand to quieten her women. At their hush my uncle looked up from his talk and paused and frowned. The air was thick with wood smoke and steam from the cooking pots and the smell of men. It was very hot. By a bearing post my grandfather sat forward a little more, with his chin on his knuckles, and stared at me from under his brows.

Behind me now there was only silence broken by a bowl set down and a dog scratching. My mouth was dry – I was very much afraid.

In the end my grandfather spoke first. 'Well,' he said, 'what is it now?'

I looked back towards my uncle. What I had to do I'd do with dignity, in the proper way.

'Sir?'

He'd not seen me since before last night. He got to his feet and his eyes narrowed and searched my face; but he showed no surprise and I thought, Someone told him, and wondered who.

'Have I leave to speak?'

Gortag moved. She half ran to Mhorged, thin and clumsy, without grace. She did not touch him, only gazed across at me, her fingers clutching at her skirts.

Mhorged said gravely, 'You know you may. In this hall any man may speak as he likes.'

I had no thoughts as to what would follow, only that I must get out the words. But there was one thing I had to do before all else, a due to pay before the reckoning. I turned to Nemair. She sat there quietly, her eyes wide, her face proud and calm as ever.

I said, 'I owe you thanks. I heard. It was brave of you – you saw what he is like.'

For a moment she smiled, no Raven-princess but a girl; her eyes were unguarded. Then she was serious again. 'Yes,' she said, 'that was why I did it.'

That done I turned to my grandfather. He stood already. For a moment it was as though we had never left the marshlands. We faced each other as so often before, in conflict and anger. But we had journeyed far since then. He'd taken a great gulp of wine, so much that it ran into his beard. He looked as he had yesterday, rough and hard and cunning.

I said, 'There's talk, Grandfather.'

About us the hall was still and quiet. Everyone watched and waited.

He stared and swallowed. Sweat sparkled on his forehead, his eyes were hot; once more the mind behind them worked.

He said, 'You'll get nothing from me.'

'Don't you know what they are saying, Grandfather? Haven't you heard their talk of witches and demons and hauntings? How the pale horse runs again. Don't you know what they call you in our hall, old man?'

He moved, quick as a striking snake, but I was ready this time and the wine he hurled from his cup splashed harmlessly on to my sleeve.

I cried out then, despairing, 'Grandfather!' But even as I

196

did he folded tight his mouth and before us all he sat. There was a plate of meat he'd put beside him. He bent and picked up his knife, hacked off a slice and began to eat.

Mhorged stepped forward. He said, 'Father?'

With his mouth full of meat my grandfather said, 'I've told you, I'll tell him nothing. Say what you like if you've a mind to. It makes no odds. He'll do as he's told him he has to.'

He turned back to me suddenly, baring his teeth, as vicious as I'd ever seen him. 'And I'll teach you to make a mock of me! You'll not walk so proud and mighty by the time I've done. And that –' he pointed to my good cheek, jabbing upwards with his finger '– will match the other!'

He would not unbend and he meant what he said, every word.

My heart gave a great thump of fear and grief. I took two steps forward till I was right in front of him, with nothing between us, only the rugs and dead heather on the floor. He straightened and stopped his chewing. I was close enough to see pulped meat before he closed his mouth on it.

Till then I had not known what I had meant to do. Now, like the trailing pattern on a cup, or a mirror, or an armband that twists upon itself and then is whole, my way was clear, the maze danced out, the dark way trod. I had waited all my life for this.

This night I had held out my arm for all the boys to see. I did so again, but for my grandfather only; this was between him and me. His eyes flickered to the mark and up again to my face.

I was quite calm. I said, 'Grandfather, since you have no help to give me, then let me cut out my shame for myself.'

Even then he did not know what I would do. For a heartbeat he stared, his heavy mouth falling open, his brow furrowed. I moved straight as the hawk, deft as the lynx when it pounces. His knife lay by his plate. I snatched it up; the blade gleamed dully; a woman screamed aloud. Then I brought it down in a long, sweeping slash with all the strength I had.

The bright blood spurted and fell in scarlet droplets. My arm was on fire, yet I'd been too slow. A hard, strong hand gripped my wrist and twisted. The blade spun and clattered on the ground and fetched up against a cup. I had meant to cut to the bone; instead the stab was ragged, and too high. The mark was left unblemished.

For a third time a voice spoke in my ear, smooth as oil.

'Little cousin, what foolery is this? What would the Clan-lord say if we gave you to him harmed?'

I did not understand. For a long moment I was only dazed and sick and wild with fear of what was to happen to me. I cast around and saw my grandfather, grim suddenly, but with the harsh hatred gone from his eyes. Mhorged looked white-faced above his beard. My aunt stood apart, her face a set mask, like clay.

I turned my head. My cousin held me still, his breath moist against my neck.

I said, 'The Clan-lord?'

'Him. After twelve years. To make his peace, for a price.'

He was smiling, gently, even to his eyes.

I said, 'No.' Then, 'No! You cannot make me!'

My uncle stepped forward. I stared at him blindly and felt his arm about my shoulders. My cousin slipped from my side like a shadow. My uncle said, 'Arawn—' but with a sudden, desperate strength I pushed him from me. I could not bear his touch. He stumbled backwards and caught his elbow on the upright of a loom. He swore a great oath and the loom crashed down among us.

I stood there. My wits were fled from me. I knew I should run, but I could not. My grandfather sat still. Now he rose, heavily, with an effort. His hands were shaking.

He said, 'The Horse-people are on the march again. They're sailing from their islands. The Clan-lord has need of everyone he can get. Even us. He will make us again what we were. Nam Dubh will rise once more. But he needs surety.'

I said, 'What surety?'

'A hostage, for our goodwill. He knows what he did to us and our pride is no quiet thing. Who better than my grandson?'

There was a blackness over my sight and a great lump in my throat. Through it I said, 'You have Hakos.'

He stared at me. His mouth opened and closed again and the silence went on and on. Then a woman laughed shrilly and her voice, cold and clear, too familiar, rose up. 'Hakos?' she cried. 'You fool! Do you think, nephew, that Aed would see the true child of his heart go to sacrifice? He has more sense than that!'

Her words were like blows. Yet, for a moment, I stood

outside their meaning, dead to it as if the blood had been wrung from me. Only the sense of nightmare, of horror beyond telling, sounded in me, distant as the sea. The blackness grew; I would have fallen. Then Nemair was before me, pale and upright, and her eyes held mine and brought me to myself. The nightmare sprang; its form rose up and the sea surged. I took to my heels and ran.

All about was confusion and the mill of bodies and men cursing. They reached to catch me but I ducked and dodged and kicked as I'd been taught, and ran through the wide doors into the yard.

They sprang after me, but I slipped off to the right. The storm clouds hid the moon but the tapers had been lit and the yard was all flaring gold and shadow. If I kept to the dark I had a chance. Panting, I crossed the place where I had fought with Arax, empty now but for the horse-trough and the molten shimmer of its water. To the side were outhouses, in front the forge and further on our hut, all streaked with flame where the tapers were set up high. Beyond was blackness. I saw this plainly, just as I heard the noise behind me and smelt the smells of night and habitation. But I did not think; I was beyond that. I only ran, as the stag before the hounds, because I had to.

I went straight on, towards the palisade with the gates that led to the pastures. Above in the gatehouse someone walked and peered and held his torch aloft; the guard, guessing that something was up. My hand was at the bolt, fumbling the stiff, cold metal, my face pressed to the rough wood. He did not know yet what he looked for. I thought I could get out. Then one sound halted me. Hideous and blaring it filled the yard: the carnyx, the war-horn whose cry will set men at each other's throats.

I sobbed out loud then and crouched by the gate. Above I heard the guard scramble to his arms and did not dare to run – even in the dark a spear may find its mark. Across the courtyard they came for me, holding torches high. The wind, rising before the coming storm, whipped up the flames so that sparks glittered in the sky. The men who held them seemed to dance lightly as they ran. Behind them the doors to the great hall stood open, thronged with the dark shapes of those who watched. And then, for the first time, thunder rumbled and summer lightning rent the sky, splitting it like rotten cloth. Briefly, high on the sheer rise of hillside, the ruins showed, frosted with light, empty, more than ever like great bones hefted from the earth.

I closed my eyes. Hot tears trickled down my face. I thought, The Clan-lord comes! and the words beat in my brain though even then I could not grasp their meaning.

I must have stayed there for but a moment. My limbs thought before my mind. Before the torches could cast their light upon me, I swung hard to the left and ran along the palisade. There was another gate that I could try.

It lay behind Nemair's chamber, a little wicker door, a bolt hole that was never used since it led out to rocks and brambles. I did not even know if it would open. It lay close to the edge of the yard where the palisade curved round. I ran towards it with the breath aching in my throat and lungs, aware of the shifting lights and shouting. Then I was there, in the deep shadows, feeling along the wood till the bolt was under my hand.

It was rusted tight into the keep and my knife was gone. I worried at it with my fingers till they grew slippery with blood. I began once more to sob and curse and suddenly it shifted.

I paused and wiped more water, tears and sweat, from my eyes. The yard was quieter now, the men drawn back, hunting by the main gates. I grasped once more at the bolt and pulled. I thought I had it but it stuck again and as, despairing, I sat back, I caught a glimpse of something white.

The dog stood there, motionless, the length of a man's arm away from me. Nemair's bitch, the big hound, the faithful huntress, whom in the night men could surely see.

I was done for. I sank back against the wood. If I moved she would have me. Her hackles had risen, a great crest of fur stood round her neck and her lips were drawn back from her teeth.

In the yard someone shouted. I turned my head and saw them pointing. They could not see me for the shadow but the dog's whiteness was lit by flames. I thought of the Clan-lord, of Nemair in her raven-cloak, Ruarch with my charm, and of my grandfather and what he would do to me for this.

The shadows moved. There was a flare of light and a figure stepped into it. I flung up my arm to shield myself and hunched away, turning into the wooden wall. There was a long moment of stillness that stretched into the night. Then came a long, low whistle and the sound of the dog moving. I shifted and stared over my arm and saw the pale form arc away and go, running through the yard and up into the pastures. The night took her, and then she showed again, making for the ruins, as lightning cracked across the sky and once again the thunder echoed on the hills. I stayed where I was, motionless and trembling, and the figure waited also. I saw who it was: Nemair, her face lit with torchlight, but still. Briefly she was there, looking down on me. Then she turned, and held her torch high into the faces of those who came running. I heard her call out and point to where the dog had run and they stopped and afterwards were gone also, surging through the yard and on to the slopes.

I felt again for the bolt. This time it worked free and I was gone, stumbling down the hillside to the darkness below.

Chapter Nineteen

I ran like a wild thing. The way was very steep and I could not
see my hand before my face; often I fell and rolled into the
undergrowth. Yet I felt nothing, only the living fear that
clung to my back, toothed and clawed, and drove me on. At
last the way opened up and the wind was in my face and I ran
on rock and grass. When the next bolt of lightning came I saw
what I knew already, that I was on the lower slopes that led
into the forest.

I ran on. I sought the shelter of the trees on instinct and
soon enough they closed about me. When I was among them
I halted, leaning against rough bark, and sucked in air and
tried to ease my aching sides.

But I could not rest for long. The lightning cracked again
and lit the trees with fire. They reared about me, then closed
once more to blackness.

Blinded, I began to run again and now my pain became a
distant thing, as if swathed in soft webs and held from me.
Instead my thoughts became my goad. I glanced behind into
the dark and with my eyes saw only black and knotted tree
trunks and the thin, curved spikes of brambles; but while the
thunder rumbled high above, my soul saw clearly. I knew the
image of the Clan-lord followed me, whooping and roaring,
riding in his war-cart, clad in gold.

Through the trees he came unhindered, the wheels
hissing, the reins snapping on his horses' necks. With him
came the Raven-queen and sometimes she was Gortag,
leaning out and screaming, and sometimes Nemair, lifting
her black cloak of wings. I heard his laughter, saw the dark
face peer after me, and I ran on in terror.

I do not know how long I ran. The branches whipped into
my face, and caught and tore my clothes and skin. I
stumbled, with my fingers clutching at the earth and my
breath thick and clogged in my throat. I picked myself up
and ran again. All my hurts came back to me: a great raven

203

pecked at my bloody arm, and my limbs were seared with fire. My legs went then. I fell among roots, scrabbling like a hare when the hounds are on it. I tried to rise while the storm lit the heavens overhead. I glimpsed blue fire and against it the tracery of branches, fine and stark. The thunder boomed and growled and I cried out and then was still.

I must have lain awhile. When I came round I was very cold and wet all through but the storm had passed. Looking up I saw between the branches of a tree the moon sailing high and the sky clear about her.

At first I was dazed and then I picked myself up and began to walk, not knowing where I should go or what I should try to do. Yet I was very calm and the calm was like a kind of death. All the wild restlessness of yesterday was past. What had been secret had been stripped bare and some pain in me was eased, like a wound wiped clean and searched.

Something was familiar. I felt about my legs the lapping of a stream and followed it, ducking beneath the branches that met above my head. I did not question why I came here, or if I found it for myself or was led. I did no more than walk until I stood before the pool.

It lay before me, the flat surface sombre and dark though lit with moonlight where it rippled. The reeds whispered on its banks, the trees were still after the passing of the storm. I saw the dark bulk of the curved stone, its outline shining silver, and I climbed on to the bank and sat beside it.

It was like a dream. I was far from tears and pain and fear. All that was gone; my mind was clear and empty. The night was quiet, the water lapped, soft as wool, shining like glass, and I was part of it, touched by the same dark breezes, the same bright moon.

Later I leant my head against the stone. Beneath my cheek I felt the rough lichen, the pits and cracks of the worn surface. With my fingers I traced the outline of the horse, and my horse, the silver horse, came back to me, no longer quenched and dimmed. Its warm breath snuffed sweetly at my neck, the rough mane brushed my forehead. I heard the stamp of its hoof and saw the soft eye's gleam. Then it slipped away, going in silence as it had come. But the night was not empty for the water was there and when I slept it was as though it closed about me, lulling me to rest.

I woke at dawn, when the mists were rising, shocked and

staring round. The wood was full of vapour which hung about the margins of the pool and rose in white columns above the surface of the water. As yet the morning was chilly and I was cold to the bone and sore and panicky. My fear had come back and I did not know what I should do. Besides, the pool seemed eerie now, and strange, and the wood full of eyes and dangers. I struggled to my feet and ducks quacked and flew, startled from the rushes. I tried to run again but my legs hurt too much and my arm jarred with every step and needed binding. I sank down once more into the tangled grasses.

Yet I could be no more the child. The boy who'd wept last night, running in terror through the woods, was gone. I knew him but could not feel as he did. Instead I thought as I must, coldly and with reason, of what I knew was true and of the odds against me.

I had no dagger and no cloak, no spear or nets to hunt with. My fate was to be killed by wild beasts or wander till I starved to death. But it would not come to that. Sometime that morning, as soon as the citadel had wakened, my uncle would loose the dogs and they would stream down the path I'd followed and hunt me out. They would not hurt me, I knew them all by name, but they would bring my uncle to me, and his men, and that was the plain fact of it.

I wondered what would happen next and when the Clan-lord would come. In my heart he had been always with me, just as last night he'd seemed to follow me – fierce and merciless, riding in his chariot. Since childhood he'd been there, the shadow, the grinning face peering from the rafters, the shape that lies under one's bed to haunt and terrify. Now they would give me to him, to pay off old debts.

The mists were like ghosts, rising and sinking on the surface of the water. I remembered my ghosts, the dead who'd borne me – my father's head bouncing at the Clan-lord's saddle; my mother given to the flames. The ruins were empty of them but this place was not. As yet they did not hear me, but they would.

My flesh was cold, the dark waters colder. The reed banks rustled and a moorhen bobbed across the pool. The air was heavy with moisture and the trees dripped dew.

I thought of other things; of Tachga hunched before her bowl, of my cousin with the wolf's head, cleaving it from its body, of my aunt scattering her stones. The dark things, the cruel things, which they laid bare before me.

I stood once more. I went along the bank and there, half hidden in the grasses, I found the carved and ugly pole set by the Clan-lord to pin the Lady in the ground. Twelve years it had held her, locked in earth and darkness. I bent to the base and pulled. It was rotten anyway and gave and splintered almost at once. Then I took it to the pool.

I looked out across the water. It was quite calm and flat. I said, 'I have no choice. I do not want to go but they will make me.'

I lifted up the pole, high above my head, and hurled it in. It sank, splashing so that the wildfowl flew up, beating their wings and honking. Then it rose to the surface and I watched it, turning its blank face to the sky.

I had made my offering. 'Help me,' I said.

I knew then. The knowledge weighed me down. It tugged at me, it called to me till my breath came thick and slow in my chest and my limbs were turned to water.

I had no words to speak. Words were not for this. What was there, what I had turned to, was something of blood and gut and bone. As the beat that runs through a song, or in verses, it echoed in the heart and in the earth and was too great for me.

I stood a while, strung out and shivering, and dimly understood what overwhelmed me.

Later that morning, just as the sun broke through, I came out on to the slopes that led to Nam Dubh. High above me the round huts sprawled within the rotten palisade and higher still the white, forsaken ruins. I set my face to it and walked on.

I went slowly, nursing my hurts. I still ached from the fight and my grandfather's flogging, and my flight to the woods had left me with more bruises and scratched all over. I did not dare look at my arm, though I'd bound it roughly with a strip of shirt.

I was in the pastures when I saw a figure on horseback riding towards me. I had to stop and shield my eyes before I could see who it was. Then I recognized Luth, spurring on his horse.

I waited for him. Presently he came up and reined in beside me. We stared at each other a long moment. Then he said, 'I got this back for you,' and flung something at me. I caught it and looked. It was the horse-charm, glittering in the sunshine.

I said, 'How?'

He shrugged. 'How do you think? Ruarch's a coward. He was squealing for me to take it almost before I'd begun. Aren't you going to wear it?'

'Would you?'

He made no answer but watched while I rolled it in its leather thong and tied it behind my belt. Then we looked at each other again.

He said, 'Why have you come back? They've been up all night, watching for you, Mhorged and your grandfather. We heard them shouting. Why didn't you stay out there?'

'I would have died in the forest.'

'Won't this be a kind of death for you? Turned over like a slave or cattle. It would for me.'

I made no answer but began to walk. The sun was warm on my back and the turf springy underfoot. Above larks were singing.

His horse snorted and started forward. He pulled it round in front of me. 'Why, Arawn?'

I gazed up, into his angry, baffled face. Nothing I could say would make it right. I was no hero to be sung to a peaceful grave and the charm was my betrayal, and his. In the end I told him the truth. 'Because I must,' I said. Presently he galloped past me, not to the citadel but out towards the moors.

The hounds bayed long before I came into the yard. I had been right; they were about to set them loose. I wondered if Nemair's white hound would have run with them.

A little later I walked in through the gate. My uncle was there, seeing to the preparations, Hakos with him, and some of his men. There were no women and none of the boys.

At first, with the racket of the dogs, they did not notice me. Then my uncle looked up and straightened slowly. After that the others did also. For a long moment nothing happened. Then he snapped his fingers and the men began to haul the dogs away.

Someone stepped behind me. Uffa took me by the arms. He held me hard, though not near my wound, and I did not struggle. My uncle started to walk towards his chamber and Uffa pushed me after.

Inside it was dark and the hearth cold and empty; my uncle bent at once to light a lamp. Uffa gripped me until my uncle said to him, 'Tell Aed,' and to me, 'Sit down.' There was a pile of heather nearby and I crouched on that while Uffa went out again. I shivered.

We waited a long time. My uncle did not speak to me. Then my grandfather's step sounded in the yard, and Uffa's, and they pushed open the door. My grandfather came in first, glaring round. He had a dog whip in his hand. He must have brought it from the yard.

They stared down at me. Mhorged said, 'How hurt are you?'

I shook my head. He said, 'I will have your arm bound properly and something for the scratches.'

He looked round and fetched a sawn log for a stool which he set before me. Uffa stood by the door, my grandfather a little way away, scowling all the time. Then, for a while, they were quiet again.

At last, leaning forward, Mhorged said, 'You must hear me out, Arawn. It is not quite as you think. We mean you no harm.'

So he had always told me. His head was down, staring at his hands clasped in front of him. But when he looked up he was smiling though his eyes were tired. 'You did well to come back to us. We'd have got you in the end. Sooner, perhaps, than you'd have thought. The dogs work well together.' His gaze dropped once more and his knuckles whitened.

In a moment he said, 'I will try to explain. It is like this. After all this time the Horse-people are on the move again and the Clan-lord is afraid. You know that much already. But there is more. The Horse-people have allies now, coming down from the north. Last spring they began to raid. We stand between them and the lands in the west where there is gold and other ores and the Clan-lord has his pastures. He needs us to be loyal and so we will be if what is ours is restored.'

He paused and now his eyes met mine. 'He has pledged already. Nemair is his niece. And now he waits for ours.'

I said, 'No.'

My uncle took a long breath. Behind me Uffa stirred. My grandfather only waited.

Still my uncle was all patience. 'Think of who you are. You

are my nephew, the old lord's grandson. For that you are important. Do you believe that in honour we would give you to him and then abandon you? You have no need to fear. And more than that: you are Macha's son. The Horse-people would not harm one of their own, and their royal blood comes through the female line. Macha had no daughter. The Clan-lord knows that. You are doubly important to him.'

I said, 'For my father, no. For my mother, no. For myself, no.'

'And for us?'

'I owe you nothing.'

There was a sound. My grandfather spat into a corner. He said, 'He'll fight you, Mhorged, however much you pretty it. I warned you. Tell him what else there is. Get it over with and let him bare his fangs. Then we'll know the score.'

I said, 'What else?'

At first no one spoke. It was Uffa who told me, speaking flatly from his place by the door.

'You'll not be hard done by, Arawn. You'll not sweat in chains or be locked away. He'll have you clad in bronze and gold and well-tanned leather. He wants to make you his foster-son.'

I stared up at him. All this time I had been cold and distant as if I only watched what went on before. Now, suddenly, I cried out to them as I had last night, the self-same words, 'You cannot make me!'

My uncle said, 'Do not say that.'

But I knew what was meant by foster-son. It was cleverly done, a sweet beguiling, a trap of honey for the bear. No doubt I would be honoured, have gold and arms as much as any man, but a foster-son was bound to his foster-father – by oaths as binding as blood, by duty, and by honour. For my gold I would swear to him that I would bear arms to no man but him, fight for no honour save his, spill my blood in no wars but his. Once I was sworn he need fear no treason. I was his, with bonds of jewels.

I came back to life as a crushed limb does, frantic with the pain of it.

I turned on my grandfather, no more the bull, a spider rather, weaving his webs of cunning. Rising up, I cried out to him, 'You knew. All the time you knew of this!'

He stepped forward. 'What of it? I would do the same again.'

'As you would for your son!'

For the first time the cold thought that had been there always, even in the yard when he had struck me down, was gone. He gasped and shuddered, blind fury in his eyes, and the mottled colour stood in his cheeks. He growled like an animal from his throat and raised his whip. I turned in time and got it full across my shoulders. The force of it sent me flying. Yet even as I hit the wall and felt Uffa seize and pull me upwards, I felt no fear, only a kind of exultation; for this was familiar, something I could stand against and madden him with rage.

The air quivered and I braced myself. Uffa exclaimed sharply, there was a movement and my uncle's voice saying, 'Leave him, Father!'

We were startled. After a moment Uffa hauled me round and I saw my grandfather standing uncertainly with the whip drooping in his hand. His eyes went from Mhorged to me and back.

I pulled myself from Uffa and Grandfather swung the whip.

'Leave him!'

'You heard how he spoke to me!'

'So? When have words ever hurt you?'

My grandfather sat down. He began to cough, not the harsh rasping of the winter but an almost silent heaving deep within his chest. Uffa went and lifted a jug of wine and poured him some and soon after he was better.

He looked across at us and wiped his mouth. He said, 'A bloody back and an empty belly. That'd put an end to such nonsense – it always did before.'

Mhorged said, 'Was that the way last night?'

They were stern and frowning, set at one another. I said, 'I will not do it.'

Uffa stepped forward. Of them all I trusted him most. He put his hands on my shoulders. 'You have a debt to pay. You have been well fed and clothed. Are you unhappy here? I trained you like a son.'

'And for that you sell me?'

'No. For what your father did.'

It was spoken plainly. I broke away. I cried out to him, 'Yesterday – you could have told me!' I had thought I had been far from tears but now, without warning, they came again. I shook with them and pressed my face against the wall and crushed my lip between my teeth that I might not make a sound.

They let me cry. They watched me, the three of them, and in the room the tension eased; with each gasping sob they thought me broken and come to hand like a mastered colt. But I was not. I turned back with fury blazing in me. I cried out to them, 'I'll tell you how it was! I'll tell you of the beatings and my belly sticking to my ribs with hunger and the feel of fish skins and the way the reeds would cut my hands as I worked. I'll tell you of Palug kicking me about the yard and how he laughed when he took Nehal away. I was frightened to speak and frightened I might show my hatred. My grandfather made me pay with every breath I took!'

There was silence. They were shaken as I was by my own anger, and staring at me; and there was more to say.

'I know what my father did. I know what he married – a witch, a filthy horse-witch, mumbling charms into the night. You taught me well. I don't remember a time when you didn't remind me of who I was and what rotten stock I come from and always with your talk of honour! Your honour! Have some care for mine!'

On Mhorged's bed, in amongst the furs, was a gaming board of bronze-bound wood set with pieces of blue and yellow glass. I'd seen it often, brought to the hall. It was one of my uncle's best things. I took two strides forward, picked it up by the corners and swung it. It crashed against the wall and splintered and the pieces bounced among us.

The room went very quiet. Outside the dogs were barking. No one moved or even drew a breath. And then, at last, my grandfather bent down and lifted a piece of glass. He weighed it in his hand then said, 'Leave us.'

They went, stepping over the threshold into the sunlight. As they left Mhorged said to him, 'Do as you must.'

I waited for him. He seemed to watch me for a long time, gazing across the hearth.

Presently he said, 'You think you'd rather die. Yet you wouldn't. I'd break you. It would take time but in the end you'd give; and that, I think, would hurt you worse than anything.'

He put down the whip, carefully, on Mhorged's bed, and let fall the shard of glass. Then he came towards me, treading on the gaming pieces so that they crackled as he walked. He

211

was very slow but when he stood over me I saw he was still the taller. I turned my face up to his. I was trembling but I did not shrink away. I had a knowledge in me that this was where we had been led – as soon a goat may shrink from slaughter as we might go from this.

He stayed with his gaze on mine, unspeaking, until at last he put out his hand and touched my face. His fingers were dry and shaky, the skin shrivelled. With his thumb he wiped away the tears and stroked the mark he'd put upon my cheek. He did it gently, as a mother would, staring at it with a kind of wonder as if it was the first time that he'd seen it, as though he wandered in his wits. A shiver ran through me. He felt it and took his hand away.

He said, 'Did you think I could help myself? Did you think I never saw them? She is there in every lift of your head. He is in your walk and your anger and your manhood. I live with it. And did you think I never hear them? She laughs in the sunlight and screams in the wind and darkness. In my dreams he calls for her. I see it all, Arawn. And I see Nam Dubh as it was and as it is.'

His eyes were blue and milky, an old man's eyes. His hands shook as he gathered his robes and pulled at them. He had to hold on to a post as before me, into the dust and heather, on to the hard, clay floor, he knelt.

Then he looked up at me. He said, 'I've begged to no man, but to you I do. Lay my dead.'

I had not looked for this. As the sea ebbs and leaves the shore empty so I was empty then, my soul a wasteland, my heart sucked dry. And more, for when the walls of some mighty citadel are breached and the defences torn down and laid to ruin, so I was then, conquered and laid bare. There was nothing I could hide. I said, 'I loosed the goddess. The white horse runs.'

He covered his face with his hands. His shoulders moved and then I too was kneeling and we clung together as children in a storm while about us was the beat of hooves and the crackle of old flames. Then he turned from me and, one hand still at his eyes, the other outstretched, sought for the stool. I helped him to it and waited, crouched at his feet, till he should speak again.

At last he did, smoothing back the hair from my hot forehead. He said, 'The gods are cruel. They mock us. Yet perhaps we shape our gods to our own image. Your mother had her Lady from the earth and the night. Our Lady is of war. The Clan-lord will bring her back to us, yet I have lived so long without her I no longer know what's right or wrong; only how each reflects the other's face and cries out for our blood.'

He was silent again, for a good while; his eyes watched far away. Then he said, 'Without them, what are we? Without them the earth is only mud and stones, the birds are bone and feather. With them we shape our lives. We see our gods' hands in the sky, in the quick slope of the fox, the entrails of a goat.'

He stood. Though he held the post he no longer shook; his step was firmer, his eyes clear. What had come for us had come too late. I knew him for the man he'd always been.

At the door he turned. 'You are our sacrifice, Arawn, our honour-price. Bear it as you must.'

It is the night and they have left me in peace, with food and my wounds bound up. Tomorrow I shall go back to the boys' hall and begin to work again when I am able, throwing with the spear, wrestling in the ring and, in a while, when the strangeness has gone, once more I shall ride out with Luth and hunt. Sometime, not tomorrow or the day after but in high summer at the time they mark for the Crop Feast, the Clan-lord will come and I will go to him. I will go in chains, as his hostage or his slave, but I will not be his son.

And in the meantime I will dream and in my dreams the white horse gallops nearer.

Chapter Twenty

He came on a day that was hot and dull and heavy with white cloud. All the afternoon Nam Dubh waited, the people sweating before the palisade as in the valley below men and chariots and carts and horses streamed from the forest. They were a horde – moving steadily, practised and at ease – and a war-band. The Clan-lord had brought a full retinue, of twenty-eight warriors, hand-picked by custom from his household, who marched with their own followers behind them. Their noise came clear to us, rising on the still air, shouts and the trundle of carts over rough ground and the sharp creak of harness. From the citadel we watched in silence – even the children were awed – and the older men, who had seen this before, smiled grimly one to another, and remembered. Into the evening we stood while they set up camp, throwing stitched, bright skins over poles for tents and bringing the war-carts round in a wide circle as if for battle.

I too watched and also remembered; but my memories were of other arrivals not so long before. Grandfather's and mine, bedraggled with the rain, soiled with dirt, and him with his bitter pride; Hakos's whooping gallop up the valley leading his men, bright in their gold and paint. My own return, one cool, sunlit morning, to face what I must, and of which it was better not to think.

Now Cernach, the Clan-lord, was come, in his own pride and splendour. Close by someone said, 'He means business,' and someone else answered, 'Well then, but it had to be.' Yet he was distant still in the valley, moving unrecognized among his men who trudged and laboured and called across to one another.

All that summer had been uneasy, with little sunshine but hot and sultry anyway, unpleasant weather that tired both us and the animals so that everyone's temper was quick. Milk spoilt by noon, meat turned green, and the midden stank and crawled with flies. In the yard the droning drove one to madness.

Yet the disquiet was fitting. Everyone waited, looking down the valley and at each other with swift sideways glances. Mhorged lost weight; his face looked haggard and bluish about the jowls and under the eyes. Uffa alternated between tyranny and a strange, anxious tenderness for those in his care. He made us practise the steps of the Fire-dance over and over till we were exhausted, panting and dripping with the warm summer sweat. He was merciless. 'You will dance it,' he said, 'for Cernach,. and dance it well.' But at night he would check us for hurts, make sure our bowls and cups were full and afterwards watch, frowning, not in anger but in thought. Only Gortag thrived. She swept by, with her head up, proud and satisfied as if already she wore fine wools. Almost one could forget her thin looks for she was full of gloating as a toad is of poison, swollen with it. I avoided her. It is not pleasant to be near one who wishes you harm, who's rejoiced at every bruise and scar upon your body and who'd pluck each nerve of you with her finger nails if only she were able.

So we waited, all of us, for Cernach to bring his hosts; and the midden buzzed and glittered, and the hot white clouds piled in the sunless sky.

That first evening we saw nothing of him. The next day was the worst. Within the palisade people stood about in groups and whispered; a woman scolding a child sounded loud and shocking. Even the geese huddled beside the dew pond. We boys sat in our hall but barely spoke and only tried a turn or two at knucklebones. Yet I found out who'd stayed my friend. It didn't take much; Nar's hand on my shoulder, Eraid smiling and passing the jug; and always Luth and Dearg and Magh, with his heavy puzzled face, watching as if I were some special pot or jar or basin that might at any time crack and break apart. Small things but enough.

Cernach had spent his first night bivouacked with his men, for all things have a time and ceremony. He'd sent a messenger to tell how he would make his entrance at noon when the sun stood highest.

At last the carnyx blew in the valley. We went out; the

gates were opened, wide as they could go. Below us the war-carts moved, slowly, in a line, pennants fluttering. Before them walked a line of men, clad in black robes with head-dresses of plumes and in front of them trundled a great cart, high on four huge wheels that creaked as they turned. Within the cart two figures stood, one a woman, her hands outstretched above her head, the other a man, bare-chested, torced, an ox-hide cloak falling from his shoulders. As they drew near we saw the woman was no living thing, but carved of wood and painted. The Raven-goddess rode before our eyes, and with her the king, the Clan-lord, her mortal consort.

All summer I'd thought how it would be. When I ate or drank or lay down at night, always he was there and I saying to him, 'I will go with you, but will not be your son.' So any boy will wish himself a hero; to see his enemy and be brave, dignified and calm, reining in his anger like the best warriors before the battle frenzy. Even the signs of fear – the tight band that seems to squeeze the breath from out one's chest, the hammer ringing in the head – are only what must be before the fight commences. Once it would have been like that with me.

The goddess' cart came on. The effigy rocked a little but the man was still and splendid, braced against the movement. I watched. Some place deep within me was the fear and anger and all there should have been; but I was cold when I'd thought to be hot, and not calm but deadened rather, like a smitten limb in the instant before it begins to hurt. All was removed and strange as though I stared out upon some dream; and like a dream some things were larger than in life, until I seemed to see clearly the grain of the wooden cart, the paint laid upon the goddess, the pin which clasped the Clan-lord's dappled cloak and the steady rise and fall of his breast beneath. Above the sky was the same hot, solid white of the day before so that the very air was flat and livid. Yet it was right that this solemn gathering of men and carts and horses should not be lit with sunlight, that there should be no glitter or sparkle such as there'd been with Hakos, or even the ordinary talk of men amongst them, real and comfortable. All was quiet and somehow eerie, with only the noise of the wheels and hooves, like watching ghosts go by. So they were to me and I thought, Rather they should have come at night.

217

They reached the gates. The black-clad men drew back, forming lines about the cart. It groaned onwards, the horses steadied for the final slope. The black feathers stained the air, fluttering from posts set in the cart's sides. Mhorged stirred, a little movement backwards, his chin lifting as if he checked himself; and the cart stopped.

Other men appeared, our own peasants from the valley, touching their brows and wailing with a low, moaning sound. One brought round a horse, splendidly harnessed. On to it the Clan-lord leapt. He was a tall man but light in his movements, arranging his cloak about him. No one spoke. Others unharnessed the heavy ponies that had pulled the cart. They led them away, leaving the traces trailing from the cart.

The men were frightened. I should have been the same only the dullness would not leave me nor let me feel anything but the pull and drag of its weight.

The black-clad men came forward. They took up the traces. On these they pulled and slowly the cart began to move once more. They cried out to the farm-folk who took the weight behind. As they drew near the inner gates swung wide. Slowly the goddess' cart entered Nam Dubh.

She was here, the Mother of the tribe, staring out at us. Close to she was crude, a rough hewing of features and heavy female body from black-painted wood, yet baleful too, with staring eyes of pebble quartz and a red, open mouth, and her torc about her neck. Her head-dress was the Raven, her carrion self, the battle-death bird who foresees the ends of men.

All the time from his horse outside the open gates the Clan-lord had watched. I'd wanted him ugly and furtive and sly, for he was all of those things to me and such are easy to hate. But take away his torc, the paint from his cheeks, his ox-hide cloak, the gold belt about his naked waist and still he would be king. I saw it and could not deny it though with all my heart I would have if I could.

One of the black-clad men stepped forward. He was wizened, old, bare-chested with breasts that sagged like a woman's, and his face was pinched and sly.

'Penance, Mhorged!' he cried. 'Penance to the Mother. Then we'll see the fitness of things and the way that things turn out.' He turned away with a spiteful little laugh, his cloak drooping from his bony shoulders, and shuffled off. Solemnly the others followed him, and we were left with the goddess staring down.

Luth said softly, 'Did you see him?'
I answered, 'Yes.'
'Did you remember him?'
'I don't know. I was three last time. Did you?'
'I think so. A little. His nose like a beak, and his hair brushed back.'
'They all wear it that way.'
We were silent awhile. Luth drew a pattern in the dust. We sat together outside by the well.
He said, 'Perhaps, if you do not remember, it will not be so bad. Mhorged promised—'
He rattled on. Once I would have hung on his every word. Now they irked and seemed a nonsense a boy would think of, to tell to adults, trying to seem of age.
It was not his fault. He could not understand. To him it was a tale or a song telling of things far off yet vivid. One knows the path the hero treads and what he faces and in one's mind one battles with self-same monsters. Yet always one can blink at firelight or mop one's plate with bread. One does not live the thing. Only for me the monster had come, splendid to the door.

I had not been harried. In the weeks before Cernach's coming, I had been left to myself, to Uffa and my duties. I kept apart. Between myself and the other boys stood the silver horse-charm and the memory of it held on the leather string. Some had some pity for me. My wounds had not been quick to heal, perhaps because of my low spirits. My cheek would be forever scarred, and the cut I had made on my arm was also seamed and raised. I do not know about my back. The weals had hurt for a long time and once or twice since, stripped for wrestling, I'd caught the others looking. I supposed that too was marked.
I nursed other wounds – deeper pains such as you'd expect; a grief for what I'd been, a young man earning his warrior's arms, torn from me like a raider's pickings. And more, my training, my friends, even the meat upon my plate, had been shown for what they were. 'See, Arawn, what you'll become, and better still when you are Cernach's son. Not bad

for the Horse-witch's bastard, the traitor's brat!'

With hot, aching eyes I saw all they laid upon me, and understood. Mhorged, in the end, would not have needed force; my grandfather had wept to bring his dead to rest. I'd do as I was told, crawling on my knees if they wanted it, a little price to pay for Nam Dubh's suffering. But that was not the worst I grieved for; the dead were mine also, slain in treachery, made my trust. For me they would not slumber. Rather they rose up, holding out their honour like bloody rags and crying: 'Justice!' I would not lay them down for Cernach's taking. Nor could Mhorged make me.

I'd made that promise, lying sick and dreary, to go so far and no further. I hugged the knowledge to me, like the memory of the horse, the talisman, the mark upon my arm. All that I was lay in those. Of the rest there was nothing.

Mhorged watched and my grandfather, for they knew what lay between us. Sometimes I could have cried to them, 'I understand. I know the suffering that was here and why you must appease him. Only let me hate him openly!' But they'd have stopped their ears. Mhorged said nothing; only he had me shut up at night, locked in the same little hut where I had spent my first night at Nam Dubh. Now a bed was set beside the wall and a fire laid for when it might be cold but still each night the bolt was shot home. He was careful. I had run once; he would take no chances.

Otherwise he treated me as if the thing was done, and I a dutiful nephew he honoured and loved. It was, 'Arawn, you wrestled well today, nephew,' or, 'Your horse is well turned out, a credit to you.' We were not fooled. Both of us remembered him walking from the hut and how he'd said to Grandfather, 'Do as you must.' And even while I did his bidding, or took my place in the hall to eat; even while he raised his cup or rode out to hunt, we each of us wondered what lay hidden in the other's heart.

As for Grandfather, he was sicker. His strength failed like a bear's in winter, all sapped and spent. He coughed and spat most nights and mornings, sometimes half the day, and his skin looked as if you could see through it and count the spread of veins. Only his eyes were bright and cunning and only he, I think, who had faced Cernach before, guessed what was to be.

So the three of us went on, like pieces on the *fidchell* board, with the King-piece in the centre and us circling round, never touching on the thing in hand.

Now Cernach, the Clan-lord, was here and the dulled, deep anger clung to me like a pelt and weighted me so that I could have suffocated, sunk into the thick stuff of it.

Later that day I sought my grandfather out. I asked him, 'What is the Summer Feast? What is to happen?'

'It is the Crop Blessing, the feast before the harvest to ask the gods for riches in the grainstores. It is a lowlands festival – what should such as we have to do with it? Yet all the tribes must attend, to make peace with the gods and goddesses. Marriages are made, and there is trade and barter and a time for the young men to show off their skills. It will last out the month.'

He paused and rubbed the bridge of his nose between his fingers, as if he caught his thoughts.

'Yet it has its dark side, as does anything concerning the gods. The deities must be appeased and old wrongs righted. It will be that way with us.'

He sounded weary. The heat of summer was exhausting him. These days he coughed, not blood, but a thick, green sputum. I looked at him and saw how today his face was filmed with a sour sweat that ran down and soaked his clothes and reeked.

Strangely these days we turned to one another. There was, I think, a sense of last things, a drawing to a close. We were enemies still, not even at truce, only familiar with each other's ways. And he would watch me, knowing me, guessing, perhaps, the close-held nature of my hatred and smiling a little for he no longer cared.

The days went on. We waited for the beginning of the Summer Feast, that would purify Nam Dubh of her old wrongs. So the Clan-lord would reap and harvest us. Till then Cernach would not eat at our tables nor dwell within the walls. But we saw the preparations; his men horse-racing in the valley, the building of great bonfires at the edges of the wood. All day it seemed the black-clad priests were about and Nemair rode down each morning to join them, trotting on a stout dun pony. Each day too more men arrived, splendid men, cloaked and booted with their own retinues. This year the Raven-tribes gathered in our forests.

At night it was different. The moon waxed. I watched, seeing it grow, no longer beautiful but yellow as a fat, rank cheese in the sky; and all the time I gave myself to the hot, dull ache that deadened my limbs and made my resolve a hidden thing, cloaked in the darkness of my soul as the moon's cloaked round by night. Now I felt, not that I was wrapped in pelts, but rather that I was under a great weight of water, pulled as the marsh tides are pulled, back and forth forever. Only in sleep was I myself, returned to life, for in my dreams my hatred burnt afresh, bright and honest as once I'd known it to be.

Two nights before the moon was full the Penance Time began – at dusk, which, like the dawn, is a magic time, neither day nor night, but in between and one of the thresholds to the Otherworld.

The first night of the Summer Feast is the time for business, for wrongs to be made right, quarrels to be sorted, the Clan-lord's judgement given. Now, after twelve years, he was to judge Nam Dubh once more.

We gathered in the yard. Mhorged and Gortag stood before the gate. Behind them, hunched on his stick, was my grandfather. Around stood our warriors, unpainted, weapon-less, their hair limp about their shoulders.

The black-clad priests gathered. In the dusk they clustered round like beetles. At first they were quiet, only shuffling their feet. Then with staves they began to beat upon the ground. At last the old one screeched aloud, darting forward and gibbering at our gate. He shook his staff at us. Then they were all at it, crying out their curses.

Nemair stepped forward. She wore the familiar raven-cloak and her hair was bound in its braids, fastened with the bright gold beads. Beside her walked Mhorged, naked and unshaven. Together they walked to the priests who fell back before them and were quiet. They passed between them under the gaze of the goddess and down towards the valley below.

The soft dusk faded. Night fell. Then, as the summer moon burnt above us, there was nothing. Only the glimmer on the empty leather tents, the deserted camp before us. The goddess stayed still and terrible in her wooden effigy. Yet she lived in it, glaring out.

The silence went on. At some time we heard screams and

cries of men from the woods below. At the great feasts criminals are put to death, strung up on trees or drowned in boggy pools according to their crimes, for how can there be justice if the guilty walk whole before the gods?

When there was silence our gates were closed. All night flames flared in the valley. Within the palisade few slept, only the very young and old. I watched from the gate-tower, with the others, and thought, Cold clay and the fire beneath; another fever sweated under furs and rugs. Soon it will be over. At daybreak Mhorged returned.

He was worn out, swaying as he walked, and his eyes looked old, but he had gone a penitent and returned a lord. A great gold torc gleamed at his neck, of thick wires twisted round; his cheeks were daubed with scarlet whorls; a new cloak hung from his shoulders. Nam Dubh and its lord were no longer outcast from the Clan. The pact was made, the promise sworn. Both sides would hold true.

They held races that day, with the war-carts and single horses. Our own young men took part, riding down to join in where once they would have been forbidden. Yet they were shy, as were we when we went down to watch. Our gear was shabby, our ponies unkempt next to what we saw; and the priests stood stern and guarded the forest pathways from our sight.

That evening I was summoned to our own great hall. I crossed the yard, hearing the laughter in the valley. The citadel was empty-feeling. Most people were drinking and eating their fill under that bright and horrid moon.

I pushed open the door and went inside. My uncle was there, and with him Gortag, a sleekness about her like a spring vixen and her thin mouth curved. Hakos and Nemair stood there also, though apart, and my grandfather, well wrapped and squatting by the hearth.

I came and stood before them, eyes down, obedient as a well-schooled hound.

My uncle said, 'Arawn.' He wore his new cloak, and his ring, and the torc.

I mumbled at him, 'Sir.'

His gaze was on me. I felt it, not hard but thoughtful. Then came a little scratching sound as he thumbed the day-old stubble on his chin.

223

He said, 'It will be tomorrow.'

I didn't lift my head, nor even close my eyes. Beneath the pelt, beneath the water, my soul held very still. But out of the dark my gaze seemed to focus. The floor where I looked was new swept. Someone had scattered fresh, green herbs. Things were kept clean these past days.

He waited, then said, 'Tomorrow night Cernach enters. You know what is expected. There is the Fire-dance, for the gods' blessing. Afterwards you will be pledged to him. Then it will be done.'

He spoke quietly, as if before a battle or some other hard thing, counting out the words one by one to hang like weights and make the men attend. I thought, He understands. He locks me up at night. What does he think I will do?

Still though I was quiet and meek, my head bent, my shoulders drooped. Almost I could see myself; and part of me cried out at him, 'It is not so! I will not do it, though you take a knife to me or string me on the trees,' while the other part, that swayed under the depth of water, that suffocated in the clinging pelt, bade me slowly, 'Not yet.'

My grandfather shifted and eased his old buttocks. Once he would have glared and snarled for me to speak up and acknowledge my good fortune. Now, seeing him stare at the fire, I thought, with a kind of wonder, He no longer cares. He is gone from all this. The Clan-lord came too late for him. And for a moment my anger did flare within me – not for his own loss but for myself and what he'd brought me to.

Mhorged spoke again, 'Take this. You must be fine as any.'

He held out a bundle, wrapped in cloth. I remembered the other time, and the bright shining blade with the edge keen on it, broken now and useless. When I only stared he stepped forward and put it right into my hands. At the touch I did look up, straight into his pouched, unhappy eyes.

My throat ached with keeping silence. When I moved my limbs seemed unfamiliar, as if I must learn afresh, like a babe, to use them. I unwrapped the gift. Fine clothes lay within – a shirt of worked leather, trousers in checks of blue and green, and a woollen cloak that would reach to the ground – fit for a prince. They'd put in a pin to hold it, a small one but worked in gold and green enamel.

'Put them on. Let us see how you will look.'

Before them I stripped. The night was warm and close

against my skin. I donned the new clothes and afterwards they stared and I felt nothing, only the strangeness of fresh cloth and stiff, unworn leather, the heavy drag of the cloak; and somewhere, far off, the fierce, bright ember of my pain.

Gortag said, 'Why the milk-face, Arawn? Why so sweet with it, and quiet? Have you a taste for finery after all? I thought that we should have to whip you to it.'

She too burnt within though her words were cold as death. Like called to like. It seemed some time we'd shared a cruel healing and paid the price as one drinks bitter herbs. I thought, We have become of a kind, you and I.

Mhorged said, 'Gortag, let it rest. Don't play the fool when you are not. Give him some peace this night at least.'

'Peace!' She turned, snarling. 'It was not I who sold him. Still, he looks well enough. Nemair displays her talents at the loom, though why for him who could say?'

There was silence. Then my grandfather barked his laughter. That much had got to him. After the silence hung them round again.

Into it Nemair spoke. 'For pity,' she said. 'And for liking.'

Till then she'd kept in shadow. Now, at her speaking, she stepped forward. She looked young tonight; a girl playing priestess, severe and soft together. Her hair was new washed and slipped from her braids. Her skin glowed, high on her cheek bones. But she was angry, and assured enough to show it. They looked at her, her chin and brows lifted.

She faced them out. Mhorged flinched. She had led him into the forest.

She came up to me. Though her eyes were on me, her words were for them. 'My uncle would not have you grudge the giving. Pay decently the honour-price. He goes for you all.'

Then, more quietly, to me, 'The *badbh* sits at your shoulder and casts her wings about you, for you are lost and in her darkness. Yet must she come to all men. Better now, with the strength of youth upon you.'

It was so, a crawling darkness. Some days I'd shivered when the sun was hot, and peered from shadowed eyes, as if before a swoon.

Her eyes were heavy, full of her own looking and what she saw. Then, as I raised my gaze to hers, they widened and her lids fluttered and she turned away. But I thought what she said was true.

Mhorged said, 'We will leave you, Arawn. Believe you have our thanks for this.' He came up to me and rested his palm upon my shoulder. 'Tomorrow,' he said, 'make sure you have some wine. It'll bring your colour back and you'll feel better. It will not be so hard.'

His fingers tightened a moment and lifted. He walked clean from me but I bore still the feel of his hand.

They went, my grandfather shuffling last of all, and I stood in the gaudy finery they had given me, numbed and weighted and sunk into the water.

I did not move. For a long time I was there, with my sight turned inwards, as Nemair's had been. But where she saw her goddess's bidding I saw only the time to come, when I should say, 'I will not be your son,' and all the trouble after. For the first time in a long while I felt the edge of fear, sliding like a whetted blade across my flesh. I wore the horse charm round my waist but it felt light, as small and ghostly as tallow flame pitted against the dark.

Someone moved. The shadows beyond the standing looms were stirred. I flung up my head on a warrior's instinct and sought for what was there. A man stepped forward, tall, well built, with the gleam of gold about his neck.

I thought, as if I had always known him, It is he.

He would have something always of youth about him, though he was my uncle's age or more. It was in the set of his bones beneath the skin, defined and generous, the lift at the corner of his mouth, some look of humour about the eyes, though he was Clan-lord, every pore and breath of him. But not as I had thought.

He said, 'When I saw you before, at the gates, you were not so fine. Did you realise I had eyes for you then, knowing who you were?'

The tides washed; I could not answer him.

'Tomorrow there will be no time to talk, so it is better that we should meet each other here and say whatever should be said.'

I stared at him mutely while my mind said, Twelve years.

Gently he said, 'There are things to talk on, surely? A child does not forget.'

I had not forgotten; but these days nothing could move me, to pity or to anger, save to what I was set on. I'd been caught by an old man's tears, a tired mourning, wept out long years ago to empty salted marshes. I was burdened and held until the Clan-lord should come. Now he was here and still my hatred waited of itself.

He regarded me thoughtfully for a while, then held out his hand, cupped as if he would take something. 'May I?' he asked. He meant he wished to see my arm. Still mute I rolled back the supple sleeve and bared the mark for him.

He looked briefly, then said, 'They have given me the right boy then. Almost I wondered, but Aed is old and has lost his cunning. Once he might have tried.'

He did not touch me, but his eyes went to the ugly scar above. 'Mhorged told me of that,' he said.

I raised my gaze to his. He put the lordly ways of Nam Dubh to shame, showing them for the empty sham they were. He was a man who had been groomed every day of his life, like the chariot pony of a favourite warrior. There was a gloss and ease about him my uncle could never have, nor Aed, no matter how often they clipped their hair and pared their nails. This man had never known poverty and hunger and the rot of his home about him.

After the silence had gone on a little longer he said, 'Will you not talk to me after all? Already they have dressed you splendid as any, ready for my fosterage. Yet Nemair, who knows such things, speaks of the *badbh* that haunts you and lingers at your side. Seeing you, I know that it is true. You have the look of the hag-ridden. Do you hate your destiny so much then?'

The waters stirred, the pelt lifted a little. Here was the man who spoke, not some idol riding by his goddess, but still I waited, struggling in vain. I was shackled, tugging at my hatred as a slave does his chains.

Still he looked at me and still I kept my eyes downturned. Then he said softly, 'Poor boy, what have they done to you? Gortag was right, that look is none of yours. Shout your curses at me – in truth I expected it – do not meet me with this emptiness.'

He named it right, an emptiness, a soul-sickness, that sucked my will away. He could not see the dark-bright anguish that all these past days had burnt within me. He saw only what was outwards, the fretting of flesh and spirit; he had not expected it. It shocked him as suddenly it did myself. He'd expected what once I would have felt, defiance and blazing rage, looking to land me as one does a fighting

227

salmon. Instead there was this whey-faced lad, adrift, no match for him, object only for his pity.

He turned to go and some part of me that was still myself, could not bear it, could not bear for me to be dishonest, to unleash my anger later without warning and mock his disadvantage.

I took a breath and felt myself tremble.

'Cernach,' I said.

He turned, and watched, and frowned a little. I let him see whatever he might. Then his mouth quirked.

'That is better,' he said, and left.

Chapter Twenty-one

The rest of the night passed long and heavy. The following day was no better. The other boys avoided me more than ever, looking across with long, sideways glances, as if ill fortune hung about my neck. Till I should be sworn to Cernach I was an outcast, the one among them, for their acceptance was not yet mine, my penance not yet made. Even Luth was quiet, withdrawing to the others, though not, I think, from fear. But they were his people and the tribe is everything. He had seen the goddess and he understood with his heart if not his mind.

Yet as night fell once more I could feel a quickening, as if the pelt stirred upon my flesh or the deep waters troubled a little. Tonight the Clan-lord would enter Nam Dubh and the young men leap again in the Fire-dance.

The moon rose and the yard fires were lit upon the walls. Uffa called us to our hall. Within were the men, to help us prepare. There were the pigments to mix and rub upon the dancers' skins, tracing out designs that wrapped and twisted round upon themselves, twining over breast and back and arms. There were amulets to hang upon wrists and ankles, little wheels and discs of gold and bronze, for the Fire-dance calls the sun to rise at dawn from the cold earth. Then came oil, smelling of resin, and the masks – a spread of antlers reared as if in life; there was a fox, a badger, a human face with bulging, staring eyes and a downturned mouth. But for me there were no amulets, no mask, no torc to wear around my neck. Not till this night was past. I had only my naked face to show before the company, and the yellow oil upon my flesh.

Afterwards we waited, kept from the others. It is bad luck to see the dancers before the feast is done. It was hot and the air thick within the hall. No one spoke. I waited, feeling Fate hold me in her hand. All around were strangers, men and beasts, of the night and the Otherworld.

The mystery of it coiled and wound us, drawn tight as serpents' bonds.

At last the drum sounded in the yard. The door was pulled open. Outside the night sky gleamed – not black but deepest blue. The flames on the walls burnt high; a great bonfire leapt and roared midway in the yard.

From the hall people flocked. The flames glimmered on daubed leather and gold and glass, on the designs freshly painted on their skin. Riches, and the right way of doing things, had come to Nam Dubh.

I saw Cernach, splendid tonight with his thick torc of kingship and his ox-hide cloak that fell to the ground. Behind him stood Mhorged and my aunt and the priests in a semi-circle.

The drums beat quicker, throbbing in the blood. The totem cart moved forward. Above the goddess glared, her paint glowed red. Nemair stepped forward to open wide her arms; the raven cloak fluttered before the flames. The first brands lifted and dipped into the bonfire. A shout like a wail went up and the dance began.

At Samhuin it drove away the dark. Here it was part of it, the flames leaping and dying, making the whole, the cycle of night and day, sun and moon together. The drums beat, the bronze charms jangled, turned to fire themselves. Naked feet beat upon the earth, dancing out the patterns; winding turns, like a river or the tracks through the trees or a pathway into the earth itself.

There is life and death in the Fire-dance. Life in the dancers who are young and strong and fearless – for no one can dance in terror of the flames; and death as the brands sink to the ground and are snuffed or quenched in the wells. And other deaths too; I remembered what I'd heard.

One could no longer see who danced with whom. The goddess stared down, one moment lit with gold and red as blood, the next gone back into the dark. But her quartz eyes watched. Now the dancers were half-men, half-beasts for the masks lived and snorted and snuffed the air, bringing forth the life of the forest and the mountain over which she ruled. Nam Dubh was part of it, taken back to her. The dance sanctified her people and gave them to her dark embrace.

Those I had known, Luth, Dearg, Nar and the rest, leapt out in turn, dancing in their pairs. Their staves clashed and sent scarlet sparks into the sky. People cried aloud and clapped and stamped – the Fire-dance brings good fortune when done with courage.

The pair before me went neat-footed. One saw the supple shift of flames and bodies, the curved backs and arcing flare of light, precisely played. The staves cracked and cracked again and the pair spun away and I stepped forward.

For a moment I hesitated, alone in the dancing space. No one had come with me. Lacking a mask I was naked before them and for a moment the place fell quiet. I stood in my own heavy darkness, beyond them all. Yet I was confused. In this I was a stranger, wandering in Tachga's old tales, in a land where there was no shape or form and where the earth was mist beneath my feet. I waited and felt my senses quiver. The goddess stood above me and then, from her shadow, my partner stepped.

He wore a boar's mask with snout and tusks and his eyes shone through the small round holes. He was blond and ruddy-skinned in the firelight. Under the oil he sweated.

Softly I said, 'Benna?' I'd danced most often with him in practice. I frowned, to try and see. He nodded, his heavy head bowing and lifting once more. Then he brought up his arm and the blazing club swung down in the first movement of the dance.

We danced well together. Fluid as water we traced the steps, well trained and smooth. Above our heads the brands crackled and spat; sparks showered up to the blue-black sky. I saw the boar's head, huge and intent, the shine of his eyes and the human mouth below, with the jutting underlip and crooked teeth.

The brands swirled down and the flames touched my shoulder. I leapt away, half stumbling. The brand cracked down again, almost in my face. Once more I lost my footing. People cried out. The boar's head reared over me, and the cruel mouth grinned.

Then I understood. The half-suspected fear became truth. It was not Benna who danced like a mad thing before me. The old foe had returned, malevolent as ever with his animal cunning. A boar indeed, with his tusks and pig-eyes and cruel, fat-lipped mouth; but a man's hatred lived within his heart and gave him up to murder.

The brand whipped before my eyes. Sparks floated and stung my flesh. I heard myself gasp, stumbling yet again, this time towards the crowd of onlookers.

Murder it would be. The song-maker's words sounded in my ear, remote and cool. 'He oiled himself too well, and so he roasted.' An ugly, agonizing way to go – a death of terror. One I would not quietly face.

I took a breath and lunged forward, throwing up my own brand before me. The flames leapt backwards, smoke billowed before. Then all was fire and roaring flame and as we leapt and cut at each other the drums began to beat once more and the people chant.

It is the nature of a sacrifice to be brought in knowledge and understanding of what is to befall. Even goats and horses in the end know as much. This I had come to ignorant as had the people, yet it was become a sacrifice. The Raven-queen looked on. I fancied she licked her carrion lips.

All the heavy pelt, the dull weight of water I had carried for so long, slipped from me. The flame of my loathing flared up, pure and free. Within my soul was naked as my body; and now – again – the two thought as one.

I was quite cool. Through the heat Arax shimmered. Still he danced but I noted what I had not before – like Benna he was heavy, slowed by his weight of muscle. His mask did not help him either. The eye holes were small. I guessed too that he did not dare unmask.

I turned and ran the length of the clear space of the yard, out of the dancing circle. It gave me room to gather my thoughts. Arax blundered on my heels. I swung my brand low so that he had to jump to save his ankles. At once he was wrong-footed. I swung the brand again and caught his mask. He bellowed and floundered back.

Some pride within me made me cry out to him. 'Arax, let's make a show of it at least!' I would go fine, leaping to the Lady, who liked her meat dead.

Then we began in earnest, in a grim play upon the Fire-dance. The drum beats sounded in our ears, the fire sticks lit before our eyes and hissed and crackled in our hearing. But the people now were quiet.

We fought well, evenly matched since his weight did not here give him advantage. Uffa could be proud. Relentlessly, unspoken, we danced together but with a killing will – each blow too near, each spin too fast and deadly. Under the goddess' eye we danced – the horse-witch's son and the mountain boar.

No one intervened. All watched, straining, caught like flies in amber; Uffa, Mhorged, Gortag, Hakos; and Nemair, proud and upright, with the gold glinting in her hair against the black feathers of her cloak. They stood in the goddess' palm, with no will of their own, only the Dark Lady's pleasing.

Arax grunted. He feinted right. I was tiring and mistook the movement. His brand caught me on the collar bone. I cried out in pain.

I ran back, dazzled and blinded. I fell and twisted and by luck flung up my brand.

I hit him hard. He rolled back, lurching, and fetched up against the goddess' cart. Above us the effigy swayed. The flame light flickered on her eyes and gaping mouth so that she seemed to cry out loud in anger. For a moment she hung there, poised like a carrion crow herself, and then she swung back, rooted to her place.

Someone screamed, a great shriek of agony that ended in a bubbling, choking sound. I turned, my brand falling from my hand. Against the cart Arax stood panting, head hung down, his mask knocked clear from his face.

Through the curling smoke and the flames a figure reeled. His hands were outstretched, his garments soaked with blood. I saw him coming and could not move. Onwards he staggered as if he walked in sleep.

He stopped. His hands groped at the air. Briefly his sight cleared and he knew me. Then his gaze went up to the Raven-queen and in that same moment he coughed. A great gout of blood gushed from his mouth, his hands pawed at his throat and he fell.

I ran forward to him, my grandfather, lying face down upon the earth. No one else was near. They all stood away as if to touch him would bring misfortune; yet he had been sick a good while.

He was very heavy but I dragged him over anyway. He should not lie face down as criminals do. He was still alive and conscious and tried to speak. I wiped away some of the blood, as much as I could, but his mouth was filled with it. I took his hand and his fingers gripped mine. Then he looked up towards the goddess. His mouth quirked, grimacing, his fingers loosened and let mine free. His hand clutched upward, groping at the air, and in his face was fear.

I leant forward, over him, and he looked at me. I saw what was in his eyes and understood; he had no need for words.

The meaning stood plain. I thought, He believes it should be me. For the last time I was his bane, his bitterness, his drink of verjuice. I shrank back and his hand moved again, grasping at my arm. His fingers dug at my flesh as he sought to pull himself up. His mouth worked; through the blood he said, 'Go to her.' Then he began to cough once more, his body flailing, and now there was terror. He cried out, 'I cannot see!' And again, 'Go to her!'

There was nothing to be done, no help for him, but I knelt beside him with his blood spewed all over my face and chest and arms. He lay and panted. Already he'd begun to wander. I took his hand as before and he let it lie in mine for a little; his flesh was cold and blue. Then his wits cleared. He looked up at me and his eyes were like a dog's; but it was not I she called. Yet in that moment I could not tell him so, only I said, 'I'm here.' I think he heard me for his lids twitched. Just at the last he said, 'Arawn,' as sharp as if I'd come in late for supper. Straight after he blinked, and belched a gout of blood, and died.

So he went, my grandfather, in fire and blood and fear; himself the sacrifice, the old, unfit lord, taken by his own Dark Lady; and he went with no say in the matter, and unwillingly, believing in another's calling; and I alone had seen how it was so.

All around there was hush and more fear. Mhorged stood, with the sweat upon his brow freshly broken out and sparkling in the flames; and Cernach, tall and grim, the torc plain about his neck, the Clan-lord, once more anointed in that moment of gushing, blackened blood. Grim though he was, he believed it for so it had always been; yet they stood in ignorance.

Afterwards there was confusion. People began to shout and crowd the body. Someone caught me by the shoulders and pulled me off and after I seem to remember how I stood while he was bundled in a cloak and borne away, and how all around there was more noise and shouting. Half the people I did not recognize for they were Cernach's men from the valley come for the feast.

Soon I was alone. The bonfire burnt still in the yard; it was meant to last till morning. Some of the dancing brands glowed, thrown down anywhere. A few of the lesser folk stood on the edges, looking and whispering since it was a great thing for them. It was cold for it was the dark hour, close to dawn. I had to wrap my arms across my chest, for I wore only the breeches I had danced in. At last I stirred, meaning to leave. As I moved some darker shadow beside the goddess' cart moved also. I paused to look and Gortag slipped out. She hesitated, drawing up her cloak and looking round as if she feared she might be seen. Then she approached the spot where Grandfather had fallen. She knelt and traced a pattern in the dust, only there was blood there also, and then she spat and I realized it was a curse she worked. While she was at it, gold glittered at her throat and in her hair and in the folds of her skirt; she was dressed for the feast. Then she stood and turned to where I was. There was loathing on her face. She had known all along that I was there and I thought, She wished me dead. Then I walked on to the little hut where I'd been shut each night.

I sat then and waited. I knew nothing of the mourning rituals here, though in the marshes the peasants had plunged their own into the waters, weighed down with stones, and let the fishes do the rest. In other places one hears of bodies set up on pallets, open to the sky, for the flesh to rot, until the soul walks free. Or the dead go into ancient barrows, gates to the Underworld, which the gods raised long ago.

I supposed I ought to weep for him yet only little things seemed real, not his death. I watched a spider spinning its morning web and counted the shields on the walls and saw a space in the roof where the turfs had shrunk back with the summer's heat; one does not weep for such. Only I was aware of a great shadow, a burden, waiting to swoop upon my soul, like a huge bird squatting in the rafters. But it stayed off, waiting, and seemed not yet to touch me. Time passed. The hut grew hot. Outside the day was fine. I could smell his blood on me; I had no water to wash it off. Later the women started wailing and kept up a good while, their cries rising and falling till it seemed there'd be no end to it. But at last they finished and shortly after I heard my name called.

I should have shown myself but instead I waited and soon the door swung open. Uffa was there. He said, 'Why didn't you answer?' And then, gently, 'They have prepared the body. You can go to him.'

I looked at him. He seemed distant and small as if seen in polished metal, held a little away. I said, 'I do not want to.' It was the truth – though I had not known it till I spoke. It was an instinct. I had held him dead, yet I wished his death a thing apart from me.

Uffa said, 'But you must, Arawn. It is the custom. His soul will be offended.' He sounded awkward and scared, like a child told of bogeymen.

I said, 'No,' and Uffa opened his mouth, then shrugged and turned away. I suppose he thought he was careful for my grief.

Uffa came twice more, once in the afternoon and once before supper. The second time, when I refused, he asked me why and when I could not tell him, lost patience and shouted at me that I should bring misfortune and my grandfather's ghost to haunt us. At that I threw one of the shields. It struck him and then broke apart against a post. He swore and left, banging tight the door behind.

Again I sat. All my thoughts were in turmoil, half angry, half in grief, so that I did not know my own mind. Still I could not mourn but I thought of the black-clad priests, hopping like crows about the body and I shuddered.

That night there came a noise. Very quietly the bolt was drawn. I was not asleep and roused at once. There was something stealthy in the sound, and the way the door moved open, stopping and starting so that it did not creak.

Someone stepped into the room but I was up already to face who was there.

It was Nemair, dressed in her mourning with a lamp in her hand and a woollen cloak pulled tight around her.

My mouth fell open. Then I said, 'Why are you here?'

She did not answer at once, only turned to set the lamp upon the floor. Then she straightened and looked at me.

She said, 'To tell you that Cernach will not ask you for your pledge. Not now. His priests have warned him. They say the month has passed into its dark half. He will wait until the moon herself has died and is reborn. You have a little time.'

I'd barely thought of this. I shrugged; I had no answer for her. I was ignorant of the priests' lore. Besides, I'd seen for myself how we were in the Lady's hand.

She looked weary, her flesh sunk a little under her cheekbones and shadows about her mouth. But her gaze was direct and clear. She said, 'Won't you go to him?'

I turned away; where Uffa could not drive I'd not be led, quiet to her hand as a silly sheep to the butcher's knife.

After a pause she went on, 'He is quite seemly. They have robed him and covered his face and honoured him.'

She had thought I was afraid of the look of him. I turned back, lifting my chin, and said, 'I wiped away the muck. He drowned in his own slime. It was green and stank. And I saw him choking on it.'

She bit her lip, discomfited. Then she said, 'Still you should go.'

I shook my head and met her gaze.

Her brows moved. She was at a loss. She studied my face but I kept quiet. In truth I do not know why I was so stubborn, only that some fear beat at my mind – not of the grief – and that to see my grandfather might give it shape and that I could not bear.

She said softly, 'Have they taught you nothing? One weeps at the parting yet it is soon over. Rejoice for him, then, as is fitting, that he will walk in the Otherworld. The dead are better off than us. Or are you so glad, rather, that he is gone that you cannot do reverence to his soul?'

'Glad?' That was so far from how I felt that she startled me. Once I would have been. Often, in the marshes, lying bloodied in the stables or the outhouse where he had flung me, I had longed to be free of him. Sometimes I'd even thought how it could be done. Now I added, 'Not of late.'

Still she considered me. She was grave, yet soft also, in her woollen robe and her brown hair loose around her. Her cloak had slipped a little and showed her flesh where she had torn her dress in mourning, all gold and shadows in the lamplight.

My throat burnt, a hard, knotted grief rose in my belly. I saw him again lurching towards me and the touch of his hand and how it had pulled at me. His fingers had been withered at the tips. I remembered how he'd looked and what I could not give him and I held it close and secret by my pride.

She waited. At last I said what I thought was true. 'He would not want me there.'

She said, 'It does not matter. He could curse you from the dead and still you should go. You are of his blood, no matter what there was between you. It is the fitness of the thing and must be done.'

It was the priestess who spoke. Suddenly I was tired out, worn thin as rotted cloth, and as like to tear apart. What had been had been. To peer at a body would change nothing. I was beyond thoughts and feelings, stripped even of the comfort of the pelt. I nodded and she smiled and wrapped her cloak about her.

'Come,' she said.

We went quietly. It was very late; the camp lay quite in darkness but, being summer, there was enough of moon and starlight to make one's way by. We skirted round in the shadow of the wall and on across scrub where the goats were tethered, to my grandfather's hut where they had laid him.

A light burnt within. I paused, wondering if anyone sat beside him; then I thought how Nemair would have warned me. Cautiously I put aside the wicker screen and stepped across the threshold.

The chamber was as he'd left it with its chest still open where he'd sorted through his clothes, and a cup stood on the rug beside the hearth. Even the wine jug had lees left in it.

He lay upon the bed. Nemair had spoken truly; they'd made him fine, as they'd made me fine, with robes of soft wool, though his were worked through with gold. He wore his jewels, and more – a torc of many intertwined strands, his belt, rings on all his fingers and a mask upon his face of sheet gold beaten into shape.

I went and stood by him, looking down. The mask stared up. It did not look like him, for it could have been the face of any man, eyes and nose and mouth, a moustache drooping above the lip, expressionless yet noble – the warrior in his own, fine, bidden death.

He seemed at peace. In death the Carrion-goddess had given back his pride. I went closer, to see the mask more clearly; a gift no doubt from Cernach, and rare. Some other Lord had worn it long ago, laid out for different rites. The work was very clever, shaped by thousands of little knocks and taps; one could see the tiny hollows, left by the hammer-head.

Nothing of my grandfather was there – nothing of his anger and passion, his hatred and fierceness – nothing that I could know and remember. All was smoothed and brightened by that gold. In death he had become what always he had wished to be, no matter how his dying eyes had looked, or how he'd choked on blood and spittle.

These last months he must have known his death was upon him. He could have looked for no more than this – to cloak

238

his bones with glory. Perhaps Nemair was right; weep for the parting but rejoice also for him whole and splendid, striding amid the painted wooden halls and feasting with the heroes. I tried to imagine him and, when I was done, I thought, It was worth it then, Grandfather, to have sold me so. His mask stared back, and held his secrets.

Nemair said, 'Let us do what is right.' She had a knife in her hand. She leant towards me, across the body, and cut a lock of my hair. Her knife was gentler than the shears. Afterwards she laid the offering on his breast.

She said, 'The Dark Lady is Mother to those she takes. See how peaceful he is.'

So he was, wrapped like a child in the Lady's black wings. Yet Gortag had cursed him, even in his death, and in dying he'd known no peace but fought against it, fearful and in pain.

My flesh crept. I felt sunk within myself, made small with fear. The moment passed. His spirit seemed close by, turning his ear to listen at our thoughts. I reached out and Nemair cried aloud and caught at my wrist with her own thin hands; she had not the strength to stop me. I touched the cool gold and raised it.

I do not know what I had thought to see – perhaps the self-same mask repeated in his flesh, or the familiar face of my childhood, grim and angry. Either would have done. I could have said, 'The Raven-queen is kind; he is at peace.' But it was not so.

He looked as he had done when I had left him. There was blood still in his beard and in the corners of his mouth, and his jaw sagged down a little, where they had not bothered to tie it. No one had cared enough to tend him further, making good only what would be seen. Even his eyes had been left staring. Behind the trappings of the warrior was this, an old man, wrecked and ruined.

As an autumn leaf blazes in its glory but crumples to dust in one's hand, so it was with him. In his splendour lay his spoilage – a mockery the worse for being hidden.

It was my mockery also that he had brought me to.

A great quiet came upon me, and a grief that was too deep for tears. It was as if I sank into a wide, dark pool whose waters closed above my head.

I put back the mask. The gold of it was fragile and very thin, yet the face seemed strong and stubborn. His dagger was in his belt. I drew it from its sheath and began to hack at my hair – the penance offering, the Samhuin gift. It fell in clumps of gold upon the golden face. I cut until my head felt light and then I said, 'You have your mourning now.'

He'd gone and I was truly cast adrift. He'd brought me here and left me, thrown like driftwood on a shore to be picked over, claimed and used; and all his splendour, the fine woollen robe, the noble, golden face which was the price of me, I saw for the lie it was, a betrayal of him as I had been betrayed.

I took his hand. His flesh felt like wax and drew no warmth from mine – rather mine grew colder. I thought, Wherever he walks we are both become the fools of others.

Together we had denied each other, even in his own last moments. So I learnt the nature of death – how it shuts the doors upon the living and beat upon those doors as we may, they will not open till it is our turn to pass between them.

There was movement and warm breath behind me. Nemair had come to stand at my shoulder. She said, 'Weep then, for yourself at least.'

His hand was still familiar, the blunt fingers, the hair at the back of his wrists, the spotted, old man's skin. Only the stiffness was new. I said, without turning, 'Weep? Do the Lady's dead expect it?'

'Wouldn't he?'

Now I did turn and saw her pity in the little furrow straight down between her eyebrows and the strained, tight look about her mouth. She said, 'I would have spared you this if I'd been able.'

I said, 'I had to see. And, yes, he'd have me weep and rend my clothes and all the rest of it. Only I cannot. I grieve, but not as he would want it.'

I had begun to tremble. The day had been long and hard and full of dreadful things. She saw and at once came up and wrapped her mantle round me, as if she nursed me still or was my sister. She said, 'I thought that this would help – to see him?' And then, after all, I had to turn my face from her and bite my lip and soon she slipped away and left me with him.

On the fourth morning, just before dawn, they carried him on a bier, up through Nam Dubh, to a high outcrop where the valley fell sheer away. The whole camp followed, both warriors and servants, and farmers from the village below.

Cernach's black-clad priests led the way, and I walked with the other boys, but a little apart, hearing their whispers.

A funeral pyre had been built, a great pile of branches laid upon the barren rock. On to this he was placed and more branches piled on top. His best things were lifted beside him, his earrings and cloak, some arms and a leather shield.

They had taken back the mask which was too old and fine to burn. Lastly they cut the throat of a hound he'd grown fond of and laid it by him with a pork joint and some wine.

Dawn was close. The torches looked less bright and the stars were dimming. The moon had lost its rank, fat look of previous days and was pale and silvery. Softly the women began to sing, crying off his soul.

The old priest, the withered, mocking one, went to stand before the pyre. He held a brand of pine roots that burnt with a red, oily flame. As the sun rose, he would light it. Mhorged and Hakos had covered their faces with their cloaks. Gortag watched on.

The air had freshened; in the valley the birds woke and began to sing. In a moment the sun would show above the mountain and the priest would raise his hand.

The mountains flamed purple and scarlet. The dawn was clear as crystal. His hand swept down. There was a crackle and a fierce, hot gust of burning. The women shrieked aloud, a wild screaming like crows around the battle field. So my grandfather started on his journey from Nam Dubh, and me.

The pyre burnt well. They had soaked it with resin. At noon the priests came to scatter the ashes and collect any pieces of bone. No one knows what they do with those. It is not done to question too carefully their rites.

Chapter Twenty-two

Days passed. No mention was made of what would happen to me. The weather changed; the sun blazed and in the valley the little fields brought forth their harvest. The warriors exercised their mounts and fought mock-battles to keep their mettle up.

It was a time to be all eyes. Whenever I could I watched Cernach. Word had it that he would leave within the month, riding back to his own citadel in the lowlands, with his men and me. Then would come the harvest and the long winter. After the spring sowings the Clans would mass and he would begin the counter-raids into the Horse-people's territories.

I learnt little more of him. What there was seemed obvious – his splendid looks, his strength, his great king's manner – all those he wore to perfection. His men were haughty, but he ruled them and would not let them give offence. In this way the mock-fights in the hall at night, the horse races and the war-cart contests stayed good humoured. Yet he let us see his power and riches; the presents he gave to Mhorged, the jewels and belt buckles and harnesses, and the weapons all said, 'See what I give back, what once I took.'

The month drew to its close. The nights grew chilly. The autumn mists began to rise, drifting in the valley, thickening round the citadel. In the mornings the air was fresh and sharp, nipping at our flesh. I looked to the west and saw the flocks of birds, starling and rook, circling in the sky, and then the wild geese flew and the swans. I had been almost a year at Nam Dubh and my spirit was restless as they were, though my wings were clipped.

I was closely watched. By day I was never alone, kept with the boys as I'd always been, and usually when we worked at arms-play, there would be some stranger looking over the ropes of the training area, or sitting by oiling his sword and spear. Once or twice when I was sent back to the tack room or the armoury and lingered longer than was meant I'd find the fellow waiting by the door. None of them ever spoke; they did not need to. Their duty was obvious in their sleek, sharp bearing and insolent eyes.

Nights they made me safe, still shut in the hut where I would lie, waiting for sleep, with Cumair's last songs in my ears. He was about. Cernach seemed amused by him though it was left to Mhorged to bid him sing. This Cumair did, long lays of heroism and the enemy defeated. His words dripped gore, praising the Raven-tribe and Cernach. Once I could hardly have borne to listen. Now I did; a wise man knows his enemy.

Nam Dubh had bowed her head, supping gratefully the lees that Cernach had brought her, but she had strong wine of her own, the sour brew born out of harder things that had been cast upon her.

Cernach's men grew no less boastful. My uncle's warriors watched with pursed mouths or limped, scowling, from some bout or other. For the most part they took it well, yet there began to be whispers. Any man may fight keenly with a belly full of meat and the best blade always sharpened.

One of the foremost of Cernach's warriors was a man named Tarvos – the Bull. He was like his name, thick-set, hairy with a long moustache and a dark growth over his neck and back and stomach. He was very vain, hung all over with amulets and tokens that jingled and caught the sun as he walked. Moreover, he sported when he could a helmet of bronze with horns stuck out on either side. We boys had had to turn away, with shaking shoulders and hands to our mouths, when he'd first strutted up in that. His arms were the width of small tree trunks, all knotted over with veins, and he could pick up a man and hold him above his head. He did so often, to much applause. One night he held up Uffa.

They had had some falling out – probably for the show of it only – and hurled insults across the hearth fire. Most people were laughing, especially round our side for Tarvos was not quick-witted and Uffa's choicest offerings bounced off his hide like pebbles from a roof. We were still laughing when Tarvos lumbered to his feet, went round the hearth, seized Uffa, who'd squared up to him, and lifted him to the beams.

Cernach's men went mad with cheering. Our own put a good face on, even Uffa who handed over a portion from his own plate to signify the better man; but he left soon after, saying he must see to his horse.

244

In our part of the hall we boys looked on. Across the way the young men of Cernach's people yelled out to us the usual things that boys will say. Then Cernach called them off. I saw him turn, lifting his brows to Mhorged, making light of the scene.

Luth bent forward – he and Dearg and Magh and I sat in our usual place and some of the others had joined us.

He said loudly, 'Bull by name and bull by nature. Great lump of meat and bone.'

There were growls from over the way and some jeering. This time Mhorged shouted at us to behave.

Meanwhile the others muttered with their heads together. They felt Uffa's honour as their own; even I was stirred by it. For a moment I hung back, but I was young. On an instant it seemed as though I had too long been constrained. I nudged Luth.

'Yes,' I said, 'like Cuthros.'

He stared at me. Cuthros was one of our bulls, a shaggy, amiable creature, much given to noise and his own importance.

Within I felt something lift and break, like a wave when you swim against it. I lowered my voice so the others couldn't hear.

'Luth, tomorrow at dawn lift the bolt of my hut. Bring a cloak and what jewels you have, only not too good, and a length of rope. And ride with me.'

He stared at me as if I spoke madly. No doubt I did. Even the idea was wild. He said, 'Arawn . . .' and then his brows drew down and he could not finish.

I knew well enough what he meant. I said, 'I will not slip the leash. Do you think I'd put that on you? I'll swear by anything you want I'll do nothing dishonourable.'

Still he looked doubtful. I looked at him and thought, I've asked too much. But it was for his own choosing. I would not plead.

All at once his own smile flashed. He said, 'At dawn?' and I grinned at him and put out my hand to his.

I was awake and ready dressed by the time he pulled the bolt back. Outside the sky was barely lightening. In the west the stars still burned and the air was damp and fresh.

Luth was there, holding a bundle. He said, 'Where are we going? What do you mean to do?'

'Work,' I said, 'with Cuthros.'

He stared a moment, then looked down at his bundle. He caught his breath and said, 'You fool!' but there was laughter already in his voice and as we slipped from the yard he went first.

We went straight off to the horse corral. The dogs knew us and came up wagging their tails and fawning. If we were seen from the watchtower Luth was unmistakable with his black hair and I kept my hood up, hoping they would take me for Dearg. They might even think we went riding. But, after all, no one cried the challenge.

For the first time in many days I slipped the bridle on Ban. I would have liked to have gentled him a while and make him know me but there was no time. It would wait till after.

When we were mounted I led the way, going up the back way along the track to the ruined citadel. I stopped before we reached it, at the old armoury hut.

Luth met my eyes. 'Come,' I said, 'it will not take long.'

Inside was just as I remembered, dust and the smell of old metal, the broken arms piled anyhow. I thought a moment of the last time I had entered with the sunlight sparkling on the floor and the gift that I'd been given. Then I put it from me. Besides, I thought, my father would not have turned his back on me for this; rather he might have cheered me to it.

The figure of the Red-lord glowered from his corner. I nicked my palm and let fall some drops of blood. We would need his blessing. All this time Luth had watched from the doorway, wide-eyed and hesitating, careful as if we trod in strangers' land.

It took a moment's searching for what I wanted. When I'd found it I threw the thing at Luth to put with his bundle. He held it up to see and began to laugh again before we ran once more to the horses.

This time we turned back again, riding as fast as we dared down the further slopes to the cattle runs.

By now it was full sunrise and the sky was pale blue and clear. In the valley the huts and pens looked hazy, like before a hot day. Already the sun warmed our faces. We took it for an omen.

'Time for breakfast,' I said, 'in the hall.'

'Yes,' said Luth, 'but not for us.'

Cuthros was grazing in his pen. I'd had no time to fetch

him bread or salt but he was docile anyway. He was used to being led away; usually it was to sweeter business.

There was a small byre close by. We got him tied up there, on a short rope so that he could only toss his head a bit and grumble. We were gentle with him and took the work slowly. It was not him we mocked.

When we had finished he looked very fine. I had brought a helmet from the armoury, as like to Tarvos' as might be found, of bronze with a similar fretwork pattern on it, in circles and whorls, and a pair of metal horns jutting up at the sides. This we'd perched between Cuthros' own, right on the poll, and tied it there, scratching his ears the while to soothe him. After that we'd laid Luth's cloak across his back and bound that on and then plaited the charms and trinkets into his thick coat. Like Tarvos, he chimed and tinkled as he walked.

By now poor Cuthros was getting restive and looking sidelong through his hair. It took more doing to lead him out and hold him while we mounted. The horses were skittish, showing their heels in turn to him. He'd begun to low and pull back against his tether.

In the end we got him to walk, crying him on and tugging at the rope, until at last we came to the hillside that looked down upon the Clan-lord's camp.

People were up. The women cooked porridge, the men sprawled in the early sunshine, cleaning tack, or moved about seeing to the horses. Their talk came clear to us on the bright air.

It was a queasy moment. Luth and I exchanged glances. He said, 'All this, for nothing?' We shook our heads at that.

We skirted the pasture, keeping to a line of trees that marked the entrance to a copse. Cuthros was quieter now, wanting only to put his head down and graze. Shortly after we halted again.

Here the ground was more level and the camp much closer so that we no longer looked down on it but glimpsed it through the trees. A woman laughed near by and made some comment on the weather. Her man, who ate at night in the hall, strolled up to lift the lid of the cooking pot. Their tent was just beyond.

We hardly breathed. Already we'd discussed how it should be done and Luth had cut himself a switch. I looked across Cuthros' ridiculous, helmeted head; for a bull he was very like Tarvos, puffing gently through his muzzle. I saw Luth swallow. He was rather pale. Then, all at once, he looked at me and a great smile lit his face. I smiled back, feeling my heart lift. I pulled on Cuthros' rope, Luth raised his hand, and the switch came down with a mighty thwack.

Cuthros bellowed; all of us shot forward and hurtled onwards. Both horses squealed and hit a gallop. I seized my knife and leant across and cut and Luth did the same. Snorting and bucking and all the time tinkling, Cuthros pranced free among the tents. We could see the flying cloak and the charms and mostly the helmet rising and falling as he careered about. Then men were yelling and waving their arms and I lost sight of Luth and Cuthros and had all I could do to guide Ban through the trees and the ropes and the tents. Then I was out, free, beyond where their war-carts were gathered and galloping up on to the hillside. I looked back. People swarmed everywhere, tents lay flattened and all to pieces, breakfast spilt upon the ground. The women had scooped up their children and headed for the trees; men grabbed nets and goads. There were screams and crashes. Then I saw Luth, kicking off a man at his bridle and urging his own pony on. He came up, flat against his pony's neck. It was the last time I paused. We rode together, madly, up on to the open high ground and beyond to the great forest.

Soon we were safe. The only noise was the stir of leaves and birdsong and the horses panting. We flung ourselves off, into bracken, breathing hard. I closed my eyes and opened them on to cool green fronds and sun dapples. Luth moved beside me. I raised myself up to look at him. Our eyes met. He said, 'That helmet!' And suddenly we were laughing till the tears poured, holding our sides and rolling back into the bracken and whenever we stopped, one of us would say, 'The helmet', or, 'Those charms', and Cuthros' reproachful head would rear again and set us off.

Later we were calm. We picked ourselves up and went to check the horses. There was time now to rest my head against Ban's flat cheek and stroke his muzzle. He felt the same as ever, flaring his whiskery nostrils and pushing with his nose.

I turned to find Luth watching. For a moment we regarded each other, all at once wary as foxes, for till this day there had been constraint between us. Nor had we spoken, except in the course of work and just last night, since my grandfather had died.

He said, 'What will happen, do you think, when we get back to the citadel?'

I considered a moment. Then I said, 'Nothing. Cernach will believe it beneath him to make a scene and Mhorged will have to take his lead from him. I suppose he'll shout, but not much else. Uffa will be the one – too proud to show he's welcomed it.'

He was quiet again, though considering all the time as one does at something new, trying to make it out. Then he said, 'Why? Why this, now?'

Not even to myself had I put the matter into words. I had gone flying on the whim, borne like a bird on high wild breezes. Yet there were reasons; and Luth had flown with me.

My heart said, 'Because I am fifteen and they mean to give me to a man who is a murderer and a great lord, to take me to a new place that I have no knowledge of, to live among strangers. I have seen my grandfather lie dead before me, and what was in his face. There is talk of war and battles. Half my nights I lie in fear. I wanted one day – one day – when there was laughter and sunshine and friendship and no darkness to think of. At least I have had that.'

But in the end there was no need to speak this. I met his look and it was enough to tap my head and say, 'Think, Luth,' and see him purse his mouth and after raise his brows and nod.

We pushed the horses on and rode a while in silence. When we reached the lower slopes we could canter again. Afterwards I said, 'This is like before.'

'Yes,' he said, 'I've missed it.'

The horses walked. We had no spears or nets so could not hunt though we skirted the woods, just in among the trees. The hot sun warmed us and the flies buzzed. There was the smell of greenery and plants at the height of their growth, full of sap, just before they turn.

Luth said, 'Have you come back to us?'

Ban shied a little, at a leaf fluttering to the woodland floor. I soothed him a moment. Then I said, 'Perhaps.'

'Before you were . . . No one could reach you.'

'The *badbh* sat at my shoulder. Nemair said so.' I spoke lightly, though my colour had risen. I felt awkward, as though we spoke of something best kept hidden.

He looked serious, legs idle at his pony's side, and rubbed his chin with his thumb as he did when he thought.

'And now?'

I said, 'I grieve, if that's what you mean. Aed was familiar, what I knew – and when I saw him, in that mask, I kept thinking, what would he have been like if Cernach had never come, never disgraced him? If he could have been what he always wished?'

Luth said, 'You are too kind. I think he'd have been what he always was; only you know how that was better than I.'

I kicked Ban on – there were memories that hurt still. The undergrowth rustled at his quarters. I ducked a branch. Then I pulled up again. I said, 'It made me think. There are things I don't understand. I wept for my grandfather, I cut my hair, I mourned for him, yet he was harsh, or cruel, or shouted every day I was with him. Yet I think on him still. He's always there. I think he always will be. But Tachga, who really cared for me, I missed for only a little. And my mother . . I was three when they killed her. Those three years, she must have loved and nursed and watched over me – yet I remember nothing of her, not her voice, or her eyes, or even the colour of her hair. All her care – for what? Does it matter how we are to one another?'

He looked at me and made to speak, then thought again and said, 'We want what we cannot have.' He leant across and slapped at Ban's rump and we cantered a little way, out of the trees to the open hillside. Then we galloped and afterwards laughed together and I thought suddenly how Luth's friendship was like the taste of good, warm bread and how I had missed it.

All day we spent together. At noon we hobbled the ponies and dozed; when we were too hot we swam. The great bare mountainside spread out before us, with its grass and heathers and fissured rock. The sky was a high, dark blue. Larks sang.

At last the sun began to sink; the air turned soft and golden. I'd been half asleep, lying on my front, feeling the sun, and the sweat gather where I rested my head on my arms and under my ribs. Now I sat up and gazed down the slopes. Long shadows lay in the valley.

I went and unhobbled the ponies, leading them back. My head felt strange from too much sun. Luth was asleep.

I nudged him with my foot. He grunted and after a moment sat. I bent and picked up my tunic and put it on.

Luth ran his hands through his hair. He said, 'It's late.'

'Yes. We should go back.'

For a while we were quiet together as we rode. Our laughter seemed fleeting and far away, like birdsong in winter. The ponies trod the little tracks through the heather. The air was still and thick, the colour of honey.

Luth went ahead. I looked at his back and took a breath and said, 'I will not go with Cernach – whatever happens – not as his foster son.' He was the first I'd told.

He reined in and turned so we faced each other. The evening sun glowed, lighting him to gold. A cloud of gnats hung and darted just above his head. Behind, in the distance, the mountains bloomed purple.

He said, 'Does Mhorged know?'

'I think he guesses. I think Cernach guesses, but they've said nothing.'

We had crested the high slopes and had begun the long ride back down into Nam Dubh's valley. The way was familiar, forest and little pastures where the cattle grazed.

I said, 'I do not know when they mean to leave. Every day I wake and wonder, Is this it? And what I shall say and what I shall do. Sometimes I think it would be easier to tell Mhorged, no matter what he did. And if I go with Cernach, what then? There'll be war against the Horse-people. What will he mean me to do?'

'You should have gone when you were able. Run away. I thought so then and I think so now.' He sounded angry, scowling down at his pony's mane, then up at me.

I said, 'Perhaps, but I did not.'

He waited, gathering his thoughts, then asked, 'Is that what they ask of you, to be his foster-son? I did not know. What will you do?'

'Anything but that. He can have what he wants of me. I'll go with him. There'll be no trouble. Not for you. Not for Nam Dubh.'

He was quiet again, then said softly, 'For honour's sake?' The words hung, empty as husks, between us.

I looked at him, seeing his pale, beak-nosed face, the sunlight on black hair. In a year he had grown older, his chin and cheeks more angular, a stubble round his mouth. Soon for him there'd be initiation, the careful, scanty spilling of his blood, the giving of a battle name to bring him clean to manhood.

'Not for mine,' I said.

We walked the horses, and skirted the rim of the mountainside, following the pathway. The horses sweated. My forehead was damp beneath my hair, my shirt stuck round my shoulders and beneath my arms.

I looked along the path. We had come out close to the outcrop where my grandfather's pyre had burned. One could see the stained black earth and some charred sticks and ash that lay there.

I said, 'I should make an offering. This is the first time I've been near, and we've talked of him. Otherwise his ghost might be angry. Uffa would think so.'

It was a little climb, though steep at the end. When we got there and had dismounted, I stood with empty hands and said, 'What can I give?'

Luth said, 'Have you nothing? Here.' He had a token pinned on his pony's cheek piece, a bronze wheel that meant the sun. He held it out.

I took it and threw it over the outcrop and watched it turn and spin and bounce upon the rocks. But it had not been mine and I had no words to fill my heart and mouth.

I turned back to Luth who said, 'He liked fine things.'

Neither of us was fooled. I'd beat a hollow drum. We hung around, not liking to go quite yet, as though my grandfather watched to see what we would do.

At last Luth, who had been thinking and scuffing up the ash, asked, 'At the end, did Aed say nothing to you?' He looked around as he said it.

'He fought his death. It was not easy for him, and he feared it.'

'No more? Not when he died?'

I shook my head. But then I said, 'There was – only not for telling.'

He paused and stared, then snorted. He said, 'I can guess. He'd have flayed you, Arawn, if it suited him, and kept you close for more. Your back's a witness. Remember that.'

I wanted to say 'Hush', for his voice was too loud for this place. Yet I did not know how to answer him. His anger seemed half at me and left me at a loss.

He wiped his brow with his arm and took a breath. He said, 'For once, why make it hard? What about us, who are

252

your friends? Do you think it's easy to see what happens? Doesn't what we feel count?'

If he had struck me I'd have been better prepared. My colour rose. But I managed to keep facing him and said, 'I am my mother's son.'

He swore then, worse than I'd ever heard him, and said, 'What answer's that!'

Shocked, I stared out from the outcrop. The citadel threw its long shadow down the mountain, the walls outlined against the sky. Below the palisade wound round beyond the hillside.

The sun was sinking. The sky was tinged pink and gold and a cool, clear green, like water. My thoughts seemed burnished by the dying rays, catching their last light, made clear and shining by them. I thought, Even at the end I angered Grandfather, denying him what he wanted. And it seemed to me, all at once, that my grandfather would be waiting for me as he used to wait in the farm yard, but with the red-gold rays the colour of blood upon him and the dog-look in his eyes.

Under my heated flesh my blood ran cold. I looked back at Luth and asked, 'What did you mean when you said we always wish for what we cannot have?'

He sighed. He looked young again and uncertain. He said, 'You've lived your life for ghosts. Even now. And all the time I've known you, you've never given in, not once. Only there's nothing bright or fine in it. It's ugly and messy and hurts. It's not what you think, and I hate how it makes me feel.'

Close by someone laughed, a thin, mocking sound that made the horses wheel and start. We had to run to catch the reins. Afterwards we stood and held them, peering for who was there.

We could hear water, the soft gurgle of a stream, running through the heather. Over the rise were the dark shapes of rocks. Amongst them a figure moved swiftly, dipping and stooping as it made its way.

It was dressed in red, a dull, thick colour like an old stain, and its hair was long and dark and streaked right through with grey.

Luth said, 'Gortag.'

She stopped and turned and raised her head. The low sun was behind her, dazzling. Her arm lifted. She threw something down, into the water. I put up my hand to shield my eyes and saw her face, and she smiled at me and beckoned.

All the hairs on my neck had lifted. Luth said, 'No, don't!' But I went forward to her, my uncle's Lady.

She waited by the stream. Her sleeves were wet and the hem of her gown also. 'Ah,' she said, 'the rider with the grey horse that treads the way to the Otherworld. What do you mourn in your heart, my lad?'

I made no answer, only looked to see what she was doing. In both hands she had clasped a fistful of ashes and it was these she scattered into the stream.

'Still proud then. And not yet foresworn.'

I started at that. 'What do you mean?'

She laughed again and bent over the water. The dark powder fell from her hands and some of it floated and some of it drifted in the bright air above like smoke.

'A quiet face, to make a fool of others. A cat purrs with its belly full of feathers. What answer will you make to Cernach, witch-spawn, when he calls to you? The bent head, the humble knee? Not you!'

My very heart grew cold. I made a sign against evil. It seemed as though she'd listened all through the long, hot afternoon to hear what Luth and I had spoken.

I said, 'Mhorged knows, I owe you nothing!'

'No. But what do you owe your grandfather, old Aed, spewing up his life's blood?'

'What's it to you? I saw you curse him!'

'Aye, curse and curse again. That was his lot, and him deserving.'

There was movement behind. I saw her look and her gaze sharpen. Luth rode on his pony to stand beside me.

I asked, 'Why did he deserve it?'

She knelt on the stream's bank and put her hands in the water. The ash washed from them and her sleeves trailed in. The red dye loosened from the cloth and curled like bloody vapour.

She stayed there, crouched upon the ground, and turned her face up to us. All the time the water flowed and took the dye and ash and mixed them and washed them away till there was nothing of them; only the fact of what had been, like her cursing.

I asked again, 'Why?'

She dabbled the water with her fingers, to make patterns. Then she said, 'He was the Lord, the Lord of Nam Dubh. We put the gold mask upon his face, the torc about his neck, but he had no rights to them. He was a coward, a hostage to his own son and his own son's wife.'

Luth said, 'Arawn, come away. I said, don't make it hard. Come away.' He put his hand on Ban's bridle to pull him round.

Her gaze snapped up at him. She lifted her hands and pointed. Her lips drew back to show her teeth. She said, 'Beware the grey horse that carries off the souls of men!'

He let go the reins. He trembled; I could feel him shake. I said, 'It's all right. She's after me.'

She watched us both, slyly, as if to catch us out in whispers. Her head tilted on one side, like a bird's and she dabbled her fingers once more in the water.

She said, sing-song as a tale-teller, 'When he came back here, Roech, with his fair, laughing smile and his quick ways, with his sword and his war-cart and his brave men about him, Aed should have turned him out. He should have cut the clothes from his back, the gold from his fingers, the sword belt from his waist. Then the Dark Lady would have smiled, on him and us.

'Only he would not. Someone else smiled – not at him. Him she hated, but at Roech, and the old man watched. He watched them always, from the doorway of his chamber, across the hall at night. Watched while Roech kissed her and she wrapped her arms around his waist. Watched while they laughed together and he stroked the bright hair from her forehead. Aed knew her for what she was – light and life to Roech, the dark breath, the poison to his people. He knew it and she knew it, seeing him peep from his corners. He should have turned them out but he let them be.'

I said, 'He was not the only one who watched.'

While she had spoken she had played with the water, watching the ripples that flowed in silver and red and gold. Now she smiled up at me, sidelong, with her mouth long and narrow.

'I watched,' she said. 'I watched with my little son held in my arms, born with his twisted leg that made him scream, born when she had come. I watched through the years till her own belly swelled, only her child was not twisted, did not limp, crying, while the others ran about him. I watched and I cursed her and I cursed Aed, for his weakness and his folly, for she bewitched him. Why else would he have let them stay?'

I was silent. I had no answer to it all, only the dark, deep, ignorant sorrow that I had borne throughout my life.

She said, 'Macha was clever. She worked her magic. She gave you to the Horse-queen. You'll bring us no luck. Her curses live on in you. So runs the white horse amongst us. Cernach's a fool to take you. He should have hung you on the trees like any common thief. In this way you owe us. You owe Aed for what your mother did to him and you owe to us for all these years of barrenness and misery.'

Suddenly she no longer jeered. Her mouth no longer spoke her malice nor her eyes their secrets. Instead she cried, with rage and anguish, the hot tears spilling down her face. I stared at her a moment while she crouched on the bank, weeping, with her hands in the red-stained water. And then I turned Ban, riding back down the hillside while the sun sank and all the soul of me seemed filled with its last blinding dazzle.

That night, when Uffa came to lock me in the hut, I said, 'You have no need.'

He gave me a close look under his brows. But I was in favour, because of Cuthros. 'Please,' I said.

Later, back in the familiar warmth of the boys' hut, bedded down in my old corner, hearing Luth softly strum and the others squabble at dice, I began to think.

All evening I'd been in turmoil, fighting with myself. My thoughts had been in chaos, remembering my grandfather, recalling my aunt's bitter words. Now they became clear and ordered, and the bitterness was mine.

It was true my grandfather was cursed. The life we'd lived in the marshlands was not fit for any, least of all the Lord of Nam Dubh. And he was cursed in the worst way of all, a man no longer master of himself. My soul shrank from the thought of his lusting and of her beguiling in secret, with her face turned smiling to my father.

And for myself I was his bane. The Horse-witch's curse lived still in me. I'd seen it in his eyes as he lay dying and I feared it – feared it for Luth and Dearg and Magh, feared it for them all as they talked and laughed and were themselves. 'You owe us,' my aunt had said. Indeed I did. I felt once more

256

the horse-charm worn tight about my waist, and once more, in secret, I wept.

Two days later I got away, on the pretext of some errand. I had made up my mind and rode down into the woods, to where the pool lay quiet and still beneath the overhanging trees.

This day also was bright and fine, the sun slanted, dark gold between the branches, the pool glimmered, turned molten and shadowy by turns.

It was very peaceful. About the banks the reeds whispered, small creatures scuttled unseen but rustling. The air had the tang that tells of autumn fires and smoky evenings and the tale-teller hunched by the cooking pot.

My heart felt full and saddened. I dismounted and drew from my bag the clothes that Mhorged had given me. Solemnly I dressed in them, fine at last. Then I pulled from beneath my cloak the horse-charm and held it up. The sun struck sparks from it; it was no less beautiful by day than by night. It ran in splendour, glittering bronze and gold and copper by turns, taking the colour of the sun and the leaves about it. I thought of the last time I had been here, beaten bloody and desperate half to madness, and of the healing I had found.

Now I must lay bare my soul again, exposed to my enemies, and give up my shield, my talisman. From my heart I prayed, 'Forgive me.'

I looked down into the water. The sun was clouded; the pool was darker now, with little chilly ripples eddying the surface.

For the last time I clutched the Horse-charm tight to me, feeling the metal warm against my body. I thought, I owe him this. I could not take his death upon me. The Dark Lady swooped for him, not me. But I was his bane, his curse. In death may he have peace.

I looked to the half-buried stone, with the running horse upon it. To the Horse-queen I spoke in my mind. 'Free me. Free me from what my mother did. Forsake me now and let me go – though I do not wish it, only know it has to be to pay the debts laid on me. For my honour's sake I go from you. Take this in my place.'

The horse-charm glinted in my palm. My grandfather had brought it from Nam Dubh on the long, shameful journey to the marshes. I understood now why he had done so. It had been my mother's, surely, and in the end he'd lost it or flung it in the mud. I could hardly bear to let it go, yet I must just as I must go with Cernach and take up whatever burden he laid upon me, even to be his son.

In the end my grandfather had bent me to his will, for a debt not of my making.

I raised my head, to judge the throw that was to cast the charm upon the water.

Chapter Twenty-three

My eye caught movement just beyond the pool, at the far bank, in amongst the trees. There was a glint of bright gold, the sombre gleam of iron, and a ruffle of black feathers. A horse snorted.

Someone was there, half hidden by the trees; one had to look to see him. He was tall on his horse, watching unsmiling from pale eyes in a young-old face.

Cernach, the Clan-lord, who had driven in the stake to pin the Horse-queen, brought by who knows what dark knowledge, to see me here in the place my mother made her own.

His own head was up, lean-cheeked, strong-browed and splendid. His gold torc shone. He wore black feathers on a brooch to hold his cloak. The Dark Lady smiled on him, and his style was showy.

Across the water my eyes met his. He was not here by chance. Quite still he stayed, and silent, waiting to see.

In that moment, I thought, So be it, and felt a kind of peace; he could be in no doubt, after. I lifted my arm, to fling the charm.

By my side there was noise, the crash of bushes broken through, wood snapped apart. A boy's voice called sharply, 'Hakos, I've got him!' Someone jumped from behind and seized me and we rolled, struggling together on the ground. Then I was pinned by their weight and someone else stepped forward and trod hard upon my wrist. I stared up, seeing familiar faces and strangers' together; then my palm opened to show what was there.

There was a gaggle of them, our young men and some of Cernach's own. My cousin was there with Ruarch and Maelduin and Sithlann and older ones who'd followed Arax. Cernach's were his rowdy ones, too young for seasoned fighters, yet curious as young wolves and with a nose for blood.

259

I struggled madly, yet all the time I strained to see; but the place behind the leaves was empty and there was nothing to show where the Clan-lord had been. Ruarch moved suddenly, to where I lay pinned. Softly he said, 'Traitor.'

He bent and retrieved the charm and weighed it as if he felt its value. Afterwards he wiped his hand upon his cloak. He said, breathing hard and smiling, 'I told you, Hakos. See for yourself.'

He hauled me up. His hands were spiteful, bruising where they could. Then he seized my hair and wrenched back my head so that I stared full at him.

First the brother, now him. What had been sport had become hatred and more. All this time he must have watched me, sneaking round with his sharp eyes and pinched, waxy face, nosing for the charm.

My cousin said, 'What were you doing?' He was serious, and curious also, honestly so, as though he'd come upon something beyond his understanding.

I shook my head. I would not tell him; I had made up my mind to that. What I did here was not for others to know but between myself and the Lady, like any sacred thing.

He walked away, under the trees, and turned his back as if deep in thought. I felt hot and cold by turns, but strangely saw everything most distinctly, from the young men gathered round, silent and watchful now, to the sunlit ripples on the water, to Ruarch who was pale and so eager his face was filmed with sweat.

My thoughts were distinct too, as clear as if I sat and pondered them in peace. I thought, The Horse-queen has heard my prayer and she has left me and this trouble now is a sign of that. But what is done here is sacrilege.

So surely it was. The horse-charm was no longer mine but hers, and the gods and goddesses are jealous of their own.

For myself, this was my punishment. She'd loosed the bonds that bound me and extracted her own price. But the punishment was just and I should bear it.

Hakos came back towards me. My arms hurt where I was held. I wished it was over and struggled a little despite myself.

He said, 'Let him go.' I stumbled forward but kept upright. Almost he put out a hand to steady me, but stilled it at his side.

His eyes searched mine. He frowned just like Mhorged,

with the crease between his brows. I thought that had we been alone we would have talked. But too many watched and knew the history of this place.

He said, 'Take him back. Let my father and Cernach see him for what he is.'

They bound my wrists with a long length of rope so that I was held like a dog on a leash. Afterwards my cousin said, 'The pack hounds like their sport.' His mouth twisted, but it made no odds. He nodded anyway to Ruarch who mounted Ban and held the rope himself.

The journey back was dreadful. Wherever it was muddy Ruarch put Ban to a canter and I was too shaken to keep up so fell and was dragged along. But he made sure I was not hurt too badly; at rocky places he walked. Still, I was bloody enough and wrecked and ruined; they had me as they wanted, shamed and once more ragged.

There was silence when we came into the yard. People stopped what they were doing and stared. Only the forge rang with the hammer striking the anvil, until someone ran to tell the smith.

I tried as best I could not to show my fear but already was beyond myself. I had been so sure that what I'd meant to do was right that there was no place left for this. I was lost, as though a fog was about me or I wandered the marsh ways far from home.

Hakos cried out, 'Fetch my father!'

Someone cried back at him, 'Sir, he's gone. Off hunting – he and Cernach together.'

Yet Cernach had watched, stern-faced through the leaves, come alone as I had once, to the Lady's place. He had not hunted long.

Someone gave a cry, pushing forward. It was Gortag. I had thought she would be pleased to hear me brought so low, but her face was wild and her eyes like a cornered hare's, scared and going from one to the other of us.

She said, 'What is this?'

Hakos said, 'Not for others' hearing.'

The look of her quietened, as if something long expected had been fulfilled. She said, 'Bring him to my chamber. Fetch your wife.'

I struggled then, for I knew there'd be no mercy. If I'd become a show for others I'd be a fine one. I fought the rope and cursed at Hakos, saying whatever first came into my head. But I spoke wildly and truly the Horse-queen was gone from me, for now he only laughed.

Within her chamber the servant drew tight the wicker screen and bolted the inner door. The room was as mean and dark as Gortag herself. A small fire sputtered in the hearth, a single lamp hung above it. She had no more lit so all about was gloomy as evening. I made out her bed, covered with a wolf-skin, and wall hangings and a worn rug upon the floor. There was a chest by her bed with little pots and boxes stood upon it, for her paint and jewellery, and her spindle cast down upon it with the wool tumbled to the floor.

It had taken several of the young men to bring me in. To them she said, 'Hold him tight.'

They did so and all the time Gortag gazed at me, holding my eyes with her own. Her face was contemptuous but there was a look about her she tried to hide, half rejoicing, half in fear.

'Now,' she said to Hakos, 'tell me of this.'

For an answer he opened his palm and let fall the horse-charm. On the rug it was small, a silver shimmer against the red and black.

She stared down. Her mouth opened and I thought she would cry aloud. Then she mastered herself and said only, 'I know it. It was hers.'

By now Nemair was here. She had entered, ducking under a spear-man's arm, breathing as though she'd run. She'd looked first at Hakos. Then she bent straight after and lifted up the charm. She said, 'Macha's?'

Her eyes met Gortag's; I remembered they were priest-esses together and that is a binding no one undoes. Gortag said, 'The witch's.'

There was silence. Then Hakos laughed. 'Caught in the act, little cousin? How provident that I too went hunting.'

Nemair said to me, 'What did you do?' She gathered her long skirts and came up to me, staring in my face.

I shook my head, 'Nothing to harm.'

Gortag said, 'She wore it always. Once I found her crying over it, though she tried to hide her face from me. She said her father's smith had made it and it reminded her of home. I watched her weeping, and I was glad.'

Nemair said again, 'What did you do?' There was fear in

262

her eyes and her hands clutched tightly at her skirts. Her knuckles were quite white.

I said, 'I worked no harm. I swear it.'

Hakos said, 'He was clad in all his finery. He was at the witch's place where Cernach pinned her horse-maned Lady. The stake was gone and he held the charm above the water.'

Again there was silence.

Then Nemair said, 'The charm is very powerful.' Hakos had it now and was turning it about, frowning down but careful with it as if he looked to see the workmanship.

He asked, 'How long have you had it?'

I wanted only truth. I told him, 'Since we set out to come here. My old nurse gave it me. She thought it would save me from harm.'

He laughed, quick and hard, and said to Nemair, 'Perhaps not so powerful after all.'

Again they paused. I scanned their faces. Each seemed taken within themselves. Then from the yard came a commotion of dogs and voices and horses trampling. Gortag said, 'Mhorged is here.'

We heard his step directly before he thrust back the screen with violence. It rocked and almost fell. He stood before us, with his cloak still hanging from his shoulders and muddy to his thighs. His face was dark with anger but he'd spent its heat. Here it was cold and thinking too.

'What is this?' he said.

For an answer Gortag stepped forward. She took the charm from Hakos and held it before Mhorged. I saw him look and his face change, wondering at first and then wide-eyed, looking back at Gortag. She met his gaze and her chin lifted. Unspoken some message passed between them.

He said, 'Tell me.'

'Hakos came upon him, by the witch's pool, working magic of his own.'

I said, 'It was not so!'

'His own magic, with this, held above the water. Did I not tell you, my lord? Did I not say what was to be?'

He ran his hands through his hair. He looked at me and then at Hakos. He said, 'Was that how it was?'

Hakos nodded. All his easy scorn was quenched, like tasting strong beer after wine with honey.

'Just so, sir.'

I cried out, 'No!'

I was ignored. Mhorged said to Hakos, 'This is your mother's doing. How did you come to be there?'

'Would you not follow the fox-cub, going to seek the vixen? He left this morning. I hunted him like any quarry. One of the boys warned me of the charm and offered to lead me to him. It was not my mother's doing.'

Mhorged came up and the young men stood away. He scanned my face.

'Now you tell.'

I said, 'Sir, I did no wrong. I meant to cast the charm away, only Hakos stopped me. It was for my grandfather's sake, to please his soul and make it right between us.'

Gortag said, 'His grandfather! Aed, whom he hated! What love was there between them?'

Mhorged said softly, 'What love indeed?'

'Some,' I said, 'at the end.'

Gortag looked to Hakos. I saw his look, considering underneath his brows. She said, 'Mhorged, the thing begins again.'

'No,' he said, 'no. Can't you see him as he is? We have taught him and fed him and made him our own.'

Quietly, from where he stood, Hakos said, 'And sold him. Father, the facts are plain.'

'Only what you have said. No more.'

Gortag said, 'There's more. There's this.' Once more she held the charm, twisting on the leather thong. She stared up, breathing into Mhorged's face. 'You see! Here is the truth of it as they have told you. See what he will bring. He carries dark times and trouble and black-tongued curses on him, soft as the down on the night owl's back, just as the Horse-witch did before him. I know, and Nemair knows.'

I could no longer be quiet. I cried out, 'It is not so! I cast the Horse-queen off, for the people. For Luth and Magh and Uffa and for us all! I took heed of you, Aunt, weeping by the water. There was a debt to pay. The charm was to go back to Her. It was an offering and to make my peace.'

Hakos said, 'Nemair, what do you say?'

She was startled, her head lifting, poised as if she questioned what was here. Hakos smiled at her but she looked like a bird caught in a cupped hand. She looked at me and then at Mhorged and I remembered her kindness. Softly she said, 'It is the Horse-queen's business. No matter what, he bears the mark upon him.'

Despairingly I asked, 'What would you have me do? I tried to cut it from me.'

There was silence. Then Mhorged stepped forward and slashed at my bonds with his hunting knife. The rope fell in coils at my feet.

Gortag cried, 'What have you done?' and Hakos said, 'Sir!' Only Nemair was quiet, watching with her great eyes from the shadows.

Mhorged said, 'It is done. Leave him in peace.'

I saw Gortag's face and the fury that she sucked down within till she was like a mould of clay hiding the molten anger.

Cold as clay she spoke. 'Why do you meddle, Mhorged? It is the Lady's business. Cernach would say as much, and his priests.'

Mhorged said, 'I believe the boy.'

'Believe him!'

Wearily he said, 'Hakos is right. We sold him. I brought him here as my nephew and he has been abused and betrayed, not least by me. Whether he is guilty or innocent, I will not try my own guilt further.'

In her anger there was fear. Her voice was harsh with it. She said, 'It is not for you to say. It is not for you to let him go. He has worked against the Dark Lady, as Macha did before him.'

Mhorged said, 'I will not have it start again. It is Hakos's word against his. What would you have me do with him?'

All her face was livid pale. She had no subtlety – only the pale scorching of her hatred. She said, 'Hakos's word and the words of those who saw. If you will give him credence, give him also to the priests. Then it would be done.'

He stared at her, his eyes grown wide and hard. She'd have soon as fashioned iron with her bare hands as him then. He said, 'You would do that? Think on this. At the least he is Cernach's hostage against the Horse-people. He is the price of our honour. Without him we have nothing to show our fealty.'

Nemair spoke. Of them all she was quiet, and deep like still, cool water. 'Do you think Cernach would stand against the priesthood's wishes? And you have proved your loyalty and made your penance. He would ask no more of you.'

Mhorged shook his head, like a great bear in pain. 'No,' he said. 'No. He is my brother's son.'

After he did not look at them, but rubbed his fingers over his brow. They held the pause. Only the young men shifted on their feet and glanced at one another.

Gortag stepped forward. She caught his wrist to pull it from his face. When she spoke it was as though she scoured the flesh from him to show the secrets of his bones.

Slowly she spoke, and carefully, as if she repeated something held long in her heart and mind.

'Your brother's son? Lucky for you he has his mother's face, for who can tell who his father was – the husband, the father or the brother?'

The flesh crept on my bones, bile rose within my throat. Shadows of old wickedness coiled about us.

Close by I heard Nemair draw a shuddering breath. Mhorged had paled. He said, 'You talk of unholy things. You shame me more than I can bear.' He looked at her as if she was some stranger, sick with plague who stretched her hand to touch him.

Then he said, 'I lay this on you: that if you work him harm or spill one drop of his blood, then it is you I will curse, by the Dark Lady, and you who will face the priests! And I tell you this too – my brother came warm from his marriage bed while I came cold from mine.'

Now the silence was deeper, like a great urn of brittle clay, hollow and dark within. Yet into it someone moved.

Cernach stepped across the threshold. No one had heard him come. He had men with him, but he gestured them back. He said, 'It is time for me to speak.'

Like Nemair he was quiet about it. He said, 'Gortag is right. He should be given to the priests and tested. This is a thing between the gods and we should not deny them what is theirs by right. If he is innocent there is nothing to fear; if guilty, then it is right to root out rotten stock.'

My mouth was dry. I said, 'You saw! You saw what I did there!'

'One sees and one interprets. But we are human. It is the gods who know what is in men's minds and for them to make it plain.'

He snapped his fingers and gestured. I found myself bundled out. In the yard the priests were waiting; he must have summoned them already. The old one was near to rubbing his hands as if the thing were done.

All of me felt shrunk in fear. I no longer struggled. Part of

266

me thought, He is right. At least this way we know the Lady's will. But I did not trust the priests, hopping and straggling around me.

Within the yard the goddess' cart still stood, as it had since the Fire-dance. Perhaps they thought it unlucky to move it until they'd had some sign. They hauled me on it and bound me to the pole so that I was tight against the wooden body and above me her face looked out, stern with her pebble eyes and crimson paint.

The drums began to beat. The gates were opened. In a little while the people arrived, up from the valley, with faces of fear and wonder. They obeyed the old call, to worship and venerate and wait the Lady's pleasure. Twelve years had passed since they had heard it. Cernach's men were there, hard and stubborn, and ours gathered too, whispering and with an old expectancy on their faces.

The blood roared in my head. My own heartbeats shook me. I thought, I danced for her in the Fire-dance. I gave the best that I was able.

The drums pounded. Above the sun burnt in a hot sky. The valley stretched away to the dark forest. The wood of the effigy felt baked and dead and old.

The old priest stepped forward into the space before the god-cart. In his hand, fluttering, he held a raven; not caught from the wild but bred for the rites. He had too a knife of gold. Arms outstretched he called upon the goddess, naming her with her many names. The raven struggled; I pulled too, against my bonds. We both were frightened, and ignorant of what would be.

He raised the knife, meaning to slash the raven's throat. I remembered him lifting the brand to set alight Aed's pyre. The raven shrieked, curving its neck and pecking at his wrist. All the time its wings beat.

I stared out at them, at their faces lifted to see, at their quiet, at their fear and wonderment.

Into the yard space someone walked, assured in her raven robes, the gold bindings in her hair. She had dressed herself on purpose in her best. She walked to where the old priest stood and said, 'I will do it.'

The old man backed off, hissing; it was plain this was a feud between them of old standing. Yet she faced him out and, in a moment, she took from him the raven and the knife.

She was very calm, her face set and thinking. She cut the

raven's throat and sprinkled the blood upon the ground before the waggon. Then she plucked out the feathers and strewed them also. Finally she pulled apart the carcase and laid the flesh in pieces, scattered round. All this she did in silence.

She approached the waggon and climbed into it. Her hands were red with the raven's blood, up to the wrists. I faced her and she came up, so close she brushed my bonds, and placed the horse-charm round my neck.

Quietly, on a breath, she said, 'Keep silent. Whatever comes, don't make a noise.' She sweated and her hands trembled. Then she climbed down before the people and spread her cloak and sat in the space before the waggon, with the raven's blood and the gobbets of flesh about her.

The sun climbed in the sky. The day grew hotter. I leant against the post, feeling my face burn and my mouth grow sore. The bonds cut my wrists; the sun was so bright that colours looked dark beside it and when I closed my eyes there was red behind my lids.

The raven blood dried black upon the ground and the flesh began to stink. Already other birds wheeled in the sky, more ravens and crows; the carrion birds. The priests looked up and murmured amongst themselves.

With a soft thump a raven landed in the yard. It walked, stiff-legged, its eye bright and knowing. Then it bent and pecked at the lump of meat. Nemair never moved, only sat with her own knowing on her, in her silence. More ravens came and also walked and pecked and squabbled. So they came to the pastures, if an animal was sick or dying.

The worst was not knowing. I had no sense of the Lady, no sense of her dark hand guiding; I was conscious only of the heat and the sun and the stink of dead flesh – and my fear of what would happen.

There was a flutter close by. One of the birds perched on the side of the waggon. It cocked its head, wicked-eyed, and hopped nearer.

In the yard was silence as if they took a breath at once. The bird paused, then tidied the feathers at its breast. Again it looked. The horse-charm with the light flashing on it had caught its eye; these birds love bright things.

Some more hopped up, each tilting its head and looking as if to say, 'What have we here?'

Down below Nemair had raised her own head; she stared

up, straining. The sun burnt so that the black of her cloak looked darker still against the pale mud of the yard. Above the sky was huge and empty.

The birds were very close. Their eyes looked dark and wise, like a snake's, with knowledge not known to men. If I had been free I would have waved my arms to scatter them. But I was tied fast against the pole. Their beaks were long and strong and bloodied where they had pecked the meat.

One fluttered to my shoulder. Its strong wings beat a moment, to finds its balance, the feathers against my ear. Its face peered into mine. I thought, My eyes!

Nemair had said to make no sound. She was the priestess; I was bound by that. But I had to close my throat against the cry that rose there. The ravens like bright things, so had I thought in my innocence; and on the battle field they pluck at whatever gleams and glistens; and if one has not the means or strength to drive them off, they cluster and wreak their carnage on him.

I closed my eyes. Behind my lids the red flowed and ebbed for my face was turned to the sun. I heard the soft thud of the birds about the waggon and smelt the blood in the yard and on them. On my shoulder the bird's feet caught in the cloth of my tunic and scratched.

I could not pray; still I had no sense of the goddess' presence and I was not hers to hear. I knew only the horror and fear of this, of knowing I could not help myself nor even take with honour what was laid upon me. There were only the long, dirty beaks and the scratching feet and the feel of the feathers.

There seemed to come a pause. There was no telling how long they'd hopped around me. Then I felt a sharp tug at my neck, where one pulled at the horse-charm, and another as they quarrelled and beat their wings.

I had to open my eyes then, straining back against the post. There was a dazzle of sunlight and black wings filling the space in front of me. Then the birds parted and I saw Nemair stood now, with her own eyes wide and her face stark with watching. The birds fluttered and beat and she was lost and then, quite suddenly, there was great cawing and birds winged into the air and wheeled and were gone, their dark shapes rising on their tattered wings as they soared and then plunged into the valley below.

Nemair stood in the yard. Behind her the people clustered,

kept back by their fear. Only Cernach waited aside, looking on, but I could not see his face.

One of the priests hopped up. He said, 'It is done,' with no good humour. Nemair nodded; she seemed too worn to speak and the priest mounted the waggon and cut my bonds. He was a straggly little man, as they all seemed. I wondered how they held such power.

I managed to get down and even to leap from the side though I was shaking all over. Already people were drifting away. I wondered what would have happened if I'd been left eyeless. But I did not like to think of that and wanted only to find myself a quiet place to go and rest. I was sore and shaken and my thoughts were everywhere. I wished I could speak to Nemair, but already she was gone.

That night I lay in the hut with the cold of an autumn night around me and a greater cold on my spirit. Towards dawn I huddled my cloak around me and stirred up the embers of the fire and tried to sleep; I think I dozed a little. Soon though I was awake again with the rotting shields looming down at me and the worn spears and swords rusting on the walls. I felt hopeless and wrung out – all the soul of me destroyed and held to wrong account.

I wondered if Mhorged believed I had worked no harm, or if he had released me only for his honour's sake. I wondered too about him and my mother though that was a dangerous path to tread. My head ached with it all; sleep seemed distant as the moon.

Then, as before, came the sound of the screen being lifted back, with the same stealth and care. I thought, Nemair, or Luth, and my heart lightened. I felt at least they would listen. I leant to stir up the fire again and then raised my head in welcome. But it was neither of those two who stood there.

Gortag said, 'There you have him.'

And Cumair said, 'So I have.'

I sprang to my feet. I could not think what to say, only looked from face to face. I saw Cumair, thoughtful as if he gazed on the spring colts, and Gortag as if she sold one. So early, then, I guessed.

My breath choked in my throat. I lurched away, till the wall was at my back.

Cumair said, 'He knows.'

For answer Gortag lifted her brows. Here, before us both,

she played the great lady; but her mouth was like a snake's, stretched thin – the great lady who slips poison in the guest-cup.

She said, 'Get it done.'

Under his fat, Cumair had muscle. He had held me before, lingeringly, like something bad that clutches and grips. I had no knife to ward him off, though I would have used one on him if I could. In the confines of the hut he was too large to dodge or trip but I tried anyway. We scuffled against the wall and I got away from him once but he caught me again and held me with his arm around my neck, pulling me tight against him.

Gortag slipped beside us, staring at me, her eyes like hollows in her face, her mouth with its same mirthless curve.

She said, 'What do you fear, Arawn? That I will kill you?'

I could not answer her, only tried not to writhe like a fish in Cumair's grasp. I had some pride still.

From under her cloak she pulled out a flask, of bronze with a raised pattern round the rim.

To Cumair she said, 'He is yours. I am held to a swearing. But take him away from here and do as you will with him, only let me not know. While he is here there is no peace for me and the shadow of the Horse-witch looms on our walls. Mhorged will not be told and so I do this, for our people, and for myself.'

The grip on my neck tightened. I gasped and choked. She reached and grasped my hair, wrenching back my head. Cumair squeezed tighter and as I gasped again she tilted the flask and slowly, drop by drop, poured the liquid held there down my throat.

They let me go. Cumair watched me with a merchant's eyes, considering. Gortag's look was far away and empty. I thought, She sought to savour this, but the taste of it is dust. Then my sight began to blacken, the bright shields on the walls swung and the floor went from below my feet. Afterwards there was only the silence and the long, long dark.

271

Chapter Twenty-four

There were spots of light, warm on my face, and jolting, and
the rumble of wheels. I opened my eyes and blinked,
dazzled, and opened them again. Above curved a low roof
of yellow hides, laced together, supported on hazel struts,
and the light spots were sun, shining through the lace
holes.

The rumbling went on, and the jolting. I lay in a cart or
waggon, quite large and enclosed. The movement hurt. My
head ached as though it had been struck and my mouth tasted
foul and dry as old bones. All about was the stink of
unwashed clothes and that close, animal smell of tanned
leather. I tried to ease myself and found I was bound. There
was rope knotted about my wrists and an iron ring about my
neck, with a chain from it, stapled into the waggon floor.
Though thick still in my wits, I remembered enough to know
I had been sold. First Cernach, now Cumair, I thought, and
something in me laughed, hard and bitter.

A while later the cart halted. I heard the creak of the
harness and the sound of a heavy body, stepping down. I
drew close against the wooden side, as much as I was able,
and waited.

There was a moment while he untied the hide flaps. As he
pushed them back I glimpsed outside trees and undergrowth
and bright green grass in a clearing, then the opening
darkened as Cumair climbed in.

He was the same as always, like a fat, greasy bird with
gorgeous, dirty plumage and that sweetish stranger's odour.
He eyed me up and already my flesh shrank from him; I had a
fear in me that I could not put a name to, since he had caught
my arm that night in the hall. He saw me flinch – I was too
weak from the drug to hide it – and his eyes went narrow in
thought.

'Well,' he said at last, 'what's come my way?'

He reached forward and pulled at the knot round my

wrists. It was strongly tied and held. He'd made sure of the prize at least. Then he tested the chain, looking sideways at me all the while and jiggling it up and down. He mocked but there was nothing I could do; only press against the wooden strut and watch him.

At last he left off and stretched through the opening to bring in a water-skin and some bread and a bucket.

'Stop looking at me,' he said, 'with those great eyes. You'd better drink, and eat something. It'll stop you being sick. Don't die on me, lad. I've plans for you.'

He came back later in the day. By then I was feeling better and determined to face him out. He squatted down, grinning, and once more looked me over. Something within him was coarse and greedy, like a man at a feast who keeps piling up his bowl and never sees the bottom. This time he was more blatant. Almost he licked his lips. He put out his hand and lifted a lock of my hair, running it through his fingers as a merchant does fine thread. At this I could not be still but pulled back, trying to fling away from him, and he smiled and in a moment tugged, as Gortag once had tugged, to bring me close and hurt as much as he was able.

My breath choked in my throat. His fingers were about my head, strong and thick and mobile. There was coarse black hair growing on his wrists. I felt his breath on my face, coming quick and hard, and saw too close his broad, flared nostrils and the bluish folds of flesh beneath his chin. His narrow gaze stripped me naked, seeing every weakness, every ignorance, and he let me know it and enjoyed that most of all.

I'd been a year in the boys' hall, listening to talk of all kinds. There were customs I'd heard of, but never known or even thought such things to be. The most I'd done was tease the peasant girls. But I thought, cold as if I'd understood forever, If he dishonours me, I will kill him. I meant it, as a vow.

He met my look and this time I did not shy. We measured each other as enemies. Then a look of sheer, black, bad temper crossed his face. He raised his hand and struck me, open-palmed, across my cheek. 'Well then,' he said, 'you'll know who's master here.'

For several days he hardly spoke to me and I lay low. At first I was ill and sleepy from the drug and always thirsty. I wanted only water and for the chain to be off. Then, when the sickness had passed, my thoughts seemed worse. I hardly dared think of what might be. I had no surety, no talisman, no hope of any god to guide my path. I wondered if my uncle would look for me or Cernach mount a hunt; but it seemed also that I had a memory, dark as a dream, of lying somewhere before this cart. Later I found that this was true. Cumair had kept me hidden in some place my aunt had known, a pit or hollow on the hillside, carried there so the dogs would have no scent. For several days he went innocent about Nam Dubh. When he had left his cart was empty and no one thought to follow and see it filled.

The horror of it struck me. I was helpless. Cumair was no warrior – I had no understanding of how to fight such a one as this. Fighting hand to hand one can always put up a good show. Here, I was lost, like a wild cat shut in a cage. Snarl and claw as I may, the cage stood fast, hot and thick under its leather canopy.

The second night he sang. Earlier he had tied back the flaps to let in some air and for me to see out; not, I think, from kindness but from cunning. He baited the trap before he sprang it.

By now I was quite desperate. To be in his presence all day was bad enough but more than anything I hated the constraint. I loathed the feel of the rope around my wrist that he would not loosen, the feeling of being forever shut up within the waggon. I was sick of the smell and the close warmth, the wooden floor and the hide covering. Worse was the iron hoop round my neck – the slave ring – and the chain that held me fast.

Now, huddled in my corner, I saw again the sky, soft and starry, and the big, low moon and the dark trees, still in leaf. The night air was cool; he'd lit a fire, bright and crackling, and put on a pot of meat to cook. The old horse grazed quietly, just beyond.

Cumair sat with his back to me, facing the fire. He plucked at a harp, just a few notes over, trying a phrase first one way, then another.

Afterwards he paused and stirred the pot and poked at the fire beneath. I could smell the stew, with herbs in. When he had done that, he took up the harp again and sang.

The song was familiar, one he'd sung often in Nam Dubh; not of war or of love but telling of a tribesman far from home.

An old trick, so obvious one would hardly credit it; only it cast its spell like any charm, woven and shaped into the night air, the notes sweet and sad, heavy with the traveller's longing.

I could not bear it. The rich voice soared and curled its notes to the stars and the moon, singing of love and cattle raids and hillsides and seashores. I'd heard it all, over and over, in the hall at Nam Dubh but now there was within me such a hard, raw longing that it tore at my soul as a dog will tear flesh from bone.

That night I went out of myself, lost to reason, pulling and pulling at the iron collar, twisting and turning within it to try and work it loose. By dawn I had opened galls upon my neck and lay exhausted in a heap on the floor to sleep.

That day Cumair halted the cart once more and came back. He stood over me, looking thoughtful.

He said, 'We'd better talk, you and I.'

I looked away, through the opening in the hides, where I could see thick-pressed trees. The chain clinked as I moved. Today we rode through forest.

He grunted, squatting down. 'Here.' He held out the water-skin, shaking it gently to sound the liquid within. There was enough give in the rope that bound me for me to stretch out my hands for it. I did so cautiously.

He said, speaking quietly, 'Does it come hard to take from such as me?'

I made no answer, only pulled out the stopper with my teeth and drank as deep as I was able.

'Aye,' he said, 'you don't despise what I can give you now. I've watched you and your kind with your fine ways – the fighters, the men with swords and shields, thinking how they're the best. Our sort, we have our pride but we end up all the same, squatting at your feet with a fancy piece of wood and gut that can't be tuned. And now, my lad, you're brought to this. Who would have thought it? Cumair the slave-owner.'

I had stopped drinking; the water at once soured as if he'd scooped it from a ditch. He reached out and took back the skin.

'Yes,' he went on, 'I've seen you, all sneers and know-how, though Gortag had your measure. Still, you're a good-looking lad. You'll bring the goods in. You'll be fine and trinket hung as any when you have to.'

He was near again. I moved on instinct, kicking out at him as I'd have kicked a snake.

Yet for all his bulk he was nimble; there was muscle under his fat and here, in the daylight, he looked less oiled and flabby. There was an edge to him, a masculinity I'd not seen before. And an anger, hidden at Nam Dubh, hidden from us all, till now.

'Ah, no,' he said, 'don't take me for a fool. I know first chance you get you'd slit my throat for me and not think twice about it. But you'll take from me because you have to.'

The rope was tight about my wrists. The chain was fast as ever. I was caught surely as a mountain pony in the spring herding. Something in me said, Be calm. And think.

I held very still. He raised his brows, a sleek, oily little man tricked up in his gaudy robes.

'There's another way,' he said.

Once more he sat, arranging his dirty robes around him with care. He had style about him, one had to give him that.

He eyed me again, cocking his head. 'Now, use your ears and save your temper for those that deserve it. And don't go edging away like that. I'll not hurt you. I reckon I've evened the score with interest. Ah, no you don't!' Once more I had kicked out at him. He lifted the chain and pulled the collar tight against my sore neck and afterwards raised his brows.

After a pause he said, 'We can go on like this for as long as we have to, but neither of us will be easy and in the end it will be worse for you. I told you there was another way. Both of us, we're outcasts, you and I. People are never sure of me. They know I've a gift, but they don't trust it. I walk too near the gods with song.'

I spat at that, accurately, and faced him out.

He wiped at his robe and went on calmly, 'Oh, I can talk to kings, lad, and they will listen. But as for you – you know better than I. They say you're cursed; I suppose for them you are. But not, perhaps, for others.'

For a moment he was busy, cleaning under his nails, but he eyed me all the same, peering sideways.

'Your own people. Your mother's people. What would they make of you, I wonder?'

Now I was silent; he had me listening after all. He paused, baiting. Like a fool I rose to it, pulling at the chain. He waited till I was done and sat once more, with my head resting on my arms, panting and worn out.

This time he did not touch me. 'Oh,' he said, 'it's a troubled, stormy soul, flying like a gull against the strong winds, the salt spray.' He crooned the words as if to a weeping child.

'Be easy, be easy. The rocks are there. Batter yourself to pieces if you must, but I think you've had enough of that. Besides, I don't like to see fine things broken.'

I hated the quiet, melodic words as much as I had the touch of him, but he had me quiet and crouched against the planks.

He said, 'I'll take you back, lad, take you back to where they came from, to the shores and the islands and the stormy seas. And if they bid a fair price for you, why they can have you. And in the meantime, serve me, Arawn. I want no thoughts of knives and rope and a cold, midnight death. Cursed you may be, but don't bring me to that, not old Cumair. I've other paths to tread.'

It was very quiet between us. I felt the throb of my blood, squeezed by the rope, and the ache in my head. Outside the trees rustled and the air was clean and mild and smelt of autumn sunshine. And there was Cumair, squatting like a demon, with the shine of sweat on his face and the pock marks in his skin and the oily beard close cut about his chin. I thought, It should not be like this, for it seemed as if he offered me a dream, long sought for, that should be brought in honour and gold and bright laughter, not tainted with his squalor.

'What gods do you serve, Cumair?' I asked him.

He smiled and tapped his nose and then at last I nodded and held out my hands and he cut the ropes and freed me.

We were together half a year; the dark half, when the sun sleeps and all the world's growing things die into the earth. There are many things I remember of that time. Samhuin we spent, not in some hall, but out in the mountains with Cumair singing wildly half the night, strange, ugly songs he said were for his gods. In the end I hid in the waggon, scared senseless at what he might conjure. After came my birth month, cold with rain and mist that got into one's bones and made them ache. But all the time we went on, with him singing at dun and farmstead and sometimes a hall with a chieftain and his men. There could be gold and food certainly and often, for him, a girl to lie with after, though he took his other, secret pleasures when he could. Perhaps for me also, some slim shadow slipping beneath my coverlet, bringing her own warmth and comfort. Once or twice it had been so, for servants take their pleasures where they can. No one thinks worse of them for, in the years to come, an extra pair of hands is always welcome, no matter how begot.

When the snows got bad we had to overwinter. There was a place at the edge of the moors that took us in. Cumair sang and put peat on the fire and worked all day at his new harp. He gave me to them for what work they could have from me while we were there. The farmer was a brute to man and beast and best forgotten; but his wife used to slip me an extra barley cake sometimes and make sure the fire was made up for the night.

It was a strange time, a fallow time, but within the earth the root curls and the leaf wakens. So, all that winter, it was with me.

Cumair was cunning. There was not a farmhouse or hall or dun that we passed by that was not lighter of some gold or bread or a goose by the time we'd done. Fat and greasy though he was, he could charm the women – not by pressing his attentions on them but by telling them what they wished to hear. Usually he cast their fortunes – as if for a favour – as he had in the hall at Nam Dubh; and he had a gift for it. He studied folk, since he lived by his wits, and had grown shrewd on it, and he had a way with words for such was his calling.

In singing he gave honest measure; it was his pride and even he would not deal short in that. He turned his songs over and over in his mind and prayed to his own gods that his gift might stay true. Plainly they heard him. It was in other things he cheated.

Always he had other finery beyond what he earnt from singing – a decent ring or an armband or a piece of clothing. At first I thought he stole; there were times when he sent me back for an extra duck or goose for if I scattered feathers enough, who was to say that it was not the fox who'd got it? But when I had the sense to use my eyes and ears I realized that there were places we reached where he was known and welcomed. Often he was taken aside and spent a while in talk with the chief or headman. I thought then how Cumair listened to everything, knew much of who would treaty with whom, or planned to raid or make marriages with. I guessed where he got his prizes from.

So we went on together and I watched him, half laughing sometimes to see him at work, at other times moved to the sore, raging longing that I dared not think too deeply on. I longed to be free but never dared, at first through fear since he was as handy with his fists as ever my grandfather had been, and then because I began to believe that one day truly he might take me back to my mother's people. Once I thought that, I was lost to him, looking down every track and beyond every homestead for what might lie there.

The sun sank and died and was reborn. The weather grew milder and then cold again but at last the first flowers shone within the snow. Then came another night when Cumair was to sing. By now I knew what was expected – that his cloak be brushed and shaken out, his boots scrubbed clean of mud, all his trinkets burnished. Throughout the day he had been fussing, going over his best songs, drinking wine weakened with water and sweetened with honey. Now it was almost time and I held the mirror before him so he could peer into the polished depths and draw a line of black around his eyes and whorls of red upon his cheeks.

I too was on edge though I could not have told why. But we had come that day to a sea-settlement, perched about the cliffs, with a broad causeway down to a harbour. The swish and hush of the sea was in my ears and the scream of the gulls. The noise seemed to echo in my head so that I was always hearing it behind the sound of talk and work.

Someone drew back the curtain – a young man, very respectful. 'Sir . . .'

It was time. Cumair swung his cloak about him, green with silver worked at the hems, a gift from an old chief holed in his lair like a grizzled wolf, puffed out his chest and walked, magnificently, from the chamber.

A little later, full for the first time in days with meat and bread and beer, I watched him. He was good, as I'd always known him to be, at first sitting easily at the special place reserved for those who sing or tell their tales. He was offered food, some white fish stewed in milk and sea-weed, and wine. He was abstemious. Later he'd eat with the best of them, but for now he knew what he was about – few better.

At my side the other servants chattered, excited at what they were to hear. We were sitting at the end of the hall nearest to the door where the draughts were, but no one complained. We had a stew-pot to ourselves.

I looked around. There were no warriors here. These were fishermen and traders, nets on the walls and barrels and boxes stacked round the room. All that were familiar were the gaming boards and the groups of women, chatting and spinning or suckling their babes. Even the talk was different, conversations growled out about tides and weather; they talked of boats as you or I would a horse – how she handled and rode.

Cumair was talking, head bent, speaking quietly to a man who'd come up to the hearth. They were a while but when they had finished both smiled at one another.

Now he stood and opened his arms in that familiar, flamboyant gesture. The hall grew hushed. The head-man, not quite used to this, was anxious to seem composed and glared at any who still spoke. Cumair picked up his harp and began to sing.

Later, when he only strummed and most were half asleep, someone said quietly in my ear, 'What's he like then, when he's not singing?'

It was a boy who spoke, younger than I and well dressed with a woollen cloak of good weave and stout boots. Those days I noticed boots again.

I said, 'A liar, a cheat and a thief. But he's good at what he does.'

He looked uncertain, then smiled as if he took it for a joke. 'And as a master?'

I shrugged. 'He knows what he wants, and how to get me to do it.'

He smiled again, and then his look sobered. He was the sort to share confidences, and eager to be kind to those he thought less fortunate. He said, 'I work. I work on the boats. Sometimes I hate it, if it's rough or raining. I saw a man drown once, falling overboard. But I am free. The boats are my father's.'

Cumair's voice soared again. People were grinning like fools. Nothing was new after all. I put my head in my hands suddenly. I was very tired. I wished it was over and quiet so I could find somewhere to sleep.

The boy looked anxious. He said, 'Are you ill? I hope not. Your master's taken passage on my father's ship tomorrow, over to the islands. He won't take you if you're ill.'

I sat up and shook the hair from my eyes. I said, 'Are there islands?'

281

He nodded. 'My father trades with them – the people work in metal, beautiful stuff, all wrought up. He brings them the ore, bronze and iron in great long ingots – and wax for the moulds, and honey, and sometimes wine. He sells on what they make. There's a market for it everywhere, especially south.'

He smirked, all at once, and leant forward. 'My father says they're good to trade with because they have to take what they're given – stuck all the way out there. But he says they were rich once and quite powerful. Some great lord defeated them. I can't remember what he was called.'

I said, 'Cernach. His name was Cernach.'

Chapter Twenty-five

The shore was long and flat, the tide far out and the sky low and grey above us. In the distance, only just darker than the sea itself was a land mass, an island. We waited to board the trader's boat that was to take us over.

It was there, moored out in the channel, a sturdy, broad-bottomed craft that looked as workmanlike as a good pony. Even now the master, the boy's father who had spoken with Cumair, was on board checking his cargo of ore and wax and honey. It would be lashed in the hold, under skins and in barrels.

We squatted on the shore. The wind was in our faces, blowing hard off the sea. There was nowhere to shelter, for the bay was flat and sandy, without rocks, stretching all around, rippled where the tide had been. Yet I'd have had none had there been any. The air tasted good, clean and cold. The sea birds swooped and screamed and Cumair huddled in his cloak. For all his stillness, he watched, as he always did, with the sharp, animal look under his lids, at the boat, at the sea and at the islands in the distance.

They sent the curragh for us, skimming like a round, brown bird. But the feel was familiar, from the marshland days, a fragile balancing upon the water. A crewman rowed us over and when we reached the boat I helped Cumair aboard, clambering over kegs and ropes and oiled cloth. Cumair cursed at the bobbing and the master showed his teeth in a grin and shouted back over his shoulder at his men.

Soon after came the rattle of the anchor chain. We watched as the leather sails filled, and the boat grew busy with shouts and the masts creaking and business all around.

Later the master came to talk. He was a young man still, though already salt-weathered by his trade. His lad, who did not after all seem to do much work, hung round with an open mouth and ears. They both seemed glad of conversation and curious, though the master had the manners or sense to try to hide it, at first asking Cumair only if he had travelled to the isles before.

Cumair shook his head so that his earrings glittered; one smelt the oil in his hair, amber-scented, given by another wolf of a bandit one would not have thought knew about such things. Here, braced against the rail, he looked stranger than ever, with the paint round his eyes dried into creases and his skin greyish. His was a world of halls and firesides and the close, hot dark of the evening. Out here, in the clear sealight, one could not forget it; it tainted him like green on bronze or old wine on the breath.

The master seemed to feel it. He hesitated, then asked, 'What brings you here?'

Cumair was all smoothness. 'My calling. I hear there's a place for songs and the memory of songs on those isles. But perhaps you would know?'

The master shrugged. 'I deal in currency a man can touch. My boy told your lad so. That's what people over there need.' They looked each other over, the master gone watchful, Cumair fat and peaceful as though he sat at supper.

The master changed the subject, nodding at me. 'Who is he? Some woman tracked you down and made you own him? His looks do her credit, though there's none of you I can see in him.' He'd have nudged him if he could.

Cumair laughed and leant forward, pulling back the cloak to show the ring about my neck.

'Payment,' he said, 'for a debt. But what of the island people? Tell me of them. You carry them honey and ore?'

'They're metal workers. Smiths and craftsmen. None finer. I bring back what they make and trade it on. Their work is in demand. And horses . . . those they breed. Good stock, if you know anything about them. But that's a tricky cargo. I stick to what doesn't move or kick or bite. But there are some who load them and take them over to the west mostly.'

Cumair grunted. For myself I could not get enough of listening.

Cumair said, 'Are they like to be generous then, to a poor tale-bringer summoned by his gods? I've heard they're a people of honour.'

The master stood to call to a crewman. The sails flapped

like great wings on their chains, the boat leaned into the wind. When he sat again he was scowling. He said, 'A poor lot. Half don't know stem from stern.' Then he remembered and answered civilly enough.

'Aye. They're mad for honour, their kind, and cold and proud. Their women – go wind that rope, lad, I've enough of your ears twitching – their women would shrivel a man useless if the fancy took them. One hears things. And their ways are not ours. I take care to keep in with them. But your boy has something about him, their look perhaps.'

There was a pause. Cumair said lightly, 'Does he now?' I met his eye and he looked away, over at the wake churned behind the boat, to the strand from where we'd sailed.

The boat plunged steadily, well under sail. I could taste salt and clean, grey air. Over the side the sea looked cold, the colour of iron, and as if it went down forever.

My mind dwelt on what the ship master had said. Part of me thought, If only they will own me, and part sounded warning, remembering what had been. Yet I was carried out of myself, a slave for selling, with no will, just like the cargo or Cumair's harp. Even a slave may hope for a good master and we are all of us borne on and on by tides drawn by a greater being, for it is the hand of the goddess that nets the moon.

There was a noise close by. Cumair had been sick, windward, over the side.

Later, when I had mopped him and made him comfortable, the master slipped up beside me. He said, 'So, where do you come from, boy?'

I was all caution; one meets any manner of types journeying. The man looked prosperous in a hard world and that makes one think. I nodded at Cumair. 'Ask him. He knows better than I do.'

The master laughed. 'Like that is it?' And slapped my shoulder. I thought he would speak again but he only looked some more and left.

The boat pitched onwards. The outline of the island grew more distinct. There were steeply rising cliffs, coves of black rock and weed and sandy inlets. Behind were mountains. The beauty of it touched me. I'd expected it bleak and barren. There were stone huts and walls high up on the cliffs and wisps of smoke rising. I thought, the place of exile, but I'd been half a year with Cumair and his waggon; this wildness spoke of freedom and set a shiver in me. Almost I reached to tug again at the ring about my neck, only the boy was looking.

We beached at last. When the curragh had been pulled up the shore as far as possible Cumair got out. He was groaning and holding his belly but once he found the land firm at his feet, he took notice, head up like a bear scenting the wind. We waited while the boat began to be unloaded. Then the master called out and beckoned. Down the cliff path came a group of men, leading pack ponies. The master nodded, 'There they are. Horse-people.'

I'd grown up with mainland folk, most of whom are of a kind, raw-boned with red hair and white, freckled skin. Some of the peasants are of older stock, darker and small, like Tachga and Palug. When they're young they're good-looking but hard work soon wears that out. Here was a different type again – people who were finer-boned in frame, strong and slender, and fair both in colouring and feature. They led their ponies on to the beach and waited, gazing from deep, fierce eyes under broad brows, their hair hanging rough upon their shoulders.

They let the master walk to them. Any welcome was given gravely. After that they gestured to the crewmen and to each other, saying how the cargo would be brought up the cliffs. For the most part I understood them, though some words they spoke differently. One had to listen hard all the time to follow.

Then they loaded the ponies and led the way. Cumair beckoned me and began to walk. There was a track leading up between the rocks, narrow but well used, with footprints in the sand and the tread of little hooves.

We walked a good way. We neither of us talked. Cumair was himself again, absorbed in everything and keen-eyed. For myself everything seemed over-sharp and clear. I could feel the steady thump of my heart and the soft hiss of breath and see very clearly the rock and the clumps of marsh grass growing through the sand.

Shortly after that the dogs came – the curs that belong to any settlement and give warning of strangers. They ran back and forth from us to the small settlement of houses that squatted on the turf, open to the winds. There were no trees here, only thorn bushes, twisted on themselves, and no high walls, just a boundary marked out in stone and a network of small fields. These were ploughed and dunged already for the spring sowings. Beyond were sheep and on some rough ground goats were tethered. From the settlement came the ring of hammered metal.

The men hallooed. At once some children came running, all wide eyes and chatter, and more dogs, obedient, going to their masters. Lastly came several women.

At Nam Dubh, even in its poor days, its days of shame, the women of the warriors made a show. They loved colour, the greens and reds and blues, and wore what jewels they had. Yet they were seemly also, kept so by my aunt, and busy with their spinning and baking and weaving. The men would not have had them otherwise.

There was nothing seemly about these women. Assurance they had, and pride in every bone and sinew, and their eyes seemed to look through us. But they were wild. From the look of them, clad in rough linen, with their hair blown about their shoulders under the grey churned sky, they could have been born of the sea wave and the wind and the cries of gulls. I was still staring when one stepped forward, a woman of middle years, straight-backed, with the lines beginning round her eyes and on her forehead. But she was handsome still and of some note. A spearman stood behind her.

'What have you brought us, Mithir? Honest goods for an honest price?' Her voice was low and firm and weary. She might have been in the market place, after a long walk, buying from the stalls.

Mithir had lost his briskness. He fingered his cap from hand to hand and shuffled. He said, 'Always honest, madam.' And, 'Shall I have them set out for you?'

She shook her head. There was grey in her hair, mixed in with the blond. Her eyes were deep-set like the men's, and the bones of her face clean and strong. My mind was full of Cumair's songs. I thought, The face of a queen, but her shift was unbelted and undyed, going down to her feet. One could not see her shape beneath.

Still there seemed some heaviness on her. She said, 'Wait till Cathal comes. He will not be long. This time he wants to see. He was not happy before. There were complaints from the smiths. Send your men back and come up to the dun.'

Mithir murmured, 'Madam,' and turned, calling orders. Cumair watched, pulling at his lip, and planted his feet, waiting to do his business.

The woman looked, first at us, then at the master. She had no need to question. Mithir said, 'A tale-teller and his boy. The man requested passage of me. I could not but give it.'

'Then we are to be entertained. Do you expect payment, tale-teller?' Her eyes were dark grey, the colour of the sea, with no light in them. It was impossible to tell if she was pleased or angry. The lines showed more clearly about her mouth.

Cumair said smoothly, 'Lady, I expect nothing. I go where my gods take me.'

Her brows quirked. She looked him up and down openly, but wearily too, like someone who's been many nights with dreams and fancies that would not let her sleep. He seemed meaningless to her, like the day.

She said, 'This is not the place for song. Nor are we a people who welcome strangers, beyond what is common courtesy. You may eat with us, but no more. Sail back, tale-teller, when the merchant goes.'

She had snapped her fingers for her spear-bearer when Cumair said softly, 'Honoured Lady, there are tales and tales. Tales of the heroes and gods and tales of men about their business. I have travelled far and through many lands. It has come to my ears that the Horse-people are once more for the world. And more things, too, have I heard which even now seek other ears to listen.'

He was at his most florid. He stroked his chin, letting her see his painted nails, grown long for the harp; but his words gave her pause.

She said, 'What lands?'

He grinned, to disconcert her.

'Lands, Lady, that once heard the tread of hooves.'

Her eyes dropped. She smoothed her palms along her skirt, but you could see her woken into thought. She said, 'You may stay. I will talk with Cathal.'

We walked further along the track, beyond the stone huts. They were very small; not one so large as the huts at Nam Dubh.

The road curved upward, following the cliff. Below we could see again the great, wide bowl of the sea and the ship moored a little way out and rocks. Further up, on a promontory, was the dun, the royal homestead, set in its cramped circle of thick, stone walls.

A well-built dun cannot be breached, except by treachery, but it is like a shackle set upon the land. Life inside is close, confined in the little bothies built of wattle, hugged against the side. I had not known of them until I came to Cumair, but these last weeks he had sung in several.

This dun was old, the stone walls weathered and displaced in places towards the top; going under the lintels we had to crouch. Inside, though, the bothies raised against the walls seemed well kept up and thatched and snug.

The courtyard was very small, with room for only a dozen or so to sit at ease. In the middle was a clay-lined hearth and driftwood burnt there with a blue-green salty flame. Cumair and Mithir sat by it where the woman showed them. I stood behind, mindful of my place.

The bothies opened on to the courtyard. Most had their curtains drawn back. Some were workplaces and byres. Others served both men and women, with looms and spindle alongside hunting slings and men's full cloaks. At Nam Dubh men and women of any rank had separate quarters.

I thought of my home in the marshlands. Here too the walls were unadorned and the floor bare earth. There was firewood piled by the wall close by the entrance and a cauldron hung over the fire with a ladle on a peg. But there were no shields or rugs or painted pillars – nothing of colour or the dark brilliance such as Nam Dubh had worn, even in her worst days. We could have sat in a peasant's house and had more cheer.

The woman took the ladle and stirred the pot. I smelt barley and boiled mutton. She fetched bowls from a stack of them, spooned out stew and handed them round. There was a portion for me. We were halfway through eating when the man Cathal arrived.

He must have been of an age with the woman, younger than my uncle, yet no longer young in himself. He'd come in as he was, in work gear, though with his hands and face damp from washing and water in his hair. He nodded at the ship-master.

We ate in silence. There was no talk of business and journeyings, the difficulties of supply and trade in general, of attacks and threatenings in the world at large. Mithir pushed his stew about and ate little. From the look of him he was nervous and on edge. For myself I had no appetite, though

Cumair as always ate enough for us both. Indeed he gestured for me to pass over my platter when he saw I did not eat. The woman noticed, though she said nothing, only her eyes dwelt a little longer on us both, and she frowned.

Cathal put aside his bowl and rose and stretched. He was a fine man, with blue eyes and a moustache covering his upper lip. Yet he was lean, not thickly built as my uncle's people were, though strong-looking for all that, as a wolf is strong. His hair was swept back from his forehead and fell straight to his shoulders, and I saw his tattoos, small signs in blue, upon his cheekbones and arms.

He looked down at Mithir. He said, 'The wax and honey we'll take. We wish to try the ore. The bronze did not work well before. We need it very fluid, with more lead, for the moulds.'

Mithir said, 'Sir, I took the supply in good faith. I'll swear to that. But it is for you to see, as you like.'

I realized now what I had suspected before, how Cathal was the chief man of these people. He nodded. 'Well then, I have ordered the ore brought up to the smithies, and the other goods outside. While the smiths make ready we will see what else you've brought.'

We left the dun. Behind were the forges, straggled anyhow, and the sheep grazed between them on the scrub land. But there was a forecourt of sorts where the grass was worn away and there a group of people had gathered, round wooden chests brought from the ship. They had remained closed. No one had touched them yet, a thing I found of note.

The people waited solemnly. Mithir stood in their midst, looking at Cathal as if he'd swallowed a mouthful of seawater.

He said, 'There's good things here, from all over, if anyone'll put up a fair price.'

He flung open the first of the chests. Within were woollen cloaks, dyed in the softest colours, reds and greens and a colour like heather, woven together into stripes and plaids. He brought them out and swung them open. The people murmured but no one moved to touch them or try them on for length.

Later came the other chests, full of leather goods, purses and belts, some pony harness, all studded and tooled – the fine stuff of craftsmen – and still later came glassware, glowing like jewels, formed into cups and gaming pieces.

Yet all the time the people only watched. At Nam Dubh

such things would have been played with already and passed from hand to hand; or thrown around in fun to make the trader gasp.

Beside me Cumair too was quiet, looking on to see the bidding so he might calculate what he might earn with singing and what other wealth might lie hidden in the dun and stone-built huts.

But no one offered barter. Instead they were still, as mountain cats are, watching for the deer to pause and drink.

Mithir stood there. He had begun to sweat and look from face to face. He said, quite suddenly, tumbling out the words, 'I have a trade to make. The goods are fair.'

There was a pause. Several smiled, though with no good humour that I could see. Then, from amongst them, there was stir and a young man stepped forward, his colour high.

'Mithir,' he said, 'do you mock us with these goods, or seek to corrupt us with such finery? What payment do you expect? You know our terms of trading.' As he said it he had half an eye on Cathal.

Mithir looked crushed and doubtful. He said, 'I meant no offence. To others they are pleasing.'

He began to pack the cases. Around him they still watched, unspeaking. But it was true; any fool could see such things had no place among them. From pride or poverty they lived hardily. As soon cloak the bare rocks with gold as hang upon these folk.

Mithir bent, hiding his face over the boxes. But his ears looked hot. Poor Mithir, I thought, and what will he tell his son?

Just then up along the track came the neat clopping of a pony at a trot. We all of us turned, watching to see who rode.

The pony was a bay, dark and polished like fine, old bronze, with a black mane and tail. It had been ridden hard. Sweat caked its chest and legs and belly. But it pulled still, eager for water and the horse run, the small head up, nostrils flared and ears well forward.

Its rider sat at ease, leaning a little back to steady it, balanced, as Uffa told us, bare legs hanging down, hands firm on the reins, but light too, giving enough to be kind.

I was trained to note such things. But the rider was a girl; I'd seen that first.

She brought the horse round to us. Her calf, pressed on its flank, was long and brown with a smooth, high curve. Her tunic hid all above her knee. She was curious; her brows arched like strong wings as she looked across and her head lifted. Cumair purred, deep in his throat.

The young man was scowling at her. She saw it and grinned, cocking her head at him and sliding from the pony.

She said, 'What is it you want, Ferbhal, that you cannot have?'

Her voice carried, pitched high with insolence. They were very alike and both already prickling at each other. Together they looked strong, and spare, and wild, like hawks, or lynxes showing their claws.

Ferbhal said, 'The man's a fool. Look what he's brought.'

She stepped up, treading carefully about the pile of stuff.

Mithir stood back, gulping and rubbing his brow. He looked wary and unhappy. The girl smiled, and bent and lifted a swatch of material, the colour of haws in autumn, and held it to her.

It was one of the best things, and had taken everyone's eye. It was made of some thread I had never seen before, very fine, like a woman's hair, and shining where it caught the light.

The girl said, 'Will you trade?' Her mouth moved as though she tasted berries.

Mithir nodded. He muttered something but I couldn't hear.

She said, 'This for him,' and pointed to the pony. 'I bred him myself, out of good stock. He is still entire.'

The young man stepped forward. He looked once to Cathal and said, 'Father!' and turned after to the girl. His face looked white, and then I saw it was with rage. He said, 'Etain, you have the brain of a goat!'

They stared at one another, the same lines of temper drawn on both their faces. Beside me Cumair shifted, enjoying it hugely.

The young man said, more reasonably, 'It's not worth the stallion, Etain. Have some sense.'

For answer she held up the fabric. Before, with her clear eyes and skin she had been cool as spring water over stone. Now, angered, her face took on the colour of the cloth. She glowed, like glass held before a candle flame. He paused, and all at once lunged for it. She jumped back neatly. In the boys' hall no one could have been quicker.

She said, 'Leave well alone, Ferbhal! Father would let me!'

'Oh, he'd skim the stars out of the sky for you and serve them on a platter!'

He grabbed again and this time nearly caught the cloth. Mithir was open-mouthed. I think I was the same.

Quietly, more than ever like cats, they prowled about each other. The cloth flapped again. She mocked her brother with it; and something else glittered. In her other hand the girl held a knife, pulled from her shift, finely honed and gleaming. She used it deftly, jabbing in front of the young man's face.

He said softly, 'Etain, give it here.'

'No!' she said. 'It's mine.'

Spellbound, I watched. Now she was all thought, and suspicion, half crouched to pounce, biting a little at her lip. Her hair was caught back roughly in a threadwork bonnet. Within it was pale like the moon or early honey.

The young man dived at her. She laughed and twisted away, in a flash of long, bared legs and goat-skin slippers. He cursed, and lunged again. Once more she whipped away and he fell, sprawling on the earth.

The next time he got her and she screeched like a vixen, right in his ear, on purpose. But she fought back after, properly, as though she knew all the moves. In the end she won. He exclaimed sharply and sat up, nursing his hand. She'd scored it right down the back with her dagger.

She had sprung to her feet. 'I mean to keep it.' She sounded defiant and sulky, like a child who's bested a playmate and is sorry for it after. The young man got up slowly, much on his dignity, and let his hand drip blood on to the mud.

Cathal said, 'Etain, you should learn to fight fair.'

She turned to face him, sweeping the cloth about her shoulders. There was just enough to make a shawl. At home there would have been trouble – the women tut-tutting and hustling her off and the men aghast. Cathal was her father, but she lifted her head to him just the same.

'A fair fight is no fight at all. You should fight to win.'

She paused, then there was mischief plucking at her mouth.

'Just think,' she said, 'of Mithir loading the stallion.'

She was right by me. I saw the answering laughter kindle in Cathal's eyes. I caught the scent of her hair, and something else. I could not take my eyes from her. She lifted up the cloth once more, fluttering the scarlet. The inside of her arm showed bare, the flesh pale and firm and lightly veined. At the crook, tattooed in its circle, was the horse-sign of her people, inevitable in this place, rightful and proud and flaunted without fear.

A familiar grip tightened on my shoulder. But for that I'd have moved. Cumair, leering across at her, said quietly in my ear: 'Hush, child. Cumair knows and Cumair knows what to do. Have a little faith at least.' His fingers slid under the hated slave collar and he pulled at it gently, just enough to tighten the metal back against my throat. 'The principle of trade is this – one wants a fair price for one's goods, and goods in demand are worth twice the price. Let us not show our hand too soon, child – lest we both be disappointed.'

Chapter Twenty-six

Shortly afterwards Cathal gestured to us. The fires were ready in the forges and smiths had begun to work their sampling of the ore.

We went over to the little huts. Inside they were rank with heat and the sour smell of the molten metal. The bronze was being melted, the ingots placed in crucibles of baked clay and then into furnaces shaped like bee skeps with a pit beneath. There were bellows, worked by boys or old men, who pumped them till the charcoal glowed.

At Nam Dubh we'd had our smithy for the ploughshares and the pots and knives and firedogs. Finer work was wrought by the journeyman smith. It was he who hammered out the swords and pony trappings. But he never liked to be watched as he worked and would drive us boys off with curses.

Here one could see it all. A finished sword or bowl or armband takes life from the one who wears it; in this place the raw metal lived. The bronze ran blazing in rivulets from the crucibles. The golden flames licked upwards as it streamed into the moulds. The huts seemed dark after gazing on it and the squatting smiths like demons casting bright sorcery from the clay. They worked naked in the smoke and heat except for their leather aprons, cracked and black all over. Everyone knows a smith has earth-magic in him and all he touches is sacred to his god.

They watched the metal, telling what we could not: the exactness of its melting, and how it flowed, even the rightness of its colour. Close by was different work. A man crouched on the floor, over a small section of bronze beaten to a sheet. He tapped out a design, working with a little hammer, punching from behind. Others shaped wax for the first setting of the moulds, etching it with bone needles and awls. Another hammered at a bloom of iron. All of it was hot and fierce with the smell of the furnaces that burnt one's throat and tongue and the noise of the hammers and the bellows and the hissing flames.

I waited till everyone seemed taken up and absorbed. One of the smiths explained some matter to Cathal and the rest craned to hear. Then I slipped out. Besides, if one is a slave one is invisible anyway, forever about one's master's business. I wished to see this land of mine. As the day had worn on I'd felt a stirring in me, like wine, or one's blood after exercise. Even the forge could not quell it. I was out of myself, running with thoughts of the sea and the mountains and how this place was home.

Outside no one was about. I went quickly beyond the huts and slowed when I was out of sight. For a time the path followed the cliff. Far below the coastline was jagged with black rocks, like beasts' backs, rising from cold, green water and great chasms where the seabirds wheeled and screeched. The sea-wind gusted. It felt strange, looking down; too small, as though seen through a god's eye, or as if you might find yourself in a moment sinking through the water or battered on the rocks.

When I could I turned inland, across the high grassland. By now it was late afternoon with the feel of the day dying. Yet the clouds were breaking up and the late rays of the sun shone through.

On I wandered. Several times I glimpsed farmsteads huddled in the valleys. Then I caught again the glint of water. I made for that. As I walked it opened up before me, a smooth sheet, black and silver with an edge of gold from the sun, and fretted a little by the wind. More than a lake, it was a long, broad loch, with smooth shores overgrown by reeds and, on the far side, trees and the mountains. In the chilly dusk the place was lonely and melancholy, yet splendid too, wild and set apart. I stood a while to see and all at once I was sad. I felt my desolation, far from man and beast, and the burden of what was to be. The slave ring was about my neck and these people not yet mine. There were other things too, longings for which I had not the words, but stirred in me by the shining light of water and the slopes with the pines stood close and the darkening air.

I began to walk along the shore. Soon the land rose and became rocky and steep with the loch far below. Sharp on the crest of the rise, black against the sky, was something that looked like a small, rectangular hut. I went closer and saw that it was so indeed, but made of wicker just as the door screens at Nam Dubh had been.

This was no screen. As I walked round I found that the fourth side, facing the loch, was open. Inside was an effigy, a small carved post, brightly painted, with holes for the eyes and mouth and pinned all over with scraps of shell and bone and withered flowers. Amongst them something glinted. I recognized it: the arching shape, the smooth, cold lines of metal, but here in gold, not silver. It was the only jewel, a talisman as I had worn it but on her who made it so; the horse-sign hung openly upon a string of leather.

I had no foreboding. I went and lifted it from the effigy's neck, bringing it up over the painted head and empty eyes, and already its shape and weight were as familiar if it had never left the place by my side, as if it had never been lost and hammered and ruined. I caught it to me and hugged it to my breast.

I put it back. I had to. Though I had been a thief for food and from necessity, I was not for this. My own I had cast away, in knowledge and understanding. It had been wilfully done and the Lady had shown me my deserving. The collar round my neck was proof of that.

I turned to go and started. In the doorway stood the woman who had greeted us. For a moment all the heavy composure of her was gone. She stared at me, almost with fear, holding very still. I could not tell how long she'd been there, only how her strong, handsome face was set, with her eyes wide and her chin lifted, and her nostrils flared as though she had taken a quick, scared breath.

I said in a rush, 'I have no weapon. I did not come to steal.'

And she said, 'I know. I saw.'

There was a pause while we regarded one another. Her deep eyes watched me. She was not the kind who is quick to question; rather the sort who asks her own mind first, 'What is this?'

At last she said, 'Did you wish to pray or leave an offering for the Lady? She is kind to suppliants.'

I stood tongue-tied. The woman came forward, though still not close, and frowned a little.

She said, 'You are the song-maker's boy. What were you doing here?'

I said, 'I was walking. I found this hut. I was curious, that was all. I meant no harm.'

'You have done none. There is no need to be anxious, or did your master not give you leave? This is our Lady, whose totem is the Horse, the Mother of our lands and herds.'

I said, 'I know.'

She paused, at a loss. Then she said, 'I am her priestess. If you have an offering to make, some flowers or a pretty stone – for anything she will be pleased.' She sounded weary, as if her duties were become a burden.

I nodded, and then on impulse pulled off the armband my grandfather had given me long ago. 'Here,' I said, 'give her this.'

She took it and looked down at it, and then at me. Again came the still watchfulness that lit behind her eyes.

'This is a fine and handsome thing for a slave to own.'

'It's mine!'

She said, 'Why so wild? I did not accuse you. But what is a slave's is his master's. Will he permit you the offering?'

Cumair could have forbidden till he was breathless; it would have made no difference.

I said, 'He would wish it.' It was, perhaps, not quite a lie. Cumair was chary of the local gods and kept to their right side.

The woman looked long at me again and I met her gaze with my colour only a little risen. Then her deep eyes dropped from mine, as though she had seen enough, and she threw back her head to shake her hair. The very movement seemed slow and worn as though, after a long day, she loosened it for bed.

'Well,' she said, 'then it is Hers.' And bent and laid it at the foot of the goddess.

'I will pray for you to Her. What is your name?'

I shook my head. 'It doesn't matter.' Now I wanted only to be gone. I felt awkward and clumsy, half wanting to tell her who I was yet fearful of her disbelief.

She must have seen me hesitate. Gently she said, 'You may go. It is a long way to the dun. By now your master will surely have need of you.'

'And now,' said Cumair, 'to our trade.'

He looked very fine. We had spent a long time working on him, so that he was oiled and sleeked and groomed. From a distance his robes were splendid, checked and worked with golden thread at the hem. He adjusted them, pushing up his sleeves and splaying wide his fingers. His nails were repolished; he used berry juice and some stuff boiled from bones that set hard. The smell alone turned my stomach.

'Arawn,' he said, 'come here.'

After all this time I hated still to be near him. I stood just out of his reach.

He looked me over. 'Pale,' he said, 'though that's no bad thing. A touch forlorn, my dear, to rouse the pity in their breasts. And a smudge of dirt, perhaps, just there, for pathos' sake, along your chin.'

There was ash in the hearth. He bent to it and afterwards rubbed his finger on my face.

'The unkempt captive, returned to his unsuspecting people. How they will welcome you.'

I shoved him off, growling. He smiled and put his arm about me, pressing himself close. I said, 'You stink!' and he nipped me sharply with his finger-nails.

The household of the dun were gathered round on the floor by the hearth, eating and drinking beer. Cumair lifted the curtain of his bothy and peered out, pausing before we were seen to gauge the audience. For now, unaware of strangers' eyes, the place felt free and easy, the people close and fond of one another. The women spun and gossiped but crossed the yard as well to speak with the men; there was banter and talk between them, though for the most part quiet.

Some of the girls were laughing together near the fire, with no pretence at spinning and no one to chide them either; my aunt would have had none of it. The girl, Etain, was holding up her shawl for them to try one after the other. Even sitting she had a wildness such as a hawk has or an eagle. She had loosed her shining hair for it to lie about her shoulders, her neck was long, her head poised, the mouth wilful. At her throat a thin torc of bronze flashed. Under it she had a necklet of shells and more about her wrists.

Cumair lifted the curtain with a flourish and went out. I followed, sullen as a lad caught stealing apples, brought for the headman's judgement. The fear had come suddenly, as when one says, 'This battle is real.' Everyone looked and the talk died. He gestured for his harp.

I sensed at once their withdrawal, like a curtain pulled

across the door. They were quiet as they'd been before Mithir's unwanted wares, courteous and watchful as well-trained hounds guarding the master's house. Even the girl, Etain, sat with her hands in her lap.

Cumair sang as well as I'd ever heard him. From the beginning he had the measure of these people; and the stakes were high. They were poor in a way that Nam Dubh had never been poor: their dun was mean and squalid, the island bleak; their lives were sheep and horses, iron and bronze, yet they had their pride and he worked it as one of their smiths would work the metal. He had his tricks, as ever, the songs of the sea and the sea-birds, of pirates, of battles and of exiles. He brought them colour and courage and wild imaginings, lands where the bright gods walked. I saw their eyes, but they did not stir or speak.

Once more I marvelled at his skill, yet hated him also. Of him there was nothing, only his voice, hard-edged or swooping, glittering against the music of the harp like drops of rain against the sun or softening to the murmur of a lover in a young girl's ear.

He had honed and crafted it, singing in the waggon or by the fire. Yet it cost him nothing; it was always there for him to give – an offering without his soul. It was too easy. It was those who heard him who suffered and lived and mourned within his songs. He had no right to hurt us in this way.

He was done at last and took up a bowl to eat and something to drink. They waited for him, respectful as though he were there at Cathal's invitation. He took his time, and all the while I crouched at his feet with my ribs feeling hot and tight and thought, It should not be like this.

When he had done and filled and refilled his cup, he looked round at them where they waited and said, 'Will you have another tale?'

He sat on a log to keep his robes from the ashes; their faces were upturned to him. He waited, just long enough before they'd stir, laid down his harp and said, 'This one I speak.'

Cathal signed to his men. Usually the women went out at such times; not here.

Cumair said, 'Get up.' I too stared at him. Now the moment was come I could not move. He knew it; there was understanding of a kind in his eyes. But he kicked out suddenly at my side and said, 'You heard!'

Shocked, I scrambled up and stood there, in the firelight,

in the open yard before my mother's people, and they looked back at me. The moment's violence was not lost on them; he'd meant it so, for them to wait like anyone does, hearing angry voices, to see what will become.

Cumair said to Cathal, 'Tell me, what do you reckon the price of a good slave, one who is strong and quick enough to learn most things?'

He said, 'It is long since we had slaves. A box of salt, a colt, a brood mare even. What do you mean by this?'

Cumair raised his hand for quiet. He said, 'Does anyone come with a fair price?'

They looked at one another. The girls were giggling and putting their heads together. The rest stayed silent. All at once there was a flash of bright colour. Something fell in the ash at the edges of the hearth. It was the cloth Etain had fought for.

Ferbhal, the young man, spoke. 'Here, song-maker. My sister gives you this. She has an eye to him.' He had snatched it from her, taunting; at Nam Dubh any decent girl would have flung herself off the walls for shame. But she was his match, and ripe for trouble. Before everyone she stood and faced us across the hearth. Then she reached up and loosed the shells about her neck, and threw them down.

'Make up the price with that. My brother is right. But I'll work him hard. To the bone, if need be.'

There was a stir and a murmur. The men laughed, not openly but with their eyes down, choking into their beer, or glancing sideways at each other and her father. Some of the girls had gasped and blushed. I was hot all over. The girl had sat, head up. Twice today she had brought them a show, and they loved her for it. Even Cathal had to wipe at his moustache to hide the way his mouth moved.

There was another pause, till they attended. Cumair spread wide his hands and shrugged. 'Yet, Lady, he is not for sale.'

She looked up and shrugged also. 'It is no matter.'

I thought, she has played her game with Ferbhal. That's all she cares about.

'Yet,' said Cumair, 'a man may come to slavery through many things – born from a pirate's leavings, taken in raiding with no one to care enough to pay the ransom.' He pulled me to him, his arm round my shoulders, a sly finger tracing at my neck. 'Sold for old hatred's sake.'

301

He met their eyes. Cathal said, 'Who are you to talk to us of hatreds?'

Cumair said, 'Do you still talk of them, Cathal, telling them over while you crouch here on this rock with the sea about you and the gulls screaming for their fish?'

'We talk.'

They held each other's gaze. I thought of knives, glinting in the dark. My skin crawled. I pulled myself away.

Cathal said, 'What do you know?'

'What others do. There were raids last spring, and the one before, against the mainland, at the edges of Cernach's territories. A confederacy of Horse-tribes and others. A few cattle driven here and there, farmsteads plundered. Not much. But enough. Enough to say "Beware" to Cernach. He's gathering his tribes. Next spring, when it begins again, he will be ready.'

Cathal said, 'You tell us things a child would know. Of course he will be ready.'

'So it begins once more. Yet that is nothing to me, beyond what I can make of it – songs, a battle field's pickings. My takings are of a different sort, Cathal.'

He settled himself. Cathal waited. There was pride under the quiet ways.

Cumair said sleekly, 'The boy. He's one of yours.'

I'd thought they might stir at that. In some of my dreams they'd welcomed me already. But they held still, and dangerous.

Cumair said, 'Things are told of the Horse-people: how they hold their own as sacred to the Horse-queen and how their women are free in all things. This last have I seen for myself. Would you take your kin into service? Or your daughter as a slave for her bed?'

Cathal frowned. He was torn between anger and curiosity, eyeing me. At her place the girl was all hiss and spit, like tinder with water poured over. I thought, She plays it one way and cannot take another. Then Cathal said, 'Who is he?'

'Macha's son. And Cernach wants him.'

One could feel it then, like a sigh welling from them, barely a sound, checked as they'd check anything that opened on their hearts.

Cumair said, 'Will you deny him or put him to shame?'

The silence went on a long time. I stared out at them,

wondering what they saw. Then the young man, Ferbhal, said, 'Come here.'

I did so slowly, to the clear place nearby the hearth.

Someone said, 'He could pass for Horse-people. He has our look.'

Cathal said, 'That is not enough. Where is the proof?' He stared at me as though he'd eat me, grim and searching, slanting up his gaze, his mouth pursed tight.

Cumair said to me, 'Show your arm.'

I did so, pulling back the sleeve, while the light from the fire glowed on my flesh so that the mark turned dark and the scar above seemed deeper and more puckered.

Again came the silence. There were other things to say, only rooted far down as weed is rooted in the stream that flows above it. Then Cathal said to Cumair, 'Tell us of him.' His words struck the quiet as the hammers had the iron.

Dully I listened as Cumair spoke. He was brief, and truthful. At the end he said, 'And Cernach wants him.'

For the first time there was a stir; they could not hold it back. I thought then, What was she to them? But the space in my mind that she might have filled stayed empty.

Ferbhal said, 'Cumair, if this is true, then it is good of you to bring him back to us. Yet you lose a servant.' He was cautious, sounding him as one sounds a wall for rot.

Cumair leaned against a post; he had made himself easy. He said, 'After all, he has a price.'

No one spoke, only their eyes gave them away. Cathal said, 'How much?'

'Metalwork. Not jewellery – arms. Your fame goes before you. Your swords and daggers fetch a good price. There are those, with whom you do not trade, who'd like to see how they are worked.'

Their breath hissed. Cathal said, 'You ask too much. For myself I will give you the price of a sound servant. No more than that.'

There was a murmur of agreement. My heart beat so loud I thought they must hear it.

Cumair said, 'Then I shall walk from here and take the good master's boat with him, and we'll be gone.'

Ferbhal said, 'Yet there are ways to stop you.'

'No,' said Cumair. 'No. He has sworn an oath and I shall hold him to it – to bide with me till I return him to his people. And if you will not have him, his oath still binds. And if you kill me, how can he in honour take his place amongst you? I tell you, he is of your own, and you dishonour yourselves in denying it.'

The girl, Etain, said, 'The price is too high. He could be anyone.'

'It stands.'

'Was it you who pricked in the mark?'

Cumair leant forward. He looked his worst, oily and sly and all the things I knew him for that his music and art could hide. He spoke quietly now, so that they had to strain to listen.

'Heed this. If I should take him back with me he will wear the slave ring all his life, and a slave's life he will lead till his days' end. And if it be with me I shall not spare him, nor shall the salt or copper mines. Is that what you wish for Macha's son?'

Again the silence; the slow consciousness of things weighed up and measured out. All at once he leant from his seat and gripped at my tunic and pulled. I jerked away, turning, and the fabric ripped, laying bare my back and the marks on it open to their sight.

I bowed my head. I could not look at anyone. I was sick with grief already and fumbled with my shirt, trying to pull it back.

Someone said, 'Song-maker.'

It was the woman of the shrine. All this while she had sat apart, at the entrance to her bothy. Now she rose and walked slowly to the hearth. The others made way for her and touched their brows as she passed.

She stood before Cumair and said, 'Song-maker, you have brought us music and this lad. You set great store by our honour, but little enough by yours.'

She turned to me and said, 'Come here.' I lifted my eyes to hers and saw again their weary darkness, and darker pity within.

Speaking softly, as though it were a thing only between me and her, she said, 'This woman who was your mother, Macha, what do you remember of her?'

'Nothing.' It was true, and the truth was desolate as the flat, grey wetlands.

I saw her consider, as she had at the shrine. The thoughts passed on her face but they were unfathomable. She said at last, 'We had no woman, Macha, in our tribe, though the name is in our tongue and once the Clan was large. Perhaps you will find your people on the mainland or on the other islands. Some of us are left.'

Cumair said, 'You will not take him?'

'He is not our blood kin. Etain is right. The price is too high. Though we work in metal, that is our livelihood, not our wealth.'

She turned away. I saw Cumair's face, white suddenly and sweating, and how he stared at her. I thought, If they do not want me, neither will Cernach. Briefly I was glad, that he had not bested her, and then I thought how it would be with him, and how she lied.

I found my voice. 'Lady,' I said, and she turned to me. 'Once, I had a token, a horse that was my mother's. The form of it is here, on the goddess. You saw me with it and I saw your face. I think you knew my mother.'

She looked long at me and then her gaze went to where Cathal sat. A look passed between them with a thread of tension drawn there, fine as a spider's silk that looks so lovely with the dew hung on it, but which traps to kill.

Cathal said, 'I'll not take Cernach's leavings.'

Still she looked at him, and it was as though within her she bore great power and knowledge but that she cloaked it tight before us.

She said, 'For Macha.'

He raised his head. I saw pain and baffled anger. 'For Macha?' he said. 'No, Echraide. For what she was.'

Then there was quiet, except for the girl, Etain, who all at once laughed shrilly and looked about her.

Chapter Twenty-seven

Cumair said, 'What will happen?'

He squatted by the hearth, almost within the circle of spent ash. He looked tired and not himself, smaller and huddled up, as though he felt the cold. In daylight his robes looked dirty round the hem and neck. Ferbhal, who sat beside him, said, 'I do not know. Echraide will seek the Lady's will.'

It was morning. We were alone in the dun. There had been some bread and meat for breakfast and Cathal had excused himself, going after to the horse runs. The girls had strolled off, about some work or other, and only Ferbhal had stayed, to be courteous. Now he was troubled and out of his depth – Cumair stirred at him as an eel stirs mud for worms.

He blinked and looked away into the empty hearth. After a moment he handed Cumair a wine-skin and said, 'We have learnt to be cautious. We are not a people who lightly offend our gods. But it will be a fine thing if Macha's son comes back to us.' He spoke politely, looking over to where I was, trying to be busy with some stuff of Cumair's, polishing it up.

Cumair said, 'Tell me of Macha. It seems to me that women have power in your tribe.' He upended the wine-skin and shook it. It was empty, from last night.

Ferbhal said, 'Should that not be so? Our women walk close to the Horse-queen. She is not the kind who favours men with secrets. But I know nothing of Macha. Only that she was a priestess, and how she was taken.'

He was clear-skinned; his face showed risen colour and he bent to play with a lacing on his boot. Cumair gave him a sly look, sideways, but he knew always how to play a man and never rushed. He said, 'And the god of your tribe?'

'The Horse-lord? He walks alone.'

Cumair said, 'This other priestess, Echraide. What she says will be accepted?'

307

Ferbhal said, 'She is my father's sister. Had she a son, he would have ruled after, in place of me. All priestesses are royal. She has much influence and we know her to be wise.'

'She speaks for the goddess? Who then speaks for the god?'

Ferbhal's lid twitched. 'The chieftain speaks.'

'But the goddess speaks first?'

'Of course. She is the people's Mother – she brings life to the land for the tribe who are her children. She accepts who may tread the land; the god decides the fitness – where a man belongs, his rank, his craft, his duties.'

'Very proper.' Cumair said it sweetly.

Once more there was a silence. I thought, This is not so different from the Raven-tribe, where the Raven-lady speaks. She too rules and the Clan-lord does her bidding.

Ferbhal stirred. He was very like his sister with the same long eyes, the straight nose and careful mouth, but his bones were stronger and more settled. He had manners. He passed a fresh wine-skin to us and rose to go, careful to seem unhurried.

The day was long. I could settle to nothing; I was neither prince nor slave, warrior nor body-servant. I was restless, yet to walk seemed to no purpose. Nor did I like to leave the dun in case I was called for. I went out only once, and watched the women pegging out a deer hide. Cumair too was impossible, watching me all the time and squatting like a toad. Even when he played snatches of raucous song his eyes never left me.

The afternoon faded. Night closed round. In the dun we took supper from the pot and went back to our bothy to eat.

Shortly after Ferbhal slipped in. He bent to my ear and said quietly, 'Echraide is waiting. My sister will take you to her. She is outside.'

I guessed they did not want a fuss. I looked out, beyond the curtain, and after a moment, when those round the hearth seemed lost in talk, I took my chance and left.

Outside the dun, in the flat yard before the pastures, there were figures; someone on a pony, who held another, and someone else standing by with a lighted taper. Their hoods were up against the cold. The taper flame was blown about. The moon came from behind the clouds as I drew near. I saw Cathal as he gestured and from the dark a clear face gleamed, cheekbone and eye and a frond of hair, and then once more was hidden.

I walked up and stopped before them. Cathal said, 'If the Horse-queen wills it, this is a fine night, and we will welcome Macha's son with all our hearts. But it is for the Lady to say. Go now and find her bidding.'

He handed up the torch to Etain and took the other pony, bringing it round, and gave me the bridle. He said, 'This thing must be known.'

I swung up. The pony felt narrow and finer boned than Ban, the mane less wiry. I glanced at Etain but saw nothing but the gather of cloak over her head.

Cathal said, 'My daughter will guide you well. She too serves the Lady.'

We began our ride. We kept to a walk or a jog trot so as not to risk the ponies. The air was salty and fresh. The clouds were whipped across the moon and shone blue-white by turns. We went up by the cliff paths and below the sea churned and roared and glimmered.

We neither of us spoke. The girl's shoulders were rigid as she guided her horse. She must remember, I thought, her words last night. For myself, it seemed that I should think beyond such things, to the Horse-lady and what she might require. Yet the rite seemed far away as ever; I thought rather of how I had seen the girl fight, with her legs bare beneath her kirtle, and the lift of her bright face and her fierce laughter.

At length we turned inland, following the track that I had taken. Soon, on the skyline, I saw the shrine, and then the black spread of the loch.

The wind blew off the sea. It lifted my hair from my brow, and the pony's mane. Etain's cloak billowed about her. The ponies jogged on and the moon's fitful light on the pathway was winter-blue and threw long shadows.

At the shrine we halted. Etain slipped from her pony and walked forward. She did not look back for me. Within was dark but by the light of the torch I saw the goddess, her little, rough-hewn figure, daubed with paint, still hung about with the scraps of cloth and trinkets.

The torch burnt redly. It touched her with gold and made darker the deep fissures in the wood. She stood in darkness. The shrine was cold and empty all around. The pitted eyes stared out from it, towards the loch, seeming to gaze upon the waters.

My back grew cold. I was a stranger, with no knowledge of their customs. It was all I could do not to turn and look myself. Then there was movement. I swung round. Echraide stood, not dressed for her Lady as Nemair did for hers, but in her shift and unbound hair. Here was no burden of black feathers. Her face was wise and calm. Her own eyes sheltered in their hollows, whatever was in them deeply hidden. Her head was raised and poised.

She said, 'I do not even know your name.'

And I said, 'Arawn.'

She said, 'Your father named you then. It is not a name of our tribe. But if the Lady accepts, you will have a new one, at your initiation.'

She had a bowl with her and some liquid in it. She set it down at the base of the effigy. Quietly she said, 'Now you must show yourself to the Lady.' I stared at her, thick-headed.

'So is a child born of the mother.'

I understood then and did as I was told. When I had done I stood with only the loathsome collar round my neck that I could not be rid of. Echraide lifted the taper and I blinked, dazzled, hearing her murmur quietly in her people's tongue that was like my own, yet not so like that I could with ease follow what she said.

She made some marks after, on my body and face, with the liquid that was cold and smelt of plants. All the time Etain stood in silence, waiting on her, handing her the sticks and cloths.

At last they gave me back my clothes. Echraide said, quite briskly, 'By this you are delivered. Now I will go and be apart and learn the wishes of the Lady.'

I was at a loss and asked, 'Where should I go?'

'Etain knows. Stay with her.'

She gathered her robe about her and turned from us. She went, striding freely across the shining heathland, crested a ridge and was lost to our view.

I turned to Etain. In the taper's light her eyes were full of shadows; she made no movement to show me what to do. In that instant she seemed remote and strange, like a room with the torch set different or a field under the moon. Almost I was scared; then I saw that her mouth was sulky, like any cross girl's.

I would have spoken at that, to ask where Echraide went,

but she put her finger to her lips and said, 'Not here before the Lady. We will wait close by.'

She led me a little way off, to a dip where the breeze did not reach. 'Sleep, if you can,' she said. I was not tired. Rather I felt light and free, but I pillowed my head on the grass and closed my eyes; but only enough that I could see beneath the lids.

I watched Etain. I wished that she would talk. I wanted to know if she was sorry for what she'd said. Besides, there was that about her which made me pause. Her hair was tugged from her face by the breeze coming off the water, her head was up and she was quite still. So intent she seemed that I followed her gaze, staring out. But the water was calm, ruffled just by the light night wind so that the black reflections in it rippled and were lit by the moonshine. But still a moment longer she watched, leaning forward a little like a young hawk from its rock, and then turned as if she made herself shake off a dream. Afterwards she looked about to see if I had noticed.

I sat up and said, 'What do you look for?'

She said, 'For the Lady's will. I too can read signs and portents. One day I will be priestess here.' She spoke it proudly, unsmiling, and tilted up her chin.

The night drew on. The whole world seemed to sink and die. Only far away I thought I heard the sea boom and suck. Then I slept a little after all, and when I woke the girl still watched with her face turned towards the loch and her hair shining like a great silver pelt upon her shoulders.

Before dawn, as I gazed up into the sky and saw the stars burn there, I felt my spirit lift and soar. I knew what Echraide would say when she returned.

Sure enough, in the early light she came. She looked weary once more, treading over the turf and rocks. Her step dragged and her face showed lined and worn. But when she saw me her face lit. She said, 'You are ours. The Lady wills it.' She put her hands on my arms and kissed my forehead and afterwards Etain came forward and did the same, only her lips were dry and hardly brushed my skin.

The smith said, 'Hold still! Do you want me to take your ear off?'

He rasped, working on through the metal of the slave collar. Outside I could hear the people gathering already.

There was laughter and little screams and scuffles. Cumair, standing apart, said smoothly, 'Well, my dear, all things are for the best.'

I said, 'Is it thanks you want, Cumair?'

I'd expected another smirk, but he said, quite quietly, 'I have that in plenty.'

I twisted round to see him and the smith swore. I said, 'Cumair, what will you do?'

'Oh, my dear,' he said, 'this song is barely written.'

After that all the day was given over to rejoicing. I was bewildered and not yet truly happy for these people were still strangers in their ways and, if they had hope of me, I did not know their expectations.

Some things stand out. At noon we rode back to the shrine. There, on the long shore of the loch, the people were assembled. As we watched they cast offerings upon the water, flowers or shining pebbles or food. Then Cathal went among them as their king. They had brought up a little boat for him made of withies. He stepped into this and was rowed a short way out. Then he stood and held high a splendid sword with a bone hilt inlaid with yellow glass. This he offered, throwing it up so that it caught the spring sunlight before it wheeled in the air and fell into the water.

There were other things also: more metal work – some wide armbands, four fingers broad and decorated all over; a shield; another sword, only not so fine. Lastly there was a flicker of bright red, the cloth that Etain had fought her brother for, quenched like a flame in the waters.

She stood near me with others of the dun. I turned to her, seeing that, and she raised her brows. She looked plain bad-tempered. 'A heavy price after all,' she said, 'for a slave boy.'

That night there was a feast, with baked fish and mutton, and dancing by the island people, singing in a tongue so old and strange I could not follow it. Ferbhal helped me with it but of Etain there was no sign.

In the time that followed I understood what it was to be honoured. Their Lady had given me her blessing according to the custom and it would not have occurred to them to do other than follow her decree. Yet it came strange to sit with the men in the first place round the hearth and to take food directly from the cauldron; to have the pick of the horses, my own spear and sling and sword. Here I felt no worse than other men, no less than the best of them.

It was a different life from that of Nam Dubh, for the dun was small with few inhabitants. Those who lived there were Cathal's family, the royal household; Cathal himself with Ferbhál and Étain his children, Echraide his sister, some others who were cousins or nephews and nieces.

Their way of life was hard. They were as much horse-breeders and fishermen as warriors. At first I went out on the boats with them, casting their nets in the little channels and bays. But I was better with the horses, herding and breaking them.

Yet they had kept their pride. When they could they practised, as we had done, with the spear and the sword. And no one could touch them for riding.

The island itself was sparsely inhabited for the ground was poor. The farmers worked little fields of wheat and rye in the sheltered places. What wealth there was came from the metal workings. The smithies were busy all day. When I asked I was told that it had always been so since first the Horse-people had come to the islands, generations ago, bringing their craftsmen with them.

Some days after my acceptance I sought Cathal out. I had watched him set off, walking as he did each day to speak with his people. They were few enough for him to know them each by name.

I found him on the shore, staring towards the mainland. He smiled as I came up.

'I like,' he said, 'to look on what once was ours. The Horse-people were always restless but our kind do not like to be driven.'

We had not yet talked, not even round the dun's hearth of an evening. Yet I was full of questions for it seemed I had received goods for no payment; and all men must pay their dues.

I said, 'Tell me of the Horse-people. I know only what my father's people said.'

'And was that bad? Could they not honour us as noble enemies?'

'When they spoke it was of my mother, and her they cursed.'

He laughed, softly, still looking over the water. 'Our ways

are not so different. But some things they did not like. We are better to our women than they are to theirs. We are proud of them. They are loyal and strong and wise. They bear fine children and rear them well. Our girls are taught to ride and handle a knife and a sling. Once, when there were enough of us, our young warriors were sent to the older women to learn their wisdom before they bore arms in combat.'

I said, 'And do your warriors stand at the loom and suckle babes?'

'Perhaps,' said Cathal, 'it is a lack to them that they do not.'

He was kind; everything he told me was as if to a child, patient and gentle. I thought of Gortag and shivered. 'It is true,' I said, 'women have power.'

He shrugged. 'Like anything, it may be used for good or ill.'

I turned and walked a little way along the shore, for my thoughts were restless and I needed to think.

When I turned back I asked, 'Why would they think my mother a witch? They hated her still, even after these years. Any man might tell a priestess, doing honour to her goddess.'

He laughed again, then bent and picked up a pebble and sent it skimming across the waves.

'In war, Arawn, anyone believes wickedness of enemies. And war we shall have again.'

He threw it in, like a chance remark, though it was a thing of import. I paused, confused, for my mind was still on my mother and it seemed that he had not answered me. Yet if I ignored the talk of war I would seem only a callow youth.

After a moment I said, 'How will it be? There are so few of you.'

He said, 'So there are. But my kingdom stretches further than this island. In the spring, when the tides race, you will see. The tribes will gather. And Cernach has enemies. He is too powerful. The People of the Sheep and the Tribes of the Fox will join us. One day my horses will run again on the mountains of Nam Dubh.'

I felt strange at that, remembering Cernach and his war-carts, his men and weapons, the gold and bronze, even the man himself with his charm and ease. Against him Cathal seemed a dreamer, a fisherman at arms. I said, 'My uncle will fight against you. You do not know what it is like, to live as a warrior in that place.'

314

He looked at me. I thought I had been impudent. 'Once,' he said, 'I did.'

He turned, beginning the long walk back up the cliffs to the dun. His boots were wet up to his ankles where the waves had lapped. I looked back along the shoreline to the place where the rocks began. A figure walked there, bending every now and then to fill a basket she carried on her arm. It was Etain, gathering the sea-weed they used to flavour stews. I knew her by her hair and the way she moved, light as the sea-foam itself. I watched until she raised her head, and then I turned and walked after Cathal. My heart was racing and I did not know why.

Chapter Twenty-eight

The days went by till it was spring and time for the seed sowing. Everyone leant a hand for, war or no, food must be grown and provided for those who were left behind. The season was wet and one had to be garbed for it, going out.

So it was that one morning Etain wished to fetch water from the well. There were few of us only taking shelter in the dun from a downpour: some women spinning and talking together, myself and other young men making good equipment. I watched her go to the entrance, peer out and purse her lips, and then walk back and fetch the cloak she'd left hanging by her place. She swung it round her shoulders and then fumbled at the neck and cursed roundly as the drawstring broke in her hand. For a moment she stood ruefully looking round but no one else had seen her plight. I thought then how I might make it better. I had my pin still, that had been given to me at Cernach's coming. I stood and called to Etain and showed her.

She took it lightly, thanking me but not looking to see its shape; and then went back to the women and bent for one of them to help her fix it. Afterwards she went into the rain and I saw her no more that morning.

That evening she sat licking her fingers from the pot and laughing with her friends. I did not like to ask her for the pin, it seemed churlish, and I thought it better to wait for her remembrance of it. In a little while she looked up and smiled and threw it over and turned back at once towards her companions. I caught the pin and stuck it in my tunic. Only later, lying in my bed, did I take it out and look at it again. The light was dim, with only a small lamp burning, but I could see how the metal was twisted out of shape at the back where she had pulled it from her cloak. I thought, She had no care of it; to her it was a trifle. And remembered how I had felt the instant it was given to me. The smell of the hall at

317

Nam Dubh came back to me and the faces of Mhorged and Hakos and my aunt and Nemair, even my grandfather sitting on his rugs with the dogs round him and his wine cup in his hand. She could not have known of it; I had no anger at her, only grief for myself that she cared so little for what was mine with its memories.

She made no mention of it and in the days that followed I worked harder than any man, trying to forget her in the tasks I did. But the dun was not Nam Dubh; there were ceremonies, and men and women talked and joked and squabbled together. I could not be free of her and there was a brightness in her that drew the eye, in her hair and her way of dressing. She was not like the others who wore their plain kirtles and cloaks unadorned with pride. She had their wildness but found ways to add colour with her shells and bracelets set with pretty glass shards from the smithies and gleaming stones from the beach.

Yet if Etain bore me no good will, Ferbhal and I had struck up a friendship. It happened almost at once. We were both of an age and of a mind. His life was horses, their breeding and breaking and riding. Indeed he had little else to do for there was no warrior training such as we'd had for nobles' sons at Nam Dubh. For myself, it was a joy to ride and hunt and fish, even to have dogs to whistle up that knew me. I had been half a year with Cumair; now, when I had freedom, I understood how tight I'd worn my collar.

No wonder then that together we were wild, choosing the bad-tempered brutes of ponies to bring to our hands, riding far into the mountains after boar – small ones only, we had some sense; bribing the fishermen to take us with them. Cathal was angry just once – when Ferbhal was thrown and knocked senseless. He was not himself for two days. After that we kept quiet about our mishaps.

One afternoon we rode to the long beach on the eastern side of the island. I could never get enough of looking at the sea. The cliffs here were high and black with deep inlets through which the water poured at high tide. It was the nesting season, and sea birds screeched and swooped or perched on their rough, untidy nests.

We had sat and watched awhile when Ferbhal said, 'The farmers and the shore-folk climb hereabouts for the eggs.'

I stared up at the cliffs. There were footholds and

handholds but the rock was sheer and tall. My spine shivered.

Ferbhal said, 'They bring the eggs up sometimes to exchange for a new knife or an axe blade, anything like that. They think that the more daring they are, the more worth there is in what they get. It's the wind that does for them mostly; it blows them on to the rocks.'

He looked at me, laughing. 'I've been up. The view's worth it. But don't tell anyone. Are you game?'

The climb was hard but it was a fine day and quite still in the sheltered places. It was less difficult once we were climbing, although the birds screamed and tried to mob us. There was a broad ledge about halfway up with sea-pinks growing where we stopped to rest.

I was glad to catch my breath and lean back against the rock. It was warm from the spring sunshine and below the sea was a clear sparkling green like glass.

Ferbhal said, 'I meant it. Don't let a word of this reach my father. Horses he can understand, but not this. It would worry him.'

'I won't. Have you done this often?'

He shook his head. 'Sometimes as a child, for dares. Etain could climb this when she was twelve. I'd try to follow her.'

I thought of her climbing, with her kirtle hitched and her face eager. I said, 'No girl would think of it in the Raven-tribes.'

He laughed and leant to flick a stone over the edge. We watched it grow small and disappear even before it hit the water. 'Etain,' he said, 'does as she pleases. Besides, in our tribes a girl is never a child. They're born women.'

Some gulls were squalling over a fish, pecking one another. Ferbhal stared at them with his thoughts elsewhere.

I asked, 'Do you mean because of the Horse-queen?'

'Oh, yes, she's for the women.'

That told me nothing. I said carefully, 'But a Clan's goddess is for all the people. She has them in her care.'

'Yes.' He flung another stone. 'So my father would think.'

We looked down once more. The sea swelled for the tide was on the turn, flowing in. It was the colour now, not of glass, but of the green stones one finds sometimes on the beach, and there were strands of red weed floating just beneath the surface.

Ferbhal said, 'We'll have to climb. The tide'll be in too far by the time we're down. We'll go up to the cliff top and round by the track to fetch the ponies.'

He paused and leant forward on his stomach, peering over. 'Do you ever think what might be down there, in the water? Some great, monstrous creature? I always wonder, when the sea's like this.'

I said, 'This is the first time I've known such a sea. I've lived in the marshes, but they were flat; the sea was distant and not like this. And in the mountains there are streams and little pools. We used to swim in the summer.' I felt cold, as though the red weed touched my back.

There was a pause. The sea swelled and sucked at the black rocks that jutted like huge fins or a backbone. I said, 'Ferbhal, tell me about my mother.'

I'd spoken quietly but he heard me. He said, 'She was a priestess and a princess. That is why you're important. Whatever my father said, he would not have let you go. The royal blood is borne by the female line though a son is chosen and crowned.'

I said, 'No, not that. Tell me of her. What you've heard. Did your father or Echraide speak anything?'

He shook his head. 'Listen, the women keep their own counsel. Whatever they do is for the goddess, and in her name. I can imagine what's been said. But I know nothing, only how the Horse-mother is.'

I said, 'How's that?'

He squirmed round on his stomach to look at me. He said, 'You'll find out, at your initiation, like we all do.' Afterwards he laughed, hard and quick, turning back to the sea. Another pebble went over, flung forcefully.

I was silent. In a bit he said softly, 'The Horse-lady's queen of the islands, not of the sea. But my father wants to make her strong again, to give back her honour. He dreams of the old lands, the plains and mountains. Etain urges him. She wants it also. For the goddess, she says. I think it's madness.'

I made some stir beside him. He moved back on the ledge and sat up. 'I'm not a coward. I'll fight, when it comes to it, as well as any. But we have our wealth here – our horses, our smithies. In a few years we could pay tribute for what we lost. In goods, not in blood.'

He looked back at the sea, and I with him. He said, 'Does the Raven-goddess have a taste for blood?'

320

There were things I remembered: the post, the feel of the feathers and the noise of them against my ear.

'Yes,' I told him.

He threw a last stone, a larger one, so that this time we saw it hit the water and sink. 'They all do,' he said. Afterwards he stood and stretched and faced the cliff, and in a moment we began to climb.

His words stayed with me, yet the worship of the Horse-people seemed clean-tasting as spring water after what I'd seen of Cernach's Lady. Daily Echraide led the women's prayers and sometimes they would leave on their ponies for the shrine. There were places for her consort also, the Horse-lord, himself powerful, who guided the ploughshare and made ready the men in strength and courage. There were the lesser gods as well, for the smiths and the fishermen, and places that were sacred in the island. Their prayers and rituals had an order and a seemliness, natural as the seasons themselves.

But though I stood with the youths and the men in the place of the Horse-lord and listened to Cathal call upon him, I did not worship. It was a thing too strange to me; these gods were not yet mine, nor did they touch my heart. It was enough to eat my fill and be warm at night, to wander with Ferbhal and no longer feel the ring about my neck. My flesh and blood and bone was given back to me. I would not lightly give away my soul.

One evening Echraide came to sit beside me. I was stitching harness for the horse I rode, a good enough beast though not a patch on Ban. She watched a while then said, 'You work well. There is a care in you for things.'

She spoke to me often. I'd grown to trust her; from the first I'd thought she had a good face. I'd learnt to tell such things.

I said, 'A horse deserves the best. You of all people should say so.'

She smiled and watched a little longer. Then she gazed round the room, seeming indifferent though not so. She was like an otter, scenting round. She rested her gaze and I too looked though I knew who I should see: Etain with some others, bent over a game of chance.

'Do you talk to her?'

I shook my head.

'Why not? You are of an age, and of rank together.'

'She has friends enough of her own.'

'Can one ever have enough of friends?'

'Perhaps she would think so.'

She smiled again and took up the leather I worked on and ran it through her hands. 'Etain has never had to lack them.'

I made no answer and did not wish to show my face so bent my head and wound up some sheep gut for my next thread.

Echraide said, 'She is a favoured child, close to Cathal and beautiful in a way that few others are. It has made her wilful.'

I threaded the gut. I'd been through worse than this and my hands were steady.

'For yourself . . .'

I said, 'It does not matter.'

'There is a set to your mouth and a way you have of looking with your chin lifted so. You too are wilful, though I think as a child you were not indulged.'

Now I did look at her, perhaps in the way that she did say, and told her, 'Lady, your calling gives you sight.'

She sighed then and made a movement as if she would put her hand on mine, but she checked and said instead, 'Etain is a flying swan, a fish's flicker, starlight on the loch. All those things. But she is a young mare too, arching her neck and lifting her tail. Or the bitch baying to the moon.' She looked at me steadily till my colour rose and we held each other's eyes.

'Arawn,' she said, 'she knows it, and so do you. If she is those things, what are you? Ask yourself that.'

She had left me bewildered and ignorant of what I should do, but in a day or two Cathal called me to him and I understood what lay behind her words.

We went out to the horse runs and I thought he wished to ask about a colt I had been breaking. We chatted a while but he seemed uneasy, unable to gather his thoughts on the matter but prowling like a big cat around the corral. At last he said, 'There are some things that I must talk of.'

I thought he meant of war and if he wanted to know the state of Nam Dubh and the number of her men – though Cumair could have told him that as well as I. But he did not go on at once, only cleared his throat and walked a little more.

At last he sat, gazing out into the field where the colt ran and looking not like a king but only as a man with trouble on his shoulders. Then he said, 'Listen to our custom. Our tribe is not a large one. We are bound to each other by ties of blood – so should you be to us.'

I began to say, 'My mother—' but he said, quite harshly, 'Macha is dead.'

He gathered his thoughts, still troubled. 'Arawn,' he said at last, 'we are the People of the Horse. Our Lady is goddess of this land and of our people; she protects and nurtures us. The Horse-lord likewise has us in his palm – to guard our boundaries and watch over us in all things. We are of the royal blood, elected by our people to serve them and our gods. Our duties lie heavy upon us. Do you understand this far?'

I said, 'I understand.' The gravity in him made me quiet, pricking to hear what lay beneath his words as an animal will prick in darkness to hear the rising wind.

'In ourselves we reflect the order of the gods. The king is married to his queen and to the land. When he prospers and is generous to those who serve him, so does the land. A niggardly coward means an empty granary and warriors with greaseless swords and a queen without her cattle. The royal women serve the goddess; it is their special duty and they must serve her well. A king should choose his wife with an eye to this, as should all of the royal blood, for when the king dies the people elect another. We have no say in this. It is as the god and goddess decree.'

I asked him, 'Why do you tell me this?'

He took a breath, half angry – with himself rather than me – and said then, in a rush, 'Your mother, Macha, was a princess of our people, and more than that. She was of the first blood – her line went back to the goddess herself, direct, first born of first born, through the generations. The bards could sing it, and to us it was a sacred thing. Well, Cernach's warriors put paid to that. And her own choosing.

'But blood will flow, from the mother to the child, however lightly she may carry it. You alone bear her lineage and her duties and so must you marry according to our custom. Do you understand this far?'

I nodded, quiet within myself, feeling his words root and stir in me like seeds in the fallow earth after winter. Yet I thought too that there was some old bitterness beyond what he told. His face was fierce and his eyes looked inwards.

The colt, which had been grazing, wheeled all at once and

ran the pasture's length. Cathal sighed and shrugged and smiled. He said, 'I look for omens. The colt runs well, and you have come back to us. I will wed you to Etain, my own daughter, who is the equal of your mother in rank, though not in blood. She will not shame you, nor you her.'

Etain was wild with fury. I saw her walk to Cathal's quarters early that evening and contrived to be near by at work. So it was that I heard her first shrieks of outrage and saw her flying from his room across the courtyard of the dun. Later from her own chamber came more cries of the rage and the sound of objects hurled repeatedly against the walls until women were running everywhere.

In the hall the men gathered round me, grinning.

'Never mind, lad. It would be the same with anyone. Let's hope you have what it takes to keep the Lady happy.' They clapped me on the back and found the whole thing funny, but I, who should have been most happy, was heartsick.

She came to me, waiting till I had taken myself off, just to the corner of the yard where I could be quiet. I was working a carving such as some of the lads used to do back at Nam Dubh. This was of Ban, a little, proud, high-stepping pony, for I thought of him often even now.

In a while I felt my spine prickle. I turned and saw her. She threw up her head at once and made no attempt to hide that she'd been watching.

I was raw-skinned already and used to different women. I said, 'Do you up the price, my lady?'

She started, furious at once. She had a fistful of some bits and pony trappings she'd been bringing to the forge, and these she flung at me.

'Here,' she said, 'since you stay a slave for all your fine blood, make yourself useful for your keep!'

They glinted at my feet amongst bits of hay and dust. She kicked at them, driving them closer.

'Pick them up!'

I did as she bade me, watching all the time. She was untidy still from her outburst at Cathal, her hair tumbled on her shoulders, skirts disordered and grimed with dust. With my eyes on her, she realized it. It made things worse. Danger hung in the air, sparking as if before a storm.

Her teeth set in her lip, her eyes narrowed. She cried at me, 'And my father would have you one of ours! Did they flog

324

you often back in your filthy mountain stronghold? What did they make you do? Clean out the midden? Stack the pile of dung? That's all you're fit for!'

Her face was white with temper; her fury beyond her reason, and mine also, for I could not tell why she should hate me so.

My own anger rose and said, Why then, give her what will make her more angry still!

I said, 'Yes, Lady. I was flogged. A slave must grovel, belly to the ground, to please his master.'

She snorted through her nose. 'And did you so?'

'And more. I tell you I polished up their boots with spittle by the time they'd done. Now, what would you have me do – lick these clean for you?'

She believed me. The contempt lit up her face, bringing the blood pink as foxgloves to her cheek and forehead. She said, 'You do defile our name.' And suddenly the knife was in her hand and darting like a dragonfly. I felt it prick my shirt and lift, cutting upwards at the cloth.

There is a movement one learns, fighting hand to hand – a quick down-blow as if breaking apart a joint of meat. It does not break the bone unless required to, but it leaves the limb numbed and useless for a time. I used it on her, before she blinked.

She cried out. The knife fell into the hay. She clasped her wrist against her breast and stared at it. For the first time, perhaps, she'd felt a fight with an enemy. Then she raised her eyes to mine.

I thought she was about to cry. For a long moment I saw the pain, and a greater one of outraged pride, and I too was halted and knew exactly, down to the last pulse and beat of her blood, how she felt this. But we stared each other out.

Then she said, 'Yes, lick them clean and bring them to me when you can.' She walked away and made no move to take up the knife. But she remembered it for she turned to look where it lay. 'Keep it,' she said, 'towards your freedom price.'

We were to be betrothed at the spring festival. Summer is the usual time for marriages and promises, but this year with the stirrings of the tribes our vow was to be sooner.

Etain would not speak to me. She kept more to her chambers with her women or else swept past me with her

325

head held high. Cumair made mischief where he could, singing of love by the fire at night. She was disdainful, lifting her bright head and open with her pride. Each day she seemed more beautiful and that was part of her defiance. She'd not be caught unkempt again. She wore her paint and her jewels in spite of me.

So I watched her till it seemed I must speak with her or go mad. My own anger had died. I understood – how could I not? – that she felt herself a hawk penned in a cage, or a young fox given to the hounds. One day, I thought, we will have this out together.

One evening, soon afterwards, she quarrelled again with Cathal. He had urged her to play a board game with him and grew cross when her mind strayed. She moved the pieces carelessly. He shouted, and she shouted back that he had no care for her feelings, and then she ran and climbed the ladder to her chamber, pulling tight the curtain.

As soon as was decent I went to my own bothy and waited there till the hearth-space emptied and people were abed. Cathal sat late on purpose. Then I slipped out quietly and looked around. It was dark save for the raked embers that made a red glow, but in the open space above the stars showed.

I did not dare try the ladder. The young women's quarters were above, and forbidden to unmarried men. But there were posts that supported the roof and the galleries, and crosspieces to take the weight. I swung up on to the range.

Her chamber was halfway round. I trod carefully on the timber floor, but no one stirred. A light burnt beneath her curtain. I wondered if she would scream and call for help, and what would happen. I'd have no rest, though, till this was made right one way or the other. And I thought also: What will she look like, sleeping?

The curtain was heavy, made of sewn skins. I lifted it and slipped inside. My heart beat quickly and my belly quivered. Lighter fabric hung behind to keep out draughts. I raised my hand, then paused, listening, for I heard voices.

They murmured, women's voices, rising and falling, some words distinct, others not.

I pleated up the cloth, just at the edge, enough for me to put my eye to. Inside the chamber was small, with a lamp on the floor close by the door and a chest for clothes, and a pile of skins in a frame of wood for a bed. Etain lay here, face down, and Echraide sat by, stroking her hair.

There was no need to hear much. I guessed already what they talked of while Echraide gave comfort as she would to a child. Yet I waited, like a thief, come to steal their secrets from the dark, and in a while Echraide dropped her hands to lie in her lap.

She said, 'Why have you taken against him? He is not old, nor brutal.' I held my breath to hear.

On the bed, near hidden in the tumble of furs, Etain shook her head.

'Why then?'

Her face lifted. She looked young and fierce and her cheeks were wet with tears. Yet her grief had rage in it still and her tears scalded.

She said, 'He is a half-breed. I remember how I saw him, with a slave's shackle round his neck and those marks upon his back. He had been beaten like a dog – and Cathal would marry me to him!'

'He is Macha's son.'

'Aye, I know it, and I know who she was. Don't you think I understand my duty? But what does it count, Echraide? What does it matter? – And him with a face as fair as any. It is not that I could not love him. If he'd come to me on a chariot in his war paint, with the gold bright round his neck and bronze on his wrists and about his ankles, then I would have cast my heart before him. Yet as it stands, he bears his shame for all to see and makes it mine! I would have bought him for my bed and had more joy of him.'

I could bear no more. I slipped from my listening place and crept back with the wounds of her tongue burning on me.

After that I wondered how I could free her. I thought that I might refuse her, only that would bring another shame to her; or to tell her how things had been at Nam Dubh, but I had my own pride.

Those days Cumair watched us slyly. He had taken against her for he preferred women soft and biddable and Etain was neither. Nor did she have much time for music but sometimes chatted softly as he played, or cursed at her spinning when it tangled, or whistled to her dogs. I prickled for her, as a dog does at danger. I knew his ways; at his tamest he was most the snake.

One night she sat brooding beside the hearth, idle and heavy. Pretending to play at the *fidchell* board I could have told her thoughts for her. Cumair began softly to strum, playing yet again some dreary tale of lost love and woe. She looked up suddenly, pulled off a ring and flung it across the hearth at him.

'Take that,' she said, 'for your pains. Now go yowl at the moon and give us peace!'

He stared at her with an odd glitter in his eye. Since we had been here he no longer oiled his beard and flesh, nor used his perfumes. All at once he was more the man. He put down his harp and bent forward, reaching for the ring. She watched and saw, I think, something in him which she feared. At any rate she started back and I rose, pushing back the board, to go to her if she needed. My movement drew her eye and she snapped at him, shrill with temper and fear, 'And take him too – who is your slave for all his royal blood!'

He had her then. I saw the understanding in his face, quite sudden, flaring as the pine root torch does in the dark. He was like a hunter who sees after days how best to lay the trap.

'A slave is it?' he said, soft as a cat after birds. 'Is that what you think him, Lady?

She stared at him, not answering; but her breasts moved with her breathing and he let his eyes rest upon them and then looked into her face.

The colour flooded there till her cheeks and throat were bloomed as red as her hair. He laughed, soft in his throat, as if he were her lover, and lifted a strand so the firelight glimmered down its length and showed the lights in it of gold and wine and amber.

'Cumair,' I said, 'let her be.'

He never turned, only played with her hair and said, 'Won't you tell her, my dear? She thinks you craven and no fit match for her. Won't you tell her of the wolf and you on your horse, outfacing it? Won't you tell her of that wicked old man, your grandfather, who'd cut the flesh from your backbone sooner than speak up for you? Come now, speak of your courage and defiance and all the splendid wildness of Nam Dubh.' Then he did turn and bared his teeth at me like a cur. 'Or won't your cursed pride let you?'

I thought, Cursed? *He* is cursed. He has us where he wants us. For I saw clearly how he shamed us, how he would hold her to ridicule for her misunderstandings and for myself – to bend me yet once more to his will.

I loved her then more than anything: more than sunlight, or the lift of Ban's mane at the gallop, or the feel of a good spear close in my hand. But he had her stricken and to fall myself would not save her. Besides, it would come better from him. She could tell herself he lied.

He stood there, with her ring already on his little finger, sleek as the granary ferret. I said to him, 'Tell her what you like.' And turned on my heel and left them.

Chapter Twenty-nine

The Horse-tribes had begun to gather. Each day the little boats would arrive bearing the island families. Around the dun tents appeared. At night we ate outside unless it rained, and I listened as they chatted and laughed and shared their news. It was a feast time and a time also to draw up plans for raiding, to seal allegiances and forge new bonds.

It was time also for the spring feast, when the animals are purified and the great fires lit to call upon the sun to burn brightly in the coming months.

Once the days were of a certain length the preparations began. Wood was hauled from the forest and stacked to dry and built into bonfires round the island, in the stockyards and the high places and before the Lady's shrine.

Meanwhile, since it was a gathering, there were games and trials of strength and boasting. There were bouts of wrestling to watch and spear throwing and long rides after game into the mountains. They were in good heart. Nights they would spend swearing how they would put Cernach and his hordes to flight and command from Cumair his fiercest songs. I thought sometimes that they were like children, foretelling fine futures – 'I shall do this, and this, and slay the wicked king bare-handed!' – with no sense of Cernach's ways.

I had to go away at times to think, remembering what had been done and how these were my people. But it was hard to think of Luth and Magh and Dearg and know how they too talked of war.

It was about this time I had a falling out with Cumair. He seemed to me a hypocrite, singing as he did for the Horse-people when once he had sung for the tribes of Cernach. I asked him one day, when we were alone in the dun, if ever he believed in what he sang? He turned on me, narrowing his eyes and almost spitting. 'What,' he said, 'is your definition of honesty? Who is more honest? I, who sing openly for gold and give the best I am able, or those who take what's given and never show there's more to sing to?'

I was bewildered and hardly knew what to say. There was more here than I had looked for; I felt as though I'd stirred at water and found a stew.

He gathered his cloak around him, though the day was warm, and rubbed at his brow with his fingers. He said, 'My head pains me these days.'

He looked well enough, not ill as my grandfather had done, sweating and white with dark marks on his skin; only his eyes looked strange, wary and quick like an animal's. He looked past me now, as if he saw something in the shadows.

I said, 'What is it?'

He came to himself, and eyed me over as he used to. 'Remember,' he said, 'even with you I took my chance. I held nothing back. I sold you openly. Call it an honour-price, my dear.'

I turned my back and went out to the sunshine, which felt clean. He made no sense, nor did I look for it then.

What was harder was Etain. I avoided her. I was as mad for her as ever but she would bring me no good. I had never asked Cumair what he had said to her; it was better not to know.

Yet I could not be forever pining. It was spring and there was joy to be found in the scents in the air, in the growing things, in being out and about after the closeness of the dun. So it chanced that one afternoon, wanting after all the noise and company to be alone, I went swimming.

There was a small bay, with a sandy cove girded round with rocks and quite safe with a long slope of sheltered shore down into the sea. I swam from there a way out though the water was cold. I was soon chilly and swam back. While I dried myself off on an old length of cloth, I looked up towards the rocks and saw Etain.

I had forgotten how she wandered the sea-shore gathering the weed that grew there. Now she stood with her hair lifted from her face and shoulders in long pale tendrils like weed itself, and her face was white as the foam. She stood quite still, looking across at me, with her woollen cloak pulled tight and her basket on her arm.

For a long moment neither of us spoke though already my heart began to thump against my ribs. The day was greying over and the wind rising from the sea. I felt it on my flesh and shivered.

Then she walked in the tall, proud way she had, stepping over the sloping rocks towards me, not smiling, defiant rather, with her chin lifted as if she scorned to look down to mind her footing.

When she was near she raised her chin still higher and said, 'Ferbhal was asking for you. He had made up a party to hunt and wants to know if you will go with them?'

'Surely,' I said, 'by now he'll be gone?'

She stood and lifted her shoulders a little and shook her head. I saw then how she was lost for words to say between us.

I said, 'It was good of you to tell me.'

'Oh,' she said, 'I did not come especially, only I saw you and thought you should know. But you are right. He will be long gone.'

Again there was silence between us, while the sea murmured and the birds called, high and shrill, above our heads.

I had never seen her so, at a loss, her harshness gone. She was like a child who has done some slight wrong that adults will find funny; too proud to own it yet on the verge of weeping.

She said, 'Well, then,' and turned to go but I was wild to keep her.

I said, 'At Nam Dubh we would swim in the lakes. They were cold but not so cold as here.'

'Here,' she said, 'one would not swim the lake, for it is sacred to the Horse-queen. You will see at the sacrifice. As for the sea, it is safe enough, as far as the bay's rim, but beyond there are currents. I would have called to you if you had gone further.'

Almost I thanked her, awkwardly, for her concern but I held off for she was like a bright, wary bird, stepping before the nets, and I was at a loss for how to hold her.

The sea churned and splashed about the rocks, for the tide had turned and was coming in. It was now quite cold and I shivered for I had only the cloth wrapped round me and that was barely enough for decency's sake. Yet I could not dress before her.

Still she paused, then looked towards the sea and drew a breath. I watched her and saw her profile and careless, tangled hair and the strong, straight shape of her set against the grey waves and black rocks – and something in me seemed to churn and break, a hard, sharp longing. I remembered my grandfather looking so at Hakos. I thought, If she turns now, she will see how I feel. I cannot hide it. Then she did turn and I was able to pretend after all that I had been watching for the tide.

She looked straight at me and she too shivered, though I do not think it was from cold; her cloak was heavy and tightly woven. She said, 'I am ashamed. Cumair told me how it was for you.'

I said, 'You weren't to know.'

'Yet still I am ashamed.'

I stood silent, for I couldn't answer her without sounding trite or as if I didn't care. Then she jumped as a wave broke on a rock behind her and glanced round, catching at her cloak.

Then she looked at me again and all at once put out her hand and touched my naked shoulder. She touched but for a moment, not long enough for me to catch her hand, and it was a clumsy gesture, the first I'd ever seen her make. She said, 'You are cold right through. Hurry and dress before the tide is in.' She turned and began to climb the rocks. She went swiftly, but looking down I saw she'd left her basket. I smiled at that, and dressed, and gave her time to get away, mindful of her pride, before I took it up and followed after.

That night, in the dun, she was very lovely. She wore her best jewels and had darkened her lashes and brows with some paste of wax and soot the women made. She laughed and played at *fidchell* with her friends so that Cathal looked at her and smiled and made plain there was peace between them; and though she did not look at me, in my heart I knew why she laughed. And I thought of the shore, and the cold, grey waves, and her warm hand on my shoulder, and my soul was content and at ease.

The eve of Beltine was soft and bright together, the sky barred with grey and pink and gold, and when the sun had sunk into the sea the moon showed very high among the stars.

No one except the children slept, but neither did we eat or drink. The time between dusk and dawn is sacred to the gods and must be spent in reverence. All the day we had made ready. There were joints already set on skewers and the wine skins brought in and placed on carts. Now we sat quiet in the dun until the night was old. And then, like one, the royal household rose and the gates were opened and Cathal led us into the yard.

The lesser chieftains waited there with their people behind them. The path from the dun stretched through the settlement, white in the moonlight.

As we walked, the people joined us; Beltine is not like Samhuin where faces are hidden in fear. All around I could hear whispers and scuffling. In the torchlight people's faces showed, eager and good-humoured.

We went steadily, the whole tribe, filling the path like a spill from the sea. Cathal led and already, flaring into the sky, the great bonfires burnt on the headlands and in the pastures.

We came to the Lady's shrine. As before it was decked with flowers and shells from the sea-shore and other things: armbands, lengths of prettily woven cloth, little figures worked in miniature – anything they thought would please the goddess.

Here the bonfires were unlit. They ringed the shrine, huge piles of wood, logs and branches and twigs, with cloths soaked in resin tucked in for the flames to bite.

Ferbhal touched my shoulder. I understood and followed him. I took no offence. I was not yet of the tribe and this was their mystery and the magic of their blood.

He took me to a higher place, behind the shrine, from which we could look down. He said, 'I'll wait awhile. It would be a long ceremony to stand alone.'

From the trackway below Cathal stepped out. He wore a shift of clean, undyed linen, bright in the moonlight. He turned towards his people and someone handed him a torch. He walked on and bent and lit the first of the bonfires. After a moment it took and began to hiss and show red and yellow within the logs.

The fires caught in turn. The flames' crackle and the snap of wood filled the air and the people shouted aloud; but afterwards were quiet.

Far off down the track, in the horse pastures, came the sound of drumming. Someone beat slowly on a tight leather skin. The noise was hollow, like old bone against bone, only deeper. Then the people took it up, clapping or stamping on the ground, but solemn and intent. The beat quickened and grew louder; I could feel it, like an echo in the earth beneath our feet.

From the pastures the horses came, distant at first, dark shapes surging like a sea-wave, lit by the flicker of the herdsmen's torches. Against the noise of drums, their hooves were a deeper thunder, and richer; living gold against the poor man's dross.

They approached, and all at once began to show clearly as the bonfires lit the night. Between the streams of flames the lead animals galloped from the dark, with tossed manes and wild, gleaming eyes. A stallion bared its teeth, neck held low and stretched. The flames defined flank and shoulder and gave them colour, gold or red or black. Then came the herd, the mares and stiff-legged, tender foals, the wicked colts and fillies. The night was filled with their heat and dust. All about was the smell of dung and sweat and smoke. They snorted and jostled – more than a wave, a pouring tide, a flood of hoof and bone and hair upon the uplands, driven by the herdsmen, riding like night fiends and screaming 'Ai-ai!'

From the shrine Echraide stepped, clad like Cathal and with a garland of flowers woven into her hair. She held out her hands as below, on the trackway, the horses streamed by.

Ferbhal was beside me. I shouted into his ear, 'The Lady blesses them.'

He shook his head. 'No. It is they who bless Her. Without her herds she is nothing. They are the wealth of this land. By them she is queen.'

The horses passed. The noise of their hooves and the herdsmen's cries died away. They had galloped through the Beltine fires that flared from the black earth in its long, winter sleep. So too comes new life with the hot blood risen, and the sun which spins like a blazing wheel from the dark half of the year.

The people were about the bonfires, setting up the spits and handing round the wine. There was laughter and the young women began to dance, circling and swaying, all rosy and gold, clapping out the beat. Their skirts swung from their hips with a glimpse of calf or the shadow behind the knee. Their arms were graceful, lifted above their heads.

The wine passed by, cool and sharp. I drank and drank

again. High above the stars were white and the moon was like a disc of quartz, hung upon the deep breast of the sky.

Now the men shouted. They too danced and leapt. Some scrambled up on others' shoulders and in pairs began to wrestle.

The drum beats began once more, closer and quicker. A carnyx blared, over and over. All round the shrine the people made a ring, within the circle of the fires.

The sound of the carnyx died. There was silence. It fell upon them. It was the quiet of the mountain cat, crouched in its lair; of the white, high-burning moon; of a dry land that lays out its dust for rain.

Into the circle a horse was led, a young stallion, grey as my Ban had been, but the mane was longer and braided with more flowers and charms. I recognized it. I had seen it running with the mares in one of the stock pens – a haughty, bad-tempered beast, but beautiful with a tapering head and strong, flared nostrils. Now it came out before us all, high stepping, pulling against the rope and jigging. Its quarters swung and the men holding it had to haul hard on its head; even so it bit one.

The people made a semicircle round it. Before was the drop to the loch, the cold, dark water shining far below. It was the sacrifice and already it seemed to feel its death upon it and reared again, dragging up the men at its head. The people murmured.

From amongst them stepped a young man, naked but for a loin cloth and charms about his neck. He had sailed over from one of the islands, with his father and brothers and cousins. I had played dice with him and two days before he had been hunting with boar spears and nets in the hills.

They held the horse. He vaulted on and held out his hands for them to bind them about the animal's neck and his feet to the belly, not tight but as if for a token. I remembered him at the hunt, telling how the crossing had been choppy so that they'd thought several times they'd foundered, and later grumbling that he'd brought too few pegs to secure his nets. Ferbhal had lent him some. My heart began to knock and my palms grew wet. I wondered how he had come to this. The horse plunged once more; he gestured that a cloth be tied about its eyes, and it grew quiet.

A great peace came upon the company. In the moonlight all the land was bleached and shadowy; the flower garlands were white, the charms shone, the bonfires blazed and crackled. From far below came the quiet lap of the water. Beyond the span of mountains showed, blacker against a black sky. .

The young man on the horse set his face to the loch. I could see his profile, calm and exalted. His brow was wide and generous, the planes of his cheek and jaw strong, the eye sockets were carved into shadow. On the white mane his hands lay loose and easy.

Echraide stepped out. She walked to the edge of the drop and opened wide her arms. She called upon the goddess in her sacred names, invoking her blessing. Still in their quiet the people waited, patient as cattle.

Echraide stepped back and now the people moved, surging towards the man and horse. They strove to touch the sacrifice, held on the ropes before them, speaking their own blessings upon it.

When each had done they drew back. The young man on the horse was alone in the circle with the loch before him. I saw his living flesh, and the proud set of his head upon his neck, and the heaving sides of the horse, ears pricked to hear, flanks quivering, breath curled upon the air.

He waited. His face was turned up to the moon. In all my life I had never seen the sacrifice of a living thing, save my grandfather, though that was between him and me.

Now I thought, I understand! In that moment I felt myself go with him. I shared in his glory, in the burning moonlight, in the hot sides of the horse. The garlands were about my neck, at my feet the loch waters lapped; the night stretched forever. The great blessing of the summer land was within me and on us all.

A great screech went up. The people screamed, a full-throated bay of hatred. They rushed forward, and now they did not praise him, nor touch him in gentleness and love. They swung their torches down upon him, and trampled the pure white flowers. His face lifted above them as the horse reared and screamed. The carved mouth opened wide, bloodied and torn; his soul looked out of his eyes. His pride died in the trodden mud and there was only anguish and a desperate, unexpected fear. All this in that moment until the horse struggled forward and lurched, falling to its knees and tumbled, plunging and turning over with the man still bound upon him.

338

They hit the water. There was a great splash and spray and afterwards a moment of quiet. The water there was deep. The people craned forward to look. Then, from the bonfire, the flames leapt and far down, upon the water, more flames shone, rippling and moving on the surface, waking the goddess in her water-form so that from the great depths she uncurled and began to swim.

Quite suddenly they surfaced. The horse began to swim, with the sodden, half-conscious thing clinging round its neck. The animal's blindfold had come off. It struck out, making for the far off shore. I thought, Perhaps he will do it, and longed for it as if the man had been Luth or Dearg or anyone I knew.

Still the people watched. At first I thought they might wish him well, but in their faces was an old knowledge. They waited, emptied of their hatred as a crucible is emptied, the hot flow moulded, the heat spent.

Now it was hard to make out the horse, for the loch was shadowy; it was the dark time when the moon dips. Yet the people had begun to murmur and to point. I strained to see also and made out the glimmering, swimming shape. All at once, far out upon the water, the horse seemed to rear, as if it had been struck a huge, upward blow from underneath, and lifted. It rolled and turned and reared again, and then it and its burden slipped from view beneath the water. We waited but there was nothing more; only a broad, long ripple that moved from where they had vanished and travelled the width of the loch until it splashed on the bank below us.

A cry went up, another baying. They rejoiced then, for the goddess had taken those who had been offered and found them pleasing. I watched a little longer, just until they went to fetch the Horse-queen from her shrine for at dawn they carry her about the fields and stock pens so she can bless them, and afterwards feast and drink and dance all day. Night broke, prised apart, and the dawn was cream and soft pinks and greens, pearly as the inside of a shell. It was then I slipped away back to the dun and sat alone, for in truth I was not yet of the tribe.

The day was bright, yellow with sunshine that shone clear as spring water in the yard. In the distance, barely heard, was the murmur of the sea, and from time to time the sound of people laughing. Once I heard footsteps run past then pause and the sound of a man and woman talking. Afterwards they walked on more slowly, so I guessed it was a couple seeking to be private.

For something to do I brought out my sword and began to oil the blade, wiping the length over and over with an old rag. They had given me one of their own fashioning, shorter than the ones at Nam Dubh, of an older style as befitted their custom. It was well balanced and beautifully worked about the hilt and scabbard with patterns like sea waves, repeated over, and swirls and tendrils branching out, etched in bronze. But it did not suit my hand as well as the other I had owned.

After a bit I heard footsteps again, this time on the flags within the dun. I looked up and there was Etain with the sunshine glowing on her hair and the flowers about her neck, delicate and withered already, and her bleached, ritual robe loose and trailing upon the ground.

I caught my breath, she was so lovely; and she in turn paused and looked at me. I got to my feet for she was of the royal household and deserving of respect.

She came towards me. The sunlight streamed in the yard, dazzling. She was a little unsteady, and stumbled on the hem of her robe. I put out my hand to take her elbow. She smelt of the incense they used and the ritual oils and on her breath was wine and honey cake. She laughed, low in her throat, and laid her fingers against my face. Her eye-lids fluttered; each lash curved, dark at the root and then light at the tip. A strand of her hair lay pale as new gold across my mouth.

Somewhere, deep within the waters of the loch, two bodies hung and drifted; the white horse and the young man bound to him, their flesh heavy with death, rocked together in the cold cradle of the goddess.

The darkness was there and the mystery; the death in the midst of life – not the death of old age, but of those who are young, in beauty and strength, with all their power upon them.

In these things we stood. They reached for us and held us fast, tied as the sacrifice, for at Beltine the sacrifice is as much for life as for death. She hung heavy upon me, with her arms about my neck, but her flesh was warm and I tasted her hair and her skin and the wine in her mouth. I caught her hand and we went up to her chamber, and she laughed once more and soon I felt the sun upon my back and the dying flowers crushed between us, and we too were held in the hands of the goddess.

Later I awoke and looked at her. She lay upon the bed, half covered by her wolfskin, her arms spread wide, her hair all over. She slept deeply, stilled and spent, but with a warmth and richness to her, like summer fruit in sunshine after rain. Her mouth was open and she snored a little. I would have liked to have teased her awake and laughed with her a while. So I had done with the village girls; all except one who had wept at our parting and said that she loved me. To her I had given a bronze charm, taken from Cumair's bag, and hung it round her neck. I'd thought it too slight for him to miss, but days later he did. And it had not stilled her crying.

Now I was restless, not tired but full of life. I went to the door of her chamber; no one was about. They were still in the fields about their own pleasures for the goddess. So I went back in and looked more carefully at what was hers. It made me smile to see how she had the best. Her wall hangings were green and red and blue; her cups were moulded bronze; even her work box had designs knocked out upon it. This was a last stronghold of the Horse-people. What was here had never been taken from them; it was their heritage and hers.

She stirred, murmuring, and opened her eyes wide. She sat up to see, then slid back against the skin. Her shoulders were white against the fur. She said, 'Arawn, it is still Beltine, for all today.' Her mouth curved, mocking. It had not been her first time. For Etain there had been other Beltines and more besides; and the women of the Horse-people have their own ways and know their own minds and bring no shame upon themselves for what they do is done before the goddess. Then in a moment I made her laugh after all. Soon after, though, she pulled the skin around us both and gasped and clung to me again.

Chapter Thirty

Beltine passed. The chieftains and their followers sailed back to their island strongholds and the dun grew quiet again. Yet soon it would be time for the spring raids. Ferbhal and his cousins spent their days practising at sword play in the yard and set up targets for their spears, or galloped along the shores and herded cattle on the mountains. The shores rang with their war cries; by night they stuck their head-dresses full of feathers and scratched charms on to the shells they wore as amulets. Cumair, meanwhile, sang more and more of victory.

I joined them, riding madly or clashing swords and making believe I meant it. Yet all to me was a dream. Those days I walked in the Otherworld with Etain by my side. What there was between us was no secret, the whole dun knew. Yet we were seemly, her for her pride and myself for respect of her – she was no light girl to have for the asking. Our times together were set apart, snatched in the sheltered coves while the sea rolled and churned, or in the heather of the moorland, hidden amongst an outcrop or a hollow. They were trysting times. Some days I hardly knew how we arrived at them; just that I would see her flying on her pony – the same that she had bartered with Mithir, only he never took it – and then she would be leaping down and running to my arms, laughing and panting and throwing back her hair. We never talked till after; she was as eager as I. But at night, in the dun, I too would work up a shine on my sword and spear and oil my shield inside and out, and she would sit with the women and spin. Yet we could have told each other's thoughts for the asking.

It would have gone on like that save for Cumair. One night when I was sitting heavy and idle, almost nodding before the fire, I felt his eye upon me. He was quite close, near enough for me to say, 'What is it?' without the others hearing. Even so, he looked around before he spoke.

Straight after he said, 'You're all spent out, emptied like a wine-skin before the dawn, while she is filled and glowing as a midnight lamp.'

My colour rose. This was something for which I had no banter.

He snorted laughter through his nose, then sang, very softly, a line or two of one of the songs he kept for the menfolk. I told him, 'Don't.'

He let his voice die away. Afterwards he sighed and scratched the side of his chin. 'When Mithir comes again,' he said, 'I will go with him.'

He'd let his beard grow longer. Some days, when we were travelling, he'd made me trim it. I hated that, with him murmuring, 'Closer, lad', or 'Steady with your hand', and his breath hot in my face all the time. I would be glad to see him gone.

I said, 'So you've picked the carcase over, Cumair. Is it fresh meat you're after?'

He glowered up at me from under his brows. 'Aye,' he said, 'better meat at least, my dear.' I shrugged. 'You've been well paid. You've no complaints.'

He pursed his mouth, considering, and all at once leant forward and snapped his fingers before my eyes. I blinked and started back.

He said, 'You're blind with love, boy. Cathal's mad for war and the women strut and preen, calling on their Lady. When can you take anything for what it seems? Strip off the skin. See the flesh and bone beneath.'

I was used to his spite, though this I did not understand. Yet I thought it unbecoming to rise to his jibes. I made to walk away but he reached out and caught me by the arm, and hissed at me, 'Take care, lad, what you are getting into.' Now I did stare. For once he sounded in earnest. He looked at me and wrapped his robe round him, sulky as an ox made to plough another furrow at the day's end. Usually he was willing to make mischief. I felt cold within and angry with sudden fear.

All at once he lumbered to his feet. He gripped my arm tighter and hustled me towards the door. It was like the old days but I could not struggle without a scene.

Outside he stopped and held me up against the wall. He said softly, 'Have you forgotten what they called your mother? There are always reasons. Only think. Do you not owe your father's people something also?'

I threw his arm off. Even so the cast went home, and hurt. Since I had come to the dun there was much I had kept back, even from myself. I had not realized the ties that bound me to what I had known before, nor how deep they went. But I had my boy's pride also.

'What do you mean, Cumair? Casting dirt with your filthy tongue?'

His shiftiness went, replaced by bad temper. He said, 'Not so long ago, my lovely lad, I'd have given that collar you wore around your neck a tug for that. You'd have felt it and known your place.'

'Know yours then,' I said, 'and speak plain.'

He scowled and looked around, but there was no one about; only the watchman, who knew us, and some girls shutting in the pigs for the night. At last he said, 'Come with me, and see for yourself.'

Almost I went; then I shook myself like a dog shaking off water. I left him standing with a scowl like black thunder and malice in his eyes.

Back by the hearth in the dun I sat awhile and ate stew from the pot and chatted with one of Cathal's men. Soon it was time to retire to the young men's chamber, yet I stayed for a bit, while the flames died in the hearth.

The next day Etain was there, wherever I looked, and Cumair lurking in whatever corner was most shadowy. He was like a piece of grit in clay that spoils the finished pot; or a bad stitch in a shoe, rubbing up a callus.

All morning I was in a dark mood. At midday Etain brought me out a round of bread spread with honey. After I had eaten it she said, sweet as the honey itself, 'You spoke a good while with Cumair last night.'

'Too long.' I did not mean to be sharp with her but she drew back, considering anyway.

'What did you talk of?' She stood close to me, on purpose. I could have reached out to span her waist and pull her close. She had darkened her lashes and a tress of hair was stuck together at the end where she had leant over the pot.

'Of this and that.'

She knew then she'd get nothing from me. Still she stood, eyeing me and pursing her lips in thought. Then she reached up and swept back her hair from her forehead and laughed and said, 'I will put a charm on him to stop his mouth and save our ears. Will that please you?'

My spine prickled; that went too close to what had been said before. I said, 'Don't make a jest of it,' and she leant then and kissed me and whispered, 'Do you think that I don't mean it?' and went off back to the dun, singing.

The next day I sought him out. He was not hard to find, sitting in his bothy stringing his harp. I watched him a moment. He was careful, twining the gut with his big fingers, and absorbed, sounding it once and then again, over and over, till it hummed just sweet enough in the air. He was at peace, like a well-fed bear licking his fur.

He must have felt my gaze. He turned all at once, with a wide stare, then lowered his lids. He strummed the harp once more and stood, smoothing out his robes. 'Well,' he said, 'my lovely. What brings you here?'

I said, 'What did you mean? What is there to see?'

The daylight streamed into the bothy. He was soothed by his task, eased in some way. Seeing him so, I thought, Last night he was frightened.

Just as I realized that he said, 'I'd have given it free before. Now it costs you.'

I cursed at him but he only held out his hand so in the end I gave him my cloak pin. He stared at the bent pin and spat; yet it had become a treasure to me.

'It's a walk,' he said, pulling on his boots.

We went out across the moorland. The day was bright and loud with birdsong. I followed him as all those months I'd followed him before, and it came to me that I was still in his hand, not free of him even yet. Soon I recognized the way, though we did not use the cliff path, and in a while the long waters of the loch stretched before us.

He paused then, and stood with head lifted. By now we were on a path that was new to me. He was listening and peering forward, his hand held up to stop my questions.

I listened also, but there was only the soft 'chuck chuck' of a blackbird calling to its mate. Cumair went on and the pathway narrowed and became a deep channel of dried mud, overgrown on either side with nettles and elder and brambles. The flies were troublesome and the place smelt rank, of tangled greenery grown thick together when the sun is hot.

The path wound down as if we went towards the loch, and grew darker. Some sun-spots shone upon the way, but mostly we walked in green shadow, single file, for the narrowness. Once I saw the glint of water not very far below.

In front Cumair breathed heavily; his weight made the going hard for him. He shouldered through while the branches parted and swung back and rustled.

On either side the banks grew higher, till the trees were growing on a level with our ears. The roots twisted through – some old and thick, mossed over; others hanging down like hair. The birds were quiet and the place felt airless. I had no fear, only wonderment that he had found such a path, and curiosity as to where it led.

At last he halted. The sweat gathered round his nose and ran from his chin. He used his sleeve to wipe it. Before us the banks had closed together so that we could go no further. Above our heads oaks and elders met. Then he bent and pulled away a strand of bramble. It lifted and drew with it a tangled clump of stems. Before us was an opening in the ground, a small hole that led in, just big enough for us to scramble through.

Cumair gestured, urging me forward and looking round once more, as though he feared that someone trod behind us. I crouched and entered and inside the opening at once became a cave, opening high as several men, with bright ferns growing about the rocks. The light was cool and green, stained by the vegetation. From the cave, going within the earth, was a passageway. I turned back to Cumair and he nodded and pointed me on.

The way led down. Very soon the light grew dim and the ferns no longer grew. I could not see the roof; it went up high and from above came squeaks and scufflings. But the floor was sanded and in the sand were other footprints going on before: small footprints; women's footprints.

Seeing those, I felt the first fear. I said, 'What is this place?' My voice spoke back at me, held within the earthy walls, close and muffled as if a great fist fastened round.

Cumair said, 'Hush.' Once more he looked back.

I said, 'Who will follow?'

And he said, 'No one. Go on.' Then, 'Wait.'

He pushed past and crouched and fumbled in his clothes. I heard a trickle of slow liquid and something cracked and hissed. There was light, a little, dim flicker in the greyness. After, it was steady. He had filled a lamp and struck a spark and lit it, having borne it all this way.

We went on. The path wound deep into the cliff, like a worm's burrow. Now we went in darkness, save for the steady flame that was like a small, pricking spear point. The walls closed round us; the roof grew low. Above was all the weight of rock.

Cumair crept, the lamp outstretched. The walls were rough, of mud and stone. Sometimes he paused and seemed to listen. I did likewise, but there was only silence, deep as you could ever think, like sleep or death itself.

I thought of what we'd come from but the sunlight and the clouds and the breeze blowing from the water seemed only dreams. Already I longed for natural things; the birds on the thorn bushes, the flowers in the fields, the push of a horse's muzzle. Then I thought how such things were unknown in this place.

The passageway broadened. Now the light was too little to shine on the walls. But beyond one sensed a great emptiness. Cumair stopped and panted. By the little lamp his face looked greenish, like a man with fever or sickness, and slick with sweat. I thought, He knows it is forbidden, and the heaviness all around seemed to gather up and fasten on us so that it hurt to breathe and my head felt squeezed and painful.

Yet he went forward, stepping on the sand while the path became a cave, unto the end, and there he halted.

The roof dipped, slimed and sparkling, and met the ground. Water oozed from the walls. Where it trickled it had formed a recess and in the recess stood a figure.

I knew her, though she was not as I had ever seen her. She was in her dark aspect – bedecked not with flowers and tokens but with the flesh of small creatures and scraps of fur. Her eyes bulged, staring. She was carved of twisted heart-wood and painted white. Round her neck was her emblem, no longer gold but silver.

At her feet lay the tools of sacrifice, the knives and the bowls. But there were piles of twigs also, with signs scratched upon them. I thought of Gortag saying all those long months ago, 'Your mother had her secret places.'

So did Etain and the women of her tribe; perhaps all

women who do not fight and openly grasp a sword and cry out their anger. But it turned my stomach, for there is worship that is lawful and that which isn't, and my heart misgave me. What is done here, I thought, that is not fit to be seen by all the tribe, or openly at the women's time of worship?

I sank to my knees. I said, 'We should not be here.' I was not scared; the cave felt empty despite the carving. We spoke no sacred words to wake the goddess. But I was wrung out, as though I'd been all day riding or back at Nam Dubh, in the practice pits for Uffa.

Cumair said, 'I told you, such as I walk with the gods, betwixt and between. It is the nature of my craft to play out tales of the Otherworld in this. My dear, I wanted you to see.'

The little flame burnt steadily. He'd set it at her feet. One could guess at horrors, looking at her face.

I said, 'Would it have been different if I'd never shown you what I thought, or if I'd kept quiet when you told the girl's fortune?'

His face was half in shadow and half lit by flame. He bent and lifted the lamp to raise it. The carved face leapt from the dark, streaked with light and blood. The artist had worked with the wood's grain, to twist her looks. Her mouth gaped, a chisel thrust; the eyes were red pebbles, picked up upon the beach.

Cumair said, 'What do you think, my dear?'

We were quiet a while, sitting before her, ourselves in darkness while the little lamp shone in a puddle of light upon the floor.

At last Cumair shifted. His outline showed, with his heavy nose and the thick chin rising from his bulk, and a touch of colour caught from his robes.

He sighed, as though he stirred from sleep, and said, 'You think me vengeful, but remember – if you look at a sword hilt, or a blade, or an armband even, when it's been worked over, you see things. Sometimes it's eyes, a man's or an owl's, staring at you; other times it's waves. Sometimes it's only a pattern, because the smith was in a good mood that day. Truth changes, Arawn.'

I could see the base of the effigy; a stick, with a long, dark splash upon it. There were things strewn round amongst the twigs, little bones, clay mouldings, a piece of gut from a harp, with knots tied in it.

And I knew what was above. I said, 'Not this.'

'No,' he said, 'not this.'

The days after were a heavy time. My mind was on what I'd seen yet there were other things to think of also, for we made ready for the spring raids to Cernach's lands. Already the little boats bobbed in the harbour; horses and their harness were rafted across to the mainland tribes of the confederacy. I thought of Cernach with his great hordes, and of Nam Dubh and of Uffa and Luth and Dearg and Magh and how they too made ready.

There was more besides. The moon waxed, fat bellied, and one evening Cathal took me aside and pointed up into the sky. He said, 'The year turns and pulls us on our way. In the meadow the Horse-lord stamps. The spring tides are running, tugging at the boats. It is time, I think, for your dedication. Are you with us?'

Cumair had left two days before. His last night he had sung, not of war, but of love and old tales. He could have been at Nam Dubh, with the people hushed before him and the dogs scratching and the ale pot going round.

I said, 'I see their faces; my uncle's, my friends'. It will be hard to bear a sword against them.'

'Is it often that you think of them?'

'Just lately,' I said, 'they've come back to me.' He drew in his breath with irritation. I did not know him very well, but it struck me he would not be one for patience.

'Well,' he said, 'put them from you, for they'd stab out your guts soon as you'd cry "welcome".'

Night followed night. The stars shone in their spring patterns; the days were warm and sparkling. Over the sea the mainland showed as a smooth green mound rising from the water; seals snoozed on the island beaches, the autumn pups grown sleek. Etain and I walked to see them and loved in the coves among the rocks and her laughter was in my ears and her hair twined round us both.

Afterwards she said, 'You angered my father.'

She lay in my arms, and twisted to look into my eyes.

I said, 'I had friends at Nam Dubh.'

'Tell me of them.'

I said a little, their names and how they'd been. Soon,

though, she slid from me and shivered, for a breeze had got up from the sea, and reached for her shift. I watched her raise her arms, and the curves of her breast and the long narrowing of her waist as the cloth fell about her.

I said, 'Come back.'

She knelt on the sand with the sea grey behind her and the sky grey above. She was just out of reach. Then she shook out her hair, from the shift's neck, and looked again at me, tilting her head. Her mouth moved, like a child told 'No'.

She said, 'Arawn, do not think of them. That time is passed. My father paid well for you, with decent goods. At the summer feast we will wed. Think of what will be.'

I said, 'Can we put away the past so lightly?'

'I can,' she said. 'I see my father with his horse herds and his head of cattle and his men. I see myself in new jewels and a fine wool cloak. How will you find me then?'

The tide was on the turn, sweeping out from the bay in long, flat ripples. The sea-birds rode the water, the seals bobbed whiskered faces and dived and bobbed again.

I said, 'First there will be the raiding.'

She moved close. Her head rested on my chest, her arms were about me. She was warm and settled, like some small, bright bird made ready for the evening.

She said, 'Fight well for me, Arawn. Tell my father you will make the dedication.'

She had never thought I might do otherwise. I laid my chin against her hair, and presently I nodded and we were quiet together.

That evening, when the dun grew quiet and drowsy after supper, I sought out Echraide. I said, 'May I speak with you?'

She rose at once and led me to her chamber. Behind the curtain the room was neat, with a narrow bed and a hanging on the wall. There was fresh hay put down and rugs laid over. She gestured me to sit, and was silent, waiting for my trouble.

I said, in a rush for I'd thought out the words already, 'Is it a heavy thing, to be brought to the goddess, even for those who are born to it and live all their lives in Her hand?'

I'd startled her; she caught back a smile as older people do when the young are serious.

She said, 'To everything its price. We eat bread but first we

351

till the earth; we cook fish but net them from the boats; we break a horse, with falls for our pains. So it is with the Horse-queen.'

'And afterwards? Must we serve wherever she takes us?'

'All things are decreed. Day follows night. One cannot be in sunlight without the shadows.'

'Do you believe that?'

She frowned, though her thoughts were slow upon her face.

She said, 'The gods hold what will be. We who are priests and priestesses show the people this and tell what is right. We must follow the omens and please our gods. Why do you ask these things? Do you not know them?'

'Can we do nothing then, for ourselves? Can we never say what's right or wrong?'

Her gaze was clear and steady; the trouble came from me, not from what she'd ever seen or done. She said, 'You ask that, as Macha's son?'

I said, 'Why did you – your people – take me back?'

'Your mother understood. The Tribe comes first in everything. By himself a man is nothing, no good to anyone. She made the mark and gave you to the Lady. She gave us back her blood.'

The hour felt late. I said, 'I will remember,' and turned to go.

She called me back, saying gently, 'What is it?'

'Nothing. I was not taught, that's all.'

I did not have long to brood. Two days later, as I rode out with Ferbhal, we were ambushed and surrounded by a group of cheering men. I recognized them and what time it was – Ferbhal grinned as though drunk already – and how I should greet them with good grace.

They took me to one of the far shores and on my skin painted the sacred signs and braided my hair back from my forehead.

Then they set me free with a spear in my hand and gave me a while before they came hunting. All day I spent lying low, keeping as much as I could to the woodlands where it was easier to hide. Twice footbands came within a spear's length of where I lay, but I had learnt quietness long ago keeping my skin whole in the marshes and it served me well.

At dusk I could in honour return to the dun. I would have

352

gone in fine heart only I recalled Etain's words. Surely, I thought, there must be more to the initiation than a day spent on my stomach in the woods? Then, as I neared the dun, I saw a group of women gathered on the road before the gates, dressed in black, and my heart began to beat more strongly and something in me said, Now comes the testing.

The women watched as I walked towards them. All the women of the royal blood were there and they looked as I had first seen them, wild and proud with secrets in their eyes. I feared them in that moment.

Echraide stepped forward and I halted before her. I did not know what to do, other than what was directed by them. In the dusk she raised her arms and invoked the goddess. I could not follow all the words; she used the old form, more ancient even than their tongue.

After that she looked at me, deep and serious. She said, 'He who comes to the land must wed with the land and the Lady waits upon him. Will you come?'

I looked round, confused, watching for some guidance, but the women only stared, even Etain who looked upon me as though I was a stranger. I guessed then that they had drunk some potion or followed a ritual to call the Horse-queen down to them. They were not themselves but truly in the Lady's hand.

I was a boy among them, earning manhood. I said, 'I will come.'

She nodded and took my arm. Her fingers felt light and thin and the cloth of her black robe fell back from her wrist to show the signs painted there. The women pressed round me and so together we went from the dun along the track that led to the shrine.

But we went beyond it. Yet it was no surprise to me when Echraide began the descent that led to the cave and held up the strands of bramble and gestured me in.

Inside they had fastened torches to the rock. The flames leapt and flickered so that the cave was sometimes small and dim and sometimes a great lit chamber. I blinked and felt the sweat of fear break out upon me. A cave is a door to the Otherworld and not to be lightly entered. Echraide led on and I followed, treading again the path that led into the earth and under the cliff, going down into the darkness. As we went the women took down the torches one by one, and snuffed them on the sandy floor. Then only Echraide's was

353

left, trailing oily smoke, the flame close and thick and yellow as a fever.

We came to the other smaller cave. I did not dare look to the shrine at first but when I did it was empty. I thought they must have taken the Lady away because it was unlawful to gaze upon her. Near to the recess there was a bed of skins laid upon heather such as we'd used at Nam Dubh. The heather was freshly gathered and springy and the hides newly tanned, such as you'd put down for an honoured guest. I looked and wondered and felt Echraide's eyes upon me; but I was too proud and too scared to ask why it was there.

Echraide said, 'The Horse-queen waits. Have courage. After the winter sowing comes the spring, when all men are happy. The Lady cares for us.'

She moved away; already the other women were drawing back down the passage.

I said, 'Echraide, I do not understand. Where I came from we had no such custom.'

She paused and looked up from under her brows. She said, 'A girl comes to a man for the ploughing and sowing all the years of their life together. So must a man come to the goddess for her to bring forth the fruits of the land and for him to be bound to her as her lord and protector. Yet it is a mystery also, a thing to be done rather than spoken. Do not question it. I told you this much in courtesy because you were a stranger.'

I waited then while she went out, taking her smoking torch with her so that for a little the glow of it shone upon the walls and the tallow smell was in the air, and then I was in darkness.

Time passed. I thought, Tomorrow I will be accounted a man. Yet for this night I was still a boy, sweating and breathing hard, making play I was unafraid yet scared to think too much in case I called up old fears and nightmares. I wished I'd thought to lie upon the heather and pull the skins about my head.

I waited a good while and began to think how the testing was only of the dark and my own imagination, and that I need only sit it out until they came for me again.

Then presently it seemed that the darkness was not so black and thick and, as I looked, the torchlight showed once more upon the walls, dim as yet but drawing nearer. With it I began to hear a shuffling sound as if something dragged wearily upon the sanded floor. As I heard it all the hairs on the back of my neck stood up. I got to my feet and faced the growing light.

It grew stronger and dazzled in the cave's entrance. The shadows sprang wavering on the rock. I saw the figure who held the torch.

It was a woman. She wore the royal robes of green and red shot through with gold, and over them a cloak of tanned horse hide with the hair turned in. It was that which had trailed upon the ground and made the dragging sound. She herself was stooped a little as if the weight had worn her down. On her head was a head-dress, very tall and slightly crooked, like a crown only taller, of worked metal, and in it was set a horse's skull.

I caught my breath and stepped back from her. Any man would have done the same. The empty eye sockets glared down; her own were masked for she was veiled with coarse black netting. Only she was not young. Her neck showed beneath the veil, skinny with loose flesh hanging, and her hands were bent and knotted.

I said, 'What do you want?' She laughed, an old woman's titter, with malice in it. Yet the sound did me good for it made her like any other.

She held the torch up, peering. Now I could see her eyes, bright as an animal's. There was a look in them I did not like. I'd seen it in Cumair's, a greed like hunger for things he meant to have. But I stood my ground. I told myself it was the same for any warrior.

She said, 'So the bridegroom is come? A fine young man. Happy the bride who takes him for hers.' She spoke softly, hissing the words though her voice caught on them once or twice. I held my breath to listen; even so I could not recognize her. Fear washed over me, like a tide on the sand, swept in from the sea.

She stepped forward. The robes dragged and shushed. The cloak was old and torn in places where the hide was thin. The hair was almost rubbed away; once it had been grey. But the gold about her neck and arms was heavy and richly worked and shone.

She shuffled again and waited. The horrid head-dress leaned further so that the horse skull lurched. She lifted her head to look at me, ducking like an old hen, and showed her scrawny wattles. I thought, Who is she?

Suddenly the fear was thick upon me. I did not know her; she was a stranger in the dun. About us was the thick cold of the cave and the smoke and yellow flame and shadows. There are tales of the gods and goddesses who walk as mortals. I thought of the Horse-queen in her shrine above and how I had seen her other face here in this cave.

Once more the woman laughed, still spiteful. My hackles rose like a dog's. She said, hardly above a whisper, 'My little colt, my little stallion, come kick your heels for me.'

I said, 'What do you mean?'

She put out her hand; there were brown spots on it among the ritual patterns, and the veins stood out. She clutched my wrist. She said, 'A pretty boy, to marry to the Mother.'

Till then I'd thought they spoke in riddles, Echraide and her kind. Now, as this creature tottered near and clutched at me, I learnt how to them the sacred marriage was the truth. The mystery caught at me and swept me up and held me in its own embrace. I thought of the skins laid down upon the bed of heather, of love and the spilling of the seed, of the ploughed earth and the corn and young animals born to the spring time. I thought of youth and age and the young man's death in cold, dark water upon the sacred horse. All this I understood, clear in my head. I was out of myself, taken to the rite. Then I looked into the woman's eyes.

She was used to this game. For her the mystery was long gone. She'd put on her robes and her crooked horse's skull and come to bed once more with a boy to make him a man. Yet there was no magic to make her quicken or young again. She was what she was and knew it, and so she chuckled and enjoyed what she did for the sake of it and the power and the fear she worked in others.

She breathed up into my face. I stepped back in horror. She smelt of her age and rotting teeth and a bad stomach. She smelt as my grandfather had done in the last year of his life.

I cried aloud. I wanted none of it. I pushed her back and she squawked like a frightened fowl and toppled, weighed with her head-dress and heavy robes. The skull cracked and splintered on the floor. The torch hissed upon the sand. She struggled, still shrieking, and kicked at the robes. Her thighs showed mottled red and white, the slack, heavy flesh of them hanging on the bone.

From the floor she spat her curses. I stared down at her; as yet they did not touch me. And the Horse-queen had not been in her. Then she grabbed the torch and struggled up and scuttled like a crab from the cave. I heard her scrabble her way along the passageway up to the night above.

Later I too made my way from the cave, going by touch. It took a good while, but in the end I saw paler darkness and felt the walls open around me. After that there was starlight and a cool wind blowing in and when I'd climbed a short while more, I was free.

Chapter Thirty-one

I lay in the shrine of the Horse-queen. I felt half dead, as if the hag picked over my brain with skinny claws. My eyes were filled with darkness; the daylight seemed a dream that I would wake from.

Above the wooden figure stood. Here she was hung with her spring flowers and pretty scraps of cloth and bright trinkets, like a girl. Though I had spurned her, yet I would make my peace, for the gods know the truth in the hearts of men. The dawn was breaking and the sky showed green as glass above the mountains and the loch was no longer black but streaked with bars of gold and silver. Already the gulls wheeled and outside the shrine a thrush hopped and beat a snail upon the ground.

My thoughts swung like the moon and crashed like tides. It was too soon to pray. Then I heard a sound and raised myself to look and saw a figure on the long shore of the loch.

I knew her at once by her hair and other little things, the way she stood, the lift of her head. She faced the loch waters, standing on a spit of ground that thrust out to the deeper part. She was casting things into the water. As I watched her my blood chilled and ran thick in my veins for I recognized what she threw – the cloak, the sword, the shield – and as she threw she keened, a high-pitched, bitter screaming that pierced the morning air.

I ran then, finding some way down from the shrine to the shore, flinging through the undergrowth and tangle of branches. I burst from the wooded slope and ran out along the empty stretch of pebbles. She turned and saw me.

She had painted yellow on her face and arms and rimmed her eyes with black. She wore her oldest clothes and had torn at them with shears. When she saw me all her body seemed to sag upon itself like someone struck across the stomach. Her mouth opened as though she gasped for air. I halted, staring, and she thrust out her arms and screamed, wild as the gulls, 'I curse you! I curse you!'

I stood, struck dumb, for till then I'd had no sense of cursing. The horror was what would have been amongst the skins and the heather in the Lady's cave. There the hag had hissed and spat, darkness in her ancient, barren grip.

Etain cried out again, 'Already I have mourned you. You are dead to me and to the tribe. And death will come! The warriors are sworn to it, to hunt you down.'

My spine prickled. I'd thought my fear was done. It was worse here, in the daylight, a wound stripped naked by this girl I'd loved and lain with.

I said, 'What is my wrong? The ritual was mine, and the Lady's. I've put no slight upon them.'

Her face was all eyes. She hugged her tattered robes and wrapped tight her arms about her body. We could have stood in ice and pelting rain, not sunshine. She leant forward, crying into the space between us, 'No slight! You spurned the Horse-queen. The marriage was not made between you.'

The fear made me sharp, like the edge on a sword before battle. I said, 'Is that what you were after – for me to lie with a withered crone in borrowed robes and call her "my Lady"? You like a practised husband?'

She cried out again and clasped her hand to her mouth. Then she said, 'You think that? What sacrilege you speak!'

My sight turned in, to the crone's eyes, filled with her age-old malice, and the Horse-queen above, waiting in her shrine. I said, 'The sacrilege was not mine, whatever you may think.'

She wailed aloud and beat her fists upon herself. Seeing her so, her pride flung down and trampled, I was all at once bewildered, lost in her anguish, and alone. Her grief possessed her. It took her up and changed her. She was strong in it, like a reef of bitter rocks, rising from the waters, and I the skiff cast on them.

I said, 'Etain—' to have it out with her.

She snarled like a mountain cat at that and cried again, 'I curse you.' Then she made a hideous little movement, hopping backwards, crouched towards the ground.

My breath caught. I guessed where she had learnt such a thing, binding up a spell. It was worse than in the cave, to see her so.

She heard me gasp and stared up, straight at me. All at

once she began to weep. Her tears made tracks down the yellow on her cheeks; water ran from her nose. She turned and paced and turned again, and never tried to stop or wipe the tears away.

At last she halted and said, 'Why didn't you? It is the custom. What a grief you've brought upon us!'

She paced again. I could not answer her. It was like treading in a mire, not knowing what was safe and what gave beneath one's feet.

She stopped once more before me, saying, 'We should have told you of the way of it. It was too hard a thing to put upon you.' She spoke half to herself, muttering.

I would have gone to her then, for she was the one in need of comfort. But as I stretched out my arms she backed away. I saw her look, as though I was dung, thrown from her horse's hooves. I thought, Truly, then, she thinks me cursed.

The knowledge weighted me like a stone. It was difficult to speak, as if I thrust against it. I said, 'Etain, I understood what should be done. I was not ignorant.'

She said again, 'It is the custom.'

Her voice had risen. She sounded what she was – a young girl crying out her pain, as if her feelings made the dark thing right.

I loved her still. Now, for that, I had properly to think, to put into words what my soul had felt and this to her, who had been bred for the ritual, who had it in her blood and mind as something sacred to the Tribe.

I told her, 'Not for me. I had no custom.'

She closed her eyes, as after pain.

She said, 'We are not children, to please ourselves. We have our duties. You bear the royal blood, more so than any. And you have wished a blight upon us.'

I said, 'I saw the shrine before. With Cumair. I saw what stood within. What binds us, Etain, to such darkness?'

She paused. Her breathing quietened. She saw me now as I was, not as the old woman had told in her ear.

We looked at one another. We knew the secrets of each other's bodies: old scars, the shape of ribs and waists and thighs, the close, naked fit of us together. But we were poor, foolish things, standing in the landscape of the gods, with their ears to listen and their eyes to see.

She said, 'You spoke with Echraide. She told you how it was.'

361

'I made my choice. I am free.'

'But we are not! And what you do, you do to us. It is the way!'

She was in agony, her hands outstretched, her teeth sunk in her lip.

I said, 'We never knew such things. We were outcasts. I had no gods to pray to, to fill the grain pit or the box of salt. We took what came because of Macha. Ask me then and I'd have done it. Not now.'

She was quiet. She brought up her hand and pushed away her hair.

I said, 'What of the other sacrifice, Etain? What of the young man in the water? Was his death for nothing? Have I undone that?'

She was staring at the loch. The sun was up now. The brightness dazzled. Her hair was burnished gold against her painted face.

Slowly she said, 'Was his death such a trouble to you? I saw you watching. You seemed cold and did not stay to feast.'

'I was not cold when you came to me.'

'No,' she said, 'not then.'

I said, 'When the Raven-tribes sacrifice it is criminals they hang – the ill-doers who have harmed and wronged. Not such as he.'

'Carrion for the crow. What merit in rotten meat?' She spoke dully, as if by rote, and I thought then how all the waters of the loch stretched between us.

I said, 'He feared his death.'

She shrugged, as if the matter was of no import. 'He is with the Lady.'

I had had no sleep. I had been frightened and angry and taken courage in both my hands to fling at my enemy. Now the weariness was upon me, binding tight, not soft but with bands of iron. I could have dropped on the sand and slept. But still I tried to make her understand.

I said, 'I've known the Horse-queen kind. One time, in a wood, where my mother had worshipped, I was sick. She gave me healing. But I am not hers.'

'Whose then? The Raven-hag's?' She spat it out. Once more I could have been a slave she cursed.

'Etain, where is the difference?'

She stared at me with her great pale eyes, ringed in black. 'It is true,' she said, 'in the Lady there is light and dark, be

362

she of the Horse or the Raven. But it is true of the god also. You make a virtue of the spear but it is tipped with blood and iron is wrought with pain and heat and blows. It is the nature of all things. You would serve the god well enough in the craft of fighting and strut a hero. Could you not serve the Lady?'

'Not in that way.'

After a pause she said, 'You have brought disgrace on me, the daughter of a king.'

I said, 'What I have done cannot touch you.'

'Touch!' she said, and began to laugh, high and wild. And then she hid her face in her hands with her hair falling about her shoulders and wept long sobs that shuddered through her body.

I stood, not knowing what to do. Yet I made no move to her for she was right and I would not insult her further.

In a while she lifted her head, all smeared about with paint. 'When my father's men catch you they will hurt you before they kill you, and I will watch, and all the Tribe will look to see how I will bear it. I will wear my finest robes and my gold and I will not flinch, for I am of the Tribe.' She drew herself straight and looked at me. Once more she was a princess. What there had been between us was gone, melted from her like the morning mist, only each of us would remember.

I looked towards the loch where the Horse-queen showed herself. Already in my heart was what I must do; not just for Etain but for myself.

I said, 'Once before I cast her off. Not willingly but there was a debt to pay. My father's blood runs also in my veins. She had a price for freedom though I did not know it then. Now I turn from her again. If there is justice in her she will understand. If not she'll punish me. But either way, Etain, she has the choice and the Tribe will not suffer. I take the price of honour freely.'

Her eyes widened. They had the colour of the morning in them, greys and blues. Her breathing grew quieter; her hands were pressed against her breast. She had understood before I'd finished speaking.

She looked towards the loch, and her brows drew down in thought. She too had been adrift, lost from what she knew. Now her path showed once more familiar, to lead her safely home.

She said, 'That too is a hard death.' Her voice was empty, like the space between sky and sea.

'Would Cathal give an easier?'

She shook her head and swallowed.

I smiled at her suddenly, trying to make light of it. 'Come,' I said, 'tell me where I should swim so she will not spy me.'

She looked at me, as though she'd speak, then out again across the water. She shook. All of her trembled; even her jaw moved, but she made herself be straight.

When she had scanned the loch she said, 'Always she takes the sacrifice there, in line with the rock across the water. If you kept to one side of it perhaps you would be safe.'

I eyed where she pointed. On the far shore there was a boulder, just glimpsed through the trees.

'Once you are across,' she said, 'there is only a little stretch of forest and a way through the mountains. When you come to the shores you will find the fishermen. Some set out from there. One will take you to the mainland. Have you something you can give them?'

Her courage helped mine. I said, 'I'll work my passage over.'

She reached inside her dress and up under her hair. When she had unfastened what was there she held it out to me.

Another charm. Once more a horse – not silver this time but gold and with a rider. The king riding in the sunlight.

I took it and held it and then I leant forward and fastened it back about her neck.

I said, 'It is not for me to wear. That would be sacrilege indeed.'

Her hand lifted, touching it. She looked up into my eyes; then she was in my arms and I tasted her mouth and her tears and the paint upon her skin. We clung together, like children in our fear. She pressed her fingers to my face and said, 'What shall I do? What shall I do? I should invoke the Horse-queen from the water and watch her take you, or else it is not done.'

I could not have held her closer. Her tremors shook me; her grief made wet my cheeks and chin; as she spoke she breathed into my mouth. But my heart said to her, Do as you should. It must be of your own choosing, for both of us are brought to sacrifice.

She knew it. Her fingers loosened. She touched the scar along my cheekbone; she used to trace it sometimes after love.

Almost she came to me again. Yet she knew her duty and her pride. She had told me what she was. She turned, hunched as she would be when she was old, and walked upon the spit of land. Then she turned again unto the water.

Now she was straight. The sunlight glittered on her tears. I thought, She cannot see. She raised her arms and called upon the goddess.

Her robes hung in tatters; the grief was taken into her like a black wick into a lamp, through and through for all her days. In that moment she was like my own shadow, or of my soul, or the heart between my ribs. But we had made our choosing, willingly of ourselves. Her voice rang clear, the words faultless, cold across the water. Her face was lifted to the sun. I went then, from her who would have been my wife, and walked into the water.

It was cold, colder than I should have thought possible though the marshes were cold and I had often swum there. The water was not clear but a deep peaty brown, full of little speckles. I waded till the water was at my waist, then took a breath and plunged forward and began to swim. I went steadily to pace myself. In front, a long way, I saw the boulder on the far shore and the shoreline itself and the rim of water upon it. The mountain rose sheer and wooded.

I wished the water was not so cold. It deadened my limbs and made them heavy and I was afraid of cramp. Swimming before, in familiar places, I had felt no fear; here every stroke was a danger, bearing me into worse. Yet I kept on and soon there was only the lift of my arms and the kick of my legs and the sparkle of the morning light on the black water, and the chill of the air upon my shoulders that was less chill than the water.

At first my mind had been bound to my actions. Now, as I settled into the rhythm, my thoughts soared free. The black cave was far away and the hag; there was greenery and the sunshine shining on the mountain. Yet I thought of my grieving Etain. Once I rolled on my back to look to where she stood. She was there still, staring out; but she did not lift her hand to greet me and I felt a great emptiness within, as empty as the water in which I swam.

I swam on. The far shore seemed no nearer. Instead there was a sense of depth, of a chasm opened beneath filled with black water. I remembered the young man drowned on the horse. Perhaps they hung there, far down in the water, bound still the one to the other, drifting like weed.

Now fear settled upon me, not of the body for I fought with the cold and the heavy water and to fight in that way was familiar, but of my soul. The goddess waited, huddled in her depths, listening for the splash of water, for the plunge of a body that was not an otter's or a fish or an eel. She was in her dark aspect, the dark of the night when the moon hides her face, or the storm cloud, or the wolf fighting for her young. So she would fight for her tribe; and she would fight also in the whispered curse, in the hidden knife, in the flickering lamp set in the cold cave walls. All these things she was, there in that water, though the morning was bright and fair and the birds called from the banks and bobbed about the reeds and the grass was a young green upon the hillside.

In my fear came a great grief, sent by the Lady. I thought, By my mother's people I should have found care and companionship; but there is only sacrifice and death and the hag-magic. And my arms grew weaker and the water seemed more cold and heavy. I thought of Nemair, the Raven priestess, and how through her there had been healing and courage, and it seemed to me unjust and a mystery that reflected the mystery of all things that in the Carrion One there should be such things.

Still I swam, and now the far shore was closer and the boulder stood out clear from the rocky banks. I began to turn a little, meaning to swim round, recalling Etain's words. I was very tired; the thoughts that had borne me up spun out and went from me like ripples circling from a stone. I was alone; if I cried out Etain would no longer hear me; there were no stones beneath my feet. The Lady whom I had always thought would succour me waited to pull me down. Sometimes in a hard winter people died or were found near death and those who did recover told how they had found that to try to live had cost them too much effort. It was easier to lie and sleep their way to death. I felt that now, with every lift of my arms and kick of my legs. Yet the debt was upon me and I had sworn to pay.

It was then, without warning, that the Horse-queen rose. There was a great swell of water that surged beneath me and carried me upwards, and after a vast suck and pull that gripped at my legs and sought to bring me under. My mouth filled with water as I cried out and the wave closed over me. I kicked my way up and the sunlight broke upon me but the fierce grip that was there would not let me go. It dragged at me again, like a huge mouth or arms that wrapped round my body and tugged. Water was in my eyes and ears and mouth. When I kicked there was only the swell of water rising from the loch depths but it had a power that was like the great flank of a horse sweeping by bearing me on and down.

I struggled, feeling death upon me. I felt no sense of mystery or of meeting my own fate, only despair and panic. Again came the suck and tug, smooth as some great beast coiled round me, for the Horse-queen has many shapes and forms. I glimpsed the sweet sky above, blue and empty, before my eyes filled with the dark.

And then, wracked out in terror, sinking against the flanks, the coils of water, my lungs burning with fire in my chest, a hammer in my head, came my anger. I kicked again, fiercely, and broke the surface and dragged up my arms and pulled against the water's weight. The Lady had had my fear and my courage, the strength of my body and all the lost terror of my soul. She had shown me her power but there was nothing in her fury that forbade me to fight.

I began to swim, battling against the current, and struggled to keep the shore boulder to my left. Anger made me strong. The young man had gone helpless to his death, perhaps willingly, yet his fear in his last moments was my fear also and my anger was his. I no longer thought, nor strove to make sense of this, only fought in baffled fury, as the wolf had done or the white hound in the water.

The water parted; the savage tug gave way. There was a last surge of water, a long wave that carried me beyond the sucking tide. I came free and my limbs were light again. Exhausted I rolled over with my face to the sun and floated. Then, chilled and wearied to the bone, I began to swim once more. At last there came a scrape of gravel at my knees and hands and feet and then the boughs of trees on the bank overhanging the water. I reached up and seized hold of one and for a moment hung there, drenched and shivering, and then hauled myself along it till I could scrabble up the bank.

I hid among the trees all morning, lying quiet in a glade where the sunlight slanted and warmed my limbs. When I had been there a while some deer came by to graze, stepping light footed and wary. There were flowers, yellow and white aconites, clustered at the roots of the trees. Birds chirped and sang in the thickets. I looked around and thought, In all of this is the Lady. And then I, who was her child, yet not her child, her victim and her hero, laid my head on my arms and wept as I had not done since my grandfather beat me. I wept for the same reason; not for pain but for my helplessness and my ignorance.

Chapter Thirty-two

Etain had spoken truly; the way through the mountains was clear and the path easy, trod by shepherds and traders on their way to the dun. By the evening I had reached the fishing port, a huddle of huts and little boats dragged up high on the beach. Far across the water was the bulk of the mainland, blue in the evening air.

No doubt I should have spun tales already in my mind to account for my needing passage. I was beyond all that. Instead I wandered in the dusk, cold and stumbling, while some men, mending nets around a driftwood fire, stared and raised their shoulders at each other.

Later one came up. He was an old salt, only interested in how many bales of wool I could load and whether I could man an oar without spewing my last meal over the side. When I had assured him on both scores he was pleased enough to take me. We sailed just before nightfall with the darkness closing in so that by the time I looked back at the island there was nothing to be seen, only a dark lump of rock stuck out from the sea.

We beached well before dawn. I slept under the oar I'd pulled on and, when the sun was up, slipped off while the master still twitched and snored and the watch played dice against himself.

The sun rose. There was a road, a proper one of battened timbers, for carts to pass along. On either side salt marsh stretched out to meet the sky. A wind blown in from the sea whipped the grasses. Later, when trees began, the road finished and there was only a track to follow, but that was plain, beaten down by long usage.

Out of the wind the sun grew hot. The broad surface of the track was pale dust beneath my feet. The trees thickened into forest bordering the path. I felt small in the sunshine, lonely as only a stranger can be, not knowing where the road will lead him, nor anyone to greet him when the day is at an end.

Once or twice thin pathways led from the track and looking down them I glimpsed clearings and occasionally thin curls of smoke drifted within the trees. I thought perhaps I should find food and water but it was too soon. I moved like an animal through the landscape. My body was tired and hungry but my instinct said 'Beware', and my instinct was stronger.

Later I came across a shrine but the gods of the place were strange and the totem different, with fox skins hung upon it. I did not like to pass without an offering and hunted till I found berries, which took a while. They were left from winter, and withered, but had kept red, like a fox, so I hoped the gods would take them.

After that I knew I should have to eat and followed the next path into the forest. If I have no harp, I thought, at least I am strong and fit and can work for payment. Soon enough I chanced upon a settlement but even as I approached the people came running and cursing with stones to throw in their hands. Yet it had not looked too poor a place; the goats were glossy.

I did not dare to try again. I walked on and the trackway grew more hot and bleak with hard, dry ruts that hurt to a walk on and the dark, close trees on either side. I came to a pond where the drovers watered their cattle on the road and drank there. I rested awhile, then got to my feet and walked once more. As the day went by Etain was more and more in my mind and there was a grief in my heart that made me bare and parched as the road that stretched beneath the sun.

The next day was much as the first, only I came out of the forest into a land empty but for some shepherds' bothies and a few scattered farmsteads. At one of these the farmer gave me bread and an egg in return for hauling wood. But he made it plain I should not stay. I lay the night between the roots of a tree and hoped the wild beasts would not come for I had no way of making fire to scare them.

Then came worse. The following evening I found myself in the hills. The hot sun had passed; the sky was white and the air cool. All day it had been chilly. I had met no one, nor seen any habitation, though I had found a stream and some wild cress growing. As the land grew more steep and rocky I thought to find a hollow where I could rest yet the place made me uneasy for there were old barrows set here and there in the landscape and once a long stone stood upon its end, marking where one of the first gods lived. They are so old no one knows their shapes or totems. It felt a land apart from men, not a good place to be alone. Even the birds seemed to watch and screech more shrilly in the skies.

I had begun to hurry, as if someone trod behind. The dusk was gathering and the place more lonely than ever. I did not even have a cloak to draw around me. I felt oppressed and all my limbs were heavy. I was tired and anxious and all the things I'd been through seemed to gather round like ghosts.

The track went on, though it had branched and my way had become thin and deep and grassed over in places. As I looked up to see where it led I saw smoke darker than the sky trailing upwards. My heart leapt, thinking there'd be some farm or village that would take me in; then I quietened and grew cold instead. The smoke hung like a pall, as if it had been a dense outpouring that only now drifted away and there was a smell in the air to catch the throat. It was sweetish and sickly and thick.

I crept forward. The land rose gently then spread downwards. On the plain below was the wreckage of a village. Not a soul stirred. The buildings, huts and byres and pens, poked up like blackened sticks. In the fields the crops were trampled. All at once I knew why I had felt so oppressed and weighted for the pall of smoke stretched over the land and the birds had quietened.

The place was deserted. Whoever had looted was gone though how far away was anyone's guess. But here on the track I'd be seen for sure if they still hunted. There was no worse danger in going to help.

The track forked again. I took the path leading downwards. The palisade had been hacked to bits. It was wattle, just to keep the livestock in.

I only stayed a little time. There was nothing I could do and I'd heaved my guts up before I'd gone five paces. Everyone was dead. Even a sow, too big and heavy to drive away, was skewered in her pen.

They needed prayers. I gabbled some for vengeance, though I could not call their gods by name. Going round I came across the headman. He'd been tortured with his legs stuck in the fire, charred away to bone. His head was gone; he must have been brave for them to take it. Close by, bound where he could watch, was a lad about my age. They'd cut his

371

throat when they'd finished. I stopped then and prayed properly, holding down my fear; they were owed that.

Afterwards the place felt better, as if their souls had heard. But I did not sleep that night, nor knew where I walked the next day, for thoughts of them.

For some days after I was fearful. Once I came across a place by a stream where the marks of hoofprints showed. I laid low for the best part of the day but the riders did not return. Gradually the land grew kinder though I was weak. I'd caught fish when I could but there were not yet fruits to pick and I had no weapons with which I could hunt game.

I no longer had any thoughts of hiding. The raiders were long gone. I followed a pathway down through forest. It became well trodden, once more a drovers' road.

The path wound on. Soon there were small painted stones, set up here and there to mark some boundary, and once the sly, soft chuckle of water, hidden deep among the trees.

The forest opened into a glade. For some way around trees had been felled. There was the noise of children laughing and shouting to one another, and someone sawing. I hid myself in a thicket and peered out. The village lay before me, snug behind its fencing. The huts were stoutly thatched; goats were tethered and a pair of oxen waited to be yoked. Beans and peas grew in neat strips of earth cleared beside the palisade.

The dogs got wind of me and began to bark. Geese cackled. I stepped out just as the children were beginning to crowd together and the women were looking and calling to the men.

The headman came at a run. He halted on the track and paused with a narrow eye. I said, 'I only want some food. I can work for it.' I opened my mouth to say more but it seemed not worth the effort and I stood mute instead.

He turned and muttered with the others. There was some arm waving. Then he walked up and looked me over more closely. He was a small man, and wiry, with a brown, lined face. After only a little silence he stepped aside and said, 'Welcome, stranger. You'd best come in.' I followed him through the gate, amid the stares, with the people fallen silent.

Once I was in everyone crowded round. I was shown to a hut and made to sit on a rug and a bowl of bean broth was pushed into my hand. They were quiet while I ate and gave me a cake of tough bread when I had finished the soup and stayed quiet while I chewed through that. At last, when they had been polite enough for honour, their headman said, 'Tell us now, who are you, and what is your tribe?'

I was dazed with so much food. I had to struggle with my wits. I said, 'I have no tribe.' And then, when they still stared, 'Not any more.'

The headman frowned. Already he was anxious, seeming the sort who's always eager to do right by his village. I wondered how he'd been chosen; not for strength. Perhaps he was best with his hands, or wisest.

Now he said, 'Yes?' with his voice going up. For a moment I wondered what he meant.

Then I said, 'My mother came from up north, from the Sheep people. She was a widow with a farm.' I spoke slowly, having to think all the time. 'She got herself a new man. When she died he kicked me out, soon as she was cold.' I spoke in Old Tongue with some of the new words, here and there, and wondered if it was convincing.

One of the women strolled over. She was middle-aged and strong, with lines across her brow and down her cheeks. Her look round at the others said plain as daylight, 'If you believe him, I don't.'

She said, 'A long way to journey, from the north.'

'I had nowhere to bide.'

'Not with your mother's people?'

'It's hard land. She'd gone against them in her youth and her brothers would not speak for what was hers.'

I met her eyes. They were a sharp, cold blue like a sky on a clear winter's day, and knowing. But I'd a good training, both with Grandfather and with Cumair. I could lie when I had to; this was less a lie than some.

I stood so they could see me better. 'I can work. I can earn a day's meals and something for the road. I'm good with animals, especially horses. I can clean tack and not get it tangled. Or drive a plough. Whatever you wish.' My voice was not quite my own. There was hunger in it still, and the memory of the endless trackway through the land.

The headman looked about him and the woman looked at him. Someone said, 'What'd you do to your face, lad? Your mother's man have a go at you?'

I nodded.

They muttered some more; I doubt if half of them believed

373

my tale but on a good farm there is always room for hands. One by one the older men of standing nodded.

The woman folded her arms. She looked stern and wry together with her mouth pursed up and her eyes less cold.

'For now,' she said, 'no talk of work. I have had sons myself. Another bowl of soup, I think, and then sleep on something comfortable. After we'll see what can be done.'

They took me in. They were good-hearted, simple people – not simple in their minds but in their souls, believing what was good. If they thought me a liar they thought also that I had reasons and did not question me. They shamed me by their trust.

In return I gave good measure. I worked till I was fit to drop but there was always a full platter night and morning, rugs to cover me where I slept, and what was best of all – tale telling and laughter and horseplay to watch and listen to in the soft light of spring's evening about the huts and yard.

The village was not large. By the next day I knew the names of each family and just a day or two after their way of talking or complaining, their work, what they thought of one another. Their kind were bound by the land, its rhythms and its nature, by tree felling and clearance, by tilling and sowing, by the feeding of their stock and its slaughter. There was no talk of warriors and their gods were kindly, dwelling in the ploughed earth, the spring that fed the woodland pools, the grove of hazel trees.

The headman Aduin and Munna his wife would have taken me in. Their own children were grown and married into neighbouring villages or with their huts built within the palisade. But I kept apart. It was enough to work and watch while gloomy Aduin fussed about the weather or his ox with a bruised foot. At nightfall I took my rugs to wherever it was quietest, often the stable. Sometimes, when I woke suddenly, I would believe I was back in the marshes with my grandfather's old pony nosing in my hair.

The mind remembers strangely. I was not with these people long, yet even now they are clear to me, only small and bright like the patterns the smiths of the Horse-people cut into the bronze. Those are etched so cleanly that you may look once and close your eyes and run your finger over them and each curve and line and tendril will spring to life. So I remember them; but bronze remains and they are rotted.

Some nights went past; the moon was in her bright half. For then I had other memories, of Beltine and of afterwards, that I recall as clearly; the fireglow, the water on the loch, the springing horse and Etain. Sometimes she seemed very close to me. Often as I started to drowse I seemed to feel her head on my shoulder and the warm ropes of her hair tumbled on my chest. Or else she was distant, as I'd last seen her, weeping on the shore with the whole deep stretch of water between us and the coils of the Horse-queen rising from the depths.

I wondered if Cathal had led his men across the sea and into Cernach's land. Before I'd left, such a little time ago, I'd seen the horses stamping on their rafts, and the jangling harnesses loaded, and the war-carts stacked in pieces. I thought, Has it begun? and if the Tribes had met together and who had lived and who had died. It could have been a dream, save that the dream passes in the daylight or haunts for just a little, but this did not pass nor could I stop from thinking on it.

There was another occupant of Aduin's hut, Barrex, Munna's father. I was wary of him, though without good reason, except that he was of an age that Grandfather had been. Yet my eye was drawn to him, perhaps because of that, while he sat to doze and gentled the hounds' ears or paused to listen to the talk. He had more time than most since he had grown frail and unfit for farm work.

Barrex himself was grandfather or great-uncle to many in the settlement. One of his grandsons, Sedd, was Munna's nephew.

We were of an age, even to our birth months, but he seemed at times a child to me, eager and quick at everything, without much thought or care. Some things, though, he was skilled at; he could shape a piece of wood and knew how best to stain it. So it was that he made a board for Barrex, who liked to play at *fidchell* in the evenings.

A great to-do was made of giving it to him. The whole hut was crowded and some honey beer poured in a jug and handed round. The board was set before Barrex' place near the hearth and he was led to it while everyone smiled and the children wiggled under their mothers' arms to see.

Sedd had worked well. He had turned it from a block of wood and bored the holes for the pegs and shaped them also, daubing them with a paint he'd made from coloured clays and resins. I looked at it. The last time I'd seen a *fidchell* board was in the dun, banded with silver and set with pastes of red and green and yellow. Then a girl's long fingers had handled the pieces, lifting them and placing them down. Her arm was graceful and her wrist narrow, with a bracelet of shells about it. But the pieces were the same, the king and the priests and the warriors held in their holes. Figures such as Barrex and Aduin and Munna and Sedd would never know and only glimpse, perhaps, at the feast meetings at the festivals when their tithe was given over.

It was then that I knew how far I was held apart from these kind and their life by what was past, and what I was. Though I might a thousand times play *fidchell* on the wooden board, always I would see what I had known and the figures to me would be real: Cernach and his black-clad priests, Uffa and Luth and Dearg. My grandfather.

Barrex was thanking Sedd and examining the gift. Sedd looked on, with a great grin on his face. Barrex was touched, nodding his pleasure over and over with gentle dignity.

Munna said to me, 'It's a fine thing and will be handed on down this house. There's many will play on it.'

I nodded. My throat had closed too tight for speech. I thought, How much longer shall I feel such things? And the bitterness was sudden, like biting on a sour herb that flavours the pot.

I stepped back, meaning to edge myself out, but at that moment Barrex looked up, straight at me. He had knowledge in his face. He said, 'Won't you set up a game with me?' Then he paused and looked some more, and I flinched.

There was quiet and glances exchanged, not hard ones, only such as any might give before sharing gossip and 'I told you so'. Then Barrex said, 'Let us be.'

When they had filed out, with the children asking, 'Why?', he beckoned me on to his rug and put the board behind him. He was firm in his manner and quiet and I thought how once he might have been headman here. His eyes under their folded lids were dark and shone.

'What runaway,' he said, 'will ever tell the truth? Or trust till faith is placed in him? A farm-boy, from the Sheep people in the north?'

The wood crackled in the hearth, beech wood to give a good heat for his thin blood. They cared well for him in the settlement.

I said, 'Do you want me to tell you?'

He'd tilted his head, like an old bird thinking what to peck. He said, 'Not now. Not like this. You are not ready and I do not think you have much liking for the old.'

I supposed that was true. I said, 'They play at being wise.'

He smiled. His gums were mostly empty. 'What's wisdom? Time to sit and watch and think a little while everyone about is busy.'

I stared at him, my colour high. I'd thought he'd meant to throw me out.

He said, 'Such sad ghosts are peering from your eyes. Young men are always sad or happy. Their girls make them so, or their horses, or the head of cattle in the pens. But they are seldom one without the other. One day you'll want to talk. Now you may go. Only promise me one thing. Some nights play *fidchell* with me.'

The next day visitors arrived. They came late in the morning as the shadows shortened towards noon. Three of them, on horses. Outside the palisade they jumped down and stretched stiff muscles and walked before the gate.

They were youngish, in their twenties – not more – with a lean, foxy look about them, something sinewy and crafty, though each apart from the others would be nothing to regard. They were shabby, yet workmanlike also, dressed in checked trousers and short cloaks. One had a battered leather breast-plate. They were bare-headed and each had a short horse-man's sword at his side.

Aduin came up, bustling and fussing. The one in a breast-plate said, 'Greetings on this house.'

They were at ease, more so than the villagers, who twittered. Another said, 'Will you give us some bread and beans? We are honest men and have this to trade.' He pulled out a cloak from his saddle bag. It was roughly worked; unbleached, with single threads of red run through, but warm and a good enough length for a man to wear.

After all, there were only three of them. Aduin fingered the cloak and gestured to his hut. 'We have bread and beans. Come and eat with us.'

They smiled and nodded. One had wandered over to the pig pen and was scratching the sow's hairy shoulders. He came back and went with them into Aduin's hut.

377

I saw no more – there was work to be done. I pulled weeds and picked stones and went in later for my portion. By then the men were gone.

Munna was washing pots. In a bit I handed her mine and helped set up the rack outside to dry them. Afterwards I asked her, carefully, 'Who were they?'

'Mercenaries, they said. On their way to the borders.'

'Is there fighting?'

She began to answer but just then one of the children called from the doorway about some quarrel with another. She went into the yard, grumbling and drying her hands on her skirt. I waited and finished the pots but she didn't come back and so I went out again to the baskets of stones and the weeds among the peas.

The afternoon wore on. Sedd joined me and when we both had backache we stopped and talked about the weather and watering the fields.

The sun was hot. Beyond the clearing the trees were cool and green and dim with shadow. Sedd yawned and said, 'I will make an offering tonight. The Lady of the stream is good to us, and the summer's sure to be fine.'

I had seen where their stream rose, a pretty place, the water bubbling through stones and mosses and over leaves. Primroses had grown there when I'd passed by.

Something glinted in the trees. I tried to see. The shimmer came again, bright and hot-looking. A horse snorted.

There was movement. From among the tree trunks and low branches a horse and rider showed. Then another and another. All around from the forest they came, the horses softly shod on beech mast, till the settlement was ringed about. Twenty men, perhaps, in all, sat still on their horses, watching.

Sedd said, 'Why, that's him who—' But already there was the supple shift of legs and hips to push the horses on, and the hands reaching across their thighs for the hanging swords. A single action done smoothly, as it should be, inevitable as the tide. That I saw, for I knew it from the practice slopes of Nam Dubh; but not their faces. I cried out, 'Run!' and caught Sedd's arm yet even as I did so there was a hiss and a hard, loud thud, and he fell with a spear driven straight between his ribs. He twisted downwards. As his face went past I saw his eyes, not frightened, wide open and astonished.

I looked back and now I did see them, and one especially, a great bear, Uffa's build, yet unlike him as may be imagined, with dark hair and a beard covering his chin and cheeks and a tight-fitting cap of leather on his head. He was laughing.

They set their horses. They came on, like a wind before the torrent or a tide against the rocks. They shrieked and cursed and I ran dodging and yelling for someone to close the gates.

They swept past. A horse's shoulder knocked me flying. A smooth, shining sweep of metal whistled over my head. I went under hooves and a belly. That saved me; they thought me done for. Somehow, though, I rolled and struggled to my feet. My thoughts were all to pieces. I stumbled on, still crying out a warning.

The gate, when I got to it, was down. Inside was terror and confusion. Already they'd got to the cooking hut and were firing the buildings. People ran screaming and rushing out with anything, sticks, rakes, spades used on the midden. They, at least, were cut down where they stood. Sedd's own brothers were there, little lads, the older putting up his fists, the younger cowering behind. The man I'd seen got them both, hacking from above.

I'd not forgotten everything. I crouched and waited and sprang, pulling off a man from behind and scrambling on his horse. I made it turn and turn about to try to hinder them. At first it worked; I caught at someone's arm and hauled the sword-blade down. Someone else I rode at and knocked on to the ground. Straight after I heard rough cursing, almost against my ear, and was fetched two great blows across the waist with the butt of a spear. As I fell, I was hit again, more viciously, so that I lay against the wall of a byre, with blackness in my eyes and a dreadful pain from my battered ribs.

When the blackness cleared it was still going on. They'd done with the men and the boys so it was the women's turn; afterwards they killed them also. But by then I'd crawled away, outside the compound, and lay against the palisade, trying to stop my ears.

Then there was no more screaming. I stared down where the grass pushed between the wattle walls and a beetle crawled. The grass was bright green and the wattle pale and dry. The palisade could have kept no one out, and they'd not even managed to close the gate.

At first there was only quiet and the sound of men talking

and moving about the compound. Soon a bird started up on one of the far walls and was answered by another. A goat bleated for milking, tethered in a copse.

Someone shrieked – thick, desperate, high-pitched cries without pause. I pressed closer to the fence and tried to stop my ears. Then I found I wept, through weakness and through pity. I knew what was happening. I smelt the burning, and I remembered from before.

The cries deepened and became bellows, frantic like an animal's, and then, quite suddenly, stopped. From the yard came cheering.

After that there was quiet again, but with a sense of them prowling and turning up this and that. Once or twice a pot lid clattered or a table overturned. They had come for what they could thieve and make their sport beside the livestock.

I tried to ease up against the wall for breathing was very painful. There were steps on the hard ground behind me. I stiffened with my eyes squeezed shut.

I waited with him unseen at my back. My tears still trickled down beside my nose and the corners of my mouth, my throat was aching agony. I barely breathed but lay against the wickerwork feeling the prick and weave of the withies make a pattern on my cheek. The sun was hot above. In the copse the goat still bleated.

There came laughter. He grabbed and heaved me up. His leather skull cap gleamed, his beard was a black mass about his chin. I thought the very touch of him would imprint blood upon my wrist.

He dragged me to the yard and flung me down. The others stood around, coughing and wiping their eyes in the drifting smoke. Some huts still burned. The bodies had been left lying, men and animals. Old Barrex was close by, his tunic ripped across his chest, a trail of blood along his breastbone.

The man said, 'More kindling.'

I could do nothing. The fire burnt outside Aduin's hut, piled high with logs and rags and a mess of rubbish. I lay stunned, like one dead already, with the knowledge of what was to come. Yet some disbelief held me – like a lad told how one day he will be old – knowing it but not believing for the youth strong in his veins like wine.

A couple of them bent and heaved something from the fire, rolling it out. A body, like the one in the other village, served the same way, only they'd left the head. Not Aduin. One of his sons, a quiet man with a pretty wife, soft spoken. He'd found his voice at the end.

I wished I hadn't seen. All at once there was a great, iron hammer in me, ringing and ringing, shaking my ribs, my heart, my spine, till I had no will, only terror like any creature's, borne helpless to its death.

Two others seized me, wrenching back my arms. I choked on a cry, because of my hurt ribs. They grinned across. One was young, bare-headed with fair damp curls and dirt on his forehead. His eyes were pale and mad. The other was older with a soft moustache that hid his upper lip. He looked ordinary, like someone you'd see anywhere, at a market, or herding cattle, or a spear-man for a lord.

The older one said, 'Young bugger. This is the one who got my horse.'

He spoke without rancour, as if I'd bettered him at dice.

They hauled me forward towards the fire and its noise and its smell of burning. With the heat in my face the young one said, 'Squeal, peasant pig! Where's Grandma's finery? Point the way to the hidey hole, or there's pork for supper.'

The heat stung; the smoke was choking and bitter. My sweat ran already to mingle with my tears.

I said, 'They had nothing. They were farmers.'

The young man whooped and capered, spinning through the flames and smoke, screaming, 'Pork meat! Pork meat!' at those around him. The other laughed and pushed me forward while the young man darted back with a length of rope and began to bind my arms behind me.

There was no place left for courage, only fear. I'd be like anyone and plead and weep for mercy. I struggled and heard my voice cry out how I was not a villager, nor ever had been and could not know their secrets, while the fire crackled and the flames leapt up, red and yellow from the blackened logs.

The young man howled, 'Put him on! Put him on!'

I writhed and twisted. They seized my legs and shoulders and hauled me on the ground. The heat beat at my flesh and I felt myself lifted and the thrust forward that would pitch me in. Men and fire roared together.

A voice said, 'He called them "They". He said, "They".'

A shadow passed before my eyes and a hard hand held my face, bringing up my chin to look. I blinked and saw someone gazing down and above him a bronze raven, wings outstretched, upon his helmet.

The world went quiet. All around life stopped and held still – even the flames seemed to pause their dance. There was only the heat and the face that stared, with a full-lipped mouth, just moistened, and small eyes that were blue and hot and cunning, and a red beard and red, raw-looking skin.

I shook all over in fierce, hard shudders; my breath came as short gasps through my mouth. No doubt my eyes showed white all round, like a colt's in terror.

He'd looked at me through flames before, and now he saved me from them.

Arax said, 'I know him. You can let him go. A scabby brooch, an armband – it'd be no odds. Cernach'll want him anyway.'

He grinned around, wolf to wolves.

'He's his foster-son. Do you think he's mucked his trousers?'

Chapter Thirty-three

They nursed me well, those mercenaries, terrified that I would take sick and die; but the muscles in my side were only torn where I had fallen and my ribs bruised. In a day or two I'd begun to mend. They'd bring me safe to Cernach.

When they realized this they let me be. By night I was guarded and by day I rode in their midst; that was all. They talked, though, of what would happen when they arrived at Cernach's camp. They were tribeless. The gift of me would be their honour-price for joining Cernach's. 'His foster-son,' they said, and pounded each other on the back. They boasted of it, and of what they would do in battle.

That was hard to hear but I held my tongue. Besides I had no words to tell a sorrow no longer sharp but wearisome and heavy from bearing it so long. Nor would they have cared.

We rode some days, living on their spoil. They did not loot. When we came to villages they were courteous, paying where before they stole, chafing the women and downing ale with the men. There was a reason. In the little shrines we came to, marking the gods of the land, the totem was the same – a painted stick, hung with raven feathers or with a corpse of a bird nailed upon it.

Already the tribes had gathered, inland on high moors, to march against the enemy at Cernach's orders. He bided his time. There had been raiding, the villagers said, on the settlements by the coast, and good heads of cattle driven off. Horse-people, looking to grow rich again. But wait till Cernach got to them.

The mercenaries were eager. We rode more quickly until, one day, Cernach's great camp lay before us.

It was like the other, outside Nam Dubh, only larger and sprawled on open ground; more tents than could be counted, the sewn hides dyed saffron or red or painted with swirls and spirals with the Raven standard raised among them.

The way led through a rough palisade of earth and gorse. At the gate guards called a challenge.

The man with the leather cap, whose name was Moccos, led the mercenaries. He displayed his arms. There was some banter. The spear-men in the tower fancied their own wit.

Moccos grinned and answered back, good-tempered as a bear after honey. When they'd opened the gates he said, 'We need to see Cernach. Where is he?'

'About. He rides round daily. Or someone will show you his tent.'

Arax said, 'And Mhorged, who rules Nam Dubh?' He was eager, the pup among the hounds, baring his teeth for them.

I caught my breath. I said, 'Is he here?' They were the first words I'd said to him since he had taken me.

He glanced across. His smile was a dog's smirk, eyeing up a bone. He said, 'Didn't you think so, peasant lover? Working the soil's made you thick. He'll be here, sworn to his Clan-lord. How will he take to you, do you think?'

We rode on. Everywhere was bustle with clansmen and traders about their business. All the time my thoughts turned on themselves like tides, in dread and hope together. I wondered who else might be with Mhorged. Familiar faces rose and shone before me, Uffa, Luth and Dearg, vivid as though but a single night had passed since we'd last spoken.

The camp went on, spread across the moor. Here and there fires burned, in pits scooped carefully from the heather.

Above them cauldrons hung or meat turned on green-wood spits while the clansmen met and talked their news. Children ran about and shrieked and laughed; women ground corn, gossiping in the tents.

Someone looked familiar, a gawky lad with big hands and broad shoulders. Arax shouted and he turned, looking up. His eyes fastened on Arax' face and his mouth gaped open. Some tents were clustered in a circle. He ran into one.

The man at Arax' shoulder laughed and said, 'What've you done to make him bolt?'

I could have told him. It was Magh who had run.

One of the tents was a little larger, made like others of dappled ox hides, quite plain, hung on poles and the edges pegged into the ground. The entrance was tied back, to let in the evening air.

Arax said to me, 'Get down.'

I dismounted and shook back my hair and waited. He

caught hold of my shoulder and the others gathered round. It was his moment. I had no time to think. He hustled me forward, to the open doorway, and pushed hard. I sprawled amid a tangle of rough, dried heather and feet.

There were exclamations and curses. My breath had gone so I had to lie a moment before I got up. They all stood round, looking at me and across to where Arax stood.

My uncle was there, and Hakos, and Uffa looking stupid with his jaw dropped open. There were others, but they were strangers. They stared and I stared back, dumb and shocked and helpless.

Arax said, 'Payment, Mhorged. An honour-price. I came to show you before I went to Cernach.'

My uncle said, 'Where did you find him?' He hardly looked at him; only the way his voice sounded this was a meal of ashes.

'Over the border lands. Digging weeds among the peasants. Grubbing in mud, where he belongs.'

Hakos said, 'Well, Arax, you should know.' His edge was there, as always, sheened and dangerous.

Arax said, pleasantly, 'Race you, Hakos.' Once he would never have dared.

There was silence, and anger in the silence, the stir of holding back, the taut lift of a head, a hand clenched and whitened.

My uncle said, 'Leave us.' Then, when for an instant no one moved, 'I would be alone with my nephew.'

Moccos touched Arax on the shoulder. They went, sauntering out, fingering what they could on the way.

My uncle went over to the tent flaps and dropped them down. The others hung about in groups outside, muttering and trying to see inside. He waited a moment, till it grew quiet. The tent was filled with a thick, dun light, coming through the seams, and the sour, leather smell was exactly that of Cumair's cart. Then Mhorged lit the tallow lamps and lifted one.

I suppose I was not much changed. Taller, by a handspan, and at that age when one is awkward and not yet filled out. My beard was just beginning and my hair was grown again, to my shoulders.

He bent and placed the lamp upon the hearth-stone. He said, 'You are back. What need to say it? You stand there and that speaks for itself.'

At his age half a year makes scarce a difference; yet it seemed to me that he was older, his eyes more deeply pouched, lines carved deeply down his cheeks and white in the hair above his ears. I thought, He is tired. It is a way here from Nam Dubh.

'Is it true,' he said, 'that you lived with peasants? They took you in?'

'They were good to me. They guessed I was not one of them, but they gave me work and food and shelter. The mercenaries killed them, in the raid when they caught me.'

He considered, scratching the side of his lip with his thumb. He was all to pieces, but hid it well.

He said, 'And you are to be their honour-price to buy their way back to the Clan.'

'What price,' I asked, 'is set on me?'

His tired mouth quirked. His eyes lit with sour laughter. But he seemed a stranger. 'The same,' he said.

He paused again, then said, 'We looked for you, when you were gone. We had the hounds and the men and the horses out, sniffing and poking and hollering. But I thought, when we couldn't find you, that you hadn't run, had you?'

'No,' I said, 'Cumair had me.'

He frowned, wrinkling his brow as if in pain. He said, 'We were in fear of Cernach, that he would ride off and leave us as we were. We ran about like ants on a kicked ant-hill. But he honoured my oath to him. He had faith enough for that.'

'So you are here, Uncle, for the rout.'

His brow cleared. 'Does it matter to you?' He sounded curious, but only as one might say, 'Have you fed the dogs?'

'Yes,' I said, 'more than ever.'

He drew a breath and looked down at his hands and then at me. 'Tell me,' he said.

I thought, I can hide nothing. He has a right to know.

I said, 'I was only with the farmers a few days, ten at most. Before that I was with the Horse-people. Cumair took me. He sold me to them, for information. It's what he trades in, as well as songs. I know what they are like. I lived with them. I know about my mother, and who she was.'

'And who you are?'

'I know what I am to them.'

'Yet you left.'

I said, 'I wouldn't have come back here, ever. Not

willingly. I owe them that. But I never betrayed you. I hated it with Cumair. I hated what had gone before. You were right to trust me, that day. I would have done what you wished. I would have sworn to Cernach.'

He was very quiet, hunched over, staring all the time at his hands. Then he said, low so that I had to listen hard to hear him, 'Was it Gortag?'

My chest felt tight and my throat full. I asked, 'Where is she?'

'At Nam Dubh. She rules while I am here. You needn't be afraid of seeing her.'

He paused and splayed apart his fingers, looking at them as though he gestured from a memory.

'That night,' he said, 'when you were gone, she came to me, and twined her arms about my neck. She was a girl again. You'd have thought some witchcraft made her so.'

He met my eyes. He laughed suddenly and said, 'You too! There's many ways to come to manhood and sweetest fruit turns mouldy quickest.' He looked away, with the same tug of pain about his mouth.

I said, 'Would you have me back?'

He sighed. Almost I thought his heart stirred for him to say 'Yes'.

But he said, 'Nothing is changed, Arawn. We stay in the hands of the Clan-lord. You are who you are. I would not want to watch you tear yourself apart.'

There was movement at the tent flaps. The evening light poured in. Moccos had cut the laces. He strode in and with him Arax. This time they bound my hands. As they began to hustle me off, Arax turned to my uncle.

'We nearly roasted him,' he said, 'and stewed his guts in barley beer!' He shouted with laughter but my uncle's face twisted.

He said, 'Wait!'

Arax' smile was sleekly insolent.

My uncle said, 'Use what brain you have. This will be better brought to Cernach through me. Leave the boy here. Tomorrow Cernach offers to the gods and the priests will tell the omens. All his lords will be there. I can hand over the boy and ask his pardon for you.'

My uncle was good to me. He saw that I was fed from his own pot and himself spread rugs for me to sleep on. But in another

387

way he was kinder still. Near midnight he said that he must take the air and would be gone a while.

I sat before the fire, hugging my knees, quite lost in thought, when the tent flaps moved again. I turned, thinking to see my uncle. Others were there.

Luth said, 'He told us you were back.'

We stared at one another. He too had grown; there was proper stubble round his chin and cheeks which a knife had shaved. His eyes looked blue under black brows and his face was thinner, bones and angles and high-peaked nose.

He said, 'Are you well?'

I nodded. I could barely speak. At his side was Dearg, his hair tousled and darkly red from sleep, sulky as he always was when unsure, and Magh, solemn as a child, eyes wide in a big, hopeful face.

Luth said, 'How has it been?'

I did not know what to say. I asked in turn, 'What have you heard?'

'That you went to them. To the Horse-people.'

He spoke flatly; one could not tell how he felt. We met each other's eyes, guarded as guests at a stranger's table.

'I was taken. By Cumair.'

'Some of us wondered, when he went too.'

They waited then. Even Magh was silent.

I said, 'Shall I tell you?'

Dearg nodded and after stared at his feet.

I began to speak, and managed a word or two; but they seemed strangers to me, as my uncle had, and I an enemy in their camp. I broke off my words and turned away.

Luth stepped behind me. He said, 'Arawn,' and I faced him at once to show I was not scared. He bit his lip. He looked first at Dearg and then at Magh. He said, 'I've missed you. We all have. We missed riding with you and talking with you. Magh missed you letting him win at dice.'

I said, 'Luth—' too raw, suddenly, for this.

'Arawn,' he said, and his voice had risen to cut through mine, 'I never knew till you were gone how like a brother you were.'

I stood there, a moment, looking at them. Luth seemed defiant, as though he expected me to laugh. Perhaps once I would have, and told him he spoke nonsense. Dearg stared straight back, and Magh looked just the same.

It was too much, like hot wine drunk on a winter morning.

All at once we hugged each other, as brothers do, brief and hard, clasping round each others' shoulders. Afterwards we grinned, shakily, like fools.

Dearg said, 'What will happen?'

I said, 'My uncle told me how Cernach will hear the omens, and will ride, if they are good.' We were silent a moment, thinking of what was to come.

Luth said, 'What will you do?'

'I do not know.' Then, like a tide bursting upon me, I told them, 'I have seen such things!'

My uncle said, 'Are you ready?' I nodded.

We went outside to where the ponies were bridled and waiting. My uncle mounted briskly and I followed him. He led the way between the little camps, picking our way across the heathers.

In a little while we came to a dip in the land, wide and shallow, like a bowl. Within lay more tents, and a large one in the middle, the size of a small hall, of skins dyed scarlet. People stood before it. Some were priests in their black robes, gathered before a smoking fire.

It was late morning. The sun stood high, hot and yellow. Flies buzzed at the horses' eyes and quarters. My uncle took the path at a steady walk. We rode into the hollow. It spread before us like a plain.

As we drew near I saw it was a gathering of the chieftains, all of them who belonged to the Clan. They stood bare-headed, their hair combed back and limed, splendid with naked chests and cloaks and belted trousers. Those we passed looked and put up a hand in greeting, but the rest held steady, looking towards the scarlet tent.

Cernach was seated before it, his great gold torc about his neck, flashing back the sun. He sat cross-legged on a platform that raised him up for all to see. But before him, more important, were the priests.

They had made the sacrifice already. There were black feathers at the edges of the hearth. Now they prepared to throw carved sticks for augury.

The old one I remembered stepped forward and lifted his arms. He called upon the goddess. The others echoed him, raising their arms towards the sun. They had painted them red to the elbow. At their feet lay a pale cloth of linen that stretched to the edge of the platform.

The old priest kept his eyes raised heavenwards; another threw down the sticks. There were nine of them, lying anyhow on the cloth. Then, with two more priests supporting him, the first shuffled forward and groped and seized one of the sticks. He looked at it a moment and passed it to the others, and repeated the gesture twice more. Afterwards he went back to where Cernach waited and whispered in his ear.

There was a pause while Cernach thought. He nodded and the priests went to stand at the corners of the platform, gazing at the sky and the land around. The clansmen waited, with the sunshine hot upon them, burning out the colours from their cloaks and trousers, striking sparks of light on their gold and bronze.

I would have asked my uncle what they sought but I sensed it was bad luck to break the silence. Some auspices they searched for from the high moor. Then birds flew past and the clansmen murmured and pointed. It seemed enough; the priest turned back to Cernach, smiling and bobbing his head.

Cernach stood. He did not need to speak. All around men roared and shook their fists and grinned like wolves. Mhorged said, 'So be it. We ride as soon as he orders. Tomorrow perhaps, if we strike camp in time.'

He stared into my face, then said, 'This way. This must be done. The sooner the better.' I met his eye and nodded. We were agreed in that.

He pushed his pony on through where men milled and talked and shouted over to one another. Outside the tent the priests were in a huddle. They straightened as we approached, smoothing their robes with their palms.

My uncle said, 'You know me, and the boy. Will you take word to Cernach that we wait upon him?'

The old one looked across, from side to side. He squinted, his eyes pouched and bright and cunning. He nodded and let us pass. His grin spoke all; there was no need for words.

Inside the tent glowed red, like a burning log before it crumbles. Cernach was by his bed. The great golden torc lay there on the bearskins. When he turned he had marks on his collar bones where it had rested.

I sensed the shock, like the rush of wind that shakes the trees before the rain. It stirred him and then he was still.

My uncle said, 'Clan-lord,' and waited.

Cernach took his time; I, after all, had kept him waiting, more than half a year. His eyes went from my face to Mhorged's and back again. Nothing showed in his. He said, 'Where did you find him?'

'Not I, lord. Mercenaries. They brought him in. One knew him from Nam Dubh. They wish your favour.'

I had thought I should be frightened, seeing him again, but it was not so. I felt nothing, or rather that I did no more than trade beans at market or tell him the state of the pastures.

There was quiet. He kept his eyes on us, not searching but sure and certain. My uncle shifted his weight from one foot to another. There was some noise at the tent's entrance, and Cernach called suddenly, 'Not now!'

My uncle said, 'The boy has been back. To the Horse-people.' He brought it out as another might tales of a lie or deeds of shame, and breathed deeply after.

The Clan-lord's look changed. The firm brows drew down, the mouth settled at the corners.

He said, 'How?'

'Clan-lord, he was taken. He did not run. He would have sworn to you, as you wanted.'

Cernach laughed. Not a belly-roar but the short, hard snort that says, 'Do you think so?'

He stood motionless in the blood red light. He was still, more than any man I'd ever seen, holding tight his thoughts.

All his movement went on behind his eyes. He was like the hot, baked road down which I'd walked, the greater part of him beyond my knowing.

He said to Mhorged, 'Go. We will talk later.'

My uncle bowed his head and left. To me Cernach said, 'Come closer.'

He'd had a rug put down, very fine, of stripes woven in blue and green. His dogs lay beyond, in the heather, forbidden the comfort. I came and stood on it, before him.

He said, 'Is this true?'

'Yes.'

'Tell me.'

I did, briefly, speaking of Cumair and Cathal and Echraide and of how I'd lived in the dun. But I spoke what I wanted; nothing of Etain, or the cave, or the long, black loch and what lay in there.

Afterwards he said, 'So you know? You know who you are. Yet you left?'

I said again, 'Yes.'

Now he leant forward and the stained light made him young, smoothing out the thoughtful clefts and hollows, turning his hair to fox-gold, deep and red.

He said, 'What will you do?'

I said, 'You can have me as your son, Cernach. I'll swear an oath to you in front of anyone, if you still want me.'

'Should I not?' At once he was careful, sensing change.

I thought, What does he understand of the gods? He is Clan-lord. What did the Raven-hag ask of him?

Outside the spear-men rattled dice. A dog pawed the rug and whined. I said, 'I am worth nothing now – not to you. Nor to the Horse-people. You cannot bargain through me. They'll do as they like. That way they'll keep their pride.'

His eyes searched me. There was no anger, only curiosity, like a priest prodding entrails.

He said, 'How did you come to this?'

'It was not of my doing.'

He sighed and waited, and ran his hands through his hair.

At last he said, 'So, at the end, you do as you were asked. You offer your loyalty freely to me. And at the same time you render it useless.'

I said what I had never dared before. 'Clan-lord, you killed them, my mother and my father. I will not turn my back on that.'

He said, softly, 'I'll hold you to it. I'll hear your promises of love and duty, and then we will ride to the battle field and watch to see which way your sword is swinging.'

I said, 'I won't fight. Do you think I could?'

He said, 'Do you bare your teeth, little hound? Would you be collared once again?'

He said it without malice. He bore his own burdens. I heard him wearily. I had reached my end, laid out like on a bleak shore after a struggle through the waves, or by a hearth of ash after a long day's toil.

I said, 'I will not fight, for you nor for them. How can I set myself against myself? I have loyalty to both or to neither – take it as you like.'

'You have run yourself into a trap. If you are scorned by them, your only hope is with us. Would you live all your days once more an outcast?'

I said, 'No. Not now.'

'Well then.'

I shook my head. 'I've bargained with the gods, Cernach. You cannot make me.'

He sat back and rested his hands on his knees. The dog sidled on its belly. He stayed quiet again; even his thoughts were stilled behind his eyes.

At last he said, 'We all make bargains with the gods. Hear mine. You will not fight for us, yet you will ride with us. Though I'll not have you for my son, yet I'll keep you by me and in splendour as though you were. Let the Horse-people howl their anger. They'll fight the better for it, and feel more keenly their shame.'

I said, 'They wish my death.'

'That is between you and them.'

The red light dimmed in the tent. The sun no longer beat upon the leather walls nor shone through the lacings. The day had clouded.

Cernach said softly, 'It works to its end. Can you feel it? The Raven-queen spreads her black wings and flies from the trees and the gate-posts across the land. She calls for blood and pale, dead flesh to glut on. She opens her beak and cries, harsh to our ears. Her eye is bright upon us. We squeak and hop, like fledglings, to her bidding.'

Chapter Thirty-four

At dawn the horde was ready. As the sun rose behind the clouds the war-carts began to move, light and swift, drawn by pairs of yoked ponies through the pathways in the heather. In each squatted a warrior, not yet garbed for battle, resting his strength, with his arms, his shield and spears and sword laid beside him. The charioteers sat also, feet on the crosspiece, hunched over the reins.

Behind came other warriors on horseback, bright in their cloaks and trousers, their swords hung at their waists, their shields held on their forearms. Some had grooms to carry their gear, and their great helmets with their crests of metal boars or ravens to wear before the battle.

Then came the rest, the spear-men and the carnyx blowers, the priests and the waggons with the wine butts and beer barrels, the sides of cured pork and beef, the sacks of beans and peas. Mingling with them and riding in the waggons were the women and children, brought to urge on the men in battle and whip their courage.

So they went, and I with them, riding in Cernach's retinue, mounted among his men, but bound in a bitter jest with iron about my wrists and ankles.

Two days we marched across the high moors and heather with the wide skies above us and the dark land before. The way was hard, between thrusting outcrops of pale, pitted rock and over the thin grasses. Above eagles shrieked; from the pine forests the stags belled. Yet this was Clan-land and the Clan-lord rode it as its master.

Then, on the third morning, with the air fresh and cold in our faces and the ponies' manes blown back from their necks, we stared down from a high cliff and saw below a long shore and the ocean, grey and deep and plumed with curls of foam. Through the mass of cloud broke the sun. The thin rays lit the water and the shore and the cliff edge.

The tribes fell quiet. Even the children ceased their chatter. Cernach pushed his pony forward, right to the margin. His standard bearer stood beside him and lifted high the iron Raven.

Then, where the cliff arced round in a wide half-circle, across the bay, there was movement. There was a distant sparkle of the watery light on metal, a glimpse of red and green; a horse whinnied, men stood small and silent and gazed on us as we on them.

Night fell. Below the sea sighed and murmured; all along the cliff watch-fires burnt with green, salty flames. Men came and went, their faces lit to stark shadow and livid flesh. The horses were fed and watered, the war-carts oiled and strung with charms, the harness likewise. 'Men honed their swords and muttered spells: 'I name this of my hand, Bone-biter. Lady, protect.' All through the camp one heard the whispers.

Near dawn Cernach called me to him. I was glad to go, wanting to know what would be. He stood outside the awning that stretched from his waggon, beneath which he slept, and he was alone.

He said, 'It will be at noon. The priests brought word, and there have been messengers between their camp and ours. Have you changed your mind? Will you fight?'

The torches looked pale. There was already enough light to see him and the outline of the awning and the shapes of pots just within the entrance.

I said, 'No.'

He sighed then and said, 'It makes no sense. Why do you persist in this? You could have honour and standing here with us.'

I stood silent. He said, 'So be it. I will have you displayed before them, my captive of their royal blood. Take your chance as to how the battle goes.'

He gave an order. Some of his spear-men stepped out and hauled me away. I was stood beside a waggon and left to wait.

I expected the morning to be full of bustle. Instead the men were quiet and prepared already. Only the horses were not yet harnessed, to keep them fresh. But the warriors were garbed. Here and there a champion strutted in his helmet, made huge by it, rearing above the others. Grooms stood by and chatted of their masters, each praising his the most. Some others stood in groups chanting their battle songs to quicken up their blood. But towards noon the camp fell silent.

The sun climbed in the sky, though shrouded by cloud. The day was heavy. I thought of how the Clan-lord had first come to Nam Dubh on a day like this. Far below the sea swelled and heaved and slowly sucked back from the shore as though a great mouth took a draught and swallowed. The sands lay broad and glistening; in places there were piles of thick black weed. High above, on the cliffs, the priests made more offerings and howled up to the skies. But the ravens already circled.

It was time. They prepared the horses. The teams were led to the carts and yoked. The bronze rosettes on the harnesses sparkled. The horses tossed their heads. Some reared. When done the charioteers crouched grim-faced on their planking and lifted up their reins.

The spear-men came for me. I said, 'Where's my uncle? Can I see him?'

'He's other things to worry about now, my lad. Hold still.'

They bound my hands behind my back and hoisted me up on one of the waggons. I stood there, stark and exposed. I said, 'What will happen?' But they shrugged and would not answer.

I waited. All the way along the cliff the men began to gather in their tribes, the little bands of warriors and spear-men and standard bearers. Everywhere I looked there was the gleam of polished horse-flesh and the flash of arms, iron and bronze. The standards were lifted, the Raven hung aloft, spreading her dark wings, her beak screaming silence.

Beside me was movement. I looked down. Luth was at the waggon's side. He rode a grey pony, lightly, defiantly, holding it with his knees. He turned his face up to mine. His eyes were wide, the pupils huge and black, his mouth taut. He looked very young and bold, like they tell in stories.

He said, 'It's all right. I've brought him. It's Ban. I'll ride him for you.'

A boy had plunged and tumbled into the loch, bound on a stallion, doing what he must for the goddess.

I said, 'Luth, you don't understand. The grey horse goes to sacrifice. They will mark you.'

He shook his head. How had I thought he did not know it?

He said again, 'It's all right. You're not the only one who knows what's best. Anyway, it's for us. For what was. None of this here is of our doing.'

He wheeled away and was gone. Some men milled past and hid him. Then I saw him again, his dark head and the fling of his checked cloak from his shoulders, and the strong, easy movement of Ban cantering to the others.

Afterwards there was no time to think. Cernach's horde, the tribes of the Raven-clan, began to move. The war-carts creaked, the waggons trundled slowly groaning on their wheels. Men clutched their spears and hoisted high the standards. The whole body of them crept across the cliff and began to descend along the pathways.

A little before noon they assembled on the beach. The tide was far out, a darker line against a band of cloud. I stood in the waggon, a little apart, set against a short reef of rocks, strewn with cockles and sea-weed. It was the quiet time, deep and strong, when one is brought face to face with what must be. There was no future, no belief in tomorrow or the day after or any time beyond. All of our lives were here, theirs in their war-carts and armour, shining like foam spun on the sea; mine in this waggon, and the rope around my wrists and the rough planking at my back. Everything was clear and bright, like little sharp chips of glass, glittering and coloured on the wet, grey sand.

Cernach was there, in his cart, with a war-helmet on which the Raven jutted its breast and wings. His cloak was bright in scarlet and green, his chest bare, the trousers laced to the knee. He wore his torc, the same as at the offering, thick and twisted and weighted with beasts at the ends. His ponies chafed at their bits and plunged. He stood steady while his charioteer brought them down, and held fast his spears and shield.

Around him stood his tribesmen, face after face with the same look, of stern, unflinching pride. Yet each was different, moustached here, clean-shaven there, one pock-marked and wrinkled, another smooth; old men and young, and every one with his burden of worry and joy, his wife, his children, his head of cattle and pastures by the stream. Other lives, that had been real, melted and wrought and refashioned to this life here, that was more real to them than any.

The shore stretched away. The gulls wheeled above and screamed. There were worm casts in the sand, close by the waggon and ripples from where the waves had been. More birds pecked at a dead crab, turned belly uppermost.

Then, as I saw all these things, the Horse-people came. Round the spit of land that formed the far curve of the bay they began to trickle. Not just Horse-people, Clan after Clan of the confederacy, with their standards of horse and sheep and fox and deer. They stood, twelve men deep, across the wide strand and faced us.

Like looked on like. They had their war-carts and their warriors in their plaids, with iron-tipped spears and well-wrought swords. Their women and children sat in the waggons drawn behind, their priests walked among them, holding aloft their smoking torches, lifting their arms to the sky.

They drew up their lines. Then they fell silent. We too were quiet, so that all about the shore one heard only the distant surge of the ocean and close by the sharp, clear chink of pony bits or the creak of carts. The moment stretched and stretched, wide as the sea, as the sky; a long, long emptiness that was as full as anything can be, of men's bright dreamings.

Cernach raised his hand. He held it high, fingers splayed. Then, in a fist, he brought it down and at the same time the air was filled with shrieks and cries and trumpetings. Everyone screamed. The women in the carts with their children, the warriors who opened their throats and howled, the priests calling on the Red-lord and the Raven-queen. The ponies started and were hauled back on their bits. The swordsmen beat their shields and stamped their feet. It hit one like a blow, so loud one could touch it, all the different noises woven to one vast overcloth of sound, strand upon strand, and, rising above, a dark, twisted cord, the snarling yowl of the war-trumpet, the animal-headed carnyx giving tongue.

From both sides the sound went up. Then the champions rode out, the favoured warriors, to boast and hurl insults and kindle their blood. They galloped across the sand, dismounted and strutted and threatened. After they fought, in single combat, slogging it out. Yet they were too far off to see properly. For a brief time they were apart from us, even as they fell or struggled on the sand.

Soon though came a new sound, a changed howling from across the shore, and a thrumming in the sand that gathered and beat as the war-carts began their charge. They came on, driven in a frenzy, the reinsmen crouched screaming at the ponies, the warriors upright, their hair streaming from their brows, lifted with lime to flow like stiff manes, their javelins poised to throw. Bright gold glittered on their necks, plumes of scarlet and green and blue fluttered from the carts, weapons shone with an oiled, cold gleam, the colour of the sea in winter.

Cathal rode at their head. He'd scorned a cart. He sat his stallion's back and lifted high his spear. He cried the cry of the herdsmen, the call of his people. He rode, enemy to enemy, with hatred shining on his face. The quiet of him was gone, burst as the bronze bursts from its mould. But the truth of the man was there, glowing in his battle light.

Now Cernach's carts leapt forward and began their own drive along the shore, and the foot men started to run and lift their swords. The carnyx blared again, till the twofold surge met and crashed and broke like a great tide, a flood of men and horses and carts that spilt in wickerwork and wood and iron upon the sand.

The battle was before my eyes. Everywhere men fought with sword and spear and slingshot. The war-carts had withdrawn, skimming light as birds, waiting on the flanks for their masters' summons. I saw Cathal stride out and lift his sword and sweep it down, splitting some man's skull. His standard bearers stayed close, raising high the Horse, to keep his men in heart. But the Raven flew too. She flashed and swooped above them. My uncle ran past with his mouth wide open, crying out words no one heard, except the men who died upon his spear. Others passed by, strangers who roared their battle fury or clutched their heads or arms or legs where the blood ran down. And all the time, against the sky, the standards rocked and plunged, the Horse and Raven gazing on the deeds of men.

I pulled against my bonds. I felt no fear, only a stark pity. An understanding grew in me until I seemed to see the goddesses themselves, tall in the clouds, urging on the tribes. They screamed as the carnyx screamed, and flapped their bloody wings, and trampled with their hooves. The shoreline stretched forever, the sea's depths were without end, the rocks were the earth's ancient bones against which men fell and spilt their brains and died. I thought how this would never finish; we were bound to it as the sun and the moon are to the sky, light and dark turning round and about forever.

A horse screamed. I turned my head and saw the grey, plunging from the battle. He ran several paces, then twisted and fell, kicking, with a jagged hole in his belly. The rider was thrown clear.

I knew them. I knew them as well as I knew any living thing, Ban dying, and Luth. He lay, too, but stunned. Already he moved and tried to rise. He lifted his head, with his black hair all sweat-soaked upon it, and his eyes wide and unfocused as though he looked upon some dream. I saw his pale face and the young flesh of his throat strained beneath. Then he brought up his hands to ward off a blow. On an instant all his body was lifted on a great thrust of iron and wood. He jerked backwards once, arched and shuddering like a speared fish. The man who had him pressed forward, pushing him back into the throng. He was a big man, a veteran, with grizzled hair and thick, knotted arms. He put his foot upon the body to free the spear before other men closed round them.

At that I cried out. The sense of awe, of looking from the heights, was gone. I plummeted, stunned as the lark before the hawk's stoop. The endless wastes, the sense of some grim pattern, went. There was darkness, thick as mud. I cried again, Luth's name, twice more. Thinking, even now I hear the echo. I struggled, wild and lost in grief, and felt the ropes hold tight and screamed through the darkness as though my own death was upon me.

From the darkness another figure rode. He sat his black mare, slight and glittering the pair of them, with the gold about his neck and arms and on the harness. He held her as once he had before, while she danced and fussed the bit.

My sight cleared. Through all the struggle, the waving heads of javelins, the plunging horses, the men that groaned and grimaced and hacked, we looked at one another; I bound helpless in the waggon, he on his horse.

I called out to him, loud as I was able, 'Hakos!'

Only for a moment did he hesitate, still in the seething horde, the thoughts naked upon his face, and then he set his spurs and the mare laid back her ears and stretched her neck. He came at the gallop, swinging in a wide arc around the waggon. He climbed behind me and slashed the ropes. He said, 'Take the knife. Take anything you find. Nothing is sacred. Not till the end.' He leapt back, pulling at the reins to bring the mare round. For all his useless leg he was quick.

I paused for a heartbeat. Before lay the darkness and the heavy swish of black wings; but already my hand had found its grip. The knife with its hilt of bone fitted to my palm. I leapt from the waggon and in my mouth was the battle-cry and the bloody croak of ravens.

When song-makers sing of battle they say, 'A whole day', or 'Two days', or 'Three days was it waged', to make men marvel. By evening this was over, barely half a day, nor was the moon quite risen before the shore fell quiet.

The sea was creeping in. We had to bring the bodies up high across the sand to where it was dry and the sea pinks grew. It took a long time. While there was still daylight the birds came; not just ravens and choughs, but gulls also. We lit fires along the shore to drive them off.

Everywhere people stooped over the fallen, to turn the bodies and peer, or work the armlets off and the rings and the belts. The big things, the shields and the swords, the harnesses, were heaped up in piles under the priests' eyes, gifts for the gods. More priests moved along the shore to tend the wounded.

Here and there a woman wailed over her man, alone or with her children clinging round her skirts. Men fetched water for their comrades. Others only wandered, empty-eyed, or clutched their swords and muttered.

The sea curled and lapped at our feet. Darkness gathered, thickening the air. The sky grew empty of birds and a clear dusk-blue. The stars began to show. Far off, round the spit of land, the Horse-people keened their dead, thin and high. The sound rose in a single note, desolate as the shore, with all this day's sorrow in it and the sorrow of days to come.

I listened awhile but there was no answering cry in my heart. The shelter of my grief was split apart and sundered, like a shell trampled on the sand, the sea-sound within crushed to silence. My soul lay bare for picking.

I walked towards the waggons. Some of our dead were there already, and Cernach waited to do them honour. They had been pulled back into a little cove. There were rocks to scramble over to get to them for the sea had come higher across the sand.

His guard had torches lit, pine roots and driftwood, stuck in clefts and in brackets on the waggons. I could see clearly, though the sea wind blew the smoke about. The pine roots burnt with a bright, red flame and the driftwood with a green, very clear and cold-looking.

The dead lay in lines; some on their shields, with their arms set out beside them. Others had cloaks pulled up, so only their boots showed. Most tribes take heads, if they can get them. I could smell the blood and the ordure and the salt weed drying on the rocks.

I looked for Luth, going round the bodies; but if he was there he was one who rested under a cloak. I could not tell him by boots, or lacings, or even an upturned palm, and would not pull aside the cloths to see.

My uncle was there, his face turned up and the gash above his eye that killed him black and gaping. His brow was split. His eyes were closed and his mouth straight and firm. Close by was Magh. They'd put him on a shield, with the best of them. He looked no different from any, stained with sweat and grime and with blood upon his sword and spears.

I thought, There is nothing. I remembered him, hugging the dead hound and weeping, and my uncle handing me the bundle that was my father's sword. I thought, What makes a man? Is it only this, that snuffs us out so lightly?

A voice said, 'Sir, my lord would speak with you.'

I turned. Some part of me was amazed to see a man stood who smiled when all around seemed only the dark gulf of night. Yet round the fires men had begun to sing.

The man led me over. He was respectful. The sword I'd used was reddened; I had killed the man who'd done for Luth, a cleaner death than he had given. After there had been others. Cernach was sitting on a rock, talking to his guard. He stood when he saw me.

He was still in his battle dress. There was blood all down the side and hem of his cloak and on his trousers; but he had washed his hands and arms up to the elbow. He wore his torc and now a crown, a circlet of iron with a spike rising up from the centre of his forehead. I remembered he was Clan-lord.

He took a torch from his guard and raised it. Sparks glittered in the breeze and floated skywards. His eyes were sunken, peering from the shadow of his brow, and his mouth thin. He had a hollow look from weariness. But the torchlight was red on him and splendid.

He said, 'We have the victory. Our dead are many, but theirs are more.'

I nodded. He watched my face, his deep eyes moving. He said, 'You are young. There will be grief, and the pain of grief, and after healing.'

'And for the People of the Horse?'

'They died well. That will be enough for them, for now.'

Cathal had not looked to die. He had thought to ride his war-cart to the horse-runs and look again at his old lands, in splendour, wearing his torc and crown as Cernach did. But I'd seen his head, tied by his hair to a waggon, with children throwing pebbles at it till the women stopped them.

A priest went by, his hands full of war-gear. There was more piled up beneath a standard, beyond where the bodies lay. Cernach watched, then turned again to me. I asked him, 'Is it then so simple?'

'A man sinks his body to the earth but his soul flies free. Flesh is nothing. A warrior goes walking with the gods.'

The Clan-lord spoke. He'd made of Magh a warrior who could not fight; and brought Luth to shudder on the spear, thinking it glory; and placed a mask of smiling gold to hide an old man's pain.

I said, 'I will not walk with them.'

His eyes grew still. I saw again the tension; the weariness put from him in the lift of his head. Across the sand some fighters cheered and passed round beer.

He said, 'You raised your sword for us.'

'Not for Her, nor for the Clan. For friendship's sake.'

He was silent a good while, with the red flames upon his face. Then he said, 'Honour you have earned this day. Once more I offer you my fosterage.'

The sea hissed on the sand. When he had bound me in the waggon I had seen true.

I said, 'Your queen wears a harsh face, Cernach. I would make a sacrifice of myself, but not of others as you have made and kings will always do. Keep your dead to her glory and your living to sing her praises. May she quicken your women and your herds and guard your citadels and the pastures round them. I will not serve her.'

His brows drew together; not in anger, only as though he'd met with something new. He said, quite softly, 'It is for you then that things are simple. But tell me, was the Horse-witch any kinder?'

I paused, but the truth had been long in me, only not in words. 'No,' I said. 'We are taught how gods and goddesses may shift their shape, to curse and mock at men. She and the Raven, they are one.'

The night spun out. The moon rode high. There was starshine on the waves; the dead lay in their heaps while the living sat and talked and drank their beer.

He said, 'It is proper for a man to fight – to save his lands, his women and his children. There is no other life than this.'

'The Raven croaks for blood, and the Horse-queen also. Blood on the battle field and blood in birth. Sacrifice and sacrifice. Do the gods never give for free? They make men what they are not, a singer to a swordsman, a humble fool with his hands upon a spear.'

He moved his head again, under his crown. He said, 'What did you see, when you were with them?'

'Dark water. A hag. Spell-bindings. What a man may fear . . . only no worse than this.'

The torch light kindled in his eyes. His skin was turned to gold, and the iron crown. He said, 'I am Clan-lord. I do as I must. Here, on this shore, is my gift to my people. This they understand. But you are not of them.'

I felt a quietness, in my mind and in my heart. All about was the night and the lapping sea. The torches hissed and flickered; men sat by the fires and laughed. Cernach was so close I could see the sweat gathered on his brow and above his lip; the crease of little lines around his eyes; the day's beard upon his chin

He said, 'To each his own. Do not try to bear the burden for us all.'

I stared at him and tried to understand.

'Come,' he said softly, 'let me set you free.'

He reached and took my arm. The flesh was naked. I had only my cloak and breeches, no tunic. His knife was plain, in a leather scabbard, with a good edge on it.

He said, 'Shall it be now?'

I nodded. The blade was lit with fire and fire flashed in my arm. He scored across the mark, clear and clean so that there was only a thin, straight line that oozed with blood.

'That much,' he said, 'have I done for you.'

The wound throbbed and stung, though he had not cut deeply. I felt no different, but he looked lighter and at ease. He paused, as if to be decent, then said, 'What will you do?'

405

I shrugged. So a slave must feel when the irons are struck off and he steps out for the first time masterless. He looked a moment more, then one of the priests said, 'Sir, a word—' and he turned and began to speak. As they put their heads together I slipped away.

I walked till the fires were distant and the only sounds were of the sea. The air was pure and cold and the shore was empty, silvered by the moon.

I was at peace. My soul felt clear and washed to brightness. Tomorrow would come the pain, as for a lost child who stumbles up an unknown path calling for his friends. I prayed, speaking to the dead by name: Luth, Magh, Mhorged, Ban. Yet it seemed they only waited, as in life, at Nam Dubh, in the hall and the pastures.

The shore stretched on. I thought, I shall walk here forever, in the darkness by the water, under the moon and stars. And for a time it seemed as though I too were dead and walking to join them; only there was the stickiness and an ache under my fingers where I clasped the wound.

Towards dawn it grew more cold. The current had washed round and thrown up flotsam on the sand. There were broken bits of cart, wheel spokes and wicker work, leather gear and harness. My quiet went. The dead seemed close again and dreadful with their wounds and agony.

I sought for shelter. The wind had risen, blowing spray. The cliff jutted, with rocks along its base. I made for those and clambered over the sticky weeds and pools. I was clumsy for my arm was sore and beginning to be hot.

There was a great slope of bare rock. I huddled up on that. I thought, What shall I do? With the dawn I should be born again, naked to the empty world and grief.

The moon had dimmed, barred with cloud; the stars, where I glimpsed them, were fading. Already the shore showed wet and grey.

Something moved along the sand, hunched and draggled, a figure who stooped under a tangle of sodden feathers. I slid behind the rock and watched and then, when it drew close, stepped out.

From the feathers a white face lifted, with eyes and mouth stretched wide with terror. I saw the hand stretch blindly, and the brown hair, still beaded at the ends. She cried, 'Who is it? Oh, who is it?'

I said, 'It is I, Arawn. Do not be afraid.'

'Arawn?' she cried. 'That cannot be. He is dead, for the Raven pecked out his eyes and left him bleeding.'

'No,' I said. 'No, Nemair. I am here.'

She turned up her face to mine. She was all dazed in her wits from the battle fever. Then she leant against me and I helped her to the rocks.

In a bit she said, 'My hands are cold,' so I took them in mine and warmed them. When the chill had gone a little I looked up and found her gazing at me. She said, 'Hakos is dead.'

I thought, When? How long after he had cut my bonds, leaping so lightly from the waggon? It seemed impossible, for I had not seen him fall.

She said, 'He had a rent in his side from a spear. When I came to him he breathed and the blood was wet. As I covered him he died. I waited till the priests fetched him away.'

She must have wandered then, about the shore, till daybreak.

We hugged together from the cold. Under her dress her ribs felt light and fragile as a bird's. The sea grew lighter, and the sky. Presently she said, 'There was a loose horse not far from here.'

I went to look and found it, grazing on the coarse sea grass, and led it back. It was glad enough of the hand of man to guide it.

When I got back she seemed better, with colour in her face and her hair pushed over her shoulders. She had taken off her cloak and shaken the sand from her dress. She said, 'You have hurt your arm. Is it wounded?'

'It is nothing,' I said, 'that will not heal.'

Her eyes had cleared. I had no need to say more. She too had done what she must and woken to a new sorrow. Perhaps in the end she had loved him. I thought of another girl, who waited to hear of the battle, with a father to mourn and maybe a brother. What shores did she pace?

Nemair said, still standing on the rock, 'There are farmsteads on the path from the cliffs. But it is a long road. Will you take me?'

'Yes,' I said, 'I will take you.'

She said, 'I am with child.'

I had known already, from the shape of her when she'd leant against me.

I lifted her on the horse and went to fetch her cloak, but she called me back. I said, 'You will be cold.'

'No,' she said, 'it is wet and dirty. And the sun will soon be risen.'

I swung up behind her for the horse was stocky and could manage two. 'Sit close then,' I said, 'and keep warm.'

We walked a way along the shore. Presently we came upon the path up through the cliffs. Soon after we reached the top she slept for she was very weary, resting her head against my breast. I halted then, to make her safe, and afterwards looked down to the sea. Below the pyres were burning, stoked with gifts for the gods. The priests ran about the sands and raised their hands to heaven. The fallen lay naked in their heaps and the shores stretched out on either side till the land curved into the ocean and met the sky.

I listened then, for the hoof-fall or the flutter of wings, the passing of a goddess, but there was nothing, only the cold wind about my ear, for who could bind her? Not man, nor the deeds of man, nor their wishes.

On the shore a man in an iron crown waited but my path turned inland to where the sea-grass fluttered, and the pony was keen for hay and water and bore us willingly till the farms came into view.